# CITADEL

## THE CONCORDANT SEQUENCE

## MATTHEW S. COX

DIVISION ZERO PRESS

# CONTENTS

# LITTLE GLITCHES

Unease circled Kiera's thoughts, melting the voice of the boring teacher at the front of the classroom into a meaningless warble. A pleasant sunny day mocked the kids for being shut up inside, even though it would kill them to spend too long out of doors. Bored and exhausted, she stared at a row of decorative pines along the edge of the school grounds, all statue-still except for *one* tree that flailed about like a spaghetti noodle in a hurricane. She caught herself nodding off and snapped upright. After wiping her eyes, she gawked at the windows, but the crazy tree had gone back to normal. The wall of greenery circling the immaculate field shifted and fluttered in a mild breeze.

Kiera had been one year old the last time any kids had been allowed to play out there.

A yawn forced its way out while video game corridors flashed by in her mind. She'd played the same level over and over again until she'd fallen asleep on her floor, not crawling into bed until sometime after twelve in the morning. She got lucky: Mom hadn't noticed how late she stayed up, but attending this class while sleep-deprived amounted to cruel and unusual punishment. Mr. Powers could knock her straight out after a good night's rest plus two cups of coffee. Going in half-zombie had been asking for detention, but he hadn't reacted to her near-faceplant on the desk.

The room full of sixth-grade students bothered her more so than any other day. Something about them right at that moment made her nerves prickle at the *wrongness*. Clothes and faces didn't match. Meredith had the same outfit down to the socks yesterday that Brittany wore today. Keith appeared to wear Spencer's shoes. She could've sworn the blue backpack on Mike's desk had been on Yasmeen's two days ago. And it still looked new. Like, right-out-of-the-store new, despite it feeling like the 5,001st day of school that year.

Kiera stared at Mr. Powers in his frumpy red sweater and beige pants. The same thing he wore every day; only the tie ever changed. Even his ramble about native tribes in the Amazon rain forest attacking military vehicles and drilling company property with spears and arrows sounded like she'd heard it dozens of times already.

Her light pen left swirls in its wake as she doodled on her QuickTab. As much as she could practically quote the teacher, she couldn't find any notes that she'd taken before. Not that she had a whole lot of interest in hearing about thousands of villagers being massacred. Powers harped on and on about how the planet was in trouble, the biosphere threatened by pollution, worsened by new wars that broke out all over the world. Small wars that lasted days or weeks, like two nations getting into a pushing match in the hallway between classes and then walking away grumbling. Resources, money, someone always wanted something someone else had. His list of nations that had collapsed felt like it grew by one every few days, but somehow also stayed the same.

*I remember writing this down already.* She leaned back and stared open-mouthed at the drop ceiling, so bored and agitated she wanted to scream. Agitated like a little brother she didn't have kept poking her in the back and she couldn't stop him. Whatever bothered her sat beyond the edge of understanding, and not being able to figure it out made her fidget. She opened a messaging application and tapped out a note to her best friend Ashleigh, who sat one row left and two seats back.

*Ugh. This sucks. I can't wait to go home. Didn't Powers give us this assignment already? He's gonna show a video of half-naked people running at trucks with spears.*

She flicked her nails on the edge of the silver tablet, wishing it could run her current video game obsession: *The Concordant Sequence.* Dad picked it up for her... a while ago, and finally, last night, she'd come close to the final level.

*Beep.*

*Powers is sooooooo boring. What are you doing later?*

Kiera peered over the top of her QuickTab to make sure the teacher wasn't watching her, and sent another message.

*Almost got to the end of TCS last night. If I don't get too much homework, I think I'm going to beat that game tonight. Do you remember this? I swear he already taught this.*

Kiera glanced out the window. Blue skies. Puffy clouds. Light breeze. Chirping birds. All of this would've been wonderful, except for her QuickTab announcing the date as October 11. It should've been blustery and chilly, leaves falling off trees but… nope. She stared at the white line along the top of her eight-by-ten inch tablet. The social studies e-textbook blinked at her from the icon tray, a passive nag scolding her for minimizing it during class.

*Shouldn't Powers have yelled at me by now?*

Most of the other students appeared to be reading along with the teacher. A longhaired boy named Steve in the back slept, head on his folded arms. Kiera looked at her screen again, noting the odd format of the date: no year.

*Ash, what year is it?*

She twisted to peer back at her friend, but froze at a glint in the sky. A passenger craft, supersonic judging by its arrowhead-like shape, hung motionless among the clouds. Flying, but not going anywhere.

*What the heck?* Kiera opened a video app and held her QuickTab up to the window to record the… *moving* plane. Sighing, she lowered her arms into her lap and frowned at the distant aircraft. *I'm losing it. Planes don't hang still in the air like that.*

*Beep.*

*That's a video game right? TCS? Is it any good? You really should work on finishing it.*

Kiera scowled.

*Ash, what's wrong with you? I asked you a question. What year is it?*

Her friend looked up at her with a confused expression for a second before bowing her head into the glow of her tablet screen.

*What kind of question is that? You don't know what year it is? Lol. You need to chill. We're gonna get in trouble for texting.*

Kiera shifted to face forward. Powers continued talking, reading from the textbook as he always did about how oil companies hired military contractors to 'control' indigenous populations. He hadn't reacted to their texting, didn't even clear his throat at her for twisting sideways. A meteor smashing in through the windows would've been less obvious than her not paying attention.

She raised her hand.

"Miss Quinn?" asked the teacher.

"Mr. Powers, what year is it?"

Some of the students chuckled.

"November of 2026, which you'd know if you were paying attention. Six months later, right-wing religious extremists attacked the Green Wall."

She sighed. "No, Mr. Powers, I mean what year is it right now?"

The boy behind her tugged on her hair. She yanked it out of his grip and gave him a quick glare.

"Since you seem to know today's lesson already, perhaps you can tell us why the Green Wall was attacked?" Powers raised his caterpillar-like eyebrows at her.

"But we haven't gotten that far," said Marlon, a bookish boy with dark skin. He glanced her way and smiled. Every day felt like the day he'd finally get up the nerve to ask her on a date, but he never did.

Powers smiled. "Precisely the point of me asking our non-attention-paying-redhead."

Kiera sighed before reciting in monotone. "The Green Wall was a group of scientists who worked to raise awareness of global environmental dangers and claimed the ecosystem was going to collapse. On May 4, 2027, five men from a fundamentalist church snuck into the audience of a presentation and shot the scientists dead. Later, law enforcement killed them during a prolonged hostage crisis. Fourteen audience members died as well. It leaked months later that the gunmen had ties to Big Oil as well as major chemical corporations, and were not in fact members of any religious group."

Mr. Powers blinked and coughed. He broke eye contact and wandered over to his desk. "Well, I suppose you *have* been reading ahead. There's a video presentation, mostly news footage for today's lesson."

*Reading ahead? No, you taught that already. I know it!* Kiera glared at the enormous monitor screen lowering from the ceiling at the front end of the classroom. A blip of white caught her eye behind the teacher's desk, an old-fashioned paper calendar on the wall open to October 2032.

The lights dimmed as the screen lit up green with rainforest. Speakers in the ceiling rattled the classroom with the roar of heavy machinery smashing down trees and crunching branches under heavy treads. Kiera slouched in her seat, gaze locked on the spot where the calendar hid in the darkness.

*It can't be October 2032 or I'd still be ten.* She closed her eyes and pictured her eleventh birthday party. Ashleigh, Kelly, Tashawna, Gerilyn, and Tamika all laughed at her when she couldn't blow out the trick candles her dad got. Sparkers. Mom had to drop them in a bowl of water to put them out.

*Okay, that's an old calendar from last year. It's gotta be 2033.*

Screaming war cries, a group of brown-skinned men and women in loincloths charged at oil company workers and their trucks. One tribal warrior died when his spear punctured an e-cell along the side of a vehicle, frying him in seconds. She had a feeling the actual footage showed it, but the edited-for-school version blurred it out. They even dubbed in a cartoony scream, like they mocked the 'dumb natives' or whatever.

Kiera scowled. *This is so racist. Those companies are ruining the planet and even the news is picking on those poor people.*

Head down, she tried to tune out the shouting, the machine noise, and the deep-voiced narrator droning on about the 'desperate but futile struggle.' Staying up too late playing games caught up to her. She slumped forward and put her head down, not caring if Powers gave her detention. The instant her forehead touched her arm, a chill ran down her back. Her hands and feet went numb. Pins and needles crawled over her skin. For a split second, it felt like all her clothes had disappeared.

"Aah!" she shouted, jumping up. Pink shirt, blue skirt, flip-flops. Check. She patted herself down to make sure her outfit was really there.

Jordan, the boy behind her, tugged on her hair again. "What's wrong with you today? You're all spacey."

Kiera twisted around to look at him. His burgundy cardigan didn't feel right. He should be wearing a flannel shirt. Thomas had the cardigan. "Stayed up too late."

"Lucky," whispered Jordan. "Gotta be nice havin' parents who always work. My dad—"

"Runs a service station and your mom's a nurse. You've told me already."

He stared at her. "Uhh, no, I haven't."

"Yeah, you did."

"When?" He leaned closer. "When did I tell you that?"

Kiera stared into his eyes, drawing a blank. "Umm. Before."

"When before? I don't remember."

"I… don't either." She whirled around to face front.

Mr. Powers started to drift sideways off his chair with no apparent cause. He stopped, floating in midair two feet to the left of his seat, not falling, and not reacting to having no chair under him.

She buried her face in her hands, rubbing her eyes. "I'm asleep and dreaming."

When she looked up, the teacher had returned to his chair. No floating.

The bell rang.

Everyone except her jumped to their feet at the same time. Kiera's sense of wrongness increased amid the commotion. A flash of memory came and went, of her rushing after Mom and Dad down a bright corridor, like something out of a hospital. Her parents glanced back at her, yelling, but their words came as indistinct blurs of sound. Overhead lights smeared by in slow motion. She didn't want to go with them. She remembered being terrified and dreading that something horrible waited for them in the room at the end of the hall, but couldn't recall exactly what.

Or if it had ever happened.

Kiera snapped back from the waking nightmare and stuffed her QuickTab into her backpack before standing, clutching it to her chest. The familiar dream had happened before, but never during the day. Always being dragged down an immaculate hallway by her parents, scared out of her mind at what lurked behind the door at the end of the hall. Irrational fear, like her mom and dad decided to donate her organs or something and they'd been taking her in to die.

She blinked at herself. Raised and lowered her toes. Short-sleeved T-shirt, skirt, flip-flops. *Summer clothes in October?* Confused, she looked up at the shrinking class. Tashawna walked through the still-closed door like a ghost. Mike got one arm into it before the door shifted to being open in the blink of an eye.

*Ugh. That's the last time I stay up 'til midnight.*

Kiera filtered out of the room with the flow of students, bumping and jostling in the crowd toward her locker halfway across school. Ashleigh hovered at her side, laughing. Her friend had a coral-colored sundress on and also sported flip-flops. The girl's shoulder-length black hair flared as she shook her head.

"You're completely out of it today, Kier. Are you feeling okay?"

"I dunno. I think I'm exhausted. I stayed up super late last night. Is it really October or is it like June and school's almost over?"

Ashleigh dodged a running eighth-grade boy and scurried to catch up. "It's October, silly. We've only been back for like two months."

"Ugh. It feels like it should be the end of the year already. Why are we dressed like this for October?"

"Duh." Her friend swatted her head. "Have you like been replaced by an alien or something? New to planet Earth? The biosphere's all messed up. It's like 109 degrees out."

"Oh." She stared down at her raspberry-colored flip-flops. "Right. Yeah. That makes sense. It hit 126 last July, didn't it?"

Ashleigh squealed. "Yes! It was so awesome not to have to go to school for that whole week. Too hot to let people outside."

"We still had to remote in." Kiera squeezed her QuickTab to her chest. "Crap. I have a test in robotics today."

"Mr. Conroy is kinda cute." Ashleigh skidded to a stop by her locker and typed in a code.

"Eww." Kiera unlocked her cubby, right next to Ashleigh's, then stashed her bag and QuickTab.

Neither spoke on the way to the cafeteria. Children sat at long row tables, assigned by grades from three up while the younger kids ate lunch in their classrooms. She ignored the roar of several hundred conversations and added herself to the end of the lunch line, standing behind a pair of tall eighth-grade boys. A short distance past the payment station, a fourth or fifth-grade boy in a green plaid dress shirt stood at the soft drink machine, holding an enormous cup under a stream of soda.

Kiera eyed pizza squares, sandwiches, spaghetti, chicken, salads, and macaroni through the glass. When her turn came, she pointed at a grilled chicken salad.

"Here you are, sweetie," said the middle-aged and somewhat chubby woman behind the counter. "How's that game of yours coming along? Beat the end boss yet?"

Thinking of her game made her tired all over again. She yawned. *Why is she asking about TCS?* "Uhh, not yet. Thanks."

The woman smiled.

Ashleigh got mac and cheese.

"You're going to get fat." Kiera grinned back at her friend and waved her hand over the silver egg by the register to scan the chip in her hand. The machine beeped, and the cashier—hired probably for decoration—smiled.

"Go to hell." Ashleigh gave her a raspberry, waving a large empty cup on her way to the soda fountain. "I'm skinnier than you and that's not easy."

"You are not. I—" Kiera turned away from the cashier, took one step, and stopped, staring at the boy in the green plaid shirt *still* filling his soda. *That's weird. Maybe he came back for a refill.* She ducked around him, grabbed a bottled water, and headed for the largest open spot at the sixth-grade table across from three boys. Ashleigh sat beside her less than a second later, startling her into yelping.

"Eep! Did you forget your drink?"

Ashleigh rattled the ice in her full soda. "No. Why?"

"You couldn't have been right behind me. How did you fill it so fast?"

The girl shrugged. "Same way I always do."

"Hey," said Jordan.

"Yo." Thomas mumbled over a mouthful of food. "You kill that alien?"

Tarik shook his head. "What's taking you so long, Kier? You're like the only one in the whole world who hasn't beat TCS yet."

She stared at them. "Uhh, not yet. Why?"

"Didn't think you'd like being the only player not to do it yet." Jordan grinned.

"She's determined to blast her way through." Ashleigh threw an arm around her back. "Oh princess of guns blazing."

Kiera stabbed a fork into her salad. "Yeah… yeah…" She bit down on a mass of leaves, Caesar dressing, and grilled chicken—tasting something vaguely beef-like. The unexpected flavor startled her into coughing. None of the other kids reacted to her almost choking. She took a single bit of chicken and nibbled on it, getting the same not-quite-beef flavor. Face scrunched with disgust and confusion, she glanced at her friend. "How's your mac?"

"Crappy, like always." Ashleigh put a forkful in her mouth.

Kiera stole a fry from Thomas, who ignored her. It too, tasted the same: somewhere between damp cardboard mush and beef. She opened her mouth to speak but her brain stalled at the sight of the kid in the green plaid shirt *still* at the soda fountain. A stream of foamy brown liquid flowed continuously into a large cup. The boy stood motionless, fixated on his task. She watched him for far longer than it ought to have taken the cup to overflow, but it didn't. Soda fell into a bottomless hole.

Ashleigh and the boys chatted about playing *The Concordant Sequence*, and beating it 'ages ago.'

Eyes narrowed, Kiera jabbed her fork into her friend's mac 'n cheese, stealing some. The girl didn't even look at her. It, too, had the exact same flavor as the salad and the fry. Not-beef.

"Everything tastes the same," said Kiera.

Thomas laughed. "Well it's school cafeteria food. What do you expect?"

"No, I mean it literally tastes the same. The salad, a fry, her mac, all tastes like liver pâté."

"What the heck is liver pâté?" asked Tarik.

"You don't want to know," muttered Ashleigh. "Something rich kids like Kier get forced to eat."

Kiera sighed. "I'm not rich. Dad's a lawyer and Mom's a VP. Well... okay they're both VPs."

"They makin' serious bucks." Jordan grinned. "My dad works in HR for Citadel. He could find out what your parents make."

"That's illegal," said Tarik.

"It ain't. He works in HR, that's his job." Jordan held his finger up like a lawyer with a killer argument. "*Telling* me what they make... that would be illegal. His finding out ain't."

The residue of mac and cheese on Kiera's tongue shifted to the taste of mac and cheese. She eyed her salad. *Can being exhausted make my tongue stop working?* She ate a forkful of salad, which tasted like it ought to have. Deciding to ignore what happened, she bowed her head and kept eating.

A thin, nerdy boy got up from the far end of the fifth-grade table behind her and hustled down the aisle. Kiera munched on romaine, watching him, fully expecting Bryce, a huge eighth-grader, to trip the kid. Sure enough, as soon as the runner passed the end of the table, the enormous fourteen-year-old stuck his boot out and tripped him flat. The scrawny kid slid about ten feet on his chest before stopping.

The cafeteria erupted in laughter—except for Kiera.

Time seemed to slow down. She looked around at all the huge smiles, closed eyes, belly laughs, and expressions of mirth. That moment had happened before. Everything as it had occurred seconds ago had occurred before, in the exact same way. *That's ridiculous. It's déjà vu. I'm tired.*

With a roar, kids' laughter leapt back to normal speed. She crouched over her salad, hurrying it along with a furtive glance toward the soda machine, expecting to see green plaid boy, but he'd gone. She sat up tall, looking around, but couldn't find him anywhere. All the overhead lights flickered.

A sudden, jabbing pain pierced the back of her head like an icepick. She grabbed the base of her skull in both hands and cringed, but the pain faded away before she could scream.

*Ugh. I'm never staying up too late again. Maybe I can sleep in English.*

"So, you gonna play TSC after school?" asked Jordan.

"Probably," mumbled Kiera. "Unless Ash wants to hang out."

"It tastes like mac and cheese," said Ashleigh.

Kiera glanced at her. "You're lagging."

"Huh what?" Ashleigh looked at her.

"You're about five minutes behind the conversation." Kiera stuck out her tongue.

"Oh, whatever." Ashleigh grinned. "You really need to catch up with the rest of like… *everyone* and beat that game."

Kiera glanced at her. *Why are they all obsessed with TCS?*

Since no one could go outside in the oppressive October heat, the students migrated to the 'fun room' after they ate. Kiera attempted to sit by herself in the corner on one of the sofas and nap, but Jordan and Thomas pestered her about the game. Both prodded her to try a 'stealth build.'

"I like being out in the open. The stealth tree doesn't have any up-front damage boosters so the PR-49 hits like spitballs. It's much faster to shoot the aliens in the face. I don't even know why they bothered putting stealth in that game. It's like they made the game as a shooter and decided to add stealth later."

"Aww, it's not. Stealth is über." Thomas grinned. "You're not patient at all. It takes finesse, but sneaky builds are basically overpowered."

After another thirty-five minutes debating game strategy, she trudged down the hall to her locker, retrieved her QuickTab, and headed to Mrs. Martin's English class. Here, she had a desk in the next to last row nearest the windows. Far enough away from the teacher to nap. On the way in, her elbow brushed a giant glass vase with water and glass beads instead of soil, a large arrangement of flowers at the corner of the desk.

"Careful!" The teacher grabbed the vase.

"Sorry, Mrs. Martin." Kiera veered away from the desk and headed down the aisle to the back of the room. She slid into her chair, set her bag on the attached desk, and put her head down on folded arms, eyes closed.

Exhaustion left her feeling like she floated, weightless in nowhere. Something tapped on her lips. *Come on, honey,* said Mom. *It's not as bad as you think. It'll feel like you blinked your eyes.* Strange fear came out of nowhere. The prodding at her lip went into her mouth, sliding down into her stomach. A sensation as though she'd swallowed a large piece of plastic shocked her awake.

Kiera shot upright at her desk, grabbing her throat and gagging.

No one so much as looked at her.

Mrs. Martin lectured about the differences between the two main characters of *Blood for Breath*, a fictionalized account of two brothers on different sides of the environmental disaster. One worked for an energy company, the other belonged to an eco-terrorist group. The teacher argued that the corporate brother was the nobler of the two, despite his actions being contrary to the planet's health, as his brother considered no act too violent to 'save the world.'

*Whoa.* She swallowed and rubbed her throat. *What was that?*

"Mrs. Martin?" asked Emily in the front row, "if someone was going to kill me, but my Dad shot him first, would that be evil?"

"Of course not, Miss Dominguez."

Emily tilted her head. "What if Nathan thinks of the planet as his child? He's defending everyone's life."

Kiera started to settle down for another attempt at napping, but stared at the vase on the teacher's desk: the water and glass beads had vanished. She leaned forward, gawking. The flowers appeared healthy and alive, but the water she'd been certain had existed when she almost knocked it over was gone.

Loud buzzing arose outside. Kiera looked away from the vase, twisting in her seat to peer out the windows at the robotic lawnmower, a giant version of the little round thing that cleaned the floors at home. Polished silver, it threw off a blinding glare in the afternoon sunlight. She squinted to keep watching the machine gliding back and forth in precise rows over the school's yard that no one dared step foot in anymore. Maybe in late December or January when the temperatures only hit ninety, someone might want to go outside.

She glanced up at the corner of the window, where holographic numbers indicated the outside temp as 109 degrees Fahrenheit. With a sigh, she slipped her feet out of her flip-flops and put her head down again, trying to remember what it felt like to walk on grass.

"Kiera?" asked Mrs. Martin.

*So much for sleep.* She lifted her head. "Marcus believed the dangers to the environment were overstated and the protestors had a grudge against Big Oil. Nothing he did violated any laws, and he even protected his brother Nathan by giving the police vague information. He didn't lie to them, but he could've told them right where to go. Nathan planted bombs that hurt and killed people who were only doing their job and had no control over the decisions made by the company."

"Can you give us a justification for why someone might consider Marcus the nobler of the two?" asked Mrs. Martin.

"I just answered you," said Kiera.

The teacher stared at her.

Kiera fidgeted under her gaze. She looked away—at the vase that had water and glass beads in it again. *This is too weird.*

"Correct," said Mrs. Martin. After a smile, she resumed lecturing about how the book, written in 2021, became controversial when Paul Allen Roberts cited it as his inspiration for a terrorist attack he carried out on oil pipelines in the Midwest.

The mower went back and forth... back and forth....

Kiera stared at it like a hypnotist's pendulum.

A sudden, blaring bell scared a scream out of her. Twenty-eight minutes had disappeared.

She scrambled to her feet, stepped into her flip-flops, and rushed out, both eager and dreading her last class of the day. Ashleigh emerged from her chemistry class two rooms to the left and on the opposite side, running to catch up. Kiera stopped at her locker, stared at her robotics kit, gloves, and safety glasses, and decided not to bother taking them with her.

"Mr. Conroy is kinda cute." Ashleigh skidded up to her locker and typed in a code.

Kiera stared at her, feeling like she'd gone back in time. "He's like my Dad's age."

"No he isn't." Her friend shut the locker door with her elbow, clutching her QuickTab. "He's only twenty-five. He looks like the guy who played the elf archer in that movie you like."

"Still eww."

"Gotta run." Ashleigh waved and zoomed off.

Kiera shut her locker, sighed, and trudged two rooms down the hall to Mr. Conroy's class. Someone had closed the door, but the bell hadn't gone off again so she couldn't be late. She grabbed the knob and turned, but pulled herself forward, feet sliding.

"Huh?" She blinked. "It's not locked...."

She slung her backpack over one shoulder and grabbed the knob in both hands. Grunting, she hauled back. The door peeled away from the frame, resisting her like she tried to open it into a pit of syrup. Kiera braced one foot up on the wall, straining with all her strength, but the door refused to open faster than a creep. She dragged it a few inches before running out of steam and sagging limp, out of breath.

Mr. Conroy walked over and pushed the door open with two fingertips. "Miss Quinn? Are you all right? You look flushed."

"I'm..." She fanned herself, staring death at the door. "Fine. The door was stuck."

"Oh." He smiled, pushing and pulling the door back and forth with one finger. "Seems you unstuck it."

Kiera grabbed the door. It moved freely, like any other door ought to. *Am I going crazy?* She hurried to her desk, sat, and huddled over her book bag. *Oh, crap. Please don't let me have like a brain tumor or something!*

"All right everyone, you won't need your kits today I'm afraid. It's test day." The class emitted a collective groan.

A period that sounded like it would be a fun time playing with robots had turned into a brain-numbing introduction to electrical engineering that should've been in high school, but Kiera managed to cling to a middling C at least, her only class not getting an A. Algebra's A- still counted as an A. This period, though, she loathed.

Everyone took out their QuickTabs. Soon, the teacher's command overrode them and locked out everything but the test. A hundred questions. She stared at the first one. Four sample circuit diagrams, asking her to select the most efficient layout for wiring a force-feedback sensor so a robot could evaluate how much strength it applied to an object in its grasp.

Cold crawled all over her body again, making her teeth chatter. Worse than the air conditioning vent above her head, the devouring freeze seemed to ignore her clothes entirely. The circular diagrams looked *so* familiar. A twinge of pain jabbed her in the left thigh before tingles ran up and down that leg.

*I've taken this test before.* She struggled to remember her crummy grade, the corrected version. *Maybe I'm still asleep at home and I'm dreaming the same day happening over and over again until I pass this stupid test.*

Forty-five minutes later, Kiera rushed the last eight questions by randomly picking buttons. The test auto turned-in at the end of the period with her finger a second and a half away from touching the submit button.

"All right, people. I know you all *love* tests, but tomorrow"—the bell rang, causing everyone except Kiera to spring to their feet—"we'll be doing something fun. Group project. Walking robot design."

Kiera stared at the clock, a hologram flickering a few inches away from the wall at the front of the room: 2:10 p.m. The only good thing about this class turned out to be its time slot as last period.

"Planning on moving in?" asked Mr. Conroy, smiling. "Time to go home, Miss Quinn."

"Sorry. I'm tired." Kiera stood, stuffed her QuickTab into the backpack, shouldered it, and dragged herself out into the hall. "See you tomorrow."

He waved without looking up.

A river of children flowed down the hall toward the front doors. Loud voices shouted about sports teams, movies, video games, plans for after school, and so on. Kiera stumbled along with the crowd toward the brilliant furnace glow at the door. She cringed as a blast of hundred-degree-plus air smacked her in the face, then darted down the stairs to the sidewalk. Blur clung to the parking lot, the surface likely hot enough to melt her flip-flops and/or burn her feet if she dared touch it without them.

Ashleigh fought her way out of the waterfall of kids coming down the stairs and trotted over, flops snapping against her heels. "Hey, wait up, Kier."

"I hate tests. Feels like there's been a million and we're not even to midterms yet."

"I gotta go to the commerce-plex with my mom today." Ashleigh tilted her head. "Are your parents still saying you can't go?"

Kiera headed toward her bus, one of twelve sleek yellow loafs lined up in front. The promise of air conditioning got her up to a jog. "Yeah. Dad says it's too dangerous there. Half the San Antonio National Guard is right around the 'Plex and there's always fighting. I heard one of the stores even had bullet holes in the window from a skirmish six blocks away."

Ashleigh twitched. "Are your parents still saying you can't go?"

"Uhh, yeah, Ash. That's exactly what I said." Kiera pushed the glowing red button by the bus door and basked in the rush of cold air when it folded in half, opening to either side. She stepped up into the wonderful coolness and looked back.

Her friend stood still, not having followed. "Are your parents still saying you can't go?"

"Ash, stop it. That's not funny."

Her friend came up the steps. "What's not funny?"

The doors closed behind her with a faint *pssh*.

"You're making fun of me for being a total zone-out today." Kiera rolled her eyes and threw herself into a seat by the window, backpack in her lap.

"Am not." Ashleigh sat beside her. "I gotta go to the commerce-plex with my mom."

"Right... I guess I'll call you later."

Kiera clung to her bag, hoping with all she had that a giant, ridiculous tumor wasn't squeezing the crap out of her brain.

# PERFECT RUN

The bus wound its way among the streets of suburban San Antonio, Texas. Kiera gazed out at the flawless houses, impeccable lawns, clear sky, and occasional pedestrian.

Her eyebrows slid closer together. All the news programs kept talking about environmental damage, mass extinction of animals, the erosion of the biosphere, countries turning their militaries on their own citizens, even militaries within the same nations breaking up into factions and fighting each other. Some big companies, mostly the ones the protestors targeted: chemical plants, mining, oil, pipelines… all of them had formed military-like forces, or hired deserter soldiers with stolen equipment.

If one believed the media, the Earth should be falling to pieces, yet here sat perfection.

*Dad says they're lying to us.*

She thought about the parents rushing her down that hallway in that recurring nightmare. White metal floor, steel walls, harsh lights. Everyone around her hurrying, panicking, worried. Hands attached to faceless people grasped her shoulders and pushed against her back, comforting but urging her to move faster toward a door that terrified her. She scowled at her reflection on the window, trying to imagine what could be in that room to scare her so much.

*It's a nightmare. They aren't supposed to make sense.*

The bus came to a stop at a traffic light. Kiera picked at her backpack, gazing at nothing in particular outside until a blonde woman walking a poodle caught her eye. The dog's legs didn't move at all. It glided along as if it had wheels for paws, but the pink leash pulling it hung slack. Kiera's mouth dried out and her throat tightened. Her lunch crawled up into the back of her mouth.

*Am I sick?* She squeezed her bag, wishing it were her mother or father.

"Ash, look at that dog."

Her friend leaned forward to peer past her at the window. "Aww. He's cute!"

"Are its legs moving?"

The instant she asked the question, the dog came to life and trotted along.

"Yeah. You really are out of it today, Kier." Ashleigh poked her in the ribs.

Kiera kept her head down, looking at nothing but her book bag as the bus drove, stopped, drove, stopped. Each time it halted, she rocked forward in her seat and students shuffled by on the way to the door. That same feeling of wrongness she'd had earlier returned, and with it, an odd scratchy feeling in her throat as if she'd stuck her finger in deep, trying to make herself throw up.

She gagged, covering her mouth with both hands. Breath stalled. For a second that felt like forever, she gasped for air, unable to breathe or even close her mouth. Something plastic wedged between her teeth, forcing her jaw open. She tried to shout, "help," but only a zombie's moan escaped.

The next thing she knew, a hand shook her by the shoulder. She lay across the bench seat on the school bus.

"Hey kid, wake up. Last stop," said the driver. His curly, wet-looking black hair hung down to his waist. Skinny, the same red-orange Hawaiian shirt with white flowers he always wore draped off him like a flag. "Come on... I wanna get home."

"Huh?" Kiera pushed herself up to sit, squinting at the windows. Her house waited three down from the corner where they'd stopped. She was the last student left on the bus. "Oh... sorry. I guess I fell asleep."

Yawning, she shuffled down the aisle, flip-flops scuffing. Again, the oven-like heat when the doors opened made her cringe. Bracing herself, she plodded down the steps. Her right foot hit the sidewalk and iced over with a sensation like thick slime oozing between her toes.

"Gah!" she screamed and jumped back up into the bus.

"Come on, kid. Hurry up," grumbled the driver.

She looked down. Dry foot. Dry sidewalk.

"This is so messed up." She lowered herself again and hesitated, toes an inch from contact with the ground.

"Don't make me 'help' you out the door." The driver chuckled. "C'mon kid... it's hot."

Kiera eased her foot down. Normal. No freezing squish. A sudden panic drove her to a sprint over lawns to her porch. After keying in the house code, the front door slid sideways and she rushed into more air conditioning.

Dad's and Mom's shoes lined up by the wall to her left, below coats that hadn't been worn in years. She kicked off her flops and padded into the living room. Her father sat on the couch, one arm over the back, watching pro speedball. He started to smile over his shoulder at her, but his head snapped to face forward. The gesture repeated again and again, sped up like a malfunctioning robot.

Kiera backed up, wide-eyed. "Dad? What's happening?"

Mom, in one of her skirt suits, walked in from the kitchen. "Hurry up, hon. You'll be late for school. Late for school. School. School. School." She twitched, her voice fragmenting into crunchy computerized scraping.

Kiera screamed.

Mom vanished.

Dad looked back over his shoulder, smiling. "Hey, hon, how was school?"

She stared at him.

Mom glided in, wearing a tank top, pink sweat pants, and white socks. "Heading to the gym, sweetie. There's some fruit if you want a snack."

Kiera stood rigid as a statue, turning her head to gawk at her mother, who only seconds before had been dressed up. Mom stepped into her sneakers by the door, then headed down a hall out of sight. Seconds later, the *whirr* of the garage door opener came from the distance.

"Dad, I think I have a brain tumor."

He laughed. "Oh, come on. School couldn't be that bad."

"No, I'm serious. I'm like hallucinating or something." She dropped her backpack and ran around the sofa to sit next to him, clinging, trembling. "I'm really scared."

Her father stroked her hair, hugging her tight. "Oh, sweetie... you're under a lot of pressure. I swear they're piling too much work on eleven-year-olds these days. When I was your age, algebra and trig didn't happen 'til high school."

Still shaking, she managed a half-hearted shrug. "I guess we're smarter now."

"There's fruit on the table," said Mom from behind.

Kiera jumped, sitting up and whipping her head around to stare... at an empty kitchen.

"What's gotten into you?" asked Dad.

Pain stabbed her midway between shoulder and elbow in both arms. Similar jabbing pierced her thighs and calves. Kiera shrieked and jumped up, swatting at the points. Her father tilted his head, watching.

"Is that a new dance or something?"

"Ow! Dad! Stop being a jerk!" She lifted her arm and examined it. No blood, no mark. Pain gone. "I'm feeling stuff that isn't there and hearing stuff that isn't there. I wanna go to the hospital."

"All right, I'll call. I suppose you *are* overdue for a checkup." Dad made a hand gesture, which summoned a holographic panel in front of him. He tapped a few keys and a dark-skinned woman with long, black hair appeared.

"San Antonio Medical Pavilion. My name is Ankita. How may I assist you?"

Dad smiled. "I'd like to make an appointment for my daughter, Kiera. She's complaining of phantom pains and hallucinations. Probably stress, but she thinks she's got a brain tumor."

"I see." Ankita glanced to the side. A flutter of beeping suggested she typed. "Has she experienced any headaches, seizures, loss of motor control, personality or memory changes, problems sleeping or remembering things? Any vomiting?"

"Uhh," said Kiera, "Does déjà vu count as memory problems? Stuff at school feels like it's happened already. I remember it, but it hasn't happened. A little headache, but it only lasted a couple seconds. I did stay up too late last night."

"Hmm. I see you're with Citadel Corporation, Mr. Quinn. We can get your daughter in Thursday at the earliest. 10:00 a.m. okay?"

"You want me to wait three days? I might have a brain tumor!" Kiera shivered.

"It's more likely you're exhibiting early signs of schizophrenia," said Ankita, deadpan. "I wouldn't worry about imminent threats to your health. Please try to remain calm and if your situation changes, contact us again. Your case number is S125197B. Have a wonderful rest of your day."

Kiera stared at the empty space where the holographic face had been floating. "Did she just call me schizo? Is that supposed to make me feel *better* than having a tumor?"

"Well, a psychological issue is less scary than invasive brain surgery." Dad smiled.

"Dad? Your sense of humor sucks." She frowned.

He stood, pulling her into a hug. "I think you're overtired. Go take a nap."

"When will we wake up?" asked Kiera.

*As soon as it's safe,* said Dad in the back of her mind.

"What?" asked Dad. "What's that supposed to mean?"

She threaded her arms up between them and rubbed her face. "Never mind... Maybe I'll take a nap and this weird stuff will stop."

Her father peeled her eyes open with his thumbs, tilted her head side to side, felt around her neck, and put his hand on her forehead. "Seems fine to me." He winked.

"Is that your legal opinion?" She quirked an eyebrow.

Dad chuckled.

"Hey, wait. Why are you home? Aren't you prepping for a case?"

"We'd be no good to the company if we worked ourselves until our brains turned to mush. Took a mental health day."

She headed into the kitchen and its icy air-conditioned floor. After snagging an apple from a thick wooden bowl at the center of the table, Kiera went upstairs to her room, scuffing her feet over the grey plush carpet for warmth. She left her backpack and the apple on the desk next to her computer and crawled into bed. Within seconds of her face making contact with the pillow, her eyes popped back open.

Grogginess told her she'd fallen asleep and woken back up. The light in the room didn't appear different, so she hadn't slept into the evening. She stretched, adoring her soft blankets for a while, lacking the willpower or strength to get up. Downstairs, the TV kept playing the sounds of speedball. A high-energy announcer screamed about something. Between his distorted yelling and the TV being downstairs, she couldn't make out anything other than the man being happy at whatever some player named Burkhauser did.

Kiera sat up, swishing her feet side to side under the soft blanket. She felt *much* better, and nothing in her room or out her window looked strange. A quick trip down the upstairs hall to the bathroom later, she flopped at her desk and pulled out her QuickTab. It synced to her home computer in a few seconds, and she opened homework assignments on her forty-inch monitor.

That eerie sense of déjà vu returned when she read over the list of modules. Every one of them had a familiarity that made her swear she'd done them before. Nonetheless, she plowed on, munching on her apple while working over math, history, programming, robotics, Spanish, and art. For whatever reason, Mrs. Martin in English hadn't assigned any homework.

"Sweet." She grinned, and glanced at the clock. Ten after five. "What the heck?"

Kiera peered back at her bed. It felt as though she'd caught more than a twenty-minute nap. After all the time she'd thrown at homework, it should've been much later. Even if she hadn't fallen asleep.

"Today is one messed up day." She glanced at her computer. "Call Ash."

A window opened, showing a still-image of her best friend's goofy smile, lips covered in hot-pink lipstick and giant, star-shaped glitter earrings dangling from her lobes. In a few seconds, the image disappeared, replaced with video of Ashleigh. The scenery behind her looked like the commerce-plex food court.

"Hey, how much longer are you going to be shopping?"

Her friend grinned, tucking a strand of hair behind her ear. "Oh, hey. You wouldn't believe this dress Mom found at Blue Barn! It's gorgeous, and they marked it down to $180. I'm gonna wear it to school tomorrow."

Kiera put her feet up on the desk, ankles crossed. "That's cool. I guess you're eating there? What time are you coming back? Wanna hang out?"

Ashleigh grinned, tucking a strand of hair behind her ear. "Oh, hey. You wouldn't believe this dress Mom found at Blue Barn! It's gorgeous, and they marked it down to $180. I'm gonna wear it to school tomorrow."

"Ash, knock it off. Stop messing with me." Kiera poked at the screen. "I'm serious. I'm having a weird day."

Ashleigh grinned, tucking a strand of hair behind her ear. "Oh, hey. You wouldn't believe this dress Mom Mom Mom found at Blue Barn! It's gorgeous, and and and they marked it d-d-d-own—"

Her friend froze again as a still image.

"Error," said a grown woman's voice, seemingly from the ceiling, drawn out into 'Err-roar.'

Kiera yelped and looked up. The call dropped. "Dad! Dad!?"

Silence.

She scrambled out of the chair and ran to the hall, shouting, "Dad?"

It occurred to her that the TV had gone silent.

Kiera ran downstairs to the empty living room, wide-eyed. "No... No... this isn't happening. I'm not going crazy." She padded over to the couch and felt the cushions. All cold. She grabbed at nothing, and the house computer's holographic terminal appeared. She pushed the button to call Dad.

He answered in three rings, seated at a desk in his work office. "Hi, hon. What's up?"

"Umm. Where are you?"

"At work. Where else would I be at this hour?" He leaned aside to show more of the office surrounding him for a second. "You know I've got a major case on the plate right now. Sorry for being a ghost so much these days, but that house isn't paying for itself. We're buried under a landslide. Can you believe people are mad at us for not cleaning stuff up fast enough? As if we made the pollution."

"You were *just* here. I got home from school and you were watching speedball." Her lip quivered.

He bowed his head, sighing. "I know I've been spending too much time here. I'm sorry. Please don't have a meltdown on me. I promise as soon as I can, I'll take two or three weeks' vacation. You'll be sick of me." He grinned.

"But you were here..." said Kiera in a small voice. "I..." *Maybe I didn't even go to school today and I just woke up?* "Ugh, this is so strange. Sorry."

"It's all right, sweetie. I should be home before you go to bed tonight."

She narrowed her eyes at him. "I'm going to hold you to that."

"See you later." He blew her a kiss and hung up.

Kiera trudged upstairs, scratching at the spot on her left arm where the phantom needle had poked. Still no sign of a puncture mark or even pain. When she reached her bedroom, she sat on a pile of small pillows arranged in the corner, facing the sixty-inch display panel hooked up to her Supernova 2 game console. No angry vid mails had arrived from any teachers or her parents, so she must have gone to school. With homework done and Ashleigh playing head games, she had a few hours to kill before bedtime.

*Why is she being like that?* Kiera felt sorry for herself for a minute or two, and got over it.

Seconds later, the title screen of *The Concordant Sequence* filled her monitor, depicting a massive armored door that guarded the final alien bunker. She'd been playing the game for-seeming-ever, running back and forth across a virtual landscape, completed every quest, hunted every achievement, found almost all the gear, and cleared everything except for that final bunker. The game had ninety-four of them, all underground complexes where a series of tunnels, creatures, and puzzles stood between her and 'beating' the game.

She'd been bashing her head into the final bunker over at least four months. The mission setup had the alien fleet in orbit, an automated group of ships controlled by the boss at the bottom level. If she took too long to get there, the creature would trigger a bombardment that vaporized all life on Earth, and the game ended with a loss... before reverting to her last saved game. Again and again, she'd tried it. Sometimes she made it *to* the end boss, but had suffered such a beating on the way down, she couldn't survive the encounter. Most of the time, she took so long in the hallways fighting past the automated defenses and aliens, the orbital fleet fired in the middle of the boss encounter, ending the game.

Cross-legged, Kiera set her elbows on her knees, gripped the controller, and narrowed her eyes.

Her character appeared in the starting room, a metal cube with glowing green lights pulsing in patterns over the walls. One door led forward. She mashed the button to skip over the "We're all counting on you to save the world," monologue from her soldier's commanding general. As soon as the cutscene ended, she rushed forward into a corridor of black metal. Dim overhead lights created lots of shadows and places to hide, but with the giant timer ticking down, she didn't bother.

Two yellow-bodied aliens, each with four arms and two rifles, opened fire from behind cover at the end of the hallway, supported by two turrets in the ceiling. She ran into a slide, tossing an EMP grenade that disabled the turrets as she skidded to a stop behind a large machine attached to the wall. From there, she traded fire with the two aliens, taking them out with ease.

Up and running, she stopped at the end long enough to shoot straight up and destroy the stunned turrets. *Experience points!* Left offered a shorter route, but it contained two sentry robots with missiles and a lot of armor. They had a good chance of dropping power up crystals, so she often risked the fight, but it took forever to kill them. The other way required traversing a much longer corridor. It didn't have any aliens, but did have *tons* of annoying turrets. They didn't hit hard, but they almost never missed. Annoyingly so. No matter what she did, they hit her. Dodging didn't work, sliding to cover didn't work, and throwing the controller across the room didn't work.

She got angry even thinking about it and headed left.

Minutes later, she finished off the second of the two heavy bots with a third of her life bar left and no more healing packs.

"Crap." She raised her arm to chuck the controller, but changed her mind. She hit the command button to reload the game and start again. "I hate this level so much. It's too damn hard." On a whim, she went to the character screen and stared at the special abilities tree. Most of her points had been spent into the combat branch, with some in survival. She'd barely touched stealth since she lacked the patience. Sneaking around to ambush enemies took like ten times as long as smashing them head on. "Okay... I get it." She flipped to the inventory page and used a Rom Flash item, resetting her points. "Game developers like stealth. I give up."

A short while of allocating special abilities later, she reworked a stealth build with enough in the combat group to enhance ambushing attacks. Her character's rifle damage dropped to 125, about one-third of what it had been, which made her expect a waste of time, but ambushing could hit for 2,500 according to the final ability at the bottom of the stealth path. That should one-hit-kill most things, and do in a single unit of ammo what it took her up-front build about twenty shots to accomplish. Counting armor, more like forty.

"Okay, you're going down, game." She pointed at it.

She ran to the bathroom and then the kitchen, coming back to her console with a squeeze bottle of orange fruit punch. *Okay, so the right side hall is better for stealth I think. It's darker and has more places to hide. But those damn turrets....*

Kiera engaged sneak mode, which made the character move slow. A vent by the start of the first hall let her skip both aliens and the turrets, so she hit the button to crawl in. She hated the speed after two minutes, but when aliens didn't attack her right away, she decided to keep going. The last time she'd tried stealth, what felt like over a year ago, she'd been obsessed with the 'perfect dark' achievement: getting to General Xax without being detected by anything. After fifty or sixty attempts where something *always* spotted her near the end, she'd sworn off ever touching stealth again.

But face-smashing hadn't worked either.

Hugging the wall, she edged up on the aliens' position, debating how to ambush them. The huge damage talent required approach from behind, but these two didn't move. After sitting for a few seconds, she remembered another ability, and used a gadget to create a noise off to the left.

Both aliens and the turret swiveled that way.

She snuck past, heading into deep shadows of the rightward corridor. Only after she got into the next section of hallway did she remember another vent that could've bypassed it. *Ugh. Almost got seen.* Kiera sat up straight, feeling insulted that she'd gone around an enemy without killing it. "Grr. They all have to die… but… She's moving so slow! Damn. The only one that I really *have* to kill is the end boss." She followed a recess along the wall where the darkness appeared thickest, passing turret after turret without being detected. "Wow… okay, maybe skipping fights is even faster than blowing stuff's faces off."

The mini-map showed cones where enemies' attention wound up pointing, allowing her to move through unwatched areas. She'd played and replayed and replayed this bunker so many times she'd stopped even looking at the minimap. Every hallway, room, closet, vent shaft, and ladder had a permanent etch in her mind. For the first time in her (relatively short) gaming life, she played the exact opposite of normal, avoiding fights at all costs.

Dark hallways glistened in the soft blue light glowing from within recesses lined with wires and hoses. The soft *tap-tap-tap-tap* of her character's boots on the metal floor made the game feel new. Usually, her entire room shook from the sound effects of plasma beams and grenades exploding. She paused to take a couple swigs of orange punch, then maneuvered her video game avatar down a vent shaft, along a tunnel, up a small ladder to another shaft. She cut through a maintenance conduit she discovered months ago but never used since it bypassed most of the third level—and she had wanted to see/kill everything.

Her character dropped down to hang at the end, scooting sideways by her fingertips to a ledge. Doing that made her fingertips hurt for real. She still hadn't recovered from the climbing gym two days ago. Dad's new obsession. Well, it would've been if he'd been home from work to go, but he paid for it and still made her go. Two hours, three days a week of 'healthy activity.' Like the endless school year, it felt as though she'd been visiting that climbing gym forever.

Much to Kiera's astonishment, she made it close to the final boss's door and still had eighteen minutes left on the doomsday timer. From what she'd read online, a *bad* but successful attempt on the boss only took nine minutes. She stopped, pausing the game.

"Crap. I can't just run into its face and be all like *blam* with this build."

Eyes closed, she pictured the boss chamber. It resembled a rectangle with triangles stuck to the narrow sides. Two floors tall but wide open, it made no sense as an actual command room, quite clearly designed as an arena for the final boss fight. A catwalk ran around the edges near the ceiling. Barrels and boxes littered the area. Lots of hiding places. Holes in the floor that she always fell into connected to vent ducts. Sniper builds went high and ran while firing. Combat builds tried to dance around the room while ducking behind boxes... those tunnels had to be meant for stealth builds. Ambush, duck down, move to another opening and try to pop up behind its back. Ten ambushes would kill it: 25,000 health.

"Well, sneaking down here was kinda boring, but it worked... and I can do that again easy."

She sucked down the rest of her orange punch, unpaused the game, and approached the final boss room. Her character held up the severed eye of a robot-alien, which the scanner accepted. Blue light streaked in an X across the giant door, meeting a circle at the middle, which spun around counterclockwise.

A heavy *thud* shook the floor of her bedroom, and the huge metal slab split in half—one part sliding into the ceiling, the other sinking into the ground. In the middle of the giant chamber stood her nemesis: Xax, the alien commander. Lemon-yellow, his enormous and malformed body floated around the room atop a wide mechanized disk. Little (by comparison) tentacles held an array of weapons, and his 'chair' bristled with numerous missiles and plasma cannons. Her soldier stared at a blob the size of a truck.

Sixteen square holes, each with a conveniently open grating nearby, dotted the floor at regular intervals. In her prior running and gunning attempts, she'd always tripped into them, gotten stuck waist-deep in the ground, and eaten missiles or some other devastating attack before she could get free. Tonight, they would help her.

Snarling, Kiera sprinted for the nearest opening and went into a slide, passing under a ripple of laser fire before her soldier fell into the shaft. The bedroom thundered and vibrated from the fury of explosions and the thrusters on the monster's pad/chair thing. Furious at not having a line of sight on her, Xax zoomed back and forth. After twenty seconds, the boss calmed and entered a slow gliding search pattern. She scooted across the room under the floor, able to catch glimpses of the enormous general from vents.

Once behind it, she popped up, aimed her big rifle, and fired at the back of its head. The ambush hit critically for 5,000 damage. Xax roared and spun, but she'd already ducked back out of sight before dozens of missiles rained down on the spot she'd fired from. Kiera leaned forward, as if doing so would push the character to crawl faster in the vents.

Small robots entered the shaft to attack her, but even the stealth build's lower up-front damage handled them with ease. They became more of an annoyance. A problem only if they snuck up on her, or happened to spawn when she tried to line up a shot on Xax.

Perhaps due to the weird day she'd had, Kiera focused on the pattern of shoot, duck, move, shoot, and didn't spare a second's thought for getting angry at taking damage or wanting to rush the clock. She had plenty of time.

Five minutes and thirty-one seconds after entering the room, her final ambush shot caused the alien overlord to explode into a gory mass of virtual splatter. His mechanical flying perch careened around the room like a rocket-powered-Frisbee during a cutscene, embedding itself into the huge computer core and destroying it, permanently disabling the invading fleet.

Kiera leapt to her feet, waving her arms. "Yes! Finally!"

She dropped the controller on her pillows and did a victory dance.

"Perfect run," said a deep male voice from the game console.

"Awesome." She grinned. "Wait, I took damage from the little ball things in the vents... how was that perfect? Huh. Oh well. I'll take it."

She plopped down to sit and picked up her empty fruit punch bottle, frowning at it.

"You reached the chamber without being detected at all," said the game console.

Kiera froze, bottle an inch from her lips, staring over it at the monitor. "Did you just talk to *me?*"

The cutscene ended, shifting to credits for the game developers.

"What the heck is wrong with me?" She set the bottle down and grabbed her head with both hands. "Am I really going schizo?"

"You're not experiencing a mental illness," said the game console.

She laughed. "Right. Voices in my head are telling me I'm not nuts."

"My origin is not from within your mind," said the game console. "Congratulations on mastering the Concordant Sequence."

"Uhh, thanks."

"I'm glad you are finally prepared," said the console. "Time was running out."

*Whatever. Even the system is making fun of me.*

Kiera picked up the bottle, which somehow had become full again. As soon as it touched her lips, her mouth filled with the sensation of plastic wedging her jaw open. She tried to pull the bottle away, but it remained stuck.

"*Mmm!*" she shouted, bottle clutched in both hands, struggling to get it out of her mouth.

The plastic extended forward into a tube that slid down her throat. She screamed, grabbing at her face, desperate—but unable—to breathe. The pain of needles jabbed her in the arms and legs. Tears streamed out of her eyes from the awful gagging sensation. Her body convulsed, wanting to throw up, but something that didn't exist plugged her mouth. Overcome by panic, she fell sideways and curled up, wheezing.

Her fifth try, she let out a real scream. The cry became coughing before she rasped, taking deep breaths until her head spun.

"Daddy!" shouted Kiera, lapsing into tears. "Mom!"

She clutched her throat, which felt like she'd tried to swallow a plastic sword. The room stopped spinning in a few seconds.

"Dinner's almost ready, hon," yelled Mom from downstairs.

*When did she get home? I never heard her come in...* Kiera choked on drool and staggered to her feet. "Mom! Help! Something's really wrong!"

She stumble-ran down the corridor, almost falling over at the top of the stairs when cramps hit both legs at the same time. Her arms locked up like chicken wings. The same sense of freezing came over her again, worse than a bucket of ice water dumped on her head. She shrieked.

Clinging to the railing, Kiera slid down the stairs on legs that refused to move. By the time her feet hit the carpet at the bottom, all the strange feelings had gone away. Crying and freaking out, she jumped up and ran to the kitchen, inhaling the smell of chicken and garlic. Her mother stood facing their huge microwave, smiling.

"Mom! Help me! Something's really, really, wrong with me. I gotta go to the hospital right *now!*"

Her mother didn't move. Kiera stared at her for a few seconds before stepping closer.

Thunder rolled overhead.

Despite not having been afraid of thunder since she'd been six, Kiera cowered at the sound. She couldn't remember a storm ever being that loud, or sounding so close overhead.

"Mom?" She crept up and put a hand on her mother's shoulder. "Mom!"

The woman didn't move.

Kiera leaned around to look at her face. Mom gazed with a vacant grin into the microwave, and didn't even appear to be breathing. The timer had stopped on 08:04. Though the machine emitted a *whirr* like it continued cooking, the tray with a huge bowl didn't rotate, nor did the timer tick down.

"Mom!" Kiera screamed, trying to shake her, but her mother had become as solid as a statue. Even her shirt felt as rigid as stone.

A blinding flash from the window over the sink made her flinch away and shriek.

Where once had been perfect green suburbia now stretched an endless field of barren brown sand. Small tornados of dirt glided back and forth beneath a dark indigo sky flickering here and there with bright green jagged lightning.

"I'm not schizo!" shouted Kiera.

She tried to hug her mother, but recoiled as her arms wrapped around a jelly-like mass of freezing slime. Mom didn't look any different. "M-Mom? What's going on?"

A peal of thunder rattled the entire house. The alien landscape outside tinted the kitchen green.

Kiera backed away from her mother. The kitchen floor squished between her toes, ice-cold gel. "I didn't wake up yet. I'm playing too many video games. This is a screwy nightmare. I'll just go back to my bed and dream that I'm going back to bed, and when I wake up, I'll be okay."

She headed out of the kitchen, trying her hardest to ignore the sensation of walking in two-inch deep frigid snot. The view from the huge bay window in the living room matched the kitchen windows—miles and miles of open sand. Far in the distance stood blackened shadows of a ruined city, skeletal skyscrapers raking at the haze.

Kiera ran across the living room to the stairs. A quarter of the way up, her feet plunged into the carpet and she sank up to her waist in freezing ooze. Screaming, she grabbed at the railing, but the wood rungs melted to slime between her fingers. Deeper and deeper she sank, no matter how hard she fought to keep her head above the liquefying staircase.

In seconds, her screams for help cut off to muffled bubbles. Icy liquid surrounded her, and the world went dark.

# 3

# WOMB

The raging *booms* of a titanic thunderstorm faded to perfect silence.

Kiera's eyes fluttered open to a blurry world of dim light in which she floated, weightless. A clear, curved window a short distance above her head offered a view of dingy drop-ceiling tiles. The dark red billow of her long hair bloomed around her. Her breathing became the loudest sound in the world, with a hollow plastic quality. A rigid band encircling her head pressed a mask tight over her mouth and nose. Between her teeth wedged a hard, rubberized nodule like a scuba diver might wear.

Kiera tried to move, but stopped at a sharp pain stabbing her forearm. She lifted her head and gazed down at her pale body, naked, glowing blue from the light outside her tank, and floating in some manner of clear, syrupy liquid. Thin robotic arms sprouted from the sides of her coffin-sized prison, impaling her with giant needles: two in each thigh, one in each calf, and two in each arm.

She stared at the insectoid, metal limbs and screamed into the mask, shaking from terror, but afraid to move.

*Dad! Help!* She started to hyperventilate. A beep came from above and behind her head, and it became more difficult to breathe. Something brushed against her shoulder. She turned her head to gaze along an inch-thick hose attached to the front of her mask. It curved around behind her, connected to the back end of the tank.

*Wake up! Wake up! Wake up!*

Whirring filled her ears. She went rigid from fright as two metal arms extended toward her from above and grasped her head with gentle, but firm pressure, immobilizing her skull. Trying to squirm made the needles burn, and her head had been locked in place. Freaked out, she screamed into the air hose. Seconds later, a jabbing pain shot into her skull from behind. Before she could scream again, the feeling changed to that of a long needle sliding *out* of her rather than thrust in. Kiera gagged, choking on the object stuck in the back of her throat she couldn't swallow.

*Please wake up! This is too scary! I don't like this dream!*

The needles piercing her arms and legs all retracted at the same time. Small puffs of blood lingered in the clear goop for only seconds before a current pulled them away past her feet. The clamps holding her head released next, leaving her floating free except for the air hose. She grabbed at the back of her head, the top of her neck, where the pain had been. One tiny point hurt, like a bee sting or bad mosquito bite. Her probing finger found nothing alarming: no gaping wound, no metal, only a tender spot that hurt about as much as the red dots the needles left on her arms and legs. She rolled over to stare at the panel that had been behind her head. Flickering lights winked and shimmered from within a nest of robotic arms all folded up like some giant, sleeping alien spider.

Screaming, she grabbed at the mask, trying to force her fingers between her cheeks and the hard plastic ring keeping it locked on, but couldn't pry it away. Her panic stopped short.

*I'm stuck in a fish tank. Pulling off the air hose is stupid. But if I drown in my dreams, will I wake up before I die?* Kiera looked around at her chamber. About half of the tank, plus both ends, consisted of solid metal, with a transparent lid sealed tight. To her, it felt roomy. A seven-foot-tall man could've fit, but would not have been happy.

She swam closer to the side, peering out at a dimly lit room that resembled a hospital. Only a few lights in the ceiling worked, tiny blue LEDs among dozens of dead tube bulbs. More tanks, all open, continued into the distance, separated by a few feet. A thin layer of fog gathered low to the tiles, drifting over dark smears beside the other pods that trailed past the foot end before curving off away from her toward the distant end of the room. The marks had the unmistakable appearance of blood left behind by dragged bodies.

Again, she screamed into her air hose and curled into a floating ball.

*Please wake up. This isn't real. I'm having the worst nightmare ever. I'm at home in bed.*

Minutes passed in silence with nothing changing. Trembling, she uncurled and looked out at the same gory room. A privacy curtain lay on the floor two tanks away. Whoever had been in the two closest tanks would've been able to see her with no clothes... *Mom? Dad?* She pressed her hands to the wall of her tank and leaned close, trying to get a better look around. The breathing mask got in the way, but she turned her head sideways to put one eye against the window. A tall metal cabinet to the left, behind the head end of her tank, held towels and folded clothes. One of Mom's skirt suits hung on the right side, covered in an epic amount of dust. The man's suit on the next hanger had to be Dad's, and it too, had collected so much dust he would've thrown it out rather than have it cleaned.

Kiera stared at the bloody smears on the floor by the tanks her parents should've been in. Only her absolute faith that she found herself in the middle of a nightmare kept her from bawling like a child. Shaking, she patted around her tank's lid, searching for any button, lever, or dial that might open it.

*It'll feel like a nap,* said Mom, somewhere in the depths of her memory.

Finding nothing except the creepy-as-hell alien spider arms on the head end gathered around the breathing tube, she rolled over to float on her back as if in bed. The dark ceiling overhead held no answers. For a while, she listened to the *whoosh-click-whoosh* of her breathing hose and flicked at the billowing cloud of hair around her head.

*This has to be a dream. That's the insecurity thing, right? Having a nightmare that you're naked?*

She stared down at herself. Aside from the red dots the needles left behind, she looked unhurt. No freaky alien modifications. Her muscles ached, but not so much that moving became painful. The feeling reminded her of the day after Dad dragged her to the climbing place the first time. She'd spent two hours clinging to fake rocks with rainbow-colored plastic handholds, dangling, falling, and trying to pull herself up. They'd been there so damn much after that, she could scale the most difficult wall without even using her legs.

Of course, climbing didn't help her get out of a locked tank.

"*Hrrlh!*" she shouted, banging her hand on the side, but the syrup slowed her fist down so much it made no noise against the glass.

A heavy *thunk* echoed in the goo. Her eyes widened. Loud mechanical whirring crawled up her spine and made her cringe. Air filled in above her, silver bubbles gathering and dancing against the glass. The clear ooze in which she floated started to drain. When the liquid reached the halfway point, the dark end of the tank past her feet snapped open—an iris door. With a loud *pop*, the air hose separated from the wall behind her, and the tank tilted forward. Smooth metal and slippery gel sent her hurtling downward in a wash of transparent fluid.

All the slime, and Kiera, plunged into a drain.

She shrieked, dropping near vertically for a few feet before reaching a bend and sliding with the torrent into total darkness. Lost to panic, Kiera flailed and shrieked as she swooshed around one turn after another.

The next thing she knew, she had stopped moving. Warm air puffed against her left thigh, in time with her breathing. She opened her eyes and found herself lying face down on a metal grating, the end of the air hose connected to her mask under her leg. Her hair, burdened with the liquid from the tank, congealed against her back like a dead, frozen jellyfish. A weird spattering noise broke the silence.

She pushed herself up and twisted around, cringing at the feeling of her jelly-hair sliding off her back. The splattering ceased as a continuous dribble of clear ooze stopped landing in her hair and fell, freezing, on her stomach. With a squeal of alarm, she scooted away from the dribble and looked up at a wide pipe in the middle of the ceiling. She'd landed in a bare metal chamber a little bigger than her old bedroom. Aside from the pipe overhead, the only way out appeared to be a square hatch high up to her left. A series of rungs like giant staples embedded in the wall offered a way to reach it. Drips and gurgles from viscous liquid came from below the grating, but the two tiny lights near the hatch didn't reach down into the murk. From the echoing sounds, she imagined a giant tank of goo beneath her.

*I guess I passed out... I don't remember falling in here.*

Shaking from the cold, she sat up and wrapped her arms around her legs. Slippery ooze clung to her like a second slimy skin.

*This dream is going to send me to a therapist.*

She fidgeted at her immobilized jaw, unable to close or even open it any farther with the mask wedged between her teeth and under her chin. The face guard pressed so tight into her cheeks she couldn't get a finger under it. Three feet of hose dangled from the front, swinging about like an elephant's trunk as she craned her neck to look around. For a few minutes, she grabbed, twisted, and pulled at it, but the device fit so snug, it wouldn't even shift. Panic rose up again, and she lapsed into short, rapid breaths. Kiera clutched the band around her head and tried to break it with brute strength. After a while of struggling, she realized it wouldn't snap and got control of herself. Eyes closed, she slouched in defeat, shivering.

"*Hrrll!*" Her voice came out the end of the hose.

*No one's going to understand me with this thing on. I'm alone in my nightmare... Don't be scared. Only a dream. Why would a mask be locked on?* She batted the hose back and forth while thinking it over. *I was sleeping underwater. Or... underslime. Whatever dream bad guy put me in that thing didn't want me to drown.* The odd notion that her parents had made her get in the tank came out of nowhere.

She felt around the plastic band and located a dial at the back, right above the sore spot. It hadn't been *locked* on, merely designed to prevent accidentally coming off. After feeling around the mechanism for a moment, she guessed two halves joined at a release switch. Kiera grabbed the mask frame with one hand and twisted the dial with the other.

*Click.*

The band clamped around her skull popped open. Relieved, she went to spit out the mouthpiece, but it dangled only an inch from her lips on a hose as thick as her finger that went down her throat.

She tried to blurt, 'Eww!' but only made herself gag.

Gingerly, she grasped it and pulled. Tubing slid up from deep inside her stomach, leaving the taste of not-quite-beef in its wake. The sensation of it coming up felt so much like vomiting that she slouched forward and heaved. Coughing and crying, she gagged, glaring at the evil thing. A trace of peanut-butter-brown goop leaked from the end that had been in her belly. Cafeteria food flashed by in her thoughts. Everything had tasted the same. Exactly like that... stuff.

The sight of it terrified her more than the spiders.

*A feeding tube... nightmares aren't that detailed.* In seconds, her brain rejected any notion that *this* could possibly be reality. She curled tighter, hugging her legs to her chest, shivering from the coating of frigid, clear ooze. Sitting on a metal grating became uncomfortable in short order. Kiera crawled to the area of smooth metal floor by the ladder. She stood, but her feet kept sliding in the slime.

She spent a few minutes wiping her hands down her body, slinging goo off to the side. Without the mask stuffed in her mouth, her teeth chattered. It took her a while to squeegee slime from her hair. When it stopped coming out by the handful, she leaned to the side and combed her fingers through it until she had a thick blanket of *ick* adhered to her back. She wrapped her arms around herself and stood there shivering.

"'Kay... This is messed up. I'm in a metal room after getting flushed like a dead goldfish, and I have no clothes." She squatted and bowed her head. The idea of sitting died as fast as she thought of it; butt plus cold steel floor equaled no way. "I'll wait here until I wake up."

A few minutes passed where the chamber only seemed to get colder.

"All right. I'll play. Stupid dream." She stood and stretched, whining from stiff muscles. "Ow. Why am I so sore?"

She examined her arm where the needle went in a few inches below her elbow. The other one hit her nearer the shoulder, so she couldn't see the puncture too well. A red dot looked only slightly nastier than a vaccine shot despite the needle being about a foot long. She reached up and felt around the back of her neck. Her hand came back bloody.

"Crap. I'm bleeding." Again, she squatted, clamping one hand to the back of her head and pressing down. "I need a Band-Aid or something." She frowned, then laughed. "Or something. Yeah. I need something... like pants. Ugh. What did I eat that's giving me dreams this bad?"

After a while of holding pressure on the back of her neck, her hand swipes didn't show any fresh blood. She eased herself standing and eyed the ladder while shivering. *Okay, dream. You're not going to let me wake up until I see whatever it is you want me to see, are you?*

About seven feet separated the bottom of the hatch from the top of her head. A dim glowing green circle at the middle looked a lot like a button. She pulled herself up the ladder, stiff muscles protesting her idea to move in a third dimension. When she reached the top, she pressed her hand into the light spot.

A loud *hiss* of air and a distinct *clank* startled a shriek out of her. The hatch sank into the wall two inches then lowered out of the way. Behind it, a squat corridor ran to the left and right. Pipes of varying size covered the far wall, awash with a grid pattern of white-blue light. She stepped up another rung and peered out.

Left held a dead end a short distance away with four large metal cabinets into which numerous fat wires connected. To the right, the corridor went a good distance before bending a corner. Reluctantly, she crawled into the dry space, which offered a little more warmth than where she'd been. Heat spread over her face, her cheeks likely as red as her hair. Of course, for it to be embarrassing to be stuck without clothing, she would have to not be dreaming. If a dream person saw her, it would all be in her mind and that wouldn't bother her.

The hatch hissed, making her jump and whirl around, too stunned to do anything more than watch it close. A green button on the wall next to the hatch looked like it would open it from this side, but the chamber didn't have any other way to go. She rubbed her hands up and down her arms, trying to warm up while gazing around at the low ceiling only inches away from the top of her head, also a metal grating. An adult would have to stoop, so she figured she'd wound up in a maintenance space below the floor. She raised up on tiptoe, peering up past the grate, coughing at dust. The hallway looked like a high-tech office or hospital with plain white doors and large windows. Dirt coated everything. Smashed, broken ceiling lights dangled from wires. Large black letters on the wall spelled, 'Basement 02.'

Kiera crept forward, gazing upward more than forward. A few times, she stopped to push on the grating overhead, but it didn't even rattle. Eeriness clawed at her back. Wherever she'd dreamed herself into being, the place looked like it had been abandoned for a long time. She tried to remember what video game had a forgotten lab complex, but the scenery didn't match anything in her memory.

She rounded a right turn at the end and sighed at an even longer section of identical corridor with more pipes along the walls and grating overhead. "Great, I'm a hamster in a really long cage with no wheel to run on."

After another thirty feet, the passage cornered left. She couldn't quite force her legs to jog, but managed a fast limping walk. By the time she reached the turn, the pain and stiffness had faded away. Again, she huddled at the wall and peeked around, intending to hide from anyone who might be there, but the hallway was empty. Some sixty feet farther ahead, the corridor cornered to the right. A quarter of the way down, a ladder on the wall led up to a hatch in the grating.

"Yes!"

She ran to the ladder and climbed. This hatch had no button, but it flipped upward with little effort. Kiera pulled herself up to stand on the metal grating she'd been walking beneath. Giant windows with frosted lettering spelling 'Citadel Corporation' on both sides looked into rooms filled with cubicles. Dim emergency lights painted everything in shades of blue, making her feel like a ghost in a dead place. None of the rooms had windows, though a few had paintings of sunny meadows. She headed for the closest door on the left, but found it locked.

A black rectangle on the wall by the handle appeared to be where someone would swipe an ID badge to open it. It had a clear plastic strip on the bottom that she worried ought to be glowing red or green. Seeing it dark didn't fill her with hope. In fact, it filled her with the exact opposite of hope.

Kiera darted across to the next plain white door, waving her arms for balance whenever her slimy feet slipped. It, too, refused to budge. She backtracked the way she'd come, checking every door. Some rooms had windows, revealing conference tables or medical labs. The majority of the doors occupied blank walls with no windows, but none of them opened. She ran to the end of the hallway and crashed into a pair of steel double-doors blocking her path.

Grunting and growling, she pulled at the handles, but couldn't get them to budge.

"Is anyone here?" She banged on the doors, sending echoing *booms* into the passageway beyond. "I need help!"

She took a step back, fuming. When she bowed her head, all her rage flashed into terror at the sight of a bloody boot print between her feet on the metal grating. She twisted, peering back over her shoulder. The trail of footprints led to the second door on the right, one she'd tried and failed to open.

Kiera grabbed her head, shaking it. "No… no… this isn't real."

She started to tiptoe around the awful footprints, but forced herself to stop. Grimacing, she squatted near one, examining it. In the dim light, she couldn't tell much by sight, so she touched a single fingertip to it.

Dry.

Her sigh of relief broke the quiet. Whoever had been here and hurt people had to be long gone, or the prints would be wet.

She stood and hurried back down the hall, past the hatch, and around a corner to a stretch of corridor with yet more windows. A short distance ahead on the left, she peered in on a shower area similar to the fitness center at her parents' office. Across the hall behind another inoperable locked door stood a cafeteria-style room with long tables and plastic chairs. Dead vending machines lined the inner wall.

"This isn't fair!" she shouted, her voice echoing over the stillness.

The sensation of being coated in cold, slippery ooze prodded her into the shower room. Dust covered the floor, deep enough to feel like she walked on powder. The small chamber had three shower stalls and a steel door to the right with a narrow strip of window that offered a view of lockers. Alas, that door refused to open. Out of spite, she pounded her fist on the dead ID badge reader. Still shivering, Kiera sighed at the showers and looked down at herself.

"Might as well... I'm already undressed."

She crept into a stall and reached for the knob, twisting a quarter of the way toward 'hot' before pulling on it. It made a sharp *squeak*, but no water came from above—not even a drop. Kiera stared at the showerhead for a moment before letting her arm drop back to her side.

"What happened here? Why does nothing work?"

The other two stalls proved equally useless, so she trudged into the hallway again, creeping along dreading at any moment someone would spring out of nowhere and she'd get in trouble (or made fun of) for not having anything on. Another double door blocked the end of that section. Kiera grumbled at it, expecting it would be locked as well, but the last door on the left hung open a few inches. She started to squeal in delight, but contained her hope of finding something to wear or eat.

"Why am I worrying about food? This is a stupid dream."

Kiera jogged to the door, the clap of her feet on the floor chasing her. A mangled handle lay on the grating nearby; bullet holes marred the door where it had been.

"Holy crap! Someone shot it!" She closed her eyes and shook her head. "No. Stop talking like this is real. No one shot it. I'm dreaming that someone shot it."

She took a few breaths to calm down and peeked in.

The space held four desks, two against the wall in front of her, two by the wall facing the corridor. A pair of tall metal cabinets stood at the narrow end. All had computer terminals similar to the one she had in her bedroom at home. Of course, the one she had at home hadn't been riddled with bullets. Someone shot everything in here to bits. Fragments of plastic littered the floor. Curiously, she didn't see any brass lying around. Just like a video game, the empty shell casings disappeared after a while. Then again, so did the bullet holes... usually.

"Yeah. I'm dreaming. This is the same computer I have."

Of course, the D-9500 terminal was everywhere. Even Ashleigh had one. Most of the workstations at her parents' company had them. Grumbling, she padded up to the cabinets, careful not to step on any sharp pieces. No lock kept the doors closed, but her hope died a quick death at spotting nothing useful inside: only shelves of computer parts and blank optical disks.

Kiera returned to the hallway, pacing around randomly. "This is a really screwy nightmare. Other than being stuck in a creepy place, it's not that scary." She frowned at herself. *That book said the naked dream is like being on a stage in front of people or dreaming that you're somewhere you'd normally be—only without clothes. It's supposed to represent fear of a situation... but there's no one here.*

A momentary image of floating in the tank with Mom peering down on her, jet-black hair framing an expression of total worry filled her mind. Her mother had turned away and removed her bra. Did they all get in tanks?

"No, that's just a bad dream, too."

Kiera squatted again, hugging her knees to her chest and sniffling. She'd had that dream before... being dragged down the hallway to the tank, her parents terrified about something but not telling her what. But every time she had that dream, she'd wake up in her bedroom and go to school. Mrs. Kee, the counselor, thought it had some hidden meaning and gave her the link for the e-book on dream meanings. Perhaps a bit advanced for a sixth-grader, but she managed to follow it for the most part.

The feeding tube haunted her, a scratch at the back of her throat. Had she felt it in school when she started to doze off? All those cold flashes, and that stuff not making sense. She grabbed the back of her head. *A needle into the brain... was I in virtual reality? The school year seemed to be taking forever, like the same few days happening over and over. It's not 2032, because I was ten. I'm eleven! I remember my birthday party!* If that life had been false, what did that mean for the blood on the ground by her parents' tanks?

She lost a few minutes crying, grief-stricken.

Eventually, she wiped her face on the back of her arm and stood.

"If this is a dream, it's not going to end 'til it's over." She sighed at the ceiling. "Yeah that was a dumb thing to say. If this is real, I'm in big trouble. I gotta get out of here."

Again, she ran around to every door, battering her scrawny body into them one after the next, but couldn't get any room to open. No one came running to check out all the noise she made, so she figured she'd wound up somewhere truly alone—and trapped. She had no way to escape this corridor. Out of breath, she dragged herself back to the maintenance passage hatch and sat on the floor, letting her legs dangle in the hole. A droplet of clear goop fell from her toes every few seconds.

"The tunnel kept going... Stay together, Kier. It's a level map, right? You haven't explored everywhere. Maybe there's another hatch. It looked long enough to go under those metal doors."

After a momentary rest, she climbed down below the floor again and faced the corridor where she hadn't gone. Hands balled into fists, she strode forward, trying to ignore fear and doubt. The only thing that made any sense pointed back to it being a crazy dream. She remembered a chapter in that book about dream triggers, something for her to find, do, or see that would end it and let her wake up. Hours of wandering this place could be only moments in reality.

Kiera scurried ahead to the next corner and into warmer air. She didn't hesitate, barreling around it at a brisk jog. A short spur ended a mere ten feet later at a dead end covered in electrical component boxes. No hatches up. She started to slouch in defeat, but spotted a square ventilation cover on the left wall.

"Wow, I didn't think places really had those."

She crept over and knelt in front of it, peering between the slats at a metal duct. Warm air blew over her face, strong enough to tease a few strands of drying hair about. Breathing tasted like dirt and the outside, as well as a faint chemical twang. A bit of determined tugging got the vent cover to come loose. She set it to the side before crawling into a dusty shaft. Five feet away, the air duct turned a left corner. A few feet past the turn, a dead fan drifted in the breeze. She lay flat on her belly, grimacing at the sensation of semidry slime squishing under her. It did, however, help her slide. She squirmed between two blades, sucking in a sharp breath when a metal edge scraped her hip.

"Ow." She rubbed the spot, relieved not to find blood.

After a long crawl, the duct ended at a T-junction. Since the warm air blew in from the right, she went in that direction. Another fan-squeeze and about thirty yards of crawling later, the vent turned a corner straight up.

She whined in frustration before she looked, but did so anyway. Her hope bloomed at the sight of a patch of sunlight at the top of a shaft. Another dormant fan sat at the midway point, low enough to reach. On tiptoe, she stretched until she got her fingers around the struts holding the fan in place.

*Thanks for taking me to that climbing place, Dad.*

Kiera froze, hands over her head gripping the bar while staring at the blank steel wall. "If that was all fake, whoever put me in there wanted me to practice climbing." She shivered. "Oh shut up. I sound like crazy Uncle Kyle."

With a soft grunt, she pulled herself up. The sides of the duct offered little traction for her feet, which mostly slipped on the smooth metal. Grunting, she wriggled up to the fan brace, lifted one knee onto it, and grabbed the walls for support. After easing her left leg up, she planted her foot on the middle of the motor and stood, wobbling. The fan mount sagged under her weight, but held.

Sunlight warmed the steel not far over her head and the wind sounded close. The shape of the duct above suggested it bent downward at an angle. One more pull-up and she might be able to slide to freedom.

Kiera grinned. "Well, that was a messed-up dream. I'm going to wake up as soon as I get outside."

# 4

# BORN OF EARTH

Kiera stared at the ledge over her head, hoping it offered escape. With any luck, only a few feet of duct stood between her and waking up. Heck, she'd even be thrilled to go back to school. She rubbed her hands together and waved them around, trying to dry them of the annoying slime. If her grip failed, she'd have a painful landing on the fan, probably cut herself, and… oh forget it, only a dream.

She crouched, took a breath, and leapt straight up. Her hands came down on the metal ridge with a loud *boom*. The sharp angle of the duct hurt to grab, but she refused to let go. Warm, dusty metal scratched at her chest as she pulled herself up inch by inch with arm power alone. Hazy sunlit dirt waited for her at the end of a short down-angled tunnel, barely six feet away. Once she got her hips past the edge, she reached a balance point that let her rest. She struggled to lift a leg up, but the shaft didn't give her enough room. Her knee kept bumping the wall and, unless a joint spontaneously developed in the middle of her thigh, she couldn't brace her knee on the ledge.

Before her arms gave out, she let herself tilt forward and lay flat, nudging ʒrself along by kicking her legs. Gravity pulled her the rest of the way in thout warning. She slid down and crashed face-first into a soft mesh cover, mpled into a tangled heap of arms and legs. Outside ground sat a short nce below, beach sand from the look of it.

ˋof!"

ˋ pushed at the edges, but the panel didn't give. A few punches broke a the screen, and she forced one hand into the hole, then the other. and pulling, she stretched the thin material apart until her weight caused her to ooze out into the day. A brief yelp of victory started, but cut short when she stopped, her hips snagged. Kiera dangled upside down, her fingertips inches from the pale beige sand. Her slime-matted hair fell around her, blocking her view of everything other than straight down.

"Argh! This sucks."

Her feet slipped over the featureless duct walls, offering no help. Grunting, she braced her hands against the vent and struggled to pull herself out. Twisting side to side, she kicked and bounced until the screen ripped wider and she fell to the dirt like a gangly newborn foal—complete with a coating of slime.

"Ow." She curled into a ball on her side, unsure if she wanted to grab where the wire mesh scratched on her way out or cradle the spot a rock got her in the back when she landed.

A few seconds later, the heat registered to her mind. It had to be over ninety. After freezing for so long, she basked in it. She sat up, pulled her hair off her face, and stood in the shadow of a ruined high-rise building, gazing up at a battered concrete and stone edifice. Past the fourth story, only tangled steel beams remained.

Her eyes adjusted to the bright light after a short while, leaving her squinting at endless open sands. Here and there, dark spots hinted at ruins, scraps of old cities on the horizon. A fragment of a nightmare came back to her. She remembered Dad's e-car screeching to a halt by the front doors of her parents' office, Citadel Corporation's main headquarters in San Antonio. They'd taken her there late at night, refusing to say why, other than she *had* to be good and listen to them. Her parents didn't even give her time to change out of the giant T-shirt she slept in.

But this couldn't be the Citadel office... it had been in the middle of a big city.

*Why didn't I wake up when I got out?* As soon as she burst out of the vent, the dream should've ended! Kiera shuddered at the tickle of clear slime running down her back. She stared at the vent she'd fallen from, jutting out of a weathered stone wall at head level. A Citadel Corporation logo adorned the opening, a flat-topped pyramid with 'CC' engraved inside.

Overhead, an angry mass of thick, dark clouds blotted out the sky. No direct sunlight reached the ground, and though bright compared to the place she'd crawled out of, the day was much dimmer than the world outside the school windows.

"No way..." She twisted around to gaze out over the desert. Swirls of sand danced in the wind. Far off, the distant sky appeared black where a standing wall of cloud blocked off the horizon. "What the heck? This better be a dream..." Again, she looked down at herself. Smears of brown marked her side and leg where she'd touched the ground. She squeegeed it off with her hand. "I'm in real big trouble if this isn't in my head."

Scuffing startled her.

Kiera leapt back, flattening herself against the scratchy, hot building. Distinct footsteps approached. She glanced around, but other than climbing the wall behind her or the massive piles of dirt to either side, she had nowhere to hide.

Expecting this to be the part of the nightmare where the monster found her, she trembled.

The head of an older man with dark skin appeared some distance in front of her, the rest of him rising into view as he ascended a hill out of the desert. Grey highlighted his afro, beard, and the hair covering his bare chest. A piecemeal skirt made of thin aluminum strips and bits of plastic, like chunks of old computers affixed to dingy canvas, clattered around his legs. Many wristwatches covered his left forearm most of the way to the elbow, and on his right, he wore a shroud of plastic fashioned into an arm guard, still with a Panasonic logo. A massive amount of necklaces dangled in front of his chest, most made of electrical cables as well as a string of DVDs glinting in the sunlight. Computer chips, resistors, and other tiny components decorated his beard. A crown of scrap metal, two wings stretching to either side studded with more computer chips and random shiny baubles, gleamed atop his head.

He came to a halt a few paces from where she stood flattened against the building, and smiled. "Child of the Earth...."

Kiera stared at his feet, also bare. She couldn't bring herself to look him in the eye—too ashamed. *I shouldn't talk to a stranger, but... I'm alone out in the desert with nothing. If he doesn't hurt me, being out here alone will.* She blushed. Lack of clothes caused conflict, a reason to seek help as well as avoid being seen. After a few seconds, fear of being alone won out and she decided to talk rather than run off screaming. "What do you want? Who are you?"

"Child of Earth, why does your face change to match your hair? I have never seen such magic before."

She bit her lip, trying to cover herself with her hands as much as she could. "I... Uhh...."

"Perhaps because you are so pale?" All the junk in his hair rattled as he tilted his head.

"Why are you calling me Child of Earth?" She managed to glance up at his face for a few seconds before shame made her bow her head again.

"*He* has sent me to find you, child." The man raised his arms to the sky in a dramatic pose, holding it for a few seconds before lowering them. "I have come to aid you. *He* told me you shall be born of the Earth this day. Come, child. Fear not."

After a long hesitation, she forced herself to look at him, face burning. He approached closer, but she couldn't lean away with stone at her shoulders.

"The planet has born you unto the world." He traced a finger across her shoulder, rubbing the clear slime between his thumb and forefinger after raising his hand. "I have witnessed your arrival, a difficult birth. You are still covered in it."

*This guy is nuts.* She forced herself to stop cringing. A little crazy, but he didn't seem dangerous. "I wasn't just born. I crawled out of a vent. I'm eleven, not a baby."

"You are born to us this day, fresh from the womb of the Earth." The old man gazed upward.

Kiera sighed, finding it odd he hadn't reacted at all to her lack of clothing. That part, she *did* have in common with a newborn. "Can I please have something to wear?"

"Follow me, child. I believe I have some cloth at my cave from which I shall fashion something for you if you desire."

"Yes, I desire." She squinted. *Why does he talk funny?* "Y-you want me to go with you? B-but I don't have anything on."

"Neither do the Sand Striders." The old man chuckled, wrinkles around his eyes deepening.

She scrunched up her nose. "What? Is that a creature or something?"

"A tribe. The Striders live in the south, near the Torment. They have no animals from which to make hides and dwell too far from the Citadel to trade."

"Tribes? There's tribes? But this is America." She glanced back at the building. "That's the Citadel Corporation… if I'm not having a big nightmare."

"America?" He blinked. "Truly, you are the Child of Earth come to save us. You speak in riddles beyond the understanding of man."

*Oh boy… he's been in the sun too long.* "My name's Kiera, not 'child.' Who are you, and how far away is your cave?"

He walked off in the direction he'd come from. "I am Legacy. We will reach my home in a few days' travel."

Kiera gasped. "A few *days*? You want me to stay like this for *days*?"

Legacy paused, glancing back over his shoulder with a raised eyebrow. "Stay like what? Is this not your true form?"

"Never mind." She bit her lip, gazing out over the endless, swirling sand. *Of course! That stupid video in class about the tribes… It's affecting my dream. Ugh, I hope I don't have to fight a truck with a spear.*

"This is a great day," said Legacy, resuming his walk.

*Umm, maybe for you.* She hurried to catch up, keeping pace two steps behind him. A constant wind from the right warmed and dried her. "Is this real or am I having a bad dream?"

"As real as you or I." Legacy chuckled. "What else would it be?"

"I was in school this morning, but I stayed up too late so I took a nap. I think I'm having a nightmare, but I don't usually talk to my nightmares."

They descended a long, sloping hill of sand, following a path of footprints that disappeared into the desert a good ways off. A traffic light stuck up out of the dirt, its top only tall as her waist. Kiera stared at the rusty metal, wondering how long it had been there. She waved her arms for balance, slipping and skidding down the dune to the flat sand at the bottom.

"What is 'school?'" asked Legacy.

Kiera stepped over a bit of concrete studded with sharp rebar spikes and paused to breathe. It had only been minutes since they started walking, but already, sweat coated her from head to toe. "It's a place where kids have to go to learn. There's teachers and lab projects and stuff. It can be fun sometimes, but mostly it's boring or difficult. It's overcrowded, too. Most of my classes have like, thirty kids."

"I find that difficult to imagine." Legacy chuckled. "There are barely ten children in any one village. What is a teacher?"

"A person who teaches."

He shook his head, making his crown clatter. "You've answered my question with the word I asked about. That does not tell me anything."

Kiera ran her hands through her slimy hair, ready to growl in frustration. "A teacher... Ugh. They like know stuff. Math, science, other languages... and it's their job to help us learn."

"Ahh, so they are your parents."

"No... not even close. They just teach us for a couple of hours, then we go home."

"Do they not nurture and guide you?" Legacy glanced at her without breaking stride.

Kiera fanned herself, gazing up at the overcast sky. Powerful sun on the other side of the clouds made the thin parts glow around roiling dark billows. *It's so hot...* "I guess, but not the same way as parents. Teachers don't love us. In fact, some teachers hate kids."

"I cannot understand that."

She laughed. "Yeah, it doesn't make sense. Why get a job as a teacher if you hate kids?"

"Job..." He blinked at her. "What is that?"

"Oh, wow. You don't know much do you?" She huffed. "A job is something that makes you leave your kid home alone all day long, but you get money for it. Most people hate them, but don't have a choice."

Legacy laughed. "I know far more than many. I seek the knowledge that time has no further use for, but may once again come to rely on... if *he* is correct."

"I have to be dreaming." She plodded on, staring down at her feet sinking to the ankle with each step in the soft silt. "Is this even sand? It feels like powder."

"We tread upon the ground up bones of what once was."

She squinted up at him. "Like cities? My parents' house is in the suburbs of San Antonio."

"Suburbs?"

"Ugh. Really?" She scowled at the sky for a few paces before taking a deep breath and chattering about her home, her parents, her school, her friend Ashleigh this boy Marlon who might like her but was too chicken to say anything, and how much she hated her robotics class, since the teacher gave hard tests.

Legacy pondered for a while in silence as they walked. He opened a satchel on his hip and removed a square water bottle about the size of a soda can. After taking a drink, he offered it to her. "Drink a sip or two. We must make it last."

She took the bottle. "Thanks." The unexpected warmth of the water almost made her choke, but she recovered and gulped down a few mouthfuls before forcing herself to stop. The taste of plastic lingered on her tongue. "Bleh."

He put the bottle back in the bag. "You have a most vivid imagination to craft such a tale."

"You think I'm making that up?"

"Or dreamed it." He chuckled.

"Okay." She hurried a few paces to get in front of him and stopped. "You said some magic voice told you to come find me, and expect me to believe that... but you don't believe that schools and houses exist?"

Legacy smiled a grandfatherly smile at her and patted her on the head. "You were right where *he* said you would be, were you not?" He gestured at the endless sands. "Look around you, Kiera. How else would I have been at that place at the moment of your birth?"

She opened her mouth, but couldn't think of anything to argue. Vast nothingness surrounded her in every direction filled with pale brown silt and the occasional hunk of concrete. Also, her emergence did bear a rather striking resemblance to birth, even down to a giant artificial womb, being covered in slime, and getting stuck on the way out. As she stared up at him, a flash of memory returned: she slid backward, butt-first into the tank, Mom holding her hand. The clear goo hadn't been cold then, only room temperature—which made it even more disgusting. A woman in a white coat approached with a syringe that would make her sleep. Another man held the breathing mask ready. Panicked tears and whining followed.

"Child?" asked Legacy, peering back at her from a few paces ahead.

Her brief daydream faded. "I think I remember before... Something scared my parents and they brought me to the place they worked, made me get in that tank. But I thought that was a bad dream." She explained going to school for-seeming-ever, and the nightmares about being dragged down the corridor.

"I do not understand." Legacy took her by the hand and resumed walking.

Kiera squinted into the wind, trying to make sense of a dark sprawl in the distance. A ruined city, skyscrapers twisted and fallen like dead trees. "This place feels like a bad dream, too. What's real?"

"Perhaps you describe the world as it was before Cloudfall."

The wind picked up, lifting her hair off her back and releasing sweat trails down her back. Moving air felt wonderful and cool. "What's Cloudfall?"

Legacy raised his arm in a grand gesture at the nothingness. "It is when the things that were became no more, and that which is became."

"You're scaring me."

He gave her a concerned look. "I am sorry, child. How?"

"You're speaking in nonsense and I don't think I'd make that up in my dream." She frowned at the sand, no longer showing any evident trail of his earlier footprints. "Are we lost?"

"I am not lost." He grinned. "Do not fear. I promised *him* I would see you safely to the Citadel."

"What year is it?"

"I understand you are asking for an expression of time, but I am unfamiliar with the answer you seek. I shall ask *him* when we reach my cave. He may know."

"He who?" She scratched at her forehead, pulling a few stray strands of hair away from her face.

"The one who sent me to find you."

"Who is he?" asked Kiera.

"*Him*." His voice sounded deeper than usual, laden with reverence.

Exasperated, she sighed. "Does *he* have a name other than he? What is he? God?"

"I have never heard *him* referred to as God, no." He bowed his head. "He is sometimes known as Thread Alpha, but I was commanded never to speak the name to any but the Child of the Earth."

"You're sure I'm this child you're looking for?"

He smiled broadly. "I am."

"How can you be so sure?" She squinted up at him. "And what am I going to do? I don't have any weapons, or training, or armor... nothing. At least you're gonna give me clothes. And I'm only eleven."

"I do not know exactly the means by which you will awaken the sleeping titans, but you shall leave a mark upon this world that generations will remember."

Kiera rolled her eyes. "No pressure then. This even *sounds* like the games I play. I am *so* having a nightmare."

"The world is trapped within a nightmare, and you shall awaken it."

"Yeah... right. So, what am I dreaming about? What are people like here? Is this place dangerous? You don't have any guns or swords."

"People are only trying to get by." He chuckled. "Most live in villages. Closer to the Citadel, they cling to the old ways. Near the Torment, they are more wild."

"Wild... does that mean they're dangerous?" She smacked her tongue a few times, parched. "Can I have some more water, please?"

"Soon. We must make it last. And not always. Wild in that they live in the ways the ancients did, long before the society that brought down the clouds."

"Oh... primitives." She glanced sideways at him. "Like you?"

Legacy let go of her hand to pat her on the back and pull her into a brief one-armed hug. "Like *us*."

# 5

# THREE MERCHANTS

Kiera walked at Legacy's side for a few hours, debating with herself what seemed the more likely nightmare: that her parents dragged her to a secret medical facility in the middle of the night and she woke up in a wasteland, or that she'd been in sixth grade for a lot longer than one year. Glitches nagged at her. The single tree waving in the breeze, the kid with the bottomless soda, the way even Ashleigh had been acting weird.

"Legacy?" She stopped walking, reaching up to feel at the back of her neck.

"Yes, child?" He faced her.

"Will you look and tell me if I'm hurt?" She turned her back to him, head bowed, and let her arms go slack at her sides. Facing the school nurse in her underwear had been mortifying, but for some reason (perhaps lack of choice) she felt at ease with him.

Calloused fingers brushed at her hair. He picked at the back of her neck, which sent a mild thread of pain into her skull. Not enough to cry out, but she cringed.

"It appears you've been bitten by a bloodfly."

"I have no idea what that is." She touched the spot again, poking at a tiny scab.

"There is some dried blood on your back, but the injury is small. A bloodfly is"—he held his thumb and finger an inch apart—"an insect about this big. They feed on blood, but are quite rare here. They are one of the few creatures the Torment does not kill."

Kiera shivered at the idea of a mosquito that size. "Umm, eww."

She sighed as they resumed walking. Heavy cloud cover dimmed the sun enough to prevent the sand from burning her feet, though it remained hot. Thick, humid air made the day miserable and left her covered in sweat. Legacy didn't perspire much, but an odd mushroom-like smell clung to him. He no longer held her hand, but she hovered close at his right side, a half-step behind.

The news had often detailed wars fought between countries, or sometimes even inside the military forces of the same country. Sometimes the reporters told of large corporations hiring mercenaries to protect against violent eco-terrorists or hostile soldiers. Yet, with all that horror on the news, her suburban home never once experienced any sign of trouble. Everything had always been normal.

A nauseous feeling stirred in her gut. Those reporters' increasing fear that the Earth was in trouble and humanity found its very existence in peril fit more with the fleeting memory of her worried parents forcing her into a bath of slime. Could a needle into her brain have plugged her into a simulation? But if that terrifying night—and *this* world—were real, that meant two things, one horrible. First: the school had been false as well as her best friend Ashleigh. How much time had passed? How long had she been floating in ooze? That at least explained why the people in white coats hadn't let her keep her underwear on: she'd have had to go to the bathroom while in the tank. Thinking of that made her scrunch up her nose in disgust.

Of course, if her suburban life had been a lie, that meant something far worse than this wasteland—her parents had been killed.

Tears ran freely at the memory of the bloody marks on the floor by the other tanks. All the rest had been empty, so why did whatever happen spare her? Why did the tank flush her down the drain rather than open to let her out? Had the killers still been there? Maybe she'd survived only because the killers couldn't open her tank.

Her game system had spoken directly to her. Everything started to feel too much like she'd already woken up.

*No. This is the nightmare! My parents aren't dead.*

Kiera forced the idea from her thoughts, wiped her face, and looked up. Legacy had gained distance due to her slowing from grief. She jogged to catch up, still sniffling, but refused to give in to despair. Three possible realities, and the one she wanted most to be true made the least amount of sense.

They walked for a few hours before squeaking and rattling came from the distance ahead. Legacy glanced toward it, but didn't show any signs of fear, so she kept going. In minutes, the clattering grew louder, and a bald man somewhere in his twenties walked up over the top of a sand hill not too far to the right. A glint flashed in front of his bare chest, a trinket, gold and shiny dangled on a chain around his neck. Furry black shorts covered his legs to the knee, and he carried a weapon that resembled a crossbow made out of metal scraps. Behind him followed two more men of similar age. The next in line had a grey plastic square held to his chest by wires, an attempt at armor. A scrap of black fur hung from a cord around his belt, serving as a loincloth. He carried an axe made from a speed limit sign.

The third man wore a skirt of tire treads and gripped a set of handlebars, though rather than a bicycle, they attached to a metal pole connected to a rickety cart full of metal boxes and plastic crates. Mountain bike tires held the wagon up off the sand. Most of the noise came from a collection of mismatched junk in plastic crates, shifting with the motion of the uneven wheels.

A spike of embarrassment hit Kiera at having three more strangers in view. She edged left to hide behind Legacy, who kept going in the same direction.

"Oy!" yelled the one with the crossbow. "Wanna trade?"

She breathed a small sigh of relief.

Legacy slowed and muttered, "Well, perhaps some water would be good… if they have it to spare." He approached the men, with Kiera reluctantly following, and stopped a few paces away. "Do you have enough water for trade?"

She peered around him, eyeing the men, not quite ready to trust them. The gleam at the crossbow-carrier's chest turned out to be a Burger King medallion on a thin chain. His companion's 'armor' chestplate looked like the side of a Dell computer—it still had the logo in the middle. If she hadn't been terrified this world could be real, she might've laughed at them for looking ridiculous.

"I was going to suggest a different trade," said King. "All your useful stuff in trade for me *not* giving you an arrow."

Kiera squeaked. *Crap!*

"Oh, and the kid, too." King smiled.

Her cheeks warmed with blush, but she stepped out from behind Legacy. "I don't have anything for you to steal. Nothing at all."

"S'okay, child," muttered Legacy. "I can handle these punks. When the fightin' starts, you run, right? I'll find ya."

"We don't want to take your stuff, kid," said King. "We takin' *you*. You make fer good tradin'."

*Daddy!* She took a step back. Her mind leapt to the cop speaking to her class about avoiding dangerous strangers, and these three appeared quite dangerous. Screaming for help wouldn't do much out in the middle of a desert, which had the crippling problem of a significant lack of authority figures. *They want to kidnap me!*

She crept backward.

"Dare you?!" roared Legacy, waving his arms. "This is the Child of Earth. You shall not interfere with her destiny!"

Kiera backed up more.

"Stop." King pointed the crossbow at her. It looked like a hunk of scrap, but the bolt loaded in it was longer than her whole arm. "I don't like running."

"You won't shoot me," said Kiera, her voice shaking. "I-if you shoot me, you can't sell me."

The other two men roared war cries and ran at Legacy. Dell raised his axe for a head-splitting swing, but Legacy caught the handle and bashed his plastic-covered forearm into the man's face. Dell staggered, but didn't let go of the axe. Legacy also kept his grip, the men grappling for control. The one in the tire skirt flung himself airborne into a flying tackle that wrapped his skinny body around the larger old man. Legacy took a step back from the weight of the hit, but kept his footing and tossed the man to the ground.

Kiera backed up another two steps, staring at the point of the bolt. *He won't shoot me. He's only trying to scare me.* Her heart raced. *This* had to be the nightmare part of the nightmare. Maybe she'd wake up soon!

"Firestone," yelled Dell. "Go low!"

The man in the tire-tread skirt dove at the old man's legs while Dell kept yanking on the axe. After Legacy hurled Firestone aside like a small boy, he shoulder-rammed Dell, managing to get the axe away from him. When he raised it, King pivoted and fired his crossbow. The long aluminum bolt pierced Legacy's right bicep and lodged, protruding from both sides, the tip bloody.

Kiera screamed and ran like hell.

Behind her, the grunts and groans of fighting continued, fading into the distance. Her feet hit the silt hard, kicking dust everywhere as she fought for traction. Like trying to run on the beach, she got tired fast, struggling not to fall over.

Growling came up behind her.

Screaming louder, she reached down deep inside herself for more speed, lost to total panic. Thumping footfalls closed in. Her lungs burned. Sweat got into her eyes, stinging. She kept pushing her legs to run faster, but the man continued gaining ground.

His shadow stretched out beside her. Rapid breaths sounded at her right ear. She yelped and veered left in a sudden turn, but he grabbed her in a two-armed bear hug, hauling her up off her feet. Shrieking, Kiera kicked and flailed. Sweaty arms on her sweaty skin slipped easily. The Burger King medallion pressed hot into her back, near burning. His bear hug became a chokehold as she slid down, too slippery to contain. Snarling, Kiera twisted, but before she could bite him, King jumped on top of her, pinning her to the dirt and wrestling until he trapped her arms to her chest with another bear hug.

"Ngh... Get off me!" she shouted. "Help! Someone help me!"

With a grunt, King dragged her upright, and then off her feet. He squeezed her wrists together, crushing most of the air out of her lungs from how tight he held on. Legs free in the air, she kicked and struggled as he carried her back toward the other two men. Legacy lay unconscious, face down in the sand. Dell rummaged the old man's satchel, taking several bottles of water and a plastic pouch holding what appeared to be yellow dish sponges.

"Put me down!" shouted Kiera, still kicking and squirming. "Get off!"

King carried her over to the cart. "Stone, grab rope. This one's a runner."

"No!" shrieked Kiera, bursting into tears and fighting harder. "Don't you dare!"

The man in the tire skirt jogged over to the cart and rifled among the junk. Screaming, she tried to punt the cart to knock it rolling, but King twisted her away from it. Firestone rounded the handlebar rod, approaching with scraps of rope in hand. She shrieked and tried to kick at him, but he gathered her legs and tied her ankles together despite her desperate squirming. As soon as the scratchy rope tightened, King flipped her over and dropped her on her chest in the sand. It took both of them to wrestle her arms behind her back. While King held her down, the other man bound her hands.

She sobbed, squirming. "Please don't do this... Let me go!"

They left her lying there wriggling for a few minutes while picking Legacy clean of anything they might be able to trade. King even took his bolt back, and reloaded the bloody thing in his crossbow. She rolled around to sit up, too terrified and angry to be embarrassed, and wobbled to her feet after a few tries.

King walked over and grabbed her after only three hops, scooping her up with one arm behind the back and one under her knees. "Don't be scared, kid. We ain't gonna hurt ya."

He carried her over to the cart and set her down on a steel-reinforced house door. The flatbed appeared to be made of two such doors somehow attached to a frame with four mountain bike tires. A plastic crate held bottles and cans to her right, others behind her had metal scraps, some knives, a rusted rifle useful only as a club, and many bundles of plastic tarp.

Out of breath, she choked and gagged on dusty air, shaking, an inch from wetting herself out of pure terror. She tugged at the binding on her wrists, grunting and gasping as it pinched. "Ow." The rope around her ankles looked ancient, like it should fall apart, but twisting her feet around didn't do much more than hurt too, so she sat still.

The men ignored her pleas and whines, loading Legacy's stuff on the cart behind her. Firestone grabbed the handlebars on her side and pushed the cart forward. She stared over her toes at his back for a little while before twisting to look at Legacy, who hadn't moved since she'd been caught. He didn't even moan.

She bowed her head, unable to stop shaking. Repetitious squeaking came from all four wheels as the cart wobbled forward. The uneven wagon rocked her side-to-side, all the accumulated junk shaking and clattering. Kiera cowered in place, begging in her mind to wake up, for her parents to hear her screaming in her sleep and come check on her. They'd both be at work now anyway, assuming she napped in the middle of the day.

Glitches. Feeding tube. Hospital nightmare. News stories of the world collapsing.

*No. This isn't real. This is* not *happening to me. I'm not being kidnapped.* She sniffled and cried.

For hours, they walked in silence, approaching the ruins of a city. Crumbling skyscrapers came into view, though most had been so damaged they'd become piles of dirt with iron beams sticking out of them. She tested the ropes every so often, but they hadn't gotten any looser. King meandered about up front, drifting left and right with a hand to his eyes, searching.

"Easy, kid," said Dell. "We ain't gonna hurt ya."

She lifted her head and gave him a pathetic, pleading stare. "Please let me go."

He stuck one of Legacy's water bottles out for her to drink.

"You didn't have to kill him." She wept.

"'Mon, kid. Gotta drink or you'll get sick." He poked her in the lip with the bottle.

She drank as much of the warm plastic-tasting water as he offered. Not that she'd known Legacy much more than a few hours, but nutty as he'd been, she had started to like him. At least he'd been friendly, and had been willing to fight these men to protect her. He could've run away.

"What are you going to do to me?" She shivered as all manner of news stories about missing kids came to mind. Most were never heard from again; some had been found dead. She trembled harder, almost throwing up the water at the thought she'd become one of those kids no one would ever find.

"Trade ya for supplies." King chugged down half a bottle.

"Trade? Like... slave?" She twisted at her hands, but the rope didn't let go.

"Dunno. Depends on who offers how much stuff for ya. Maybe someone who wants a kid, they be nice to ya. Maybe it be someone who needs a worker. Maybe they not be so nice." He stuck the end of the bottle in her face.

She opened her mouth and he poured the rest of the water down her throat. No one spoke for another two hours or so. Most of the time, she kept her head bowed in shame, somewhat covering herself with her thick hair. Whenever she looked around, desert stretched as far as she could see all around. When the clouds overhead darkened, King pointed, and they rushed off in that direction. Her butt bounced up off the old house door again and again as the wagon hurtled over ridges and dunes in the silt. She threaded her fingers through the mesh of a crate behind her to hold on so she didn't go flying and land on her head. Firestone slowed when they neared a giant mound of rubble, mostly dirt studded with concrete bits, easily two stories tall. One side had an opening, which they used to enter a C-shaped hollow.

Firestone pulled the wagon a few steps past the middle and stopped. King set his crossbow on the front end before scooping her up and carrying her to the innermost part of the area where he set her seated on the ground with her back against the twenty-foot high mound of rubble.

"Don't go nowhere." He pointed at the opening in the wall. "Only one way out. We hear ya. 'Sides, you gonna get trouble on your own."

She peered up at him. "Are you going to make me sleep tied up?"

"Yep. You a runner." King walked out of sight. "Don't want'cha gettin' hurt."

She lay there, sweating in the humid oven the world had become, barely able to move. "This is really rude. You're not being very nice at all. Can you at least give me something to wear?"

The men exchanged glances as if she'd asked them to paint her green.

"Whoever buys you can worry 'bout that," said King, from over by the wagon. "Don't make sense ta give you somethin' we can trade for stuff we need. Sides, you a kid, what'cha need armor for? Don' be stupid."

She scowled, deciding not to bother explaining the difference between armor and clothing. Frustrated, she stretched her legs out, grimacing, trying to squeeze one of her feet loose. A few minutes of struggling left her out of breath and drenched in sweat. *It's so hot...* Weary, she let her head plop back in the soft dirt, but sleep was impossible.

Plastic crinkles, muttering, and chewing came from her abductors.

*Are they going to give me food?* Her stomach growled. *How long was I in that tank?*

The sky blackened over the next few minutes. Soon, she couldn't even see herself it had gotten so dark. She twisted around, trying to reach the rope around her ankles, but couldn't quite get her fingers to touch it. A light winked on by the cart, startling her. Kiera shuffled around to lie flat again, hoping they hadn't noticed her escape attempt. King approached her with a flashlight and squatted nearby before setting the clear plastic pouch with those yellow slabs in it down nearby. She cringed from the sudden, bright glare, shying away from him. Only the expression of total calm on his face kept her from screaming in panic at being so defenseless.

He took one of the yellow objects out of the pouch and held it up. It looked about the size of a dish sponge, wrapped in plastic. After setting the flashlight on the ground by her knee, he opened the package and peeled the wrapper back, releasing a smell like scrambled eggs and chicken soup.

"What is that?" asked Kiera.

"It's food. Eat it." King held it out for her to bite.

*That looks modern. This isn't making sense again.* She leaned forward and bit off a piece. It had the texture of an omelet, but a much stronger flavor, like over-seasoned chicken soup. Though not awful, she'd never *want* to eat it if she had any other option. "Where did you get that?"

"From that old guy." He chuckled. "Just food, nothin' special."

"If the world is broken and everyone's living like tribals, where did you get a protein bar?" She bit off another hunk.

"Trade for 'em at the Citadel. They sell it for numbers."

"Numbers?" She leaned forward and took another bite, trying to finish it before he changed his mind and walked away.

"Yeah... 'ow many numbers ya have is like bein' rich. Lot of numbers makes you rich, but only in the Citadel. People out here don't trade in numbers."

"Oh, like a bank account?" She chomped the last piece, chewing and swallowing too fast to taste it.

"Ain't no idea what you' talkin' about." He crumpled up the wrapper and wandered back to the cart.

She twisted at her hands, tugging. "What year is it?"

"What'cha mean?" asked King.

Firestone yawned while unrolling a foam mat, upon which he stretched out to sleep.

"When is it? Like what date?" Kiera twisted and pulled at her arms. "I remember it being 2033."

"Twenty thirty what?" King scratched his head with the flashlight. "You talkin' funny."

"Please don't kidnap me." She squirmed. "Will you untie me?"

"Sure," said King, unrolling a foam mat.

Kiera blinked and sat up tall. "Really? You will?"

"Yep." King sat on his bed. "Soon as someone trades for you. We ain't givin' away our rope. That stuff is hard to find."

"Grr!" She writhed. "You're mean!" After struggling for a few seconds, she flopped limp and looked across the camp. "Dell? Will you at least untie my hands? You're scared I'll run away, but I can't if you leave my feet tied." She poured on the pleading stare.

"Uhh." Dell scratched his head. "Umm. Okay."

*Wow...* Kiera squirmed around so he could reach her hands more easily, but King grabbed his arm when he'd made it halfway across the camp.

"Leave 'er tied." King shook his head.

"Jes' her hands. She cain't run with her hands loose." Dell tried to take another step, but King tugged him back.

"What's the problem?" asked Firestone. "Dell's right. Kid can't run wif her hands, an' kinda hard ta sleep like that."

Kiera kept smiling innocently.

"You more-ans!" King sighed at the sky. "If 'er hands are loose, she can untie her feet."

Dell blinked, staring at Kiera for a long moment. He looked clueless.

"Go stand watch." King shoved him back toward the gap in the debris wall.

*Grr.* Kiera scowled at his back. Dripping sweat itched her nose, but she could only wipe her face with her knee.

Dell marched over to his spot and settled down to rest.

King threw a small rock at him. "You got first watch. We can't all sleep."

Grumbling, Dell dragged himself upright again. He trudged to the cart, picked up the crossbow, and plodded back to the gap in the wall.

Kiera lay back, sweltering in the baking heat, too miserable to move. Without the flashlight, the world became total darkness for a while, until her eyes managed to scrape the tiniest bit of moonlight out of the clouds, enough to perceive basic shapes at a distance. She stared down at her body, never having felt so vulnerable and helpless before, and never wanting her parents so much.

*It'll feel like you're taking a nap, and you'll wake right back up,* said Mom in the depths of her memory.

Her stomach grumbled. She stared at her navel, wondering how long it had been since solid food had been in there. The egg-bar hadn't been exactly solid. Still, it had more substance than the brown slime from the feeding tube.

"We try an' sell 'er 'round Norz?" asked Dell, sounding half-awake.

"No." Firestone stretched and yawned. "Too close to the Citadel. Them silver men kill slavers on sight."

"We ain't no New Dominion." King extended his arm toward her. "We are rescuin' a little feral what wants ta run off an' get hurt. If anyone ask why she tied, we say she's wild and kept tryin' to run off 'lone. We didn't want 'er ta get hurt."

"I'm not feral," yelled Kiera. "You're kidnapping me."

"Yeah, kid. Time to take a nap," muttered Firestone.

Kiera squirmed, gasping from the pinchy rope. Lying in the dirt, she stared up at the dark valleys between clouds backlit by the moon. *This isn't really happening. This can't be real.* The humid heat left her covered in sweat that wouldn't evaporate, and made each breath of the thick, wet air difficult. Her nightmare had gone on for far too long. As much as she begged the universe to let this be a bad dream, she kept finding doubt. In school at the same grade for way too long, repeating coursework, Ashleigh being weird, the glass beads in the vase appearing and disappearing. A needle in the brain, the tank, that old nightmare she'd almost forgotten.

Her one chance at possibly understanding anything lay off in the desert hours away and most likely dead. Her parents, too, had probably been killed. She wondered if her mother or father had even woken up before they'd died. No one who might protect her knew she lay here with only ropes to wear, kidnapped by men who she most definitely did *not* trust. Everything—and everyone—she'd known was gone.

Trembling with dread, Kiera gazed into the sky, tears streaming down the sides of her face.

# 6

# A PLACE TO HIDE

Time slipped in and out. Kiera tracked motion amid the shifting cloud ceiling, following thick spots or dark patches as they glided by. In the stillness of the camp, it occurred to her that there had been a continual breeze before they went inside this rubble wall. Aside from sand wisping off the top of the debris around them, the huge mounds of rubble shielded them from the constant wind howling above. The lack of moving air left her miserably hot, even in the dead of night with nothing on.

*They're going to sell me. Who does that?* She fought to keep herself from crying again. *I don't want to be a slave.* Horrible ideas came and went at what she might face in the coming days. Scrubbing floors, farm work, laundry, perhaps even sent to dig in a mine or something. Maybe, like the man said, someone who really wanted a child would buy her and take her in. If her parents had been murdered, finding a new family might not be so bad—but what if someone awful bought her? Could she run away, or would they keep her tied up all the time, too?

*I gotta get out of here!*

She wriggled hard for a few minutes before collapsing out of breath. Sweat dribbled down her sides. Dell glanced back at her from his watch post by the opening in the wall. He eventually looked away and yawned. She stared at him, heart pounding, lungs on fire from her futile effort as well as pure fear. No matter what these men said, she refused to trust anyone who would treat her like this and attack an old man.

After a while of utter silence, Dell nodded off. She kept watching him, nervously tapping her big toes together. He popped awake in under a minute, looked back at her, glanced at his two companions, and faced forward. Soon, he slumped forward again.

Kiera lay quiet and still, watching the man pass out, wake up, and pass out over and over. Each time he slept, he stayed out longer. Whenever his head slumped, she held her breath, sensing opportunity but having no idea what to do with it. The cart might offer help, especially the crate full of knives. *No way... I'll make so much noise.* She twisted left, shoving her arms out to the side so she could look at the rope. He'd wound the cord around a few times, before tying it off between her wrists. No way for her fingers to get to the knot. The rope also looked older than dirt, frayed, and ready to fall apart—but not so brittle she had the strength to break free.

*I need something sharp.*

She debated her odds of hopping to the wagon again, but felt certain the rickety thing would make a whole bunch of noise and wake all three of them up. Tears gathered in preparation for a storm at feeling trapped, but a glint caught her attention to the left. She swallowed her panic and squinted at a rusty spar jutting up from the rubble about six feet away.

Dell remained slouched over against the dirt, out cold. He'd wanted to sleep instead of stand watch, so maybe if she stayed super quiet, he'd remain unconscious. She pressed her hands down, lifting her rear end off the ground, and shimmied to the side. Like a sidewinder snake, she scooted over to where a broken signpost stuck out from a hunk of concrete. Though the flange didn't look sharpened, it had a thin edge loaded with rust, which might wind up working like saw teeth. Bending forward, she raised her hands up behind her back and pressed the knot between her wrists to the metal.

Her stare locked on Dell, she worked her arms up and down, grinding the ancient rope against the spar. Within seconds, her hope soared at faint snaps and rips. Dell mumbled and shifted. She froze, leaning her head to one side, pretending to be asleep. He adjusted his position and settled down against the dirt without looking back.

Again, she raked the rope up and down, clenching her hands into fists. Fear shifted bit by bit into anger and determination. A stink like burning hair wafted by, but it only made her scrape harder. Sweat dripped from her nose, patting on her thigh. She kept her jaw clenched tight so she didn't breathe too loud. Twisting and pulling at her arms, she ground the rotting cord into the metal for over a minute more before it gave way.

Perhaps the *snap* of it breaking made a little too much noise.

Dell sat up.

She kept her hands behind her back, head lolled to the side, and pretended to sleep, watching him past a curtain of hair over her face. He looked around, muttering incoherently. Kiera shivered from nerves. Moving slow, she worked her hands free and dropped the cord, but held her arms like she remained tied so he wouldn't notice she'd gotten loose. *Hah. I broke your stupid valuable rope. Take that!*

Dell snuggled up to the dirt once more and rested his head on his arm.

She waited another minute before reaching forward to untie her feet. The poorly tightened knot gave way with ease, making far less noise than sawing. Triumphant, Kiera kicked her legs free of the rope and hurled it aside. She shifted to all fours, staring at the wagon like a predatory cat. Something she could wear might be among the junk, but if the snap of rope startled Dell awake, he'd definitely catch her trying to steal from the cart.

Her gaze settled on the plastic pouch of yellow protein bars. *Ugh.* Still, food was food, and they'd foolishly left it close to her. She crawled to it, picked it up, and eased back against the rubble. Dell guarded the opening in the C like they couldn't even comprehend that anyone could simply scale the pile of dirt and concrete bits. If not for them trying to kidnap her, she might have pitied them for being idiots.

Kiera bit the food pouch, holding it with her teeth so she could use both hands to climb, careful not to grab anything rusty or sharp. Free of ropes, going up the wall proved a simple task. Hunks of concrete sticking out here and there made it as easy as the baby version of the climbing wall at the gym. At the top, the continuous wind again blew over her, bringing a momentary shiver as her sweat-soaked skin cooled. Dried slime from the tank matted her hair into a sticky mess, but a few threads fluttered in the breeze. She perched at the peak of rubble and peered back at the men to make sure none had noticed her. Relieved to find them all sleeping, she shifted around to descend the outside feet-first. At the bottom, she took a few steps backward before turning around, gazing in horrified awe at a sprawl of moonlit ruin.

The rubble ring in which they had camped sat at the edge of a former city, probably a downtown section. She couldn't recognize the place compared to the world she once knew. It looked more like a scene from one of her games than any place that had ever existed for real. The emptiness frightened her in a way being kidnapped had not, worsening her feelings of being small, alone, and vulnerable. A yawn forced its way out of her.

*I need to hide.*

Despite pouring with sweat, she trembled from a chill. It had to be close to midnight or past it. Between walking with Legacy and the cart ride as a captive, she figured she'd been awake since early morning. As much as she wanted to run and keep running until the sun came up, her exhausted body wouldn't obey. *I've been sleeping for at least a whole school year in virtual reality... I should be able to stay awake.*

She yawned again.

Kiera sprinted away from the rubble, heading toward the shadowy buildings. A short section of paving warmed her feet, still clinging to the heat it had baked in all day. Towering monstrosities of concrete and steel loomed over her on both sides. Gnarled, twisted struts of I-beams raked at the air, greedy fangs waiting for a meal. She jogged onward, staring side to side at every shadow.

She followed the path of what had once been a street for about ten minutes before catching sight of an old building that still had three intact floors. It stood near a few others that also remained recognizable as structures and not mounds of rubble and junk. It would've been dumb to hide in a single intact place with nothing nearby. If they had five or six buildings to check, the kidnappers might get frustrated and leave before they found her.

A short dash into the wind chased the oppressive heat away and brought her to a crumbling window frame. Any trace of glass had vanished years ago. She climbed up and into an alien landscape of furniture covered in windblown silt. The sand everywhere had the feel of talc, soft and cushy to walk on. The air tasted like dirt but smelled of mildew. Weak moonlight didn't penetrate far into the building, but her fear at being abducted again forced her onward down a corridor into total darkness. She slid her feet over the floor to avoid stepping on anything that would cut her, and kept one hand on the wall. Soon, her toe jabbed into something spongy. She squatted and felt around, guessing that she'd discovered a foam ceiling tile.

The wind howled in the upper reaches of the building, frightening a shiver out of her. She felt her way along the corridor, venturing deeper while climbing over soft rubble. Something plastic shot out from under her foot, making her fall flat on dry, scratchy/crumbly material. Nothing collapsed further, and after a few seconds of listening to silence, she pushed herself up to stand again, and continued.

She swept the wall with her hand and found an open doorway. After a moment of consideration, she decided to enter and stepped on grit. A few paces in, the floor became smooth. Waving both arms around in front of her, she stumbled blind until she grabbed a smooth, flat surface about chest high. Patting and feeling about, she soon recognized a countertop with a sink above a row of cabinet doors.

She squatted, grabbed the first tiny knob her hand met, and pulled open the door. Probing around in the dark, she slid her hands over smooth, empty surfaces. The space inside held only the smell of damp wood. The bottom felt like Formica, or something clean and un-rotted. Far from soft, but the enclosed space would hide her. She turned around and sat inside the cabinet, slid backward, and pulled the door closed behind her.

Kiera stretched out on her back, grasping her wrist to her chest and rubbing the sore spot where the rope had been. *I did it! I got away!* She wanted to cheer, to cry from joy, but dared not make even the tiniest sound.

For a while, she lay with her eyes closed, willing to sleep but unable to.

Her mind roamed to Legacy. *Maybe they didn't kill him. I didn't see any blood by his face, just from the arrow. He's a bit crazy, but nice.* She scratched idly at her stomach, wishing that he'd be okay. She caught herself wanting to be with him instead of her parents, and teared up. Though they often spent long hours at the office and hadn't been with her as much as she would've liked, they did love her. Had school been a lie? She grasped the back of her head and rubbed a finger over the tender spot. Those parents had been there for her. Dad even skipped work sometimes to do fun stuff. Had she been living with software, or had her parents in the other tanks logged into the same VR world?

She tried to remember what she had spent so long believing to be a nightmare: her terrified parents dragging her into a strange hospital in the middle of the night and not answering any of her questions. There had been other people beside the ones in white coats, but no other kids. She recalled standing next to the pod watching faces drift by the gap in the privacy screen, no one she knew by name. One or two had seemed familiar, probably met them at 'take-your-kid-to-work' day. Someone argued with Dad about her being there, ranting about it being too late, and they shouldn't have brought a child *here*.

Dad had shouted, "I'm not leaving her out there," followed by a stream of nasty words.

The more she thought about all the little glitches and the unnatural sense of strangeness over everything that day, the more she came to the reluctant conclusion that her present situation had to be actual reality. Mom had faded out of existence by the microwave not too long before Kiera wound up in the tank. *Someone unplugged them before me!* She decided to disbelieve her memory of bloody drag marks on the floor and tried to cling to the hope that her parents might be out there somewhere.

Shivering from worry, Kiera curled up and closed her eyes, waiting and hoping that her exhaustion might overpower her fear.

# 7

# THE FALLEN

Kiera awoke to a stifling enclosure lit by sunlight shining past gaps in the doors. She lay on her side, her left arm curled up under her head for a pillow. Sweat squished between her skin and the white Formica floor of a cabinet. Droplets ran over her face and neck, creeping down her sides like spiders. A cluster of PVC pipes connected a drum-shaped component to the underside of a steel sink a short distance past her feet.

She let out a groan of misery at being so hot, and, for a fleeting instant, didn't so much mind having nothing to wear. After stretching, she sat up and pushed the nearest door open. The room outside had a relatively clean floor of bland grey, another set of cabinets to the left, and a giant steel fridge next to a broken hole where tattered drywall fringed a gap in the cinder blocks. A whiteboard dangled by one corner on the opposite wall, near a row of windows that somehow still had glass. Ruined city outside baked under the glow of an invisible sun, hidden beyond the ceiling of dense clouds.

Urgency in her bladder got her moving. She crawled out from her hiding place and stood, bouncing on her toes, knees pinned together. In all her life, she couldn't remember *ever* having to go as bad as she did at that moment. Maybe it hurt because her body hadn't been used to holding it in the tank? Cooler air in the room compared to the stifling cabinet made the need even worse. Kiera hurried to the doorway on the right and peered out. Debris of crumbled walls, drop ceiling tiles, and old furniture formed a mudslide in both directions, the rubble up to her hips in places, though it looked possible to climb over. White tiles covered the wall inside another door a distance away.

*That has to be a bathroom!*

She wound up crawling on all fours to get over the pile of junk. A few times, she bit back yelps of surprise when the debris shifted under her and she went sliding. Eventually, she reached the doorway she'd been aiming for. The debris halved the height of the hallway, forcing her to stoop to avoid hitting her head on the ceiling. Perched with her feet together on a concrete block, she grasped the wall for balance and leaned in to look. The room beyond was indeed a bathroom, but urinals on the wall to her left said men's room.

"Ugh. Who cares!"

She skidded down the debris hill before speed-limping around fragments of tile and broken sinks to the stalls. All the toilets had a thick coating of dirt and plaster dust; not one had any water. Cringing, she forced herself to sit, knowing she'd never make it outside before having an accident. Dry or not, the toilet offered a sense of normality. She melted with relief into a slouch, elbows across her knees, head down as the pressure released. No water meant the plumbing had to be broken, so it wouldn't take long for it to stink, especially in the heat.

*I don't care. I'm not going to stay here. I can't... I'll starve.*

When she finished, she felt too relaxed to move for a minute or two. Freedom from such discomfort made her smile in spite of her situation. Perhaps it would've been smarter to stay with those three men and try to escape from whoever bought her instead? *No way.* She'd rather be on her own instead of with people who wanted to *sell* her.

Kiera stood and stretched. An empty toilet paper holder on her left horrified her with the sudden realization that in all likelihood, this primitive world had no idea what TP even was. "Oh, eww!"

Once the disgust at that thought wore off, she crept out of the bathroom and returned to the spot she'd spent the night, idly wondering about how those tribespeople who'd attacked the corporations dealt with not having toilet paper. No one ever really mentioned that in school. Maybe they had it despite being primitive? Leaves? Or did they simply jump in the river and take a bath every time they had to go?

"Bleh."

She sat on the floor in front of the cabinets and nibbled on another protein bar. Between color and texture, it reminded her of tamago sushi, but the overpowering chicken soup flavor would take a lot of getting used to. While munching, she examined the wrapper.

"Chicken flavored protein supplement bar. One thousand calories. Recommended usage: two per day." She froze, staring at the flat-topped pyramid logo at the corner of the wrapper with 'CC' on it. Citadel Corporation made it. She stuck the spongy bar in her teeth to hold it and turned the plastic film around, frantically searching for a 'best by' date. Alas, the label offered nothing of the sort. It didn't appear old, nor did the block taste stale. In fact, it had an overabundance of moisture, almost as if it had been designed to provide water as well as protein... though finishing it off left her thirsty.

She stared at the faucet over the sink and sighed. "Yeah, that'll work...."

"Dammit!" shouted a man out in the hallway.

Kiera froze like a mouse under the gaze of a hawk.

"It ain't my fault," said Dell.

*No!*

She grabbed the pouch with two remaining protein bars and crawled back into the cabinet as fast and quiet as she could. After pulling the door closed, she cringed away from the light leaking in, hugging her legs to her chest and shaking. Footsteps tromped closer in the room outside. At the far left end of the cabinet, a large slab of Formica-covered wood lay flat, something that had once divided the space into separate sections. She crawled over it into the deepest corner, a space between where two sets of cabinets met, then lifted the board into position so she could hide behind it. After wedging it in place against the top and bottom, she curled into a ball huddled against bare cinder blocks.

"Kid's gotta be in here somewhere," said King. "Tracks don't go nowhere else."

She put a hand over her mouth to stop from whimpering. All the soft dirt outside, of course she'd left a clear line of footprints straight to this building. Kiera tried to become part of the wall as the three men entered the room outside. Her hiding spot occupied a dead space in the corner, not part of either cabinet. She closed her eyes and begged the universe not to let them find her.

"Gotta be here somewhere," said Dell.

A meaty *slap* rang out, making her jump and shiver.

"Wouldn't need ta be running after the kid if you did your job!" yelled King. "Sleep on watch, you could'a killed us all."

"Kid ain't dangerous," muttered Dell in a meek tone.

Another *slap* followed, but she didn't move.

"No, you more-ran. Not the kid. Damn dust hounds, or bandits."

Kiera narrowed her eyes. *You're the bandits!*

"Kid was here," said Firestone. Plastic crinkled. "Found this."

A cabinet door opened with a squeak.

She held her breath, trying to stop shaking. Shadows moved to the right, dark spots shifting in the gaps around her temporary wall. *Please don't see me. Please don't see me.* A metallic clatter of a heavy amulet tapped against the floor.

"Hmm. Smells like kid in here, but ain't nothin'." King's voice filled the cabinet. "Bet she slept here."

"Hole?" asked Firestone. "Hole in the wall there. We ain't fittin'."

King grumbled. Light shifted as the cabinet door slammed. "Damn it, you idiot!"

She squeezed herself into a tighter ball, toes curling, the rage in the men's screaming voices paralyzed her with dread. If they found her, they'd probably hit her.

"You owe us what we would'a got for 'er," yelled King.

"Do not," said Dell. "You always take first watch. I used to sleepin' first. Not my fault. Why don't ya blame Firestone fer not tyin' her good."

"I tied her good," yelled Firestone.

Rapid scuffling footsteps and grunts preceded a body slamming into the cabinets. Kiera clamped her second hand over her mouth, huddled in the stifling, enclosed shelter. Despite becoming lightheaded from baking, she kept herself still, refusing to even wipe at the tickles wherever sweat ran down her body.

"F'ya tied her good, why she get loose?" yelled Dell.

"She got loose 'cause you sleepin!" shouted Firestone.

"It's comin' outta your share. And for the rope she broke!" King kicked one of the cabinet doors with a splintery *crunch*. "Damn!"

Kiera managed a tiny smile of self-satisfaction, then narrowed her eyes, wishing she'd destroyed the other rope, too.

"That's crap," yelled Dell. "She ain't worth 'at much. Who'd buy her? She too small ta do any real work."

"Naw, you dumb," said King. A slap rang out, and a second later, another. "Think! She's dora bull. You see that look on 'er when she begged ta be let go? Someone what wants a kid would'a give up half their house. Spirits ain't bringin' lotta babies around no more. Villagers all want kids, can't 'ave 'em."

Kiera's eyebrows scrunched together. *Dora bull?* It took her a second to figure out he meant 'adorable.' Simultaneously terrified and indignant, she scowled.

"Ya. You's smert," said Firestone. "Ain't lotta kids 'round the villages here'n this parts."

She bit her lip. An elderly news reporter babbled on in her memory about declining birth rates due to toxins in the environment. Terror gave way to a shred of hope. If she could reach a village, maybe the people there would be nice... assuming she could get away from these three. King had run her down with ease. She couldn't risk being spotted, or she'd get caught again. *He didn't see me... All I gotta do is stay quiet until they leave.*

"Come on..." King tromped across the room. "You go outside and look for more tracks. 'Stone, come wit' me and check 'round here."

The men walked out, grumbling amongst themselves.

Kiera stayed put, face mushed into her knees, staring down her legs at her feet. Fear kept her still, afraid to even breathe too loud. Over the better part of an hour, the noise of the men kicking in doors, flipping over desks, and searching any possible hiding place grew faint. A few times, they shouted bad words and hit things. Her mouth became dry and she found herself licking the sweat off her arms and even legs where she could reach. She scratched idly at her foot. The quiet stillness made her think of her parents again, and the awful idea that she'd probably become an orphan. She lost a while crying, her brain torturing her by trying to figure out if they'd died in the tanks before they woke up, or had been beaten and dragged away alive. So much blood smeared the floor in that room, she doubted anyone could have survived.

She hid her face against her knees, shaking with sobs. The parents she'd lived with for the unusually long school year had been much different from the ones she remembered in that other nightmare world. Not that they'd been mean or neglectful, but they'd both been so busy with work they left her alone with her video games more often than not. Could she cry over fake people? Except for the last day or two, it had seemed *so* real. Ashleigh, the rest of the kids at school, had they existed at all? Overcome by grief as though everyone she'd known had died at once in some horrible accident, hid in silence, too sad to weep.

*I shouldn't keep crying. I'm wasting water.*

She languished in the cramped, uncomfortable cabinet, roasting until she hadn't heard any signs of activity for a long time. A few bumps of her hand knocked the slab of wood loose, and she eased it down flat. One of the cabinet doors had been kicked in, littering the area with fragments of particleboard. She froze at the sight, even more frightened of King and those men. If they found her again, they'd be mean to her, probably stuff her into one of those crates.

Kiera crawled out of the cabinet, stood, and fanned herself. It had to be over a hundred degrees in the room, but the hiding place had been hotter. She crept to the door and peered into the hall. The building hung in silence except for the constant ghostly wail of the wind. One thing she knew for sure: staying here was a bad idea.

She headed out and walked past the bathroom, climbing over the debris to an open area where the buildings' walls had collapsed. Windblown sand slid across rusting desks and office chairs that had rotted to their frames. Dark mold clung to the walls in splotchy patterns that almost resembled a pine forest. Crusty brown muck covered the floor, crunching wherever she stepped. She squatted and picked at it, figuring it to be silt that had been wet and dried, become wet again, and dried again countless times.

Creeping around in search of anything she might be able to wear, she explored cabinets, desk drawers, doors, and rooms for a while, but turned up only some plastic sheets with so much mold on them she dared not touch them at all. The last room in the hallway held a ten-person conference table, but no chairs. Green marker writing on a whiteboard read, "Evacuation and Cairn Assignments – Phase 3: May 2040."

Kiera crept up to the board, stretching up on tiptoe to touch the writing. "It can't be 2040... I'd be eighteen. I'm eleven..." She examined herself, certain she didn't appear any older than she remembered being. Still scrawny, still in sixth grade. Though the muscles on her abdomen looked a bit more defined than she remembered. "If..." She gulped. "Was that tank like cryonic or something? Did they freeze us?"

She backed out of the room. Losing hope that the building offered anything useful, she clung to the pouch of two protein bars and made her way to a section of collapsed wall where the room became the outside. Kiera crouched and crawled up behind the debris, peeking out at the ruined city. When she spotted no sign of the three men who'd kidnapped her, she breathed a sigh of relief, stood, and walked out into the street.

Wind pushed her hair off her back, the heavy, sticky mass somewhat fluttering. She squinted at a brushing of dust on her face and body, and turned away so the pelting hit her in the side instead. Creaks and groans came from concrete far overhead, protesting the motion of the breeze. Every way she faced promised more ruined city and desert beyond. She decided to go in a random direction that didn't blow sand in her face. Most of the buildings she passed had collapsed into piles of dirt and chunks of concrete, no longer structures as much as mounds.

She stepped on something hot that made her yelp and jump back. Brass casings, corroded to a dark green color, littered the dirt around her. Kiera squatted and picked one up, tossing it back and forth between her hands as the sun made the metal painful to touch. Her vast experience with military equipment (from video games) told her it had come from a rifle. Fighting had happened here. She dropped it, as she had no use for spent ammo. Not that live ammo would help her either since she had no gun.

A short distance later, a long, segmented shape sat in the dust. Curiosity pulled her toward it, and she again squatted, brushing powdery sand away from what appeared to be a track, like from a tank, that had been blown off and left behind. She looked around, but no sign of the vehicle it came from remained. The metal appeared partially melted, as if it had been exposed to acid.

"This used to be part of San Antonio? What happened?" She stood, clapping dust from her hands. "Okay. I can't panic. I'm in trouble, but I need to keep calm. I've got two meals left, no water, no weapons, no armor..." She looked down and sighed. "No clothes...."

Granted, as hot as it was, she only needed clothes to protect from embarrassment. So far, everyone she'd met appeared to have made their own garments out of junk. Some kind of fur, plastic, power cables, computer cases, tires... Their utter lack of reaction to her absence of clothes bothered her the most. They hadn't even pointed and laughed.

"People have blown themselves up back to being cavemen." The irrational sorrow of no longer being able to play video games seemed like the worst thing in the world all of a sudden. She kicked a puff of silt into the air. "What's wrong with me? There isn't even toilet paper anymore and I miss video games?"

She refused to think that she'd spent more time with games than with her real parents. With the wind at her back, she followed the ghost of a city street. Twisted lampposts stuck up out of the ground here and there, barely taller than her. *The city's half buried...* She glanced down where she stepped, wondering if cars and stuff lurked below her.

Thunder crawled across the sky. Bright emerald lightning snapped and faded far off in the distance where the dark clouds formed an inky curtain.

"What... the... hell?" She stared at the wall of darkness. "Lightning isn't supposed to be green." *Clouds aren't supposed to go all the way to the ground either.*

The unending breeze made the heat tolerable, perhaps even comfortable. *It's not as hot as I remember running from school to the bus. Guess it's cooler because of the clouds.* She walked onward for a while longer. Eventually, she spotted the corner of a red stone building that remained upright, three walls but no roof. Kiera approached the ruin, carefully navigating a pile of concrete scraps, wincing whenever she stepped on a rock. Much to her disappointment, the area inside the walls held only more of the same: rubble. She scanned back and forth, sighing at the uselessness of it all, and swallowed spit.

"I need to find water."

Sunlight flashed from something shiny when she started to climb back down. She stared at the debris around that spot and made out the shape of a head among the rocks: a shiny, silvery head with dark hexagonal eyes.

"A robot?"

Kiera pulled herself up over the hill, stumble-sliding down the short incline to the ground inside the walls. She approached the gleam, having to circle around the bulk of concrete chunks to where a man-sized figure made of metal and plastic lay buried to the waist under the collapsed remains of the missing fourth wall. It didn't move or react in any way to her approach. She crouched behind its head, poking and prodding at anything that looked like a button or switch. A small blue square depressed with a faint *click*, causing a panel at the back of its head to flip open.

She recognized micro circuit breakers; two of eight had tripped due to a short. Also, a white plastic connector had popped loose from its socket, probably from the force of the wall striking it in the face. Kiera stood again to peer over the collapse, studying the way the rubble trapped the machine. Steel rebar had punctured the chest, and one of the legs had been crushed like a soda can under a car tire. Even if it turned out to be a bad guy, she doubted it would be any threat, even to a kid.

*Yay for robotics class. I guess I did learn something.*

"I wonder..." She squatted again and plugged the wire back into its socket before pushing the two blown breaker switches back to the left. "Does it still have any power?"

A few seconds after the last switch clicked, the robot beeped. Eyes divided into hundreds of tiny hexagons by thin gold wires lit up blue, a yellow glow at the center simulating a pupil.

"System error. Mobility functions impaired." The robot twitched, trying to move, but lacked the strength to shift the rubble. "Operator query?"

"Hello," said Kiera.

It leaned its head back to look at her, upside down. "Greetings, human child. Which tribe do you belong to?"

"I'm not from a tribe."

Its eyes simulated blinking by darkening from the edges inward. "Your attire suggests that you are from one of the tribes in the area. Though the chromatic signature of your hair is uncommon. Also, your skin possesses an unusual pallor. Are you sick?"

"No. I'm a ginger."

It blinked again. "You are not a root."

Kiera sighed. "Is everyone in this place stupid?"

"The average education level among the tribespeople outside the Citadel is quite low, so your assessment is close to accurate. Though there is a difference between lack of intelligence and lack of education."

"Do you know where I can find something to wear?"

"Villages or the Citadel would be the most likely source for apparel. Where are your parents?"

She frowned at the dirt. "Dead, probably."

"I suggest you locate a village. You are a child and in need of a caretaker. The Citadel does not allow access to members of the tribes without a work permit."

Kiera decided the robot didn't look like a threat, and stepped around in front of where it lay, sitting on a flattish piece of warm concrete that left her about eye-level with it. The machine lifted its head with a whirr. Instead of a mouth, it had a rectangular display screen, scratched and dusty. A straight bright green line gave off a neutral mood. Its shoulders bore a Citadel Corporation logo.

"What's the Citadel? Do you mean the corporation?"

The robot shook its head. "The business entity known as Citadel Corporation has not existed as such for a long time. There is only the Citadel left. It stands at the center of this refuge zone and keeps the contamination down to levels compatible with human life. The Citadel is a self-contained arcology where society continues to attempt survival. Venturing more than one hundred miles away in any direction would be harmful to you."

She dug her toes into the silt and bit her lip. *A hundred miles?* "Umm. What year is it now?"

"The current date is Thursday, February 11th, 2094."

Kiera gasped. "No! That's impossible. I... I... it's only 2033."

"My systems are accurate. I am certain the date is correct."

She buried her face in her hands, shaking her head. "It can't be. I shouldn't still be alive or I'd be an old woman."

"You have injection marks." The robot raised its one exposed arm to point at her thigh.

"Yeah." She tilted her arm to show off the red dots there as well. "And one in the back of my neck. The needles were *huge*."

The robot's green line mouth bent upward to a smile. "Did you emerge from a chamber full of liquid?"

"Yeah... that's why I don't have any clothes. This old guy thought I was just born."

The robot chuckled. "Ahh, primitives can be amusing. The injections were stimulant shots to restore your muscles after a long period of inactivity. It is likely that you were preserved in cryonic suspension."

"So it's really 2094 now? I was like frozen? How was I awake...?" She explained her friends, parents, house in the suburbs, and all.

"I calculate that you were frozen for the majority of the time you spent in the pod. The virtual reality you experienced would have likely occupied only a few weeks or months, though it could have felt like years at the speed of electronic communication with your brain."

She wiped sweat off her forehead, fidgeting, struggling to believe her ears. "The game told me I was almost out of time. I saw weird stuff happening."

"The life support system would have been close to running out of power after so long. As you may have determined, there is no infrastructure left. Because you are still alive, it must have had backup systems, but they do not last forever."

"Why did it wait so long to open? What happened to everyone else in there?" She started to tear up over her parents, but swallowed her grief.

Crying could wait until she didn't need to worry about staying alive—or losing water.

"Insufficient data."

"Are you from the Citadel? Wait, that's a stupid question. You're a robot. Of course you'd be from there if it's the only technology left."

"That is correct. My function is law enforcement."

She scratched at her shin, chasing a trickle of sweat. "Why are you out here so far?"

"I was in pursuit of four individuals who abducted several villagers for the purpose of enslaving them. We encountered them nearby. One of the men had an improvised explosive device, which he employed against me."

"You're a cop?" She bounced, her trust for the robot growing. "Some guys tried to kidnap me!" She rushed an explanation of the three men and pointed out the red marks on her wrists.

"I do not think it would be the same individuals. My system logs went offline in 2087. I have been here since, and likely will remain indefinitely. If I were not trapped, I would be obligated to escort an unaccompanied child to civilization."

"Can you call for help? Cops have radios."

The thin green line bent into a frown. "I am sorry, human child. My frame has suffered extensive damage."

"Where is the Citadel? How do I get there?"

"The refuge zone experiences a constant cyclonic wind effect. It rotates around the Citadel's position counterclockwise. To find the center, you would only need to put the wind to your left side and walk forward. If the wind is at your right, you are traveling away from it."

She jumped to her feet. "Awesome. So all I need to do is get to the Citadel."

"They will not let you in, child. Tribal individuals require work permits to gain entry."

Kiera stomped. "I'm *not* tribal! I know I have nothing on, but if they talk to me, they'll understand I'm not."

"Perhaps. You do seem intelligent. You may be able to convince them."

"Wait… work permits?" She raised an eyebrow. "That sounds a lot like slaves."

"Oh no. Slavery is highly illegal in the Citadel. Technology is closely guarded. Outsiders who wish to enter the Citadel to work must be screened. They are issued identity documentation. Administrator Sokolov has outlawed slavery with a death penalty. Alas, it does still occur out among the uncivilized. Primarily in the northeast area of the refuge among the New Dominion."

"Those guys who tried to kidnap me said something about that… New Dominion."

"A tribe. Violent and warlike." The robot shook his head. "You should avoid them. They would surely harm you. However, you are relatively close to the Citadel, so the odds of your encountering them are low."

"I need to find water and clothes... and food. Can you help me?" She pulled her hair away from her eyes, summoning her most endearing smile.

"My present condition renders that unlikely. You lack the strength to remove the rubble trapping me here. Your best chance for survival would be to go to a nearby village. There is one north of here, close enough that you should be able to walk there before you die of dehydration."

Kiera stared at it. "Wow... uhh thanks. That's not scary at all."

"Turn so the wind is meeting you at an angle." It traced a circle in the dirt, made a triangle at the center, and another dot close to the midway point between the edge and the triangle. "You are approximately here." It poked another dot into the dirt closer to the center but not in a straight line toward the middle. "The village is here."

She squatted by the map, pointing at the triangle. "That's the Citadel?"

"Correct."

With the wind rotating around the Citadel counterclockwise, if she faced diagonally into it, that would put her on course for the village. Straight into the wind would roam around the circle without getting closer to the middle. If the wind hit her from the left, she'd walk toward the center and miss the village.

"Okay. I got it. Thank you. Sorry I can't get you out of there."

"It is pointless to apologize for not doing something you are incapable of doing. It would take multiple adults to pull me free. I do not worry for my existence. I am curious though, how a tribal girl reactivated me."

Kiera growled. "Stop calling me tribal. I'm not. I went to school." *Even if it was fake.*

"School? Out here?" It tilted its head. "Power cell critical."

Its glowing eyes and mouth went dark as the head sagged to one side.

She sighed up at the clouds. "Figures. I'm alone again."

# 8

# DUST AND ASH

For a while after the robot went dark, Kiera paced around inside the shelter of the three remaining walls. Part of her begged the universe that this wasteland came out of a nightmare and she'd wake up safe in her bed soon. She hugged herself, shaking from the despair of wanting her parents back. Tears threatened to overtake her, but she kept fighting them off.

"I can't stay here…" She frowned at the two protein bars. No water, nothing to wear, no weapons to defend herself with, little food. "I'm not going to last long alone."

Kiera bit her lip while thinking about the village. The kidnappers said that people struggled to have babies, and someone might sell their entire house for a kid. That sounded like someone would be willing to help her… if she could handle the embarrassment of streaking around.

*Well, I can hide or I can starve to death.*

She took a deep breath and climbed a debris pile at the edge of the ruined building, careful not to scratch herself on jutting metal rods. At the top, she paused long enough to peer around at the endless desert in hopes of seeing any sign of civilization or another person who could help her, but every direction offered only more dust. Kiera stared down at herself and brushed dirt from her stomach, shaking her head in total disbelief that her present situation could possibly be anything other than a horrible dream. Living in a world where she needed a breathing mask to go outside would be easier to believe as real.

*Maybe I'm still in virtual reality. When I noticed the dog glitching out and sliding instead of walking, it fixed itself.* She concentrated on how wrong it was not to have any clothes, hoping the computer would pick up the error and correct it, but nothing happened.

When no amount of wishing helped, she made her way down the other side of the rubble, stepping with care over chunks of concrete to a flat area of soft silt. A few turns in place to feel the wind against her skin oriented her in the direction the robot told her to go. Alas, the ruins objected to her path, forcing her to detour around ruined buildings and divert along old streets for a while. Kiera gazed around in awed horror at what remained of buildings, traffic signs, and unidentifiable junk. Everything had an odd molten quality, as if a giant had carved a model city out of chocolate and left it in the sun too long. She touched one of the walls to confirm it as actual concrete, but jerked her hand back not wanting to get any bad stuff on her. Something that could dissolve rock would likely hurt her.

At least the powdery grey stuff under her feet proved nice to walk on. She followed as straight a line as possible while going around buildings or mounds of rubble in order to keep traveling in the general direction she wanted. Best of all, she found no sign of the bandits.

After a few continuous hours of walking, a building emerged from the whirling dust up ahead that looked in better shape than all the others she'd seen. Barriers of sandbags blocked off the front, and the façade had numerous gouges from bullets. Otherwise, the tall building still had the majority of its walls, though none of the windows remained.

Inspired with hope, she ran to it, puffs of dust blooming whenever her feet smacked the silt. The constant wind soon swept the line of haze she left in her wake into oblivion. Kiera jumped a thick aluminum pipe, perhaps a former traffic light, and rushed to a halt at the door. She hesitated, looking back over her shoulder at her footprints fading fast enough to see. About a minute later, no one could tell a person had walked there.

*No wonder those guys gave up trying to find me.*

The lobby held a thick, humid atmosphere, heavy with the stink of mold. Dust covered a floor of marble tiles in swaths, like a tiny scale model of desert dunes. She kept to the clear spots to avoid leaving footprints, heading around the reception desk to a pair of double glass doors with the name 'Meade, Wilson, and Dunn, Attorneys at Law' on it. Kiera grabbed the handles and tugged, but they refused to open. She growled, shaking them harder, more as a statement of protest at their being locked than a serious attempt to get in.

Kiera didn't bother trying the elevators and headed for the stairs. On the second story, she found a bunch of windblown rooms, exposed to the elements for so long nothing of any use remained. Footprints here and there suggested others had been and gone, likely collecting salvage long before her. A moldy piece of paper had a printout of an email with phone numbers to call for those inquiring about the status of family members in the armed forces.

Red lettering at the top proclaimed, "No information is available for service members who have deserted with units not loyal to the United States."

She dropped it and went up to the third story.

Upon finding a bathroom, she crept in and decided to relieve herself. A robot calling her tribal didn't make her tribal. She'd try to be civilized as much as possible. As soon as she sat, the floor crunched, the toilet sinking an inch or two. She screamed, grabbing the sides of the stall. With great care, she pulled her weight up off the seat, hanging by her grip on the empty toilet paper holder on one side, a handicapped-assistance railing on the other. The toilet shifted again, fell through the floor, and smashed to pieces on the ground level, leaving her suspended over a hole, her toes gripping the edge of the break.

Kiera dangled there, whimpering in shock for a second before her brain engaged. She leaned toward the toilet paper holder before shoving herself to the right, grabbing the railing in both hands and hanging. The partitions between stalls shook from her landing, threatening to rattle apart. A nasal wail of fear leaked out of her as she climbed hand over hand to the left. When she reached the end of the bar, she stretched one leg out and got her left foot up on solid floor. She grasped the edge of the stall, and, clinging to the cool metal, pulled herself to safety. A few more bits of tile fell down the hole, landing with sharp *cracks*.

She backed away, staring in horror at the broken floor. *Holy crap!* A few seconds later, she ran to the corridor. *I'll pee later.*

When she ceased trembling, she ventured into the hall and resumed her quick search, hoping to find curtains, fabric, or anything she could wrap herself in. All the rooms contained dust, broken furniture, and occasionally, smashed electronics. Old computers too damaged for the earlier scavengers to bother with remained as well as a mini-fridge or two that had long since been looted. Desk by desk, she pulled open every drawer, but someone had beat her here. Finger smears in dust indicated where a prior scavenger had taken things.

One small office still had vertical blinds, but the plastic slats would never work as any kind of garment. As soon as she touched one, it crumbled in her fingers. Whatever toxic mess it had been exposed to left the material as brittle as a cobweb. Scowling, she stormed across the hallway to the next room and flung the door open. At least ten skeletons slumped against the far wall on their knees, plastic ties around their wrists. All had holes in the backs of their skulls.

Kiera screamed and jumped back, hands clutched at her chin. After a few seconds of horrified staring, she bolted down the hall to the stairs and up again. Empty rifle brass, bones, and a skull littered the landing at the switchback, near a hole in the wall where a rusted bolt-action rifle remained lodged. Bare footprints in the dust, much larger than her feet, recorded the steps of whoever had looted the dead person. They hadn't bothered taking any of the empty casings.

She crept forward and peered out the gap between rifle and concrete, which looked down on the old city street over the sandbags. *Sniper nest.* The remains had broken apart so badly, she couldn't tell how he died other than not being shot in the head—the skull didn't have any holes in it that shouldn't be there. The gamer in her came out. She took a knee, hefting the rifle to her shoulder and pretending to be a sniper camping in a high-rise building. Alas, the scope had turned opaque grey, the lens having fallen victim to whatever corrosive substance had ruined everything else. Since she pointed the weapon at nothingness, she tried to fire it, but the trigger didn't move at all.

"Wow… guess the gun's rotted inside." She set it back as she found it and wiped her hands off on the wall.

When she noticed she'd put her knee down on a patch of dried blood, she winced, leapt to her feet, and tiptoed past the dead guy, back to the stairs.

The door to the fourth floor creaked, sending a screech of rusty metal echoing in the stairwell. She cringed at the loudness, but kept pushing until the fire door jammed on something inside. Enough space had opened for her to attempt squeezing by. Cinder blocks scraped at her backside, cool metal along her front, as she wedged herself past the gap into a hallway full of smashed rubble. The floor above this part had collapsed in, leaving her staring up at the ceiling of the fifth.

*Uhh, maybe I shouldn't be in here at all. This whole place is going to fall apart.*

A doorway straight ahead led to a giant spread of office cubicles. Another pair of bathroom doors flanked vending machines on the left side of a short hallway. On the right, an archway opened to a break room.

Kiera crept down the hall to the cube farm, grasping at a thread of memory, how her father used to keep a spare suit in his office 'for emergencies.' Maybe one of the employees had stashed clothing in their workspace. She went from cube to cube, searching dust-coated desks and drawers. More handprints and swipes in the grime told the story of other scavengers who'd already gathered everything shiny, electronic-looking, or useful.

After a while of searching, she took a break, sitting on a padded office chair in one of the cubes. The crusty, damp fabric scratched her skin and reeked of mold, disintegrating as she put her weight on it. Pictures tacked to the grey cube wall showed a smiling man a little younger than her father and a pair of two-year-old boys. Some of the photos had a strawberry-blonde woman with the same man and kids. A handful looked like they'd been taken at Disneyland, with a row of militarized police officers in the background.

She swung her feet back and forth, thinking about a news voice mentioning anti-corporate terrorists attacking the theme park. The woman reporter made a comment about how could people still bother going to amusement parks when the world was falling to pieces. Her co-anchor started an argument on air, which had caused the network to go to commercial.

Out of sheer randomness, she sat up straight and set her hands on the keyboard connected to nothing, muttering as she typed, "If this is a nightmare or if I'm in virtual reality right now, please let me wake up."

She waited a second, not really expecting anything to happen—and nothing did.

"I'm wasting time... and this building is going to fall apart."

More searching brought her to the end of the room by a long window. Cubes took up most of the fourth floor, and fortunately, only that one section of hallway by the stairs had collapsed. She stepped up on a slab of crumbled wall to get closer to the window without entering the field of glass shards all over the carpet. Balanced on her knees, she grasped the top of the concrete chunk and peered out between two twisted bits of rebar at the ruins of downtown.

"Mom, Dad... are you dead?" Tears came without warning. "Where are you? Please... I don't want to be alone anymore."

The ruined city went on for several more blocks before giving way to open desert again. At this height, her view of the surroundings made the cloud cover appear dome-like. The robot had told her a hundred miles out from the Citadel, the world became toxic. She pictured a bubble of 'good air' pushing the clouds away.

Off in the distance, smoke trails suggested the presence of other people, perhaps the village that robot mentioned. Her stomach growled, so she put a hand to it. The protein bar she'd had before didn't fill her up, but it was concentrated. Eating more than two a day would be both wasteful and unhealthy.

A laugh belted out of her. *Are tribespeople worried about getting fat?*

She pictured a pair of loincloth-clad spearmen stopping at a Starbucks on their way to the campfire, and cracked up giggling at the ridiculousness of it. Laughing soon became crying at the worry she might not be dreaming. She slid to the bottom of the slab and curled up on the rug, sobbing.

No amount of wanting made her parents appear out of thin air.

# 9

# SMALL

Kiera rested her chin on her knees, staring down her legs at the clear plastic pouch by her toes. Two protein bars represented the entirety of her worldly possessions. She heaved a sigh and wiped her face dry. Her parents were probably dead. The ghosts she'd been living with in virtual reality didn't behave like her parents. They'd been programs made to act like parents. Her real parents 'gave her space' since she'd become older.

She made a sour face. 'Giving her space' had been a nice way of saying she had to cook for herself when they didn't come home from work until after her bedtime, or how they left her alone with video games every day. Her grief over their loss darkened to anger at them for ignoring her.

"So what if you're dead! You already were!" She leapt up to stand, hands balled in fists. "You ignored me. I'm not sad you're gone!"

Another wave of sobbing gathered in her chest, but she forced it down.

"Think. I gotta think. I'm going to die if I'm stupid." She gulped. "I can't be stupid." Her lip quivered as tears fought to come out. "This isn't fake. I'm not dreaming."

She slapped herself on the thigh hard enough to sting.

"Aww, crap." She cradled the spot, limping to the side. "Ow. Nope. This is real." When the pain faded, she stooped to grab her protein bars, and sighed. "Double crap. I'm in deep crud."

Creeping along, she made her way out of the cube farm and back to the stairs. The rest of the floors up could go to hell. Her fear of the building falling apart overpowered her curiosity. Anything that might've been here had been taken already, no sense risking her life on the small chance prior looters missed something. She hurried down the stairs to the first floor and ran straight into the door—which didn't move.

"Oof." She backed up, rubbing her arm. "Ow."

Again she pushed on the bar, shoving until her feet slid backward over the floor.

"Oh no... what happened?" Her heart thudded in her chest. "It opened before...."

Kiera flung herself against the door over and over, bouncing away without budging it even an inch. She considered shouting for help, but still feared those three men more than being stuck in the stairwell. *Did the ceiling fall in when the toilet broke?*

"What am I gonna do now?" She paced around in a circle, debating between another set of stairs down to a basement level or heading up to the second floor and looking for a way to climb down outside.

Basement didn't seem likely to offer a way out, but the idea of going out a window on the second floor scared her. *I should at least check.* She edged over to the stairs and peeked around the corner. Metal-capped concrete steps brought her to the opening of an underground garage. A few cars remained in parking spaces, many she recognized. That, of course, meant the cars approached sixty years old. Dried stains on the ground below them didn't bode well for their odds of working. Not that she had the keys anyway. She grumbled, about to give up, but froze at a sudden thought.

"Cars! That's awesome! There's gotta be a ramp!"

Kiera jogged into the basement, finding herself shivering at the unexpected chill. Like a cave, the underground concrete structure had made the area a shelter from the oppressive heat. She proceeded past a row of parking spaces, forty in total, before the room bent rightward at a corner and continued to a ramp blocked off by two guard booths and a steel garage door.

She shook her fists in victory. "Yes!"

The clap of her feet striking smooth concrete echoed as she jogged across the length of the garage. A golf cart with security markings sat parked near the booth. She hopped in the driver's seat, cringing at the sensation of dry-rotted fabric crumbling beneath her, scratching as she moved. She grabbed the wheel, but turning it didn't do anything, nor did stepping on the cold pedals.

"Duh."

She twisted a small key in the dashboard to the on position, but the cart remained dead. Frustrated, she folded her arms across the steering wheel and put her head down on them. "Ugh. What am I thinking? It's been sitting here for like, ever. The batteries are gone."

Reluctantly, she abandoned the cart, brushing fabric bits off her rear end, then ducked under the yellow-and-white striped arm of the security booth. Ancient dried blood spattered the inside wall. She cringed away, not wanting to see what might be inside there, and scurried over to the exit ramp.

A rolling steel door covered the three-lane-wide opening, with a few inches of gap at the bottom. Warmth breezed in over her toes, almost pleasant compared to the chilly basement. She got down on her hands and knees and peered under at the outside, grinning at her almost-freedom. Grabbing the bottom of the door and pulling succeeded only in making a large amount of clattering noise.

"The button's in that nasty booth, isn't it?" she asked no one in particular.

Hoping not to have to go anywhere near where someone died, she looked around for another option. The flexible door unspooled from a long, cylindrical housing along the top. On the right end, an electric motor connected to the spindle, but it also had a chain over a spoked wheel that hung down near the floor—a manual backup.

"Yes! Luck!" She grinned, but frowned a second later at being stranded in a destroyed world with nothing to drink, or wear, and only a couple of protein bars to eat. "If this is *good* luck, I don't want to know what bad luck looks like." She thought of the bandits carting her off to slavery. "Okay, I take that back. I've seen bad luck."

She dropped the protein bar pouch on the floor and took the chain in both hands. Pulling lifted her up on tiptoe, but didn't move the door. *Maybe I got it backward?* She grabbed the other side of the chain loop and tried again, but couldn't budge it. *Grr. I hate being so weak.* Kiera frowned at her arms and chest... both of which looked more sinewy and muscular than she remembered. *Huh what?* She even almost had abs. *I've been a couch potato forever... why do I look like I've been taking gymnastics? That climbing stuff was in VR....*

Grumbling, she stared up the length of chain at the spoked wheel. If it connected to the spindle without some funky gear system, it would need to rotate counterclockwise to pull the door up. She grabbed the inner part of the chain loop again and lifted herself up off her feet, hanging on it. *Grr! Come on!* Kiera wrapped her legs around the chain and climbed it like the rope in gym class for a few feet. She pulled herself up until her fists reached her stomach, then dropped to hang by her hands, using all her weight to heave at the chain. The door shook in response. *It's stuck.* She repeated the process of pulling herself up and falling.

"Come on, move!" she yelled, and did it again.

The fourth time, the mechanism gave way, rattling as she glided down until her toes touched concrete. While the chain had moved several feet, the door had only gone up two inches. Grumbling, she tried to climb again, but the chain didn't resist enough for her to leave the ground. A little while of pulling raised the door, creating a gap she could fit through. Eager to flee the deathtrap building, she didn't bother wasting the time it would take to open it enough to walk out, preferring to lay flat on her chest and scoot under.

Once outside, she ran well away in case the old office decided to spite her escaping by collapsing on top of her. As soon as she felt safe, she stopped to rest and took a seat on the soft dirt. She picked at her hair, still sticky from the dried residue of the tank slime. Taking a bath ranked low on her list of priorities (and also required a whole bunch of water she didn't have), but she still spent a while pulling the matted slab apart into separate strands at least so air could move across her back.

Confident that the silt wouldn't collapse out from under her like the last toilet had, she ducked behind a pile of rubble and relieved herself on the ground, blushing despite having no other choice. *Do the villages have toilets or are they like, super native?* Fortunately, she didn't have to do the other thing, so not having any toilet paper didn't present an immediate worry. With any luck, maybe those high-efficiency protein bars would make it so she didn't have to go for a long time.

"Eww."

Using the wind to aim herself toward the village, she walked on. Soon, she left the dead high-rises behind for shorter ruins. Light faded far faster than she expected it to. In barely three blocks' distance, she almost couldn't see twenty feet away from where she stood. Despite the pitch darkness, she continued walking with her arms out in front to catch anything she might stumble into.

A glimmer of moonlight ahead led her to a demolished building that consisted only of two fragmentary walls barely a full story tall, a broken wedge pointing into the wind. Kiera figured she could find shelter there for the night. Traveling alone scared her plenty enough when she *could* see. Having no desire to roam blind, she scurried into the remnants of a structure so far decayed she couldn't tell what it had been. In the corner where the walls met lay a mildewed mattress. Someone had made a home of this place some time ago, but she spotted no sign of recent use.

The wind whistled overhead, shaking the flimsy walls. She tested the mattress with a foot, finding it damp. A spring poked out here and there, but enough area looked safe for a kid to sleep on. She sat on the edge and opened another protein bar, nibbling on it while thinking about how much she missed her home, even if it had been fake. No matter how hard she tried to remember where she'd lived in the real world before, she couldn't picture anything—only that her parents had never been around. Faint memories of breathing masks and plastic ponchos flickered in and out, and something about school being cancelled for a long time due to poison in the air; the government didn't want children going outside.

Clouds thickened, dimming the moon even more. She might as well have closed her eyes, for it had become so dark she couldn't see her arm an inch in front of her face.

After finishing the bar, she eased herself back and curled up on her side in a fetal pose. Her bed smelled like a sneaker that had been left out in the rain. Indirect wind tousled her hair against her back, though the temperature remained uncomfortably warm. She had trouble falling asleep without at least a sheet on her, more out of habit than being cold. All her life, she'd slept in air-conditioning with winter blankets up to her chin. 'Snug as a bug in a rug' as Mom always said.

Mom.

Kiera sniffled, but refused to cry. "I'm still mad at you for ignoring me."

Curled up with her hands at her chin, she gazed into the darkness, and shivered out of worry despite sweating. For the first time in her life, she felt completely alone and unprotected. No parents to stand between her and whatever wanted to hurt her. No bedtime, no rules, no school. She sighed. No video games. No food. No clothes. No friends. No idea if she'd be alive in three days. Her throat scratched with every breath. She'd gone a day without water. Miss Lentz in biology said something about that. How long could a person go without water? Two days? Three? Four? The robot told her she could make it to the village before she died from no water. But he didn't expect her to waste hours exploring an old building.

*Tomorrow, I'll go straight. No stops.* She smacked her lips, worrying at how dry her mouth had become.

A while after lying down, the cloud cover thinned, brightening the weak moonlight enough to suggest the basic shapes of her surroundings. Of course, her pale skin practically glowed blue in the dark. Feeling conspicuous, she looked around for something to cover herself with, but the only option involved burrowing under the powdery silt—or lying on top of it; the pale grey substance took on the same luminous blue as her body. Hoping that the rubble and the walls would keep her safe, she closed her eyes and tried to stop worrying enough to sleep.

KIERA AWOKE IN A MIRE OF SWEAT. DAYLIGHT BROUGHT INTENSE, HUMID HEAT. She rolled onto her back and stretched out flat on the rotting mattress. Part of her knew she should get up and continue walking, but part of her also thought she'd already messed up by wasting so much time. No matter what she did, she would die, so why bother? Dead is dead; why die tired?

Her mother's voice needled at her ear. *Come on, hon. You've got school today. You can't sleep all the time.*

"Why can't they have school later? I'm a night owl," said Kiera. "I hate waking up early."

She stared up at the clouds, tracing her fingers around her stomach, scratching her hip, swishing her feet back and forth. Remaining here might not be a great plan, but it appealed to her lazy side. The realization that she didn't have to pee started her worrying. That worry built until it pulled her up to sit. She couldn't ever remember waking up in the morning and not needing to go straight to the bathroom.

Kiera eyed her last protein bar. *I'll save it for tonight.*

With a groan, she stood and swatted bits of rotten mattress off her legs. As soon as she left the shelter of the joined walls, the wind dropped the temperature to tolerable levels. The urge to lie there and die faded along with the overwhelming heat, though her mouth still felt like she'd packed it with cotton balls.

*Ugh. Someone please help me....*

She trudged onward, facing diagonal to the wind, and walked for hours. Buildings became more and more sparse. A blast crater on the left glittered with fragments of metal and glass. She diverted away from it, fearing it might've been a nuclear bomb and had radiation or something. Not that walking another fifty feet farther from it would have mattered.

Well past noon, a still-standing building emerged from the dusty haze ahead on the right. The green, white, and red pattern of a 7-11 convenience store teased her with hope. She loped up to a run, heading for the doors. A short distance from the building, something hard caught her toe and tripped her flat on her chest.

She yowled in pain and rolled over to grab her foot, cradling her throbbing toes while glaring at a mostly-buried concrete parking space bumper. Gritting her teeth, she stood and limped into the store. Bare metal shelves held a few empty cardboard boxes while cases by the register remained packed full of useless scratch-off game cards. She approached the counter, gazing up at empty racks that used to hold cigarette packs. Gritty sand scuffed under her feet while she roamed around the shelves on the way to the cooler case. That, too, had been emptied of everything. Chances are, the looters that hit this place had done so long before humanity went tribal.

In a back hallway, a tangle of chairs blocked a heavy door covered in dents. It looked like someone (or several someones) had spent quite a while bashing at it with the chairs, but didn't manage to get it open. A little way to the right of the door, a former looter had taken a sledgehammer to the cinder blocks, bashing a few apart and creating a small hole. The broken-off sledge head still sat on the floor nearby.

Kiera padded over to the smashed wall and got down on all fours to stick her head into a stock room. It contained more empty shelves, but against the wall, a rotting wooden pallet held two six-packs of bottled water.

"Ooh!"

She flattened out on the floor and pulled herself through the hole, offering a quiet mutter of thanks to whoever had broken their hammer trying to make a new doorway. She grabbed at the floor, wriggling forward. As soon as she cleared the opening, she scrambled for the water, not even bothering to stand up all the way.

Like a feral creature, she clawed at the plastic. After tearing a bottle loose from the pack, she ripped the cap off and chugged. It might've been seventy years old and stale, but it was awesome.

About a quarter of the bottle dribbled down her chest in her haste. She swished a mouthful around her gummy, dried-out mouth, and spat. Another swig she held in her mouth while imagining her tongue soaking it up like a sponge. The second bottle, she drank with care not to spill any, finishing the whole thing as fast as her need to breathe would allow.

She glanced back over her shoulder at the hole. "Okay, maybe it's good to be small."

Once she caught her breath, Kiera forced herself upright and explored the storeroom. Rust crescents marked the surfaces of three freestanding steel shelves in the middle of the room, ghosts of ancient canned goods. A single package of Devil Dogs cakes remained along with a scattering of old magazines. One desk against the opposite wall had a computer that looked out of date, an antique even before the world fell apart.

She grabbed the cakes and headed to the desk with the magazines under one arm. Warm, brittle material cracked against her skin as she sat, the steel chair with fake-leather cushion creaking under her weight. In the drawers, she found pens, markers, rubber bands, paper clips, a stapler, five boxes of staples, pushpins, a whole bunch of copy paper, and three-ring binders. Nothing to eat, drink, or wear inside.

Kiera sighed. She leaned back in the chair, put her feet up on the desk, and feasted on Devil Dogs while leafing through a hunting and fishing magazine from 2029. She chucked it aside in only minutes, nauseated by pictures from the last legal deer hunt before they became officially endangered. A teacher or newscaster in her memory mentioned deer becoming extinct in 2032.

Another magazine had many pictures of celebrities, a few of whom she recognized. Most of the articles were interviews with actors and directors calling on people to challenge the government and stand up to the companies responsible for poisoning the environment as well as 'big banks' for working with corporations linked to major disasters. She tossed the magazine on the desk and ate another Devil Dog.

"Guess they didn't stop."

While working on water bottle number three, she browsed a news magazine from 2031. Most of its articles talked about worldwide war, though rather than a true World War, fragmented armies picked fights with themselves or other small factions in neighboring countries. As pockets of habitable Earth shrank, the people who remained fought for survival.

"Ugh." She threw that one into the corner. "I'm already sad and scared out of my mind. Don't need to make it worse."

*This room is safe. I could live here for a while.* She picked at the cardboard snack cake box. *I'll run out of food and there's only nine bottles of water left.* An hour or so of attempting to make a skirt out of ripped up magazines ended in a giant useless mess. With a sigh, she crawled back out the hole and ran around behind the store to relieve herself. Shredded magazine made for uncomfortable toilet paper, but it beat nothing. After burying the evidence, she stared up at the late afternoon sky.

*I'll sleep here tonight... keep going in the morning.*

A hole only a kid could squeeze through offered a sense of security she hadn't felt since being home in her own bed. Even if that bed had been a computer-dream. Kiera spent the rest of the daylight time exploring the store, searching every cabinet, shelf, and cooler case, but aside from a long-expired bottle of bleach and some cat litter, found nothing of interest.

Once it started to get dark, she crawled into the storage room, ate another Devil Dog, and curled up in a ball on the office chair, the only thing in the area with any degree of softness. Loneliness crashed into her anger at her parents for leaving her alone, and she cried herself to sleep.

# VOICES OF THE DEAD

**K**iera awoke to a loud *bang*, arms and legs flailing in panic as she slid across the floor, sweaty skin gliding with ease. She came to a stop on her chest and stared into space for a few seconds until her brain finished waking up. *Why am I on the floor?* With a groan of pain, she rubbed her shoulder and twisted around to look at the desk. The chair had broken at the strut, dumping her over. Grumbling, she shifted around to sit and yawned, barely able to keep her eyes open.

Two small windows in the wall above the shelves looked out at a predawn sky, only a hint of light glowing in the clouds.

"Okay, I'm up." She groaned, wiping crumbs from her eyes. "This isn't fair. No school and I'm awake at like, six in the morning."

The plastic pouch that held the protein bars had enough room for the remaining Devil Dogs plus two bottles of water. That left one unopened six-pack and a stray bottle. She carried her treasure to the hole, pushed it out. and crawled after it. The L-shaped building gave her a little privacy around back to pee. That done, she sat on the sidewalk in front, sipping water and munching down the last protein bar while watching the sun come up. Or at least, watching the cloud dome brighten. She stretched her legs out and yawned again, annoyed at waking up so early. Her legs remained pale as ever. *No sunburn. Wow. Guess those clouds are thick.*

Today, she'd walk without giving in to any distractions. No collapsing buildings. Any food or clothing she stood a tiny chance of finding in ruins, she had a much better chance of begging for at the village. The only problem being, begging a villager for clothing would require walking into the village first. Merely thinking about that got her blushing.

"I don't have any choice. I'm in trouble." She stood, dusted herself off, and picked up her supplies. "Someone's gonna help me, right? *Everyone* can't be mean."

With the six-pack dangling from her right hand, the pouch under her left arm, she marched down the street, hair trailing off to the right in the steady breeze. Having gone a few days without air conditioning, she found the heat less bothersome, but today had a new level of humidity that turned walking into a chore. She popped another water bottle after less than an hour of travel, sipping it gradually as she went.

A droplet patted her on the head. She stopped and stared up. Another droplet hit her in the cheek. Seconds later, the skies unleashed a driving rain that turned the silt around her feet to mud in an instant and left an odd metallic flavor in the air. Visibility shrank to a short distance in all directions, mere shadows of ruined buildings appeared here and there in the murk. Soon, the roar of falling rain became so loud she'd have to shout to hear herself.

Kiera sighed. At least the raindrops were warm.

*People run to get out of the rain so their clothes don't get soaked.* She shrugged. *Oh well.* Ashleigh's giggling came out of her memory. She and her friend had dashed from the awning in front of the school to a waiting bus in a downpour much like this, soaked to the skin after a mere twenty yards. At the time, they'd both found it hilarious.

Her throat tightened and she felt like crying over her best friend. Not knowing if the girl ever existed didn't make her homesickness better. That entire life had been a lie, but such a believable one... Her mom once told her she sometimes missed characters from books after finishing them, but Kiera had thought it ridiculous. If Ashleigh had been a character, a computer program, a mere NPC in a virtual world, how could she pine for her friend so much?

*I guess I understand now, Mom.*

She trudged onward in the rain, eyes squinted, feet splashing with every step in ground that had become goopy pudding. Eventually, the sadness of loss retreated, leaving behind her determination to stay alive. Sticking out her tongue found the rain had a nasty, metallic taste. She didn't dare drink it, but wound up enjoying the sensation of playing in the storm. For a while, Kiera jumped in puddles, spun in circles, and enjoyed the rain washing all over her while pretending to be a forest elf from *Shadow Kingdoms*, a fantasy-themed game she finished right before Dad got her *The Concordant Sequence*. That game had been too easy. She'd gotten to the end and killed the main boss in only a week. The lore said the elves lived as one with nature. Frolicking in the rain touched something primal deep in her soul, a freedom she had never imagined possible.

The downpour continued for hours, but at least it fell at an angle because of the wind, making it easier to keep going in the right direction despite not being able to see too far. Thunder rolled back and forth overhead, accompanied by green lightning high in the cloud dome.

*Standing around out here wet is probably stupid.*

No sign of shelter appeared amid the wasteland as she hurried forward, only more mountainous piles of rubble full of tiny waterfalls. Her amusement at playing in the rain had vanished, replaced with a hurried panic to get somewhere away from the lightning as fast as possible. At every flash of lightning or crack of thunder, she bit back squeals of alarm. After a while of slogging as fast as she could move through shin-deep muck, she reached a river of muddy water crossing her path. Based on the robot's directions, going to the village required her to cross it. Kiera took a few breaths searching for courage, and stepped into a fast-moving flow that came up to her thighs. Twice, the current swept her off her feet, but she fought to keep her head above the surface despite being pushed along quite a bit off course. Fear got the better of her near the midway point when the current dragged her under. She screamed and tried to swim, accomplishing little until the river swept her into a smashed traffic light. Ignoring the pain of crashing into it, she flipped around and wrapped her arms and legs around it, stopping herself before the torrent swept her onward.

She clung there, unwilling to let go of the pouch or the six-pack of water bottles and unsure how to rescue herself from the flood with her hands both full. About six feet of rushing water stood between her and solid (relatively speaking) ground. Gripping the pipe with her legs, she hurled the plastic pouch as hard as she could, landing it in the muck well past the raging flood. She transferred the water to her right hand and threw it as well. The heavier object landed at the edge of the river, but came down with enough force that it stuck in place.

Her hands free, Kiera climbed up onto a pipe that had once dangled a traffic light out over a road, the rain clearing her of mud in seconds. Bobbing up and down on her perch, she felt like someone had locked her in a shower stall and turned the water on high. It had been fun initially to frolic in the rain, but having no way to escape the driving downpour made her want to get away from it.

She crept along the spar to where it met the post. *This used to be a traffic light, like way high up. The river must be following the street.* It scared her that only a little bit of it remained visible, suggesting this whole area sat buried under like ten feet of powdery silt. Kiera stood, balancing with both feet together on the cap at the top of the pole. From here, she could jump down clear of the raging runoff—if she could find the courage. At another *boom* of thunder, she screamed and jumped. Slick mud made for a clumsy sliding landing, but it didn't hurt. She snagged her water bottles before darting over to the clear pouch, almost slipping three times in the deep mud.

Pelted by the driving rain, she hurried onward, leaving the rapids behind. Her stomach churned from the battle of Devil Dog and protein bar, creating a sensation somewhere between hungry and sick. A chocolate chicken soup burp almost made her throw up. She didn't think eating one now would work too well. If she opened the plastic around one of her remaining cakes, the storm would turn it into a mushy mess. Plus, the rain tasted dangerous.

Shin deep in muck, she trudged along under the downpour. A constant battering of rain soaked her for hours. Lightning and thunder continued every minute or two, making her jump and shriek every time, terrified the next lightning bolt would hit her. Eventually, a flash of lightning illuminated a tall shadow ahead on the left. Curious, she headed for it. A few minutes later when another flash occurred, she made out the form of a destroyed high-rise, eight or nine stories tall. None of the outer walls remained intact, allowing her to look straight into the interior of every floor. Cascades of water ran down the side facing the rain, spilling off each jutting concrete slab.

*No buildings.* She kept marching, intending to ignore it, but stopped at the sound of voices inside. *It's going to be dark soon... and...* she sighed and veered to the left, facing straight into the wind and rain. A puddle she stepped in turned out to be a pool, and she plunged underwater in a giant pothole. She swam back up, an iron grip keeping hold of the six-pack like her life depended on it. Fortunately, while deep, the pit only spanned a few feet across. She set her water and the plastic pouch on the ground in front of her face, then grabbed the old pavement to pull herself up.

Wary of puddles, she navigated a serpentine path over the rest of the distance between her and the tower and scurried in out of the rain. She stopped a few paces away from the edge where the downpour didn't blow in, and stood there dripping. Whatever this building had been, no clue of its former purpose remained. Only rubble and mounds of dirt littered an otherwise barren area between columns. Plaster had crumbled away from the supports, exposing I-beams. This building felt even less safe than the one with the deadly toilet, but it hadn't collapsed yet.

*I am not going upstairs.*

A conversation between two men came from deeper down one of three corridors leading out of the room. She blushed, hesitating, but her need for help kicked her embarrassment to the side. A short sprint into the murky corridor brought her to a door labeled 108. Under that, a card had 'Mr.

Lamar' on it in black marker. The small room held a metal bed frame with side-railings, but no mattress. It bent upward in the middle, evidently broken. A steel framed chair-thing with a bedpan stood nearby, an adult-sized potty. Someone had constructed a bed of plastic scraps under a window that looked out into a tiny courtyard at the core of the building. Another charred bedpan next to it held ashes and burned bits. Not far from it, a cigarette lighter sat on the floor next to a can of lighter fluid. Beside them, a tiny digital music player connected to a little solar panel radiated the sound of two men raving on about someone named Wilkins.

Her hope crashed into the pit of her gut as she listened to them discuss his point-earnings and season performance.

Scowling, she stomped over and turned the player off, bathing the room in silence.

She set her hands on a radiator cabinet and leaned close to the window on tiptoe, peering up at a hollow shaft in the center of the building. Rusty wheelchairs and picnic tables stuck out of deep sand dunes, flowing with mud. Sheets of rainwater poured off the exposed edges of all the floors above in loud, splattering streams. Green light flashed in the courtyard, in time with another *crack* of thunder so loud she screamed from the suddenness of it. Hands clamped to her chest, she scurried away from the window, breathing hard for a few seconds. Once the shock wore off, she sank to her knees, shaking.

"That was loud. I shouldn't go back outside 'til this stops."

Kiera crept across the hallway and peered into the next nearest room. A group of skeletons lay scattered around, two on a metal bed frame, more on the ground. The bare footprints of adults crisscrossed the dirt on the floor, and one of the skeletons had been broken apart, probably by someone taking its clothing. All the dead wound up with their skulls facing right at her. Again, she shrieked and scrambled away from the grisly sight, running back to the safety of the room with the digital music player. She flopped on the floor by the bedpan-turned-campfire pit, and decided not to look in any more scary rooms.

While nibbling on a Devil Dog and sipping the last water bottle from the first six-pack, Kiera sat for a while in silence. *The robot said I could make it to the village without dehydrating. I have six bottles left. I'm gonna be okay.* She shivered, hating being alone more than she'd ever hated anything in her life. Even robotics class.

Chin on her knee, she stared down at her feet while tracing lines in the rain she'd dripped all over the floor. Daylight began its rapid retreat, likely early due to the awful weather. Kiera leaned over and turned the digital player back on before crawling into the nest of plastic scraps. Even if they talked about sports she had no interest in, the voices of two dead men echoing off the bare concrete walls made her feel less alone.

Ashamed of herself for wanting to cling to her parents like a little kid, she closed her eyes and tried not to let the thunder frighten her.

# 11

# NIGHTMARE'S TEETH

K iera's bladder woke her up early the next morning. A heavy blanket of humidity saturated the room, turning it into an oven. Sticky from sweat, she peeled herself away from the plastic scrap bedding and stood. The pouch held five Devil Dogs, two of which she planned to have right after finding a spot to pee. Considering she felt like the last person left on Earth, a suitable spot wound up being ten paces outside the building in the dirt. After, she walked only far enough to find a hunk of concrete to sit on to stay out of mud, and downed two Devil Dogs plus the first water bottle of the second six-pack.

Her meal done, she hopped off the rock and strolled across the goopy mud. The rain had ceased sometime during the night, leaving the cloud come bright again but the air wet. What had been soft, powdery silt had become like walking in ankle-deep pudding. The steady wind would probably dry most of it out before the day ended, helped along by the ninety-ish degree heat. The all-day shower did have one nice benefit: her hair floated free, no longer caked into a mass from the dried-up slime.

Howling wind far off in the sky worsened her feelings of loneliness. She kept her gaze down, sometimes kicking mud to the side or sweeping her foot around to make patterns. Bands of grey and brown smeared in the sludge like one of those pretty rocks from science class. Kiera grinned at the thought it looked like melted rocky road ice cream.

She got thirsty an hour or so on, and drank another bottle while walking. *Is it wrong to litter?* Kiera stared at the empty bottle, thinking of Legacy telling her the water had to last. *I can't be that far away from the village now.* She tossed the empty and kept going.

After an hour or two, she began muttering to herself, complaining about the robotics test or the epic boredom level of Mr. Powers' class. The wind continued without end, every so often gusting hard enough to knock her a step or two sideways.

"We found this cute little blue dress for only $180," said Kiera in an imitation of Ashleigh. "Mom's gonna buy it for me so I can wear it to school tomorrow."

"Oh, that's cool," she replied back in her normal voice. "I've got a new ensemble from the Birthday Suit collection. It's really comfortable and great to wear in the rain, too. I can even go swimming in it."

She did an impression of Ashleigh's excited face. "Oh wow! How much did that cost?"

"It was on sale! Only a couple years locked up in a tank full of frozen snot." Kiera sighed. "Is talking out loud to myself a sign that I've gone crazy?"

Her lip quivered and she sniffled into tears again, but kept on walking. The loneliness of a wasteland gnawed at her. She hadn't ever been apart from people this long before, nor so lost, confused, and frightened. Her parents or Ashleigh were always no farther away than a text message or phone call; she'd never truly been alone. Now, she had no way to contact anyone, and no parents to protect her. Even those three bandits started to feel like a not-so-bad option.

Kiera grabbed her throat, too choked up to speak, and sobbed in silence. She could barely see through her tears, but it didn't matter. Not like she'd walk into anything out here.

"I'm sorry." Her voice wavered with sorrow. "Mom, Dad... I'm sorry for saying those mean things. Please come back. I don't want to be alone."

Overcome with loneliness and grief, she stumbled to a halt and squatted, arms wrapped around her legs, head to her knees, listening to the faint howl of the wind everywhere. Her hair danced across her back, reminding her of her need to find clothing. That, in turn, reminded her of her need for water and food. Giving in to sadness and just sitting there would only get her hurt. She stood, wiping her eyes, and trudged on. Head down, she stared at her feet disappearing in the muck with each step.

Hours drifted by in a haze of random memories of home, school, friends, and her parents. Eventually, the constant wind hardened the ground to a texture like clay. Given the humidity, it would be a while before it dried once more to powder. A hint of blacktop emerged from the mud up ahead, with a line of utility poles on one side and three crumbling high-rises on the other. The dead buildings all had the same basic rectangular shape. Their uniformity suggested apartments, but the middle tower leaned away from the street, ready to fall over if even a single pigeon landed in the wrong place. The most distant structure had split apart, leaving one face by the road with the rest of the building scattered out across the desert to the right like a stack of plates that had fallen over. Since the scrap of road almost matched the direction she wanted to go, she decided to follow it.

Kiera moved to the utility pole side of the street, shying away from the dangerous structures. She walked about in a turn, begging in her mind for someone nice to find her. Another day alone, and she'd scream. Maybe go crazy.

Growling came from her left and behind. At first, she disregarded the sound, assuming it a figment of her imagination. When it got louder, she looked back over her shoulder. A shorthaired black dog resembling a cross between a Doberman and a wolf stood by a mound of debris that had once been a building. Stark yellow eyes stared straight into her soul as it bared large teeth.

"Be a good dog, okay?" She walked a little faster. "I can't play right now."

Another dog walked out from behind the rubble, staring at her. It, too, snarled.

A flash of black on the right made her whirl. A third dog crept closer from between two of the apartment buildings. Dog number four peered out of the shadows by the end of the last building, a distance in front of her. The pack stalked into the open, surrounding her.

Kiera screamed and ran, heading for the nearest utility pole. She dropped the pouch and water bottles, leaping to grab on to the metal studs sticking out from the sides of the pole. The dogs came charging, snarling, and jumping after her, their teeth snapping shut far too close to her feet. She kept shrieking as she climbed all the way to the top where bits of old power lines still dangled from porcelain insulators.

Clinging to the damp wood, she stared down at a group of seven dogs gathered about the bottom. One stood on its hind legs, forepaws against the pole, drooling and growling.

"Heeeeeelp!" shouted Kiera. "Please! Someone help me!"

Her voice echoed over the ruin.

Dogs paced in circles around the base of the pole. Two sat, staring up at her, seeming content to wait for her to fall.

"This isn't real. *Now* I'm having a nightmare. Stuck naked up a telephone pole with evil dogs trying to eat me. This is the worst nightmare I've ever had." She cried herself to laughing. "Evil... Devil Dogs. Yeah. I ate too much sugar. These things are here because I saw Devil Dogs. Now I know this is a dream."

The animals kept circling, waiting, watching, snarling.

She hugged herself tight to the ancient wood, shaking. "These kinds of dreams mean people are afraid of stuff… yeah, like getting eaten by wild dogs."

It didn't take long for her legs to cramp up and her hands to go numb from clutching the metal step rods. Silence offered hope. She opened her eyes and peered down. All seven dogs sat there, patient, as calm as if they waited for her to throw a tennis ball. The second she made eye contact, they resumed snarling. It occurred to her that their fur looked an awful lot like King's strange hairy shorts. Had he made them from dog leather?

She shivered.

Killing dogs seemed so wrong, but at the moment, she might not have minded these particular dogs having something bad happen to them. Like a random city bus coming out of nowhere and running them over.

"Help!" she screamed again. "Is anyone there?"

Even if the kidnappers found her, being forced to work for someone probably wouldn't be as bad as becoming dog food. She cried out for help a few more times, but only her voice echoing back answered. The dogs' ears perked up. Two wagged their tails like they smelled her fear and expected dinner time to be arriving soon.

*I can't stay up here… my hands kill already.* She shifted her weight enough to let go with her right hand. Opening and closing her fingers a couple times helped a little, but it hurt as soon as she grasped the metal rod again to do the same for her other hand.

"Go away," she said, downward. "Shoo. Bad dogs!"

One leaned its forepaws on the pole again, licking at the air.

Kiera whined. She glanced up at a thick wire running from the pole to one of the apartment buildings, connecting to the wall about where the third story became the fourth. *Oh, no way.* She wiggled her toes, trying to get feeling back into her feet. Clinging to the side of a telephone pole wouldn't last much longer before her muscles gave out, no matter how scared she was.

*I can't believe I'm really thinking about doing this…* She stared at the wire. *I'm gonna fall soon anyway.*

The dogs paced around below, almost appearing docile, staring up at her like they wanted to play.

"Nice try. I don't believe you."

She stretched up and grabbed the wooden cross spar where the wires connected. If she thought too much about doing it, she'd never do it. After pulling herself up to hang by her hands, she edged to the left until she got a grip on the wire, legs pedaling at open air. The dogs migrated a little to the side, staying under her.

Kiera rotated to face away from the building and shifted her left hand to grab the wire from the other side. With a grunt, she bent up and hooked her legs over for support. Hand over hand, she pulled herself along, swaying in the wind. The snarls and groans of dogs stayed below her, but she didn't dare look down. Only the wire existed. Inch by inch, she crossed, tilting her head back enough to gauge her distance to the ancient apartment building. The wire swayed and bobbed, but held her weight.

A torturous few minutes later, she reached the crumbling wall. Kiera took a few breaths to get ready, tightened her grip, and let her legs slip free so she dangled by her hands. She hung from one arm long enough to grab the wire the other way and rotated to face the building. A leg stretch got her toes on the sill of a third-story window. She planted her right foot on a vent fan cowl, and with a kicking shove, released the wire to grab the top of the window frame. A rush of terrified adrenaline came and went while she hung off the side of a building. The glass was long gone, so as soon as the fear-paralysis faded, she eased her hands down the frame until she squatted on the sill, refusing to look down at the pack of growling animals.

The fragment of an apartment didn't reassure her much. About a third of someone's living room remained, a triangular-shaped section of floor suspended on the inside of two walls. The rest of the building had collapsed away into a debris field. Kiera crawled in and sank to sit on moldy wooden floorboards, a ledge hanging thirty feet off the ground. To her left, a spread of mushrooms and toadstools grew out from the wall. She had nowhere to go, but better, the dogs had no way up here unless they could fly. And, huddling in the corner with solid floor under her proved far more comfortable than clinging to a telephone pole. She pulled one foot into her lap and massaged her sole where the metal rods she'd been standing on left a red mark.

Snarling and growling came from below, along with the snapping of twigs and rustle of small bodies moving among debris. Scratching, claws on brick, followed.

Kiera hugged her knees to her chest and bowed her head. All the fear of scaling a wire crashed on top of her terror of the dogs. She trembled, muttering, "I'm having a nightmare," over and over, trying to convince herself of it.

Eventually, she abandoned her hope she might be having a nightmare and huddled in the corner, resigned to waiting the dogs out. She wanted them to give up and go away soon, since she'd dropped her water and food out by the pole.

"Please, let me wake up. I don't like this dream. I want to go home."

# 12

# NO BETTER OPTION

Kiera sat motionless for hours, wedged into the corner against crumbling walls as far away from the edge of the broken floor as she could get. She tried to move as little as possible, shivering in fear that her perch, part of an old living room, might fall at any second. The wind tossed her hair about, a chaotic storm trapped within the hollow space. Eventually, she lifted her face away from her knees, disappointed to see the world unchanged. She hadn't been dreaming. A pack of wild dogs really did want to eat her.

The growling from below had stopped and the sky gave off the sense of late afternoon. She'd wasted most of a day, barely having covered any distance. Worse, she'd dropped her water. Not that she'd gone too far from it, but the dogs might be watching.

She let her feet slide forward until her legs lay flat, and looked around. The triangular section of floor sagged in the middle. A bit of wall jutted out from the left, enough to show where a doorway had once connected to the next room. Dreading that she'd have to climb back across to the wire to get down, she rolled onto her hands and knees and crawled to the edge. Her motion made the floor under her wobble. Fear leaked out her nose on a faint whine of apprehension. Still, she kept going until she reached the broken end and peered past it at the ground.

The area two stories down contained the first green plant life she'd yet seen since waking up, mostly weeds and creeper vines growing in the shelter of the first floor walls. Nothing a person could eat. She didn't notice any trace of dogs, nor any obvious way down aside from jumping. Nothing existed of the second story, giving her a thirty-foot drop to deal with. Straight ahead, the greater part of the building stretched out as a long line of rubble where it had toppled over. Little remained recognizable, as though the atmosphere had once been corrosive enough to dissolve bricks, wood, metal, and furnishings into a mismatched mound of debris.

"Guess that's why there's so much nothing." She stared off at the seemingly endless field of pale grey silt. "It's like the whole city turned to dust."

A *creak* came from the floor directly under her.

"Eep!"

She scurried back from the edge and crawled to the other corner. There, the wall offered a little more hope. A beam at the second story stuck a few feet out of the wall, and a large metal fuse box reasonably close to it looked like it might support her weight. If she could climb onto that, she'd only have a small distance to drop to make it to the ground. It looked less dangerous than going back across the wire to the pole.

Kiera turned around and lowered herself over the edge feet first to hang by her hands. She crept to the left until she could reach a metal pipe running along the wall. She transferred her grip to the pipe, then shimmied across to the giant wooden beam, stepping in holes wherever the wall offered one. When she reached the beam, she tested it with one foot, bouncing a little before trusting it with her full weight. Confident it wouldn't break, she stepped up onto it and dusted her hands off.

*This is kinda like that climbing place Dad took me to, only with more death.*

Bright plastic-colored handholds had been a lot more comfortable to grab than old wood and thin metal pipes bolted to bricks. Plus, there, she had a padded floor and harness to save her if she slipped. Losing her grip there had meant only the shame of failing in front of people who would probably laugh at her. She squatted on the beam and backed up a few inches. The only way she could think of to get to the fuse box involved a leap of faith.

After a preparatory deep breath, she jumped forward, flying at the wall and landing with both hands grabbing the top of the metal cabinet. Kiera nearly bounced off when she crashed into it, but clung so tight her fingers hurt. Once the shock of slamming chest-first into a metal box wore off, she braced her feet on the exposed bricks.

"Ow." She cringed before peering down.

A narrow metal pipe ran below close enough for her to get her toes on and take her weight off her aching fingers. After catching her breath, she sank into a dangling squat off the bottom of the metal cabinet, then stretched one foot to a fat but short pipe, leaned to the right to grab a windowsill, and made her way down via a series of holes, wire conduits, and one more jutting beam. When the ground got close enough to jump, she pushed away from the wall to avoid clipping any protruding wooden spikes or pipe fragments, and fell into tumble upon landing.

Flat on her back and surrounded by weeds, she stared up at the churning clouds overhead, breathing hard. After a moment, she held her hands up to examine her throbbing fingers. They hurt, but fortunately, she hadn't cut herself. No bleeding. Kiera sat up and brushed dirt off her stomach. A quick check of her body found no splinters or scratches.

The plant life didn't look like anything she'd ever seen before, as though some mad scientist had crossbred rose bushes with ivy. Most of the twisty vines sported one-inch spikes. Still, she'd made it to the ground without breaking her neck.

"Okay... that wasn't *too* bad... but I shouldn't stay here. Those dogs might come back."

Kiera scrambled to her feet and looked around. Climbing out the first-story window facing the street appealed more than a naked march through thorny vines that came up to her waist. She made easy work of jumping the windowsill, then darted across the street back to the telephone pole as fast and quiet as possible to retrieve her water and snack cakes.

*The dogs didn't eat them... does that mean they're bad?* She shrugged. *They didn't taste bad. Maybe they couldn't smell them through the plastic.*

Not wanting to even see those dogs again, Kiera took off running in the direction she'd been going and left the tiny island of ruins behind for open desert. She kept sprinting until her lungs caught fire—or at least felt like they did. After stumbling into a channel between dunes, she flopped on the ground and fanned herself. Another water bottle went fast, leaving her three. Hunger overpowered restraint, and she scarfed down her last two Devil Dogs.

Kiera rested for a few minutes, flat on her back in the soft silt, swishing her feet side to side, amazed at how comfortable a bed the ground made. This powdery stuff wasn't exactly sand. Eventually, she got back on her feet and walked for hours, wondering if those tribespeople in Mr. Powers' video felt as ridiculous as she did for walking around without any clothes.

*I guess it's all they knew, so they couldn't be embarrassed.*

Eventually, her stomach announced hunger with a rather loud grumble. She guessed it close to six in the evening due to the dimming light, and nursed another water bottle while trudging onward, hoping her two remaining ones would be enough to allow her to reach help.

Not long after she tossed the empty aside, smoke trails came into view up ahead where the ground became hilly and rocky. A handful of cactuses grew scattered around the area, and beyond that, the shapes of strange buildings dotted the ground in front of a stretch of pine trees. They didn't look like any sort of building she'd ever seen before, put together from pieces of trailers, scrap metal, and wood. Almost nothing had straight edges, evidence of past corrosion eating the materials away.

*The village!*

She jogged closer, keeping to the low areas between dunes in the windblown silt until the sounds of voices ahead confirmed the presence of people. At the outskirts of the village, she climbed to the top of a hill and dropped to a crawl, scurrying up to hide behind a giant boulder. For a few minutes, she couldn't bring herself to move, too embarrassed to let anyone see her. At another growl from her stomach, she let out a resigned sigh and leaned around the side to peer down the hill.

The village contained a few tents as well as trailers and scrap homes. Near the center, a large building made of cinder blocks had 'TRADE' painted on the front in huge red letters. A bent sign near it read 'Exxo,' but she recognized it as a damaged Exxon gas station. Whoever lived there now had added to the garage and turned it into a store of some kind. Various men, women, and children roamed about. About half of them wore cloth garments, many decorated with odd things like computer chips, hexagonal nuts, coins, and the like—anything shiny. Most of the men went shirtless, a few having skirts or pants that appeared to be black dog fur or another type of leather with reddish-brown hair.

Nervousness gripped her at the idea of strolling into town with no clothes. Her stomach demanded food, and the promise of no longer being alone made her shake with anxiety. She debated sneaking in and trying to steal food, but after another few minutes of watching the townspeople act so *normal*, she developed some hope that they would help her instead of trying to sell her.

*I gotta do this. Come on. Those rain forest people weren't embarrassed. I'm not in the modern world anymore. We've gone back to living in tribes. Old rules don't matter. Some of those women don't have tops on, and no one is staring at them... Maybe they don't care.* Her cheeks warmed. *I'm blushing so hard.* She fanned herself. *Okay. I can do this. I'm gonna die if I don't get help.*

Kiera swallowed her embarrassment and forced herself to stand. Hands clutched into fists at her sides, she walked around the boulder and followed a dirt trail down the hill toward the heart of the village.

*Please let me find someone nice.*

# EXXO

A man in tire sandals, a dog-fur loincloth, and a leather headband pulled a wagon made from the rear end of a rusty pickup truck. He glanced casually at Kiera as she went by, no more shocked by her presence than if she'd passed the janitor at school in the hallway. She managed a weak smile, but he kept going before she could work up the nerve to speak.

An old woman in a cloth poncho glanced curiously at her from beneath a porch of corrugated metal, but made no move to approach. Two younger women, Mom's age, went by, both in thin, beige cloth dresses, barefoot. They gave her cursory glances, but didn't stop to talk.

She spotted a few villagers here and there who also had no clothes, but only tiny children no older than three. Everyone past toddler age had at least a loincloth. *Not like they make diapers anymore.* Come to think of it, aside from those dogs, she hadn't seen any wildlife—nothing to make leather from.

She drifted deeper into the village, gazing around at people. The vast majority wore scavenged things like Legacy's skirt of metal, bits of plastic, or even circuit boards. One man had shorts made from an old US flag. Unable to stop blushing, she held her chin up and forced herself to keep going. Everyone's utter lack of reaction to her state of dress helped calm her somewhat after a couple minutes. She debated approaching one or two people who looked the friendliest, but no one held eye contact long enough for her to get up the nerve.

Eventually, her fear of being made fun of or getting in trouble lessened enough for the trembling to stop. She continued walking among the huts, but no one paid her much mind at all. While she no longer shivered, being confident enough to *speak* hadn't happened yet. Every time she almost made eye contact with an adult, she flinched away, managed a weak smile, and kept on creeping forward.

Whirring machinery near the middle of the village attracted her to a contraption that looked a bit like a fountain standing under a massive umbrella of purple fabric stretched out over metal pipes. The cube-shaped heart of the machine perched above a basin with two spigots leaking feeble streams of water into the pool. A tall column of thin black mesh rose three times her height from the center with most of its length up past the 'umbrella.' Inside the column, a dangerous looking set of sharp, rotating vanes swirled in the wind. Water droplets crawled down the mesh, inching toward the collector at the bottom.

Two boys, one about her age with black hair and brown skin, the other only about seven with blond hair and a deep tan, filled buckets. The older boy had a scrap of white cloth tied around his waist and through his legs like a tiny sumo wrestler, while the younger wore a dog-fur loincloth so wide on him the front and back pieces touched, making it a skirt.

Kiera froze, bracing for mockery.

They looked at her with curiosity, neither showing any trace of amusement, surprise, or alarm at her lack of clothes. She inched up to the fountain while looking around, waiting for someone to chase her away, but no one did.

Kiera set her two remaining bottles on the ground at her feet, stooped forward, and cupped water in her hands. It tasted clean, so she drank several handfuls. The boys collected their filled pails and walked off without saying a word, though the smaller one kept smiling back at her.

Adults strolled by giving her curious glances, but each time someone got close, she blushed and bowed her head, too ashamed to try talking to them.

*Come on. They don't care. They're tribal. It's not a big deal. Grow a spine. Oh, this is so weird.* Not having people running straight up to her to either make fun of her, yell at her, or worried to death that something bad happened felt surreal. Then again, people spending time outside at all, not simply sprinting between pockets of air conditioning, felt odd too. This village had no power lines, so she doubted air conditioning existed anymore.

"Well, it *is* February, so it's only like ninety degrees. What do they do in the summer?"

She turned on her heel and marched up to the giant cinder block building marked 'TRADE' in painted letters. Leather strips formed a curtain in the doorway. She stuck her hands between two, brushing the scraps aside while stepping into a room that made her feel like she'd found the standard town merchant from every fantasy video game she'd ever played. If the guy had swords and hammers on the walls, it would've been perfect. Most of the stuff appeared to be scavenged junk. Pots, pans, plates, forks and knives, a couple pairs of handmade boots far, far, too big for her, and a smattering of clothes.

"Welcome to Exxo!" called a bearded man in his thirties from behind the counter. "I don't think I've seen you before."

Kiera approached the counter and stood in as polite a posture as she could manage. "Hi. I think I'm an orphan. Can I please have something to wear?"

"Sure, sure." He smiled. "Do you have anything to trade?"

"Umm." She looked down, raising and dropping her toes. "I don't have anything at all."

The man scratched at his beard. "Hmm. Well, sorry kid, but I'm not in the business of charity. I could pay you with a bit of clothing if you're willing to do some work."

"Okay. Will you give me the clothes first?"

"And have you run off? I know how you cute ones are... think we're all saps that'll fall for the wide blue eyes."

"But... I'm"—her voice fell to a whisper—"naked."

"Aha! A smart one!" He snapped his fingers. "I like that!"

Kiera scowled. "It's not right."

"You're tryin' to get one over on old Norven, aren't ya? Someone put you up to this, right? Half the tribes in the south don't even bother scrappin' for clothes. Why's it matter so much to you?"

She folded her arms. "Because it does. People are supposed to wear clothes unless they're taking a bath."

"Hmph. You want something to wear or not?"

"Yes!" she shouted.

"Then that means you want work." He smiled.

Kiera narrowed her eyes at him and grumbled, "What's the job?"

Norven pointed at the wall. "There's a pre-Cloudfall ruin bit west o' Exxo in a ravine. Been tryin' ta get someone to head out that way, but they're all afraid of it. Some nonsense about it bein' cursed. Take the trail into the woods. Left at the split and keep goin' 'til you see a hole on the left. It ain't far."

"Cursed? You think the place is *cursed* and you want a kid to go look at it?" She set her hands on her hips. "I'm eleven. I have no provisions, no idea where I am, no weapons, and no clothes. Are you serious?"

"Something's different about you. I don't think you'd be afraid of the curse. Y'aint talk like anyone I seen before."

"I don't believe in curses. I may be a kid, but I'm not stupid. There's no such thing as magic." She ground her toes into the floor. "Can't I just sweep or wash dishes or cook or something?"

"Ehh." Norven shrugged. "It's the job I got. I ain't runnin' a cook place."

"Ooh." She stomped, fumed at him for a few seconds, and stormed out in a huff.

"If ya change yer mind, bring back anythin' ya find there fer trade," yelled Norven.

Too angry to feel shame, Kiera marched past the bizarre fountain, following a path between dwellings toward the other end of the village. Perhaps a furious scowl wasn't the best face to wear when hoping for charity. Most people gave her the same 'oh, someone new' look, but didn't try to talk or even look remotely concerned about her.

"What an idiot!" She came to a stop a few minutes away from the store and seethed at the kind of man who'd try to squeeze a desperate eleven-year-old for money. She glared back over her shoulder at the distant trading post. The idea of shoplifting had never once before entered Kiera's mind, but she'd also never been stranded with nothing to wear either.

*I'll wait 'til dark and steal something.*

# 14

## TERYN AND MALA

I n search of a hiding spot to wait for nightfall, Kiera weaved around trailers converted to permanent homes, other huts made of cinder blocks and corrugated steel, a few tents, and a couple scrap-and-wood dwellings. Walking around nude bothered her more than it had in the days since she'd been spat out of the cryo chamber purely because no one reacted to it. Not one villager from toddler to grandparent seemed to care. She may as well have been back home in 2033, fully dressed, strolling down the street. Well, except for it having been too hot to go outside then.

*The world is broken.*

At least no one tried to grab and sell her. The village had that on the three idiots if nothing else. *I'm not acting like I'm as scared as I feel. Maybe they all think I'm okay?* She turned in place, searching for the first adult with a friendly expression. Perhaps if she started crying or begging, someone might realize all was not right in Kiera world.

The scent of cooking food wafted by on the wind, some manner of meat or beans. It triggered an immediate growl from her belly and got her salivating. She swallowed and hurried along the road in the direction the wind came from. The last building at that end of town, a wide structure half camper trailer, half cinder-block-and-scrap, sat near a significant collection of junk, piled in rows behind it.

She edged up to a waist-high wall of concrete hunks and old car parts surrounding a front yard. An opening, a few feet to her left, looked like it should hold a gate or something, but didn't. A woman in her later twenties with brown skin sat on an orange plastic trunk, tending a pot at a fire pit, also made of cinder blocks, midway between the house and the wall. Her long black hair flowed in the wind, brushing a dress of pale tan cloth.

Near the back of the house, a man with a similar complexion leaned over a folding table full of tools and appliances. His camouflage shorts looked old and ready to fall to pieces, though numerous bits of decorative wood and wire held them together. He whistled to himself while tinkering with something that buzzed.

Kiera headed to the gap in the wall, entered the yard, and crept up to the woman. She clasped her hands in front of her and asked in a meek tone, "*Hola. ¿Puedo tener algo de comida?*"

The woman jumped, startled by her approach. "I'm sorry. What?"

*Oops!* "Can I please have some food? I'm alone and hungry. My parents are dead and I have no place to go."

"Oh, you poor thing." The woman got up and grasped her by the shoulders. "What happened? You're far away from home, aren't you?"

"Yes." Kiera nodded.

"Here, sit." The woman indicated another trunk.

Kiera flopped on the warm plastic, arms crossed in her lap. The man at the table looked back, spotted her, and set down a tool before walking over. After ladling out a portion of food that resembled stew into a metal bowl, the woman sat again on the orange cooler and handed her a plastic spoon.

"Thank you." Kiera stirred at the offering, unsure what sort of meat she looked at, but it smelled like beef. Too hungry to care, she dug in. As soon as she bit into a piece, she realized it to be large cubes of mushroom.

"I am Mala," said the woman, "and this is my husband Teryn."

She hurried chewing her current mouthful. "I'm Kiera."

Teryn wandered off to grab another plastic cooler. He dragged it closer and used it as a seat. "What's your story, child?"

"I don't know what's real and what isn't." Between mouthfuls of stew, she explained waking up inside a strange tank, getting flushed, finding Legacy and the bandits who tried to kidnap her, then her long walk here. "I think I might have been in virtual reality for a while. I had bad dreams, but I can't tell if they might be memories, not dreams."

Teryn and Mala exchanged a glance.

"I think my parents are dead. The floors had so much blood. None of the other tanks had anyone in them."

"Aww." Mala put a hand on her shoulder. "That's quite a story."

The way she said it didn't come off accusing, but the woman didn't appear to believe her, radiating confusion and concern in equal parts.

"I know it sounds made up. I promise I'm not lying. Have you ever heard of some 'Child of the Earth' prophecy?"

Teryn shook his head. "Nope. I'm thinkin' that old man was out in the sun too long."

Kiera giggled.

Mala stared at her husband for a long moment. He nodded. She looked back, squeezing her shoulder and offering a warm smile. "Kiera, if you don't have a hearth waiting for you, we invite you to join ours."

She scraped the spoon at the bottom of the bowl, chasing the last bits of sauce. "Hearth? What?"

"Umm. Our hearth." She pointed at the trailer/cinder block structure. "We offer you to become our family."

"If you are without parents or anyone to look after you, we want you to know you are welcome to stay with us if you want." Teryn leaned forward, elbows on his knees, concern on his face.

She stared into the bowl. Hope and sadness collided. Admitting she needed someone to take care of her felt like declaring her parents dead. But... all that blood. Hours ago, she'd turned on a digital music player not to feel like the last person left alive in the world. Choked up, she managed only a nod.

"Are you still hungry?" asked Mala.

Kiera nodded again.

The woman gave her another ladle of stew before portioning out some for herself and Teryn. Kiera stared down as she ate, gripped with sorrow for the loss of the life she thought she'd been living. Scenes from her endless school year came and went. How could she miss people who never existed? The robot mentioned that weeks in VR could've felt like years. Perhaps her parents had been dead far longer than she knew.

"I spend most of my time hunting for scrap," said Teryn. "And fixing up some stuff people trade for. It's been enough to get by, trade for some Ponics and whatnot. Mala grows a few things here, but the dirt's no good."

The woman shook her head, sighing. "We need to fix the holes in the awning. The poison rain is getting in. If I could only get approved, it would be so much easier for us."

"Approved?" asked Kiera.

"For a work permit." Mala sighed. "It is difficult. I have been reading, but the test is not easy."

Kiera scraped up more stew and shoveled it into her mouth, careful not to spill any of the hot substance on her bare legs. She'd almost forgotten how it felt to be full. "What are you learning?"

"The Citadel has many machines. I am trying to fix the ones that make the air cold and clean it. The books will start, but to really learn, I must work the basic job. Many people try for jobs, but they take only so many. I will keep trying." She smiled.

"So… what do kids do here? I'm not sure how to be in a tribe. Where I came from, it's different."

"You're a bit small to work yet." Teryn winked. "You'll help around here. We could use a hand with keeping the place clean. Maybe I'll teach you a bit of tinkering. You'll have to play though. Make some friends."

"Okay." *That sounds… normal.*

"We already have a room set aside." Mala stood with a smile, though it appeared strained. "You can have it."

Teryn put his arms around Mala, holding her for a moment before kissing her cheek and muttering, "You will have a child soon enough. And it will need to be a boy, as we already have a daughter."

"I will keep trying," whispered Mala.

"*We* will keep trying. Do not blame yourself." He kissed her again before smiling at Kiera. "I will be back soon."

Mala's smile became genuine. "Come, Kiera. I will show you."

She got up, set the bowl on the cooler where she'd been sitting, and followed the woman to the front door. The right end of the room (the camper trailer) had a tiny kitchenette cluttered with junk, a big sofa, coffee table, and a recliner chair older than the Earth itself. A small square table occupied the center of the dwelling with four metal-framed chairs around it. The red fake-leather cushions made them look salvaged from a pizza shop. On the left, a large bed sat tucked into a cinder block alcove by some shelves holding plastic storage boxes, and a steep stairway—more of a ladder—went up to a second-story room.

"Up there." Mala gestured at the ladder. "Is the room you will call yours. You are perhaps a bit old to have night scares, but if you are frightened and wish to share our bed, you would be welcome to."

"Thanks." Kiera hugged her new mother. "I'm sorry you haven't had a baby. Are you sure it's okay I steal his room?"

Mala patted her on the back. "You have stolen nothing."

She led Kiera out a back door onto a low porch made of wooden planks decorated with a few plastic chairs and one wicker chaise lounge. A path made of hubcaps and metal plates led about thirty feet to a narrow cinder block building with a shower curtain for a door, currently slid all the way to the side to reveal a wooden bench with a toilet seat on it.

"Wow. An actual brick crap house." Kiera laughed.

"I wish your father had built it a little farther away. Whenever he makes use, we will know."

"Ugh." She scrunched up her nose.

"Go on and see your room. I need to preserve what we did not eat."

"Okay."

They entered the house together, though Mala continued out the front door while Kiera ascended the ladder. The small area at the top had barely a third the space of her old bedroom. A wooden bookshelf on the right held two toys: a grungy teddy bear next to a rocket ship made from pipe segments and scrap metal. Opposite the shelf, a thin mattress sat on the floor in the corner. Above it, two missing cinder blocks in the otherwise solid wall formed a window with a sheet of clear plastic hung over it on the outside to protect from rain.

The room smelled like wet wood, but nothing felt damp. She crawled in and sat on her new bed, the toy rocket ship at eye level.

"New bedroom…" She scuffed her feet back and forth on the floor. "No TV… no *Supernova 2* game console, no Ashleigh…."

Pining for her friend who probably never existed, stuff she never really owned, and thinking about her other friends from school brought silent tears. It might have been completely fake, but that life felt more real than a few fleeting glimpses of running down a hospital corridor in the middle of the night with two frantic parents she barely spent four hours with a month. She pictured the tank, how terrified she'd been at the sight of those robotic arms and needles, and stopped crying.

"None of them were ever real." Ashleigh's contagious giggle danced across her memory. "She was so stereotypical tween. Boy bands and obsessed with clothes. No wonder. She was a program… someone's idea of what an eleven-year-old girl is like. All the kids at school were characters. That nerd they kept picking on, the sports kids… everything was so perfect." She wiped her face. "I'm not going to cry over programs."

On top of that, she felt utterly ridiculous sitting in her bedroom without a stitch of clothing on. *Duh. They want me to be their kid… I'm going to ask them for something to wear. Maybe they think I like this.*

"Kiera?" called Teryn from downstairs. "Come here, please."

She stared at the ladder, all of a sudden wanting to be alone with her grief. A sigh leaked from her nose. *Will they kick me out if I don't listen to them?*

"Kiera? Are you up there?" called Teryn.

"Yeah. Coming." She got up, crept to the opening in the floor, and stared down. The ladder looked too steep to walk on like steps, so she turned around and climbed with her back to the room below.

Teryn met her at the bottom, smiling. "Got you something." He held up a piece of hide with a hole at the middle.

"What is it?" She reached out and felt the material. Soft leather on the inside, short fur on the outside… like a Doberman.

"A poncho." He pulled it over her head and spun it a bit to the right. "With a hood."

The poncho fell around her to the knees, loose, comfortable, and soft enough to feel like a dress with long sleeves. She raised her arms, only her hands sticking out past the edges. It took her brain a few seconds to process that he'd given her clothing. These people who had offered to welcome her into their home and adopt her had already started to take care of her. When that realization clicked, she looked up with fresh tears in her eyes.

After staring at him for a breath and a half, she flung herself into a hug, muttering, "Thank you," over and over.

He picked her up, holding and rocking her side to side. Unable to remember the last time her actual father had held her like that, she broke down and sobbed. After losing everything, nearly being sold into slavery, almost being eaten by a pack of wild dogs, and spending several terrifying days on her own, she finally felt safe.

Kiera closed her eyes and clung tight to him, overcome with gratitude.

*I'm not alone anymore. I'm not gonna die.*

# 15

# THE GATHERING

Kiera spent her first night in her new room curled up on her side, staring at the dingy wooden bookshelf. Teryn made the toy rocket ship in expectation of having a baby, but it had spent years sitting on a shelf in an empty room. She thought back to the bandits who tried to kidnap her, how they said villagers would've given up half their home to have a kid. Maybe they had been right, and perhaps they would've traded her to would-be parents instead of an owner. Still, she couldn't trust people who'd kill an old man and throw her in their cart like some other piece of junk they'd found out in the desert.

She fanned herself with the dog-leather poncho. No trace of a breeze stirred in this room and she missed her air conditioning. After a while of tossing and turning, unable to sleep in the heat, she stood on the mattress and pushed at the plastic covering the hole in the wall. She spotted a metal clamp inside the opening on either side, angled upward like something you'd stick a flag in. A moment of searching around with her hands located two wooden poles, a broom handle cut in half, on the floor between the mattress and the wall. She stuck them in the sockets on either side of the window to prop the plastic sheet outward like an awning, letting in air.

Relieved, she lay back down and closed her eyes.

Her dreams mixed the school that never happened with the scary corridor in the basement of the Citadel Corporation office. Ashleigh and Marlon ran alongside her screaming that the world is dying and they had to hide here. She reached the tank and found her game console floating in it.

"It's about time you got here," said the console.

Kiera shot upright in bed. She blinked at the cinder block walls and the dingy mattress beneath her. "Whoa. That was weird."

Since the sun had come up, she rolled off the bed to her feet and climbed downstairs. Mala stood by the small table in the middle of the room, setting a large bowl at its center.

"Good morning. Teryn is fetching bread. I was about to wake you."

"Morning..." Kiera wasn't quite sure what to call her. Using the woman's name didn't feel proper, and after being here only hours, Mom might be overdoing it... but these people wanted to take her in. Again, she thought of the digital music player, not wanting to be alone. "...Mom."

Mala's huge smile caused a moment of guilt, like she'd tried to take advantage of the woman's desperation for a child by calling her that. But she needed a home. It would take a while to get over the fear of being stranded alone in the desert with nothing, not knowing if she'd live three more days. This couple welcomed her into their home, barely knowing her, offered a safe place, protection, and even the promise of love.

Legacy and his Child of Earth stuff sounded crazier and crazier. *Save the world? Yeah right. I'm safe here.*

This place had the emotional warmth she'd been missing in the real world, her old life. The fake life tried to make up for it, changing her parents, but it went too far. They didn't act like real people, more like the perfect family from a TV show.

Kiera hugged Mala and walked to the outhouse. She stepped from hubcap to stone to a piece of old computer case, avoiding a line of pill bugs as big as a man's thumb. The shower curtain doorway slid aside with a *shht*. She stepped in, closed the curtain, and sat on a modern toilet seat bolted down over a medieval bench. A small shelf on the left held a collection of old books, most rotted or water damaged to the point little of the text remained.

*Those aren't here to be read...* She bit her lip and giggled. *Guess they really are better than e-books.*

Within seconds of her returning to the house, Teryn walked in the door. He'd gone into town, trading a couple of vegetables for a loaf of bread. Another villager, Errol, farmed wheat. His wife worked in the Citadel and brought home seeds as well as some manner of treatment for the soil that allowed plants to grow.

Kiera sat with her new family, eating a breakfast of bread and sliced raw vegetables. "Are there still eggs?"

"Eggs?" asked Mala.

"Yeah, eggs. Like scrambled or fried or omelets?" Kiera gnawed on a tough carrot. "They come from chickens."

"There is chicken from the Citadel," said Teryn. "You can buy it with numbers. It's food. Blocks..." He held up his hands to indicate a brick-sized shape.

"Omelet, too." Mala nodded. "Also blocks. Wrapped in clear."

"Like the protein bars?" Kiera cringed. "So... fake-o eggs."

Her new parents looked at each other, shrugged, and resumed eating.

"Guess there's no actual chickens left." Kiera stared at her plate, at the pitiful vegetables, and smiled. "This is good. Thank you for the food."

Teryn leaned over and ruffled her hair. "You are our daughter now. Oh... that reminds me... the Gathering."

"Yes." Mala nodded, eyes wide with happiness. "We must."

Kiera looked up. "What?"

"Elder Lonna holds the Gathering once each month. Our whole village meets in the center and we talk about things, vote, plan to build new houses if needed, and so on."

Mala grinned. "Whenever there is a new baby, the parents present them to the village during the Gathering. We must present you."

*Uhh.* The woman looked so excited to finally be able to present a child, Kiera swallowed her initial *no thanks* reaction, and forced a smile. It couldn't be any worse than when she had to sit on the lame saddle thing for her ninth birthday at that steakhouse. "Okay."

Teryn tapped a finger on his chin. "I wonder if we will need to present her to the Sky Spirits. She's a bit big to hold way up in the air."

"What, like *The Lion King*?" Kiera giggled.

"The what?" asked Mala.

"You've seen the New Dominion?" Teryn looked horrified.

She shook her head. "No, it's a really old movie. A baby lion is born and they hold him up to show everyone."

"A lion?" asked Mala.

"Umm." Kiera stared at them. "It's a big cat." When that further confused them, she sighed. "Forget it. It's an animal that's not around anymore."

"Oh." Teryn exhaled. "I suppose something like that. Since you're no baby, I don't think they will insist on it."

"The village is close." Mala reached across the table and squeezed her hand. "Once they all know you, everyone here will protect you. When you are an adult, you will do the same for any child here."

She smiled. "That's kinda nice. Where I came from, most people didn't even talk to their neighbors."

"After we eat, I'll show you around the garden. It will be nice to have a helper." Mala smiled.

Kiera looked at her hands covered in dirt, black lines around her fingernails. Somewhere in the back of her mind, Bio-Mom scolded her for getting filthy and sent her off to the bathroom to wash. "Garden? I'll get dirty." She stuck her tongue out with a giggle.

Mala tilted her head.

"I'm joking. I'm already dirty. My other parents were neat freaks. If they saw me like this, they'd faint."

"Oh." Mala nodded. "We are sorry for your loss."

Kiera swung her feet side to side. "Thanks. I... don't think I really even knew them anymore."

"Enough sad." Teryn patted her shoulder. "Go and help your mother in the garden."

THREE DAYS LATER, MALA WOKE KIERA AT SUNRISE AND LED HER ACROSS THE scrap field behind the house to the sands beyond it. Five minutes of walking later, they arrived at an artificial waterway that stretched as far as she could see to the left and right. About twenty yards wide, the enormous concrete trench held more water than Kiera had ever seen in one place before, not counting video or pictures of the ocean. To the right, it disappeared into the endless silt desert. To her left, the canal entered the pine forest outside Exxo.

Mala walked with her to the edge. The manufactured river had a shape similar to the bottom half of a stop sign, the walls beneath the surface covered in patches of green algae.

"Is it safe?" asked Kiera.

"If it has not rained within a few hours, you can drink this, yes. The rain is not healthy. It takes some time for it to become pure. This water comes from the Citadel. We are here to clean ourselves. Today is the Gathering."

Mala removed her dress and slid into the water. The calm current created vees around her where she broke the surface, but didn't push her along. Kiera dropped her poncho near her mother's dress and jumped in. As soon as she entered the water, a constant vibration and high-pitched mechanical noise seeped into her bones. She clung to the wall, the angled part too far down for her feet to reach while keeping her head above water. The flat section at the middle of the bottom had to be at least twenty feet deep.

"What's that sound?" asked Kiera, shivering at the chilly water and clinging to the wall so the current didn't sweep her away.

Mala poured handfuls of water over her head. "This river goes across flat ground. You are hearing the machines that push it."

"Oh. Is it dangerous? Do people get sucked up by the pumps and hurt?"

"I have never seen such a thing happen. But we only swim and bathe here by the village. I have never been in the river closer to the Citadel where the machines are."

She relaxed, treading water while her mother washed her hair. Due to the special occasion, Mom used some of their precious 'cleaning elixir,' which Kiera figured to be liquid soap from the Citadel. The purple gel smelled flowery and lathered a lot more than expected. She gazed along the path of the river into the barren distance.

Far away from Exxo, a dark shadow rose over the ground. Its trapezoid shape reminded her of the Citadel Corporation logo, but she couldn't remember them ever building any actual giant pyramids. A ropey twist of clouds, like a captive tornado, whorled above the dark spot. She gazed upward, following it to the sky and the cloud dome overhead.

"That's the Citadel?" Kiera pointed.

"Yes. It's a long way. It would take days to walk there."

She gawked. "How big is it?"

"It made me feel like an ant. Much bigger than any of the ruins." Mala finished with Kiera's hair and began washing her own. "We do not have much time. Hurry and make yourself clean."

"Okay." Kiera did the best she could with her hands and no soap.

They air-dried on the walk back to the house. Teryn had breakfast waiting for them, having awakened before dawn to bathe himself and be ready. Kiera, still damp, slipped into her poncho as Mala put her dress back on. Together, they sat to eat.

After breakfast, they left the house and walked down the path to the village center where people had already started to assemble. A long folding table like the ones from her school cafeteria had been set up near the water collector. An older woman with grey hair and long robes of dog-hide stood upon it, holding a staff made from a broken floor lamp. Beads, fuses, and wires hung from the top. She wore a headdress of metal shards that resembled bird's wings, and held herself with an air of authority.

Kiera almost laughed at the sight of her, but having come from civilization didn't mean much when the world had gone primitive. Mr. Powers' class spent a few weeks on mythology, and she remembered how some cultures reacted with violence if anyone mocked their superstitions. Hopefully, these villagers wouldn't burn her alive if she laughed at an old woman in a ridiculous outfit, but she decided to keep her head down and pretend to accept it.

Teryn and Mala walked with her into the crowd, coming to a stop near the front close to the table. The old woman smiled like a kindly grandmother at them. Kiera found herself returning the smile and clasped her hands in front of herself, waiting patiently.

Before long, the village center filled with about a hundred adults of varying age. She spotted the old woman who'd watched her walk into town from her porch, the idiot shopkeeper who 'didn't do charity,' and the two boys she'd seen at the collector. Constant murmuring surrounded her, but no one sounded annoyed at being here.

A tickle on her foot made her look down—at a nine-inch-long black centipede flowing over her toes.

She let off a gasp, froze rigid as a statue, and pressed herself against Teryn with a whine leaking out of her nose.

When he looked down, she pointed.

"They eat other bugs. It won't sting you if you keep still. Always check any clothes you leave on the ground for firelegs before you put them on. Their sting hurts, but they only bite if threatened."

"Uhh." She shivered as it crept over her left foot and onto the dirt. As soon as it no longer touched her skin, she stepped away and clung to him, staring at the creature as it crawled off into the crowd.

Other adults shied away from it, which further freaked her out.

Teryn picked her up. "Unless you get one stuck under your clothes, or wind up stepping on one, they won't sting you."

She shivered. "Why is everyone afraid of it?"

"Because when they *do* sting, it hurts a lot. People are afraid because they believe they bite all the time."

"Oh." Kiera decided she preferred not having her feet near the ground for a little while, and held on to him.

"Welcome," said the old woman, who she assumed to be Elder Lonna. "Is everyone here, other than Menaeus, who is too sick to leave his bed?"

Murmurs of agreement spread over the crowd.

Elder Lonna raised her hands. "I know you've all been eager to discuss Jeral's water diversion request, but before we move on to that, we have a wonderful announcement." She beckoned toward Teryn and Mala.

They approached the table.

Mala climbed up to stand beside the elder, and faced the villagers. "I announce a daughter to the village." She quivered with joy. "Her name is Kiera."

Teryn hefted her up and set her standing on the table.

All the villagers, except for some toddlers, looked at her. She gazed out at the sea of faces, most smiling. A Japanese-looking girl close in age to her wearing a poncho of thin tan cloth peeked out from behind her mother and smiled. After an initial spike of insecurity at being the center of the entire town's attention, Kiera waved and smiled.

The elder leaned over. "Child, Teryn and Mala have opened their home to you, and with it, our village. Since you are no infant, it is customary for you to declare yourself, and you shall be regarded as though you came from her womb."

Kiera turned her head to meet the elder's gaze. "Declare myself? What am I supposed to say?"

Elder Lonna patted her cheek. "If you consider yourself part of their family, declare that they are your mother and father to everyone as witness."

"Okay." Kiera took Mala's hand and faced the village. "My name is Kiera. I am the daughter of Mala and Teryn."

"This is my daughter," said Teryn.

Mala wiped a tear of joy. "This is my daughter."

The village all said, "Kiera" at the same time, except for a few of the smaller children. A chaotic murmur followed, with some saying "Welcome," others clapping, and a few muttering praise to the Sky Spirits.

Elder Lonna placed her hand on the back of Kiera's head. "We know this child."

"We know Kiera," chanted the villagers.

The elder bowed her head at them, with a friendly glint in her eyes. Teryn lifted her back to stand on the ground before helping Mala climb down. Villagers shifted into a procession. One by one, every adult approached. Women bowed at Teryn and hugged Mala before hugging Kiera and speaking their names to introduce themselves. Men shook hands with Teryn, bowed at Mala, and either patted Kiera on the head, hugged her, or simply bowed before speaking their names.

After they had all met her, the villagers formed again into a crowd, facing Elder Lonna. When they quieted, the old woman explained a request by a farmer named Jeral who wanted to construct a small pipe to divert some water out of the river so he could expand his farm. The discussion of his offering vegetables in trade for help building it followed the general opinion of the village being in favor of doing it.

The Gathering continued for a short while more with discussions of small issues mostly about farm production or who received acceptance for a 'job' in the Citadel. Elder Lonna eventually announced the assembly over, and the crowd dispersed, heading back to their respective homes.

Kiera looked around at everyone, lost in a swirl of hope and sadness. This place, this feeling of community, was like nothing she'd ever imagined. Even in the ideal suburban falsehood she had thought to be real, the people in the next house never talked to her or her parents. In less than an hour, she'd been welcomed, smiled at, and embraced by around a hundred people.

In the midst of a destroyed world, she dared think she might be happy.

# 16

## A STRANGE NEW LIFE

Over the next several weeks, Kiera fell into a routine around her new home. Some of her days went toward chores like cleaning pots, tidying up the house, tending the garden with Mala, or assisting with meals. About once a week, Mom went off to the Citadel, trying to retake the test for a work permit. Whenever that happened, Teryn cooked, usually timing it such that their evening meal wound up being ready within minutes of her returning home. Still, she hadn't managed to pass whatever test she had to take, but her spirits remained high. Kiera tried to help, but her sixth-grade robotics class felt like two-plus-two compared to the material in the book.

The couple who'd taken her in treated her well, and she soon stopped thinking about Legacy or his Child of Earth prophecy stuff. This home may have been primitive, but her new family's warmth made up for it. She tried not to hold it against her bio-parents. They had lived in another world, a world that ended around sixty years ago. A world of corporate executives, lawyers, and fourteen-hour workdays. In their way, they did as best as they could for her. What Teryn and Mala lacked in money, they more than made up for with emotion—and time spent with her.

She'd come to learn that they'd been trying to have a baby for about ten years, ever since Mala turned seventeen and they had been able to marry. He was older by five years, but none of the other women had any patience for the 'crazy tinker who roams all over the place.' He'd often disappear for days at a time, his pack laden with things he referred to as 'pre-Cloudfall relics' when he returned. Other times, he'd spend most of a day in the forest hunting boar, sometimes wild dogs. He spoke of other beasts, enormous creatures with red-brown fur. They posed no threat to people beyond accidental trampling, but his bow and arrow wouldn't kill them. Once in a while, he'd find one a pack of dogs had taken down, and skin what he could. The villagers called them mammoths, but they sounded more like bison than giant elephants.

Kiera recognized almost everything he brought back: flashlights, e-book readers, laptops, toasters, all manner of consumer electronics. That she understood ancient technology so well fascinated him, and the two spent many hours together at his tables trying to fix things.

Dad—for simplicity's sake, she'd accepted calling them Mom and Dad—taught her about electronics and circuits. Her knowledge of what devices had been used for acted like a key, allowing him to figure stuff out he'd been stuck on for years. Within a month of living there, the two had become almost inseparable. That bond she'd always missed with her biological father swooped in out of nowhere, catching her quite off guard. But she didn't mind. Bio-Dad was dead, and couldn't be jealous. He probably would've been happy she found these people.

Kiera never imagined a world without video games could be anything but permanently boring, but she only thought about them for a little bit while trying to fall asleep each night. Despite being silly, she did kinda miss them. Video games had been a huge part of her life before jumping into a tank of slime—and even while inside it. Heck her *entire* life that she remembered basically *was* a video game.

After breakfast two days into her fifth week, she perched on her father's lap watching him fix a toaster oven at the table in the scrapyard behind the house. Much to her surprise, his tools didn't appear primitive. The soldering iron he presently wielded had a self-contained power cell and looked futuristic compared to anything she'd remembered from her pre-tank life.

She fanned the poncho at her chest, trying to get some air moving under it. Early April brought temperatures past a hundred some days. Dad thought the heat unusual for the season, and said it didn't get too much hotter, even in the middle of summer. Whenever the temperature became unbearable, most of the town would go swimming. The artificial river ended at a lake in the middle of the pine forest to the northwest of the village. Sometimes, people would even jump in the river if they didn't feel like walking all the way to the lake.

He took a familiar black box with angled sides out of his pack and smirked at it while looking it over. "Hmm. Not sure what this is."

"It's a Supernova 2!" Kiera bounced. "An old one...."

"A what?" He patted her head.

"A video game console. I used to have one like that." She happily explained what it did, as well as the idea of video games in general. "That's where the power cable goes. Those two are USB ports. That's HDMI, and that little one there is fiber optic audio, like if you wanna connect the sound to a big stereo."

Teryn beamed with pride, patting her on the back and ruffling her hair. "That's wonderful! Where did you learn all this? You've seen things even I haven't and I've roamed all the way to the Torment and back. I wonder if you were taken from the Citadel." His joy faded.

"No, Dad." She leaned into him. "I've never even been to the Citadel. I lived before Cloudfall. I was born in 2022."

"How is that possible?" He ran his hand over her hair. "You're not even twelve yet."

Kiera stared at her arm, unable to tell where the needle mark had been. "My other parents worked for a big company. They were always at the office. The news kept talking about the planet being sick and war and stuff. One night, they woke me up and dragged me right out of bed to the car. Didn't even let me get dressed or pack or anything. They took me to where they worked and we went into the basement like a hospital. I didn't want to go, but they pulled me down the hallway. A man in a white coat gave me some shots, and they made me get undressed then get into this tank. Mom said it would feel like I fell asleep and woke right back up. They were both so scared I thought they were lying. They wouldn't tell me anything. I don't remember much before that... friends or school or anything. I know I played a lot of video games. Then I was in this virtual world. We used to live in an apartment building, way up high. I never went outside and don't remember if I even *had* friends. But in the VR, we had a house in the suburbs."

He snugged his arm around her. "That's a big story, but I believe you. I can't think of any other way a kid your age would know what all these things are. There aren't a lot of people, even those inside the Citadel, who even care what the world was like before Cloudfall."

"What was Cloudfall?" She twisted to look at him. "Do you know?"

"Only the stories. I'm not that old." He winked. "They say that the world was much different before the Sky Spirits became angry. The people angered them, so they grabbed the world and squeezed it until the clouds fell to the sands. Everything died, but the Sky Spirits knew regret, and brought back a small group of people and gave us a place to live where the Torment cannot touch us."

She furrowed her eyebrows. "Do you believe that?"

Teryn laughed. "When I was your age, I did. You find enough things like this"—he gestured at his table full of junk—"and the Sky Spirits start to sound like magic."

Kiera leaned against him while he tinkered with the old game console, taking the screws out to open it up. Aside from being packed full of silt, it didn't appear damaged. She tried to remember more of her life before the VR lie, which several weeks removed, felt more and more false. Maybe being frozen for so long hurt her brain that she couldn't remember things like grandparents or real friends or even what her non-VR home had looked like. That the place cost a lot of money to live in stood out, but nothing else about it came to mind. A scrap of memory floated up from the nothingness, her and her mother scurrying through a crowd, everyone wearing masks to breathe and plastic raincoats to keep... pollution from touching their skin or clothes. Ninth birthday... going somewhere to have fun, but the air had made her sick.

"Pollution," said Kiera.

"Hmm?" Dad stopped puffing air at the machine and glanced at her. "What's that?"

"Cloudfall... it's pollution," said Kiera, staring at the Supernova 2.

He gave the machine a shake, knocking dirt out of it. "Oh. I can understand that."

"I remembered. We had to wear special stuff to go outside." She held her hands over her mouth and nose. "A mask to breathe and plastic coats to keep the poison off. The air could burn us, and made our stuff fall apart if we left it outside too long."

Dad set the machine down, tapping his fingers. "It sounds like the Torment, but not as bad. Going into the clouds is deadly. Even with masks. They say the Sky Spirits' venom floats like mist in the air. It has only to fall on your skin and it can kill you."

"I think that's what my parents were running from. They knew the pollution was going to get worse, too bad for people to live. They figured it out before everyone else did, so they tried to hide in the tanks." She nudged a bolt back and forth on the table, frowning. "Lots of people died. I guess everyone who's more than a hundred miles away from the Citadel. The whole world."

"Hmm." He scratched his chin.

Whispering caught her ear from behind. Kiera turned to look. The two boys she'd seen at the fountain (which she had since learned to be a water extractor that pulled moisture right out of the air) stood by the front yard wall, alongside the Japanese girl about her age. The other girl's poncho had no hood and had been made of the same thin, coarse fabric as Mom's dress. The kids had come by a few times, though they only lingered by the wall and had yet to speak to her.

"Dad?" asked Kiera.

"Hmm?" He looked up from the game console. "This is a fascinating device, but I don't think it will be of any use. There's no electrical power out here, and I think a piece is missing."

"It needs a TV, and controllers... and the Internet. Pretty sure that's gone."

She nodded toward the front yard. "Why don't those kids talk to me? Is it because I look different? Or did they hear that Child of Earth thing, too?"

He laughed. A few weeks ago, she'd told him of her crawling out of the vent and the old man seeing it and believing her to be a giant baby being born. Dad had chuckled on and off for over an hour after that. "Most people in Exxo are a cautious about the things I have back here. Something… exploded a few years ago. No one got hurt, but they're all afraid of being too close. That's why they don't come in the yard. I don't know why they haven't spoken to you… but there's no law or tradition or anything."

"Huh…" She shrugged. "That's weird."

Dad fluffed at her hair. "You *are* the only person I've ever seen with hair this color or skin so white."

"I promise I won't take your soul."

"What?" He tickled her side. "What's that supposed to mean?"

She grinned. "Something people used to say about redheads."

He set the game console on the table to his left, grumbling about it being useless.

"Can I have it? If you can't trade it?"

"But it doesn't work."

She shrugged. "I know, but it's like a memory."

"All right. Maybe someday I'll find a TV for it. And that other thing."

"Controllers? It's okay. I guess I can live without my games." She grinned.

Mala walked up behind them and set a plate of burritos on the table. "I'm going to try the test again. Maybe if I have the right vitamins from the Ponics, we can have a boy."

"Ponics?" asked Kiera, before biting her lunch.

"Big, clean vegetables," said Teryn. "Grown inside the Citadel. Most of the permit people work so they can get numbers to buy Ponics. Little grows out here, and what does is sickly."

"Oh… *Hydro*ponics." She chomped another mouthful of burrito and licked a dribble of bean sliding down her arm.

"Hydro… ponics?" Teryn ate a quarter of his burrito in one enormous bite, earning a scolding look from Mala.

"It's where they grow things in liquid instead of dirt… the robot said there's still technology inside the Citadel."

"Yes." Mala nodded. "Their law enforcers are all metal men. The ones who give the tests are metal men as well. I could buy Ponics without a work permit, but I do not have a way to get numbers without working inside."

"They don't trade stuff?" asked Kiera.

"Sometimes, but there isn't much they need or want from outside." Teryn took a smaller bite. "You'll pass it this time."

Her parents kissed. Mom hugged Kiera and headed off across the yard on her way to the middle of the village.

*Grr.* Being unable to remember much more than bits and pieces of what happened before the tank left her with sudden doubt if that had been real. The life she remembered most—and still somewhat missed—didn't make any sense for her to have been put in a cryogenic pod. That world hadn't had a trace of pollution or war. It had to be fake, but why would anyone bother giving her a made up reality, especially one so perfect?

"Dad... do people dream when they're frozen? Why would they make me have a fake dream?"

He mumbled, his mouth full, and held up a finger until he swallowed. "Good question. Maybe they wanted you to be happier, letting you have a nice world for a while?"

"But why? It's worse to wake up from that in... this. If I remembered the Earth dying and everyone about to die, waking up to this would've been *much* better. Am I stupid for feeling like those people were real? Like my friend Ashleigh?"

"I can't imagine what it was like to be in... vee-arr."

Kiera fidgeted at her poncho. "It felt so real."

"Are you unhappy here?" He looked at her, his expression going serious.

"No." She hugged him. "I'm *really* happy you adopted me. I'm only trying to figure out what happened. All this stuff in my head, and I don't know what's fake."

He ruffled her hair. "You're smart. I'm sure you'll succeed."

She puffed out her chest. "Yeah. I'm the Child of Earth, right?"

Teryn's laugh sprayed refried beans.

# 17

# CLOUDFALL

K iera spent a few hours roaming the far end of her new Dad's scrap collection, crawling among old ductwork, playing with random objects, and running around pretending to be the soldier character from the game. Passageways between mountains of junk resembled one of the early maps, and a length of pipe with a small metal box on the side made for a decent pretend rifle.

After spending most of the day playing alone in her best non-electronic recreation of TCS, she decided to help out when Teryn got ready to prepare dinner. Her mother returned about twenty minutes before dark, looking worried. Kiera and Teryn sat by the cook fire in the front yard warming up the last of the beans for another round of burritos. Mala sank to sit on her orange cooler and slouched.

"You passed," said Teryn.

Mala picked at one of the resistors sewn into the neckline of her dress. "I don't know. I scored processing."

"Processing?" asked Teryn.

"That's what the metal man said. I need to go back in a week."

Kiera grinned. "I think you passed. I bet a real person inside the Citadel has to look at your test now, and it takes a while."

"I hope." Mala accepted a plate from Teryn. "I am so tired of taking that test."

Kiera thought about her robotics class. "Yeah. I know how that feels."

At the confused look from both of them, she explained about having to take the same difficult hundred-question exam in that robotics class over and over. At least, it had felt like she'd taken it numerous times before. Maybe the simulation only had so much content, and it kept resetting.

*Did I repeat the entire school year like sixty times?* She cringed.

After dinner, they sat together on the back porch with a nice view of the forest. Teryn took an e-tablet out from under the cushion, and read her a story about a bunch of tween witches trying to stop a demon (who had possessed their principal) from destroying their school. He stumbled over a few words, but she kept quiet and listened. 'Real Dad' started to feel like 'Bio Dad' and Teryn like 'Real Dad.' *Did he ever read to me? He might have... I can't remember.*

A little while past dark, he announced bedtime.

"How does that thing have power?" asked Kiera.

"Got a little solar panel hooked up to a battery. Can get 110-volt AC for about two hours off it... then it's gotta bake in the sun for a day or two. I made a charging wire for the reader. Power to one pin and the negative to the metal bit. Darn small stuff. It's amazing that the ancients could make something so small, but I bet there's even better in the Citadel."

Mala hugged him with Kiera caught between them. "If I did get a permit, I'll look... but my numbers are going to food before toys."

After hugging her parents, she went inside and climbed up to her bedroom. She'd decorated it with a few flowers she'd picked from the edge of the woods and two brightly colored panels from the sides of old PC cases. One white with zigzags of red, the other black with a weird little creature on it that appeared to be a yellow pill with eyes. The Supernova 2 held a place of honor in the middle of the top shelf.

She stretched out on her mattress, closed her eyes, and had no trouble falling asleep.

ONCE SHE'D FINISHED CLEANING UP THE BREAKFAST DISHES THE NEXT DAY, Kiera headed with Mala to the left side of the house where the garden spread out below a huge tarp held up by metal poles and rope. Gutters made from sliced-open PVC pipes surrounded it, carrying rain a safe distance away so it didn't poison their food. They examined the plants, plucking off any vegetables that appeared too shriveled. According to Mala, the bad ones sucked energy away from the rest of the plant and would make more vegetables die on the vine.

The chili peppers grew the best, looking almost like what she remembered. The tomatoes resembled red prunes, undersized and wrinkled. Scallions didn't do too bad, but the poor potato plants all looked rough. They didn't dig any up to check, and spent most of their time on the cucumbers and corn.

"Your friends are here," said Mala, smiling.

Kiera looked up.

Four kids stood by the wall, staring at her. The two boys and the Japanese girl she remembered, but not the older black-haired boy in a cloth skirt who had to be about thirteen. The eldest also wore a necklace of circuit board fragments on a thin cable, maybe an old mouse wire.

"They're not my friends," muttered Kiera. "Not yet, anyway. They don't even talk to me... just stare."

"Why don't you go talk to them?" Mala gave her a light pat on the rear end. "Maybe they're hoping you will?"

"The vegetables...."

"I can finish this. Go and play if you like." Mala winked.

*Okay. Fine. Let's talk.* Except for the few days where she had nothing to wear, she never considered herself a shy person. She marched right up to the wall, standing opposite the other kids, and put her hands on her hips. "Hi."

"Hi," chimed the seven-year-old boy with blond hair.

"Hello." The other girl smiled.

"She *can* talk," said the brown-haired boy about her age. He still wore the cloth tied around his middle that wound up resembling something between a tiny bathing suit and a diaper.

Kiera rolled her eyes. "I thought you couldn't talk. You've been watching me forever."

"Stuff makes bangs here," said the small one.

"Can I touch your hair?" asked the other girl.

"It's just hair." Kiera leaned forward.

"How is it red?" The girl pet her like a cat.

Kiera held her arms out to either side, making her poncho drape wide. "The great Sky Spirits took me as a baby and dipped me head first into the river of roses."

Three of them gasped in awe, but the oldest squinted at her.

"I'm teasing." She dropped her arms and laughed. "It's always been this color."

"What do we call you?" asked the boy in the cloth scrap. "I'm Osc."

"Oscar?" asked Kiera.

"Your name is Oscar?" The blond boy blinked.

"No... I'm Kiera. His name is Oscar?"

The boy shook his head. "Osc."

"Oh." Kiera shrugged.

"I'm Peter," said the oldest.

"Sparrow." The small boy grinned ear to ear.

"I'm Mei," said the girl.

"You from 'a Sand Strys?" asked Sparrow.

Kiera blinked. "What?"

Osc, the boy with the 'wedgie shorts,' smiled. "You're a Sand Strider, right? From the other tribe."

"No." She shook her head. "Orphan."

"Oh. Where do they live?" asked Osc.

"Umm. Orphan's not a tribe. A kid is an orphan if both of their parents are dead and they're all alone."

Mei looked downcast. "Oh, sorry. Such sad. Make many cries."

"Many cries." Peter bowed his head.

Kiera ground her toe into the dirt. "Thanks… I'm okay now. I'm not an orphan anymore. I live here now."

"Can you play?" asked Osc.

"Don't go too far and be back for midfood," called Mala.

"Okay." Kiera climbed over the wall and jumped down among her new friends.

Peter led the way along the path, heading for the village center. Near the water collector, deep tire tracks marked the sand where a large vehicle had pulled in and later backed out.

Kiera ran over and squatted next to them, her poncho draped to the ground. "What did this? There's still trucks?"

"The Passage," said Peter. "It brings work-permit to Citadel, and returns in dark."

Kiera stood and walked along the tread for a few paces, before gazing off into the desert. The marks faded once the buildings and hills stopped shielding the ground from the wind. She muttered, "The Citadel still has technology."

"It!" yelled Sparrow, an instant before leaping into her from behind and clapping both hands onto her back. Laughing, he ran off.

*Tag? Seriously?* She blinked. *No video games. They want to play tag? Geez, what am I, six?* She laughed, but decided to chase him anyway. Osc slipped in a mud patch left over from the rain, allowing Kiera to catch him for the tag. Sparrow had climbed onto the roof of a trailer to hide, while Mei relied on her speed. They ran around dwellings and tents, clambering over junk piles and up dirt hills. From the Gathering, Kiera knew the village had fourteen children not counting her. Aside from Peter, Osc, Mei, and Sparrow, the rest were all three or smaller.

They split up to return home for lunch—or 'midfood' as her new parents called it—after Peter made her promise to come back so he could show her something. Kiera chatted happily of her adventures running around the village over a meal of dark brown paste smeared on bread. It tasted like beef and came from a plastic jar, so she assumed they'd gotten it from the Citadel. Probably from the trader who wouldn't help her. He'd been friendly at the Gathering, but she still thought he was a butthead.

After lunch, she ran off to meet the others by the water collector. The eight-foot tall column of twisted vanes whirred around in the breeze. Water droplets on the mesh of wires inside it gleamed in the sunlight, all trickling down to collect in the basin. She understood the reason for the giant umbrella over it now, keeping the toxic rain out of the clean water. After drinking a few handfuls, she wandered back and forth, waiting.

Peter arrived first, still munching on a baked potato.

She looked up at him, head tilted. "What did you wanna show me?"

"You'll see." He winked. "Once everyone's here."

"Is it dangerous or scary?"

He scratched at the side of his head. "Yeah, it's dangerous. But not if you're careful."

"Okay."

Mei arrived next, jogging down the street, arms out to the sides flapping her cloth poncho, pretending to be a butterfly. Sparrow and Osc walked up a few minutes after her, both gnawing on sorry-looking apples.

"C'mon." Peter waved for them to follow and rushed off down the dirt path.

Kiera jogged after him, still feeling like she'd stepped into a fantasy world at the sight of homes so close together on a 'street' only as wide as a footpath. No cars could ever drive around the west part of town.

The kids weaved among scrap metal buildings, trailers, and a couple of long structures made from semi-truck trailers. Most had small gardens, some big enough to count as farms. All of the plants appeared to be struggling to exist. Those closer to the pine forest had healthier growth, and perhaps with the new pipe the people planned to build, the farms would get better.

Peter headed out of the village along a trail into the woods. The ground changed from soft powdery dust to damp soil. A forest without chirping birds felt *wrong*. A sudden scamper of small boars in the distance startled her, but the others didn't react. She ducked branches and stepped around patches of weeds, sticking as close to where Peter went as she could. It would be her luck that of all the thousands of plants to die off, poison ivy wouldn't be one of them.

The trail went down a long overgrown hill to a grassy ravine that had a line of mud running along the bottom. Kiera leapt over the muck, as did everyone else except for Sparrow who jumped into it with both feet. Peter followed the gully for a few minutes before moving to the far side and climbing it. Kiera grabbed grass and roots, planting her feet deep in the soil as she made her way up.

At the top, Peter grasped her hand and pulled her up into thigh-high grass in the shadow of a huge metal tower. She leaned back, almost falling down the hill while staring at the lattice of steel that had to be fifty feet tall. Scraps of wire drifted in the wind, dangling from struts made of black segments, like a bunch of giant ceramic coasters stacked on top of each other.

"Whoa." She crept forward. "I think it's like for power lines."

"What?" asked Peter.

"Electricity." Kiera pointed up. "Those wires used to carry electricity."

"Oh." He grabbed Mei's hand and pulled her up. "I guess. It's not the best part."

"How'd the old ones catch lightning?" asked Mei.

Kiera giggled. "They didn't catch it, they made it."

Osc and Sparrow scrambled over the top, ignoring Peter's hand while Mei stared at her in awe.

The thirteen-year-old took the lead again, walking up to the base of the tower where a ladder hung. Without ceremony, he hopped on and climbed. Osc raced up behind him, as did Mei and Sparrow.

*Well, he did say dangerous...* She bit her lip. After scooting across a wire to escape the dogs, this didn't seem *too* bad. Kiera grabbed the warm metal rung. As soon as she touched it, a tingle spread down her arm and made her hair fluff. *Eep!* She let go. It couldn't be electricity. None of the wires connected to anything, all broken short and drifting in the wind. Again, she touched it, and again the tingle needled at her fingers. *Lightning?* Maybe the tower had a charge the way scuffing her feet on a rug used to cause sparks. She stared up at Sparrow. The younger boy had no fear whatsoever, and kept swatting at Mei's feet to get her to go faster. Osc took his time going up, appearing to share Kiera's distaste for heights.

She shook her head. *This is dumb.* For no reason she could think of, she decided to climb. The hot metal rungs under her soles made her wish for the sneakers she didn't have, left behind in the world that didn't exist. When she neared the level of the treetops, a stiff wind whipped her hair to the side and made her poncho flap around like a flag. She clung tight to the ladder, squinting at the wind.

The climb ended at a narrow catwalk about forty feet off the ground, below the wide arms that supported the wires. Fortunately, Peter didn't continue trying to scale the tower itself, and sat on the grating, letting his feet hang over. Mei sat beside him, legs curled to the side, and clamped onto his arm. Osc also sat with his feet dangling, as did Sparrow. Kiera stepped off the ladder, but kept holding on to the side rails.

Forest stretched out below, continuing for miles in a shape that resembled the top of a tree with the artificial river as the trunk. She imagined the water spilling into the Earth and the ground soaking up life like a paper towel.

"Wow... It's pretty." Clinging to the railing, she twisted to look back at the village. The change from forest to desert was so abrupt it looked fake. She faced forward, mesmerized by the wavering trees that all leaned in the same direction. The hiss of the breeze among the pine needles soothed her.

"Look there." Peter pointed to the right.

Kiera stared into the distance. The silvery-grey shimmer of the Citadel gleamed in the early afternoon light. From forty feet off the ground, she had a clear view of the immense pyramid. The tornado danced upon the flattened top of the structure, the top inhaling trails of fog from the cloud dome above. The constant circular wind matched the robot's explanation. When she faced the Citadel, the breeze hit her on the left shoulder, pushing her hair off to the right.

"The Citadel," said Mei. "My mom makes numbers there and brings food. She says it's nice. They have cold inside. It's not hot. There's metal men and glowing things. They put people in little windows."

"Little windows?" asked Kiera.

Mei nodded. "Mom has one at home. It's a little box with a window on it, and there's people inside it that talk. Sometimes they shout at each other and stuff blows up."

"Sounds like she's got something that plays movies or video," said Kiera.

"Huh?" asked Osc.

Kiera eased herself down to sit, and explained movies.

"Maybe." Mei nodded.

"Dad says sometimes they put stuff in the water to grow." Osc pointed at the trees. "That's why there's forest. Seeds an' stuff swim down the river."

"The Exalted live in the Citadel, and they don't come out." Peter glanced at Kiera. "I saw one once. He had strange clothes. Same color like your eyes, and they made noise when he moved."

Osc scratched his stomach. "Is like before Cloudfall happened inside. I wanna see it."

"Silly." Mei nudged him. "They don't let kids inside. You not old 'nuff to get a permit."

"I get permit when I older." He folded his arms. "Work like my dad."

Kiera gathered her fur poncho close, guarding against the wind. Most of what she could remember from before had been scary. War, poison, people frightened all the time, her parents always away at work. The primitive life she'd stumbled into had none of that. "Maybe it's better this way... but I kinda miss my games."

"Better what way?" asked Peter.

"The village." She shrugged. "This. Farming. Parents home all day, not going off to work. It's quiet."

"Was it loud where you came from?" asked Mei.

Kiera picked at a burr in her poncho, a spiked seedpod she must've collected on the walk in. "I don't remember, but I think so. There were so many people and cars and riots and... war."

"We had a war." Osc swatted a giant fly off his arm. "Bandits try ta steal from us. My dad an' everyone had ta fight 'em."

"Much bads," said Mei, nodding. "But we win."

The ponderous insect, as fat as a green grape, seemed to be struggling to stay aloft, and buzzed around the kids.

Kiera stared at the circling bug, pulling her knees close to her chest, hiding as much of her skin as possible under her poncho. "Do bandits attack often?"

"Who's often? Why'd bandits wanna hurt him?" asked Sparrow.

"A lot. Do bandits attack a lot." Kiera cringed when the fly thrummed past her face. "Do these things bite?"

"Sometimes." Mei swatted at the bug, her hand making an audible *thump* on contact. Like a crashing plane, the fly spiraled down into the trees before recovering and darting off. "They bite."

"Only one time bandits," said Osc.

Peter pushed himself upright and moved to the far left end of the catwalk, standing with his back to the others. Kiera watched him until he lifted the front of his skirt, at which point she turned away, blushing. "Dad said the bandits had a king, and a lot of them made a big group. After the war, there aren't enough bandits to try again. As long as we stay near the village, we're safe."

"I saw some bandits," said Kiera.

"You did?" Mei gasped. "What happened? Did they try to steal you?"

Peter returned to sit where he had been.

"Yeah." She told them the story.

The four of them stared at her in awe the entire time.

"I bet they were *sooooo* mad," said Mei, grinning.

"Yeah." Kiera explained how she hid in the cabinet listening to them slam stuff around.

Peter laughed. "You were right next to them and they didn't know."

"What game do you miss?" asked Mei.

"I had a lot of them, but I was playing TCS most."

"Tee-cee-ess?" asked Sparrow.

"*The Concordant Sequence*. A video game."

All four of them stared at her like she'd spoken a foreign language.

"That's the name. It's about aliens invading Earth, and you control this soldier who's the last one left from her squad. You gotta fight all the aliens yourself."

"How do you do that?" asked Osc. "What's a video game?"

Kiera tried to explain as best she could, but her attempt only confused them more. None of them had ever seen a TV or a computer or a gaming console. "It's like that window with the people in it, only they're not real people... just drawings that move around, and you control them."

"Okay." Mei shrugged.

"What's that?" When everyone looked at Osc, he pointed. "Over there by the white stuff."

Kiera crawled to the edge of the catwalk. A spread of wildflowers ran along the top of a ridge near a boxy, metal object with tracked treads facing up. "It looks like a tank... upside down."

Peter scrunched up his nose. "Tank?"

"A war machine," said Kiera. "Like from the Army."

Osc scrambled to his feet. "I wanna see."

"Umm. It could be dangerous." Kiera leaned away from the edge.

"So is being up here." Peter grabbed Sparrow before he could lean too far forward, and carried him to the hole in the grating. "Go down."

*Yeah. Down is good.* Kiera crawled to the ladder, stepping on as soon as Sparrow gave her room. The wind flipped her poncho about and tried to blind her by whipping her hair into her face. She kept her eyes shut and descended by feel until the trees shielded her from the gale. Osc ran off as soon as he could jump to the dirt without hurting himself. Sparrow took a few steps, but waited for the others. Once Peter reached the ground, they headed off in single file behind him.

After about ten minutes of walking, they found Osc squatting at the top of the ridge amid tall grass and white wildflowers. Once he noticed the others approaching, he climbed down out of sight. Peter jogged after him.

Kiera halted at the top while the others slid down a dirt hill to where the rusted hulk of an old Army vehicle lay at the bottom with its tracks in the air, entombed in a cluster of weeds and vines. Some plants even grew in the dirt that collected between the tracks. Above it, a divot in the far side of the ravine showed where the earth had collapsed, dumping the tank over the edge. The dead war machine tilted at an angle, propped up by a turret. A large square hatch at the back end had opened upward. What had been a ramp became an awning.

Sparrow tripped on a root and rolled down the ridge face like a log, screaming. He spilled out at the bottom, flat on his back, and his screams became laughter. She let out a sigh of relief, turned her back to the gulley, and climbed. By the time she reached the bottom, Osc had already gone inside the machine.

"Wow," said Mei. "That looks old."

"It is." Kiera walked around the nose end. The gun sticking out of the turret looked way too tiny for the size of the tank. She kept going around to the back. The interior had two bench seats along the sides, now on the ceiling. "Oh… it's like an APC or something."

"What's that mean?" Mei sidled up next to her and grabbed her hand.

"It's not dangerous. It's a umm… personal carrier. Armor personal carrier." Kiera nodded. "Or something like that. Soldiers used to drive them to the war."

Osc dug at something in the back. He pulled up a helmet, still attached to a skeleton. A shake knocked the bones loose and he put it on. "Look. I found a hat! It's heavy."

"Eww!" shouted Kiera. "That was on a dead guy!"

"So?" Osc shrugged. "He don't need it."

Mei crept up to the back, staring up at the ramp. Peter climbed on top of the old vehicle, watching their surroundings. Kiera glanced up at him. *He's trying to protect us… but from what?* Mei crawled inside. Sparrow sprang upright holding a combat knife.

While Osc pulled crumbling camouflage clothes out of a box, Mei rummaged a well-rusted assault rifle from a gathering of dirt in the back corner. Two pea-sized mushrooms grew out of an opening in its side. Kiera remembered empty bullets flying out of that spot from one of her FPS games, but that rifle fired its last shot a long time ago.

*No amount of skill points in repair is gonna fix that.*

Osc grumbled in frustration as the camo fabric disintegrated into a rain of crumbles.

Content with her find, Mei walked back outside, jumping off the end of the vehicle and carrying the relic over. "Do you know what this is? You know stuff."

"Yes. It's a rifle. Or was. It's junk now."

"A rifle?" asked Mei.

"Do you know what a gun is?"

Mei shook her head.

"Okay… For war, people kill each other."

"I know that." Mei rolled her eyes.

"A gun is something that kills people from far away. It throws bullets, little pieces of metal, really fast."

Mei gasped and dropped the rifle. "I don't wanna kill anyone."

"The only way you'd kill anyone with that is if you hit them over the head with it." Kiera crouched, poking at it. "It's rusty, and all the inside parts are stuck."

Sparrow scampered over to her holding a moldy paper book bound with black spiral plastic. "I found it in a box! What this?"

"A book." Kiera took it to examine. The plain white cover had no pictures, only words. She could make most of it out under the deep mold stains.

"Soldier's manual and trainer's guide for M2 Bradley Fighting Vehicle... something."

Inside had some pictures, drawings of the truck, like how to take stuff apart.

"Can I give this to my dad?" asked Kiera.

"I found it." Sparrow pouted. "Is good for pooping."

"You got the knife." She pointed at it. "And this might have information in it that could help the whole village."

He sighed. "Okay."

From far off, Dad's voice echoed, calling Kiera's name. Soon after, a man shouted, "Mei."

"They're calling us," said Peter before turning toward the voices. He held his hands to his mouth and yelled, "We're coming back."

Kiera looked down at herself, covered in dirt, wearing a dog-leather poncho, living in a tribal village somewhere in a place that used to be Texas. If her bio-parents wanted her to come home, they'd have called her smartphone. She'd gone weeks without even thinking of one, and couldn't even remember where in her room she'd left it. Then again, it's not as if she ever went anywhere that they'd have had to call her home. Few memories of her *real* home remained inside her head, but she did remember that going outside could be deadly.

*Weird. I don't even miss my phone much.* She hurried after the others to climb the dirt wall. Living in a village so small she could walk out the door, shout the name of anyone she knew, and they'd hear her kinda made phones needless. At the top of the hill, she paused to stare up at the dark clouds. A thin strip of green lightning snaked along without sound. All the humans left in the world lived in a 200-mile wide circle.

That kinda made a lot of things pointless.

## STOLEN GOODS

**K**iera spent the rest of the day before bed sitting with her father on the sofa, poring over the book she'd brought back. Unfortunately, the information in it would likely never be of any use. However, he found it fascinating. Mostly, it explained how to operate the old war machine and maintain its various systems. Some handwritten notes indicated the vehicle had belonged to the National Guard, and was quite old even before Cloudfall. She also learned it had been a *personnel* carrier—not 'personal carrier.'

When bedtime came, she scrambled up the ladder to her room and felt her way in the dark to her mattress. Content and happy, she drifted off to a dreamless sleep. Mala's hand on her foot patted her awake in what felt like an instant. The stifling heat so early promised an uncomfortable day, and she wasted little time climbing down to the much cooler ground floor.

They shared a breakfast of vegetables as well as bread covered in jam. That, too, came from a modern plastic jar. She couldn't identify the flavor beyond it being fruit.

"I'm going to Norven's in a bit to trade. Want to go?" asked Teryn.

Kiera snarled into her bread. "I don't like him."

Mala looked up. "Did something happen?"

"He's cheap." She explained begging for clothes and him wanting her to work.

"The man probably thought you were playing." Teryn shrugged. "I've known him for years. I'm sure if you'd asked for food, he'd have helped."

She shrugged.

After helping clean dishes, Kiera accompanied her father on the way into the village, his backpack loaded with items he'd managed to fix. A handful of homes had working solar panels, so a few people could make use of appliances like toasters or small lamps. He'd also made an armored vest out of dog-leather and metal plates taken from other junk he couldn't fix. Kiera didn't think it would help much against a real knife, but it looked cool.

Norven greeted them both with a smile. "Morning. It looks good on her." He winked.

Kiera glanced up at her father while tugging at her poncho. "You got this here?"

"You're surprised?" He chuckled. "Only one place to trade. I didn't run across the Refuge to another village."

*Grr. He had this and could've given it to me all along.* She kept her scowl aimed at the floor as her father set items out on the counter for Norven to examine. Kiera hovered close, watching the men discuss the value of various gadgets. Bored, she scratched at her shin with her toes, close to falling asleep.

"What'cha lookin' for?" asked Norven.

"Some solder if you have any, but mostly need Citadel food. Garden's strugglin'. Could use some wire, too."

Kiera tugged on his arm. "Dad, that old Army truck. There's gotta be wires inside it."

"You ever gonna check out that place?" asked Norven. "Ain't too far off ya know. In the woods a ways. Can't seem to get anyone interested."

"Not since Kal tried it and stayed gone." Teryn muttered something about Sky Spirits. "And you tried to send my daughter there?"

"Aww." Norven waved dismissively. "Ain't no tellin' what happened to him. Of anyone in Exxo, you ought'a know 'cursed' means good stuff they don't understand."

Teryn shook his head and pushed the toaster toward him. "Maybe if I ain't got another choice."

Footsteps scuffed over the dirt outside. Kiera glanced back at the leather strips serving as a door. She raised her arm to wave at whoever walked in, but froze in panic when King brushed the scraps aside. Dell and Firestone followed him in, looking around at the shelves. Dell carried a plastic crate full of junk, Firestone had the crossbow, the bolt in it still smeared with Legacy's blood.

Kiera clamped on to her father, shaking.

He looked down at her, confused.

"Hey!" yelled King. "That's ours."

"No!" yelled Kiera. "Don't let them take me!"

The bandit rushed toward them. Kiera wedged herself between her father and the counter, barely keeping her breakfast from flying out of her mouth.

Teryn shoved the man back a step. "You're the ones... She's my daughter. Don't touch her."

"That kid's stolen," said Dell. "She belongs ta us."

Kiera leaned around her father and shouted, "You tried to kidnap me! I escaped. You can't *steal* people!"

Firestone pointed at her. "She stole herself. Belongs us."

"I thought I wasn't a slave," snapped Kiera. "Some feral thing you were 'rescuing?' Well, I'm safe and civilized here. Go away!"

King thrust out his chin, getting in Teryn's face. "We found her. She stole herself before we could bring her to trade. You owe us trade value."

"You're slaver dogs." Teryn gripped the handle of a knife on his belt. "Your kind has no place in Exxo. Get gone while you can still walk."

Norven grasped Kiera from behind, hands under her armpits. She jumped at the sudden touch, but didn't make a sound as he lifted her up and over the counter. As soon as he set her back on her feet, he grabbed a sledgehammer from pegs on the wall behind her. Kiera crouched, peering over the countertop.

"That kid's worth a lot. Not sick, all her limbs on," said King.

"She kinda sick," said Dell. "People ain't s'posed ta be that white. Got fever er somethin'."

Firestone raised the crossbow. "Best be reason bull. Pay owed and no blood."

"Pay, or she's ours," snarled King.

"Go away," said Kiera.

The waver of fear in her voice got the muscles in Teryn's arm bulging. "You got no claim to her. All the village knows her. You dogs won't survive ten steps."

King went to lunge past him and reach over the counter for her hair. She screamed and leapt back, bumping a shelf and knocking over a few small cans. Teryn yanked the knife from his belt and jammed it into the bandit's chest too fast for the bandit to react. King's face reddened as veins in his forehead swelled. His expression of rage melted to shock. Kiera screamed again and ducked down to sit on the floor, huddled against the wall.

The crossbow fired with a *twang*. Teryn shouted in pain. Norven jumped the counter with his sledgehammer, roaring. Feet scuffled. A body thudded to the ground. Teryn staggered to one side. Daylight flared brighter in the room with the rustle of leather scraps as men burst outside.

Norven's shout carried over the village, "Bandits! Tried ta kill Teryn and take Kiera for slave!"

More shouting arose, becoming distant, but continuing. Soon, the thumps and wails of a fight started.

"Stay down there. Don't look," rasped Teryn.

"What happened?" whispered Kiera. "Are you okay?"

He leaned on the counter. "Arrow in the leg. I'll be all right. Don't worry."

She stood and grabbed his arm, hiding her face against his shoulder. "I'm sorry."

"It's not your fault. Bandits. They're the ones who took you?"

"Yeah," she sniveled. "They killed Legacy, too. He might've been nuts, but he was only an old man."

She held on to him. Minutes later, the riot going on outside faded to silence. Norven tromped back in, a spritz of blood across his face. Kiera stared at him, shivering, unable to speak.

The shopkeeper walked around behind the counter, set the sledge down, and patted Teryn on the shoulder. "Come on in back."

Kiera clung to her father's forearm while he limped around to the gap in the counter and stumbled after Norven. A doorway led to a room with plain cinder block walls and a long wooden table that took up most of the space. Shelves full of canned goods, satchels, and other bottles lined two walls. Another corridor led to a smaller room with a bed in it.

Norven helped Teryn climb up on the table and lie down before heading over to search one of the shelves. Kiera stayed by her father's side, still shaking. He'd killed someone, right in front of her, but he could've died, too. That he'd risked his life to protect her got her crying in silence.

Teryn let out a sigh and chuckled. "I don't like bows."

"Ehh, no sense worryin' 'bout them." Norven walked over with two bottles and a pack of gauze. "You were a little off on yer count. They got about thirty steps."

Kiera stared at the aluminum shaft sticking out of Teryn's thigh. "They're dead?"

"Yep." Norven put his left hand on the leg and grasped the bolt with his right. "Very dead. All right, on the count of three."

Teryn closed his eyes. "You're going to—"

Norven ripped the bolt out.

Her father shouted a whole mess of bad words, banging his fist on the table. Blood welled up from of the hole in his leg. Fortunately, the crossbow bolt had a thin point, and left a neat finger-sized puncture. Norven tossed the weapon aside, pulled the end of Teryn's shorts out of the way, and wiped at the wound with gauze. The shot had broken one of the wooden rods decorating the old army fatigues. After tweezing splinters away from the wound, Norven opened one of the bottles and dribbled clear liquid into it.

Teryn howled in agony, his face reddening.

Kiera wrapped herself around his arm, muttering, "I'm sorry," again and again.

"Hurts a bunch, but it keeps away the sick." Norven squeezed the leg, forcing it to bleed, and dribbled more liquid in before it could fill back up.

Again, Teryn screamed.

"Almost done." Norven opened the other bottle, which had a dropper on the lid. He applied the dark brown fluid within to the injury site, which milked over in seconds. The white spot shifted toward pink as the liquid solidified into new skin. "There."

"Wow…" Kiera stared at her father's leg. "Is that a healing potion?"

Norven chuckled. "No idea what that means, but this stuff grows back skin real fast. He's still got a hole most the way through 'is leg, but this'll keep blood in and bad stuff out." The shopkeeper closed up the bottles and grasped Kiera's shoulder. "You all right, child? Seen them bandits before?"

"Yeah, I did… I'm scared, but okay." She squeezed her father's hand while telling Norven about her day of captivity.

He grumbled. "Well, they got what they deserved. You stay here with your dad. I gotta clean up out there. Nothin' for a li'l girl ta see."

"I will." Kiera leaned against the table, clutching her father's arm.

Norven put the bottles back on the shelf and headed for the door, pausing halfway across the room to pat Teryn on the shoulder. "Let me tend to matters. I'll give ya a hand gettin' home after."

"'Preciate it," gasped Teryn.

Norven brushed aside the curtain in the doorway and headed out front.

Teryn reached up to place his hand on her cheek. "You sure you're all right? You're still shaking."

"You killed him." She gulped. "A-are you gonna go to jail?"

"What's jail and why would I want to go there?"

Kiera let out a nervous giggle. "A bad place. For bad people. You're not bad, but the cops… Forget it. I'm being stupid."

"Cops?"

"Police," she murmured.

"The metal men?" Teryn brushed his thumb at the corner of her eye. "They'd have killed slavers, too. Much faster with their firelight."

"Fire light?" asked Kiera, wide-eyed. "Light that makes fire? They have real lasers?"

Teryn let his arm drop. Sweat ran down the sides of his head. "Is that what they called them before Cloudfall?"

"I think so, but they didn't use them as guns then. Not small enough to carry around." Kiera glanced at the shelf. "How much will he want for the medicine?"

"He won't ask trade. It was necessary." Teryn chuckled. "And the bandits brought that cart full of junk, which he'll keep."

She frowned. "Sorry for thinking he was mean. I really wanted clothes."

He mumbled, nodding. She stood by his side for a while, holding his hand as they waited. Eventually, Norven returned. He put Teryn's knife back in its sheath and helped him to his feet, bracing an arm across his shoulder. Kiera followed them out past the store, taking a long jumping step over the blood where King fell. The sight of the rickety cart she'd spent most of a day on a short distance away from the store brought back the memory of tight ropes. She shied away from it, keeping her gaze on the ground until they'd walked past it.

Mala's cry of alarm carried over the village from the end of the northwest path. She ran down, meeting them near the edge of the village center. "What happened?"

Norven explained on the way up the trail. A range of emotion radiated from Mala: rage, satisfaction, and finally worry. She grabbed Kiera in a protective embrace and followed the men past the yard and inside, where the shopkeeper eased Teryn into his bed.

"Is there danger?" asked Mala.

"Shouldn't be." Norven pointed at the leg. "Gave him some bottle skin and the wound cleaner. Be a while 'fore he can walk again without help, but ought ta be right soon. Watch the spot fer yellow or if he goes fever. May gotta take him to the Citadel."

Mala sat on the edge of the bed, grasping her husband's hand. "We don't have the numbers for their medicine."

"Fever ain't much if we get it early. Can use my numbers if need be." Norven grinned at Mala, ruffled Kiera's hair, and walked out.

She watched him go, thinking about the Gathering. Everyone here knew her by name, and most of them had descended upon the bandits to protect her. She tried not to imagine what it looked like for fifty or so villagers to swarm the two idiots and beat them to death, but as much as the idea horrified her, it made her feel safe.

"Will you get some water?" asked Mala, handing her a large pitcher. "He will need to drink."

"Yes, Mom." Kiera took it and started for the door, pausing a few steps later when she realized it hadn't felt strange to call her that. She stared into the empty plastic jug.

*This is home now.*

# PETABYTE

K iera gathered parts and components from the worktable out back, sorting them into wooden trunks. It would be a while before her father could tinker again, and this stuff couldn't be left to sit in the rain. Computers or electronics went in one box, appliances another, mechanical parts a third box, and anything else, the fourth.

Her parents' voices carried out the back door. Mala hadn't yet returned to the Citadel to check on her permit, and worried their garden wouldn't provide enough to keep them going with him stuck in bed and unable to scavenge. Teryn suggested she go to Norven and pick up the food he'd traded for.

"That will help, but it won't last forever," said Mala.

Teryn groaned. "You worry too much, woman."

Fear knocked a giant chip out of her new life. They could run out of food and perhaps starve, or merely get sick. Her new tribal existence lacked the flaws of the life she'd almost forgotten: school, taxes for parents to complain about, jobs to keep parents away from her, pressure to get into a good college. However, her biggest worry had gone from not getting so much homework she had no time left for video games to 'will we have enough food not to die?'

She ground her toes into the dirt. *I have to help. I can't just be a child* all *the time. Norven's ruin! I'll go check out this cursed place. Probably just a door they can't open or something modern and scary-looking.* She hurried along, packing the rest of the components in their boxes. Mala emerged from the back door and walked over, offering two thick pieces of bread and a pair of tomatoes the size of apricots.

"I'll be back soon. I'm going to see Norven." Her mother failed to hide the worry in her eyes as she looked away.

Kiera took the food and sat on one of the chests. "We'll be okay."

"I will try to share your hope." Mala hugged her. "You are probably right. He will get better and I may get a permit."

She grinned. "Yep."

"Your father is asleep. Try to let him rest."

Her mouth stuffed with bread, she nodded.

Mala walked around the trailer end of the building to the front yard. Kiera ate the tomatoes in three bites each, stood, and closed the remaining trunks with her foot while chomping down the last of the bread. With her lunch done, and the salvage safe from an unexpected rain, she dusted her hands free of crumbs and headed past the garden to the trail that would take her into the forest. Her home stood at the northwest corner of the village, the last building at the edge. Norven told her the ruin sat to the west, after a left fork in the trail. He made it sound close by, so she didn't carry any provisions other than an empty canvas satchel in case she found stuff worth bringing back.

She crossed a field of powdery silt that ended at a patch of coarse grass with twigs that hurt to step on. Soon, she found a noticeable trail headed west. It took about three minutes of walking to reach the edge of the pine forest. The air remained warm, but either she'd gotten used to ninety-degree heat plus humidity or the trees blocking even more of the sunlight than the thick clouds made it cooler. Still, she couldn't claim to be comfortable, and after walking for a while more, wanted to find that lake so she could jump in.

Somewhere up ahead, the artificial river ended at the center of the spreading growth, creating a lake. She wondered if any fish lived in it, or if they had also disappeared. Over a few minutes of walking, she tried to dig up memories of the world as she remembered it, like reports of animals going extinct on TV two and three times a week. She paused where the trail split with a fork up ahead. Remembering Norven's instructions, she veered left.

A heavy grunt came from the foliage nearby. Kiera froze. *Dogs!*

Barely moving, she eased her head around to the right, searching for the source of the sound, and stared into the eyes of a great, shaggy mass. The beast had to be thirteen feet tall at the shoulder, covered with reddish-brown shag. Its overall shape resembled that of a bison, but it lacked the hump behind the head, having more of a bull's stature. Black horns, tiny compared to the animal, curved upward from its head. Strands of greenery dangled from its chewing mouth.

"Uhh, hi." She waved at it. "Please don't step on me."

The massive animal twitched at the sound of her voice and took a few steps back.

*It's afraid of me?* She blinked in disbelief.

The creature stared at her for a few seconds more before hurling itself into a turn and bounding off among the trees. The ground shook, and its passage knocked pinecones from high branches. Scars along its hindquarters made her imagine a pack of wild dogs biting at it while it fled.

"Wild dogs. They're out here, too." She looked around. "Maybe this was a bad idea. I can get up a tree... maybe. I'm not too far away. I can scream and someone will hear me. If I don't find it in another five minutes, I'll turn back."

Kiera hurried along the road, looking around for any trace of motion. Before her nerves got the better of her courage, she spotted a large gully on the left, almost a gorge. Trees continued on the other side fifty or sixty yards away. She approached the edge and peered over. A steep, rocky wall studded with tiny bushes led down to a shallow creek dotted with round stones. Two of those bison-like creatures lay a distance farther to the west, exploded into gore. From the look of it, they'd slipped and fallen and popped like water balloons when they hit the ground. She cringed from the gruesome spectacle, and caught a flash of silver closer on the far side.

A metal plate shaped like a trapezoid bore the Citadel Corporation logo as well as a door with a steel half-sphere protruding above it. The video gamer in her saw a laser defense turret, but she giggled at the idea. *It's only a camera.* Two ventilation grates occupied the bottom corners of the metal wall section, probably too small for a man to fit into, but maybe she could.

She squatted, turned her back to the canyon, and lowered herself over the edge. Fingers and toes sought solid rock for purchase. Though steep, the ridge wall never became a vertical drop. It felt a lot like the climbing place, and looked *much* safer than the inside of that apartment building. She scaled down with ease, barely worried about falling.

Upon reaching the ground, she rested for a moment, flexing her hands and rubbing her feet. From here, the vents did look big enough for her to crawl into, if she could get the covers off. A few dents and dings didn't give her confidence, as it appeared someone had already tried that.

*Maybe they were too dumb to understand screwdrivers?*

Once she caught her breath, she got up and walked over to the door, staring at the camera ball. The place radiated an odd sense that didn't strike her as being abandoned. Like standing next to a turned-on stereo emanating silence, it felt as if power somehow still existed here.

"Whoa." She crept closer, reaching out to touch the metal door. "What is this place?"

The sphere rotated, revealing a black lens that trained on her.

"Motion detected," said a robotic voice. "Do not tamper with facility entrance. Lethal force is authorized."

She gawked. "That *is* a laser?"

It didn't respond. She pressed her hand against the cold metal.

"Please move away from the facility or provide authentication," said the robot voice. "Aggression will be met with force."

"I'm Kiera."

It didn't react.

"Hmm. It's not an AI like that robot... or it can't hear me." She felt around the door. When her hand reached the middle of the right edge, a chirrup beeped from overhead.

"Authentication accepted. Welcome, Quinn, Kiera A."

She gulped. "Whoa. What the heck?"

The door emitted a hiss and slid sideways into the wall, revealing a hallway of brushed steel. Lights along the corners of the ceiling winked on in sequence, banishing the dark, segment by segment, into the distance.

She stepped in, the floor smooth and neither warm nor cold to the touch.

"What is this place?"

When no answer came, she walked in farther. A door on the right led to a room with four cubicles. Computers, chairs, a printer, art on the walls— everything looked clean, functional, and from her era. Most unusual, none of the cushioned chairs or cube walls appeared decayed or rotted. Whatever contamination had affected the world outside hadn't leaked in here. She crept forward, mystified by the sensation of carpet on her bare feet being simultaneously foreign and familiar. A peel-away calendar on one desk displayed June of 2034. She touched a finger to the screen and it winked on showing a news website. A yellow error at the bottom read 'No Internet connection.'

Kiera climbed up into the chair and started reading. The article was dated 2026, and had a panic-stricken tone. The reporter spoke of mass unrest among citizens at widespread damage to the environment. People became divided into corporatists and environmentalists. Both sides hated the other so much it blossomed into actual war. Militaries split apart on the same lines as well as a third faction still loyal to the governments they served. The article described the systematic breakdown of world order and nations fragmenting into independent regions and towns, everyone shooting at everyone.

She stared at pictures. One showed dusty rioters screaming at the camera somewhere in the Middle East, the center man's face covered in a blood-soaked bandage. In another, college-aged men and women sat on a curb, bloodied and handcuffed with plastic ties. The caption read, 'Unrest at UC Berkeley.'

When she tried to scroll down, the page went blank with a 'server not found' error, and suggested she contact her network administrator for help. She laughed at it.

Kneeling on the chair, she rummaged the desk, tossing a calculator, pens, a notebook, a stapler, a small digital clock, and a few other gadgets into her satchel before repeating the process at the second cube.

"It's take your daughter to looting day," said Kiera in a singsong. Desk two had some jewelry in the drawer, a couple of pairs of earrings, and two bracelets. She'd never had any interest in getting hers pierced, but they would trade for food. People always wanted gold. "Nice." Into the satchel they went.

Desk three had a printout on the wall with a picture of an iceberg. The article below, dated August 18th, 2030, described panicked citizens fleeing inland from the US coasts. A giant chunk of polar ice had fallen off, melting into the ocean. Rising sea levels surged inland, despite the corporatists' continued insistence that the scientists lied about the danger. Between the first and ninth of August, hundreds of thousands died as the sea altered the coastlines. Hawaii vanished except for mountain peaks.

She looked away, taken by a sudden memory of hiding under a table while her parents screamed at each other about some project they'd been involved with. Dad had been frustrated at endless lawsuits trying to shut them down. The corporations had been afraid Citadel's effort to clean up the planet made them look bad. Mom wanted more time before 'those idiots kill us all.' He hadn't been angry with her, rather angry in general, but the screaming had frightened her. Kiera almost remembered being about eight at the time. Mom kept mentioning the coastal flooding during that argument.

Desk four surrendered two wristwatches and a flashlight to the satchel. The big drawer on the left contained a cloud of silvery mold oozing out of a box of donuts. She gently closed it while holding her breath.

Sitting in front of a computer felt weird while wearing a dog-leather poncho and nothing else. So much like the world she remembered, yet so different. The computer had clearly been an office machine. The only games on it had come with the operating system: solitaire, something with little squares to click on, and a cheesy 3D pinball game. Temptation got the best of her. She played pinball for a little while, but got bored of it in minutes.

Cabinets held copy paper, toner cartridges, and staples—nothing that seemed useful to tribals. She headed out of the room and stopped at a door on the left a few paces away, which turned out to be a bathroom. Five rolls of toilet paper went into the satchel without a second thought. *Mine.* Some things had too much value to trade away. She also snagged four plastic pouches of hand soap from wall dispensers.

The next door on the right opened to a break room where she examined a few horrifying vending machines, science projects in what happened to fake food after half a century passed. Finding nothing of use, she hurried down the hall to a corner. Another group of office workstations filled the next room on the left. She took a couple more solar calculators and a clock, as well as two e-readers and three smartphones with their charging cables, none of which had any battery life left. If Dad could charge them, one might have a game or something that still worked.

Her satchel grew heavier as she explored the second, much larger, office area. She rounded the plain grey fabric wall into the seventh workstation, stared for a second at a corpse slumped over in the chair, and screamed with a mixture of surprise and disgust.

A grey jumpsuit covered a dried out and blackened body. By the right hand lay a white and silver gun made of plastic. She would've thought it a toy, if not for the neat hole in the cube wall on the other side of his head. Once the initial horror at finding a dead man weakened, she crept closer. He'd lost his grip on the weapon after shooting himself. Kiera cringed, but reached up and grasped the pistol. She pulled it back, making his arm bump the mouse, which woke up the screen. The shift from black to white startled a yelp out of her. She patted her chest until her heart resumed beating. An email had been the last thing the man read.

*To all employees: We have received confirmation that the air quality over most of the continental United States has reached a point where life is no longer possible outside managed environments. Our scientists have been unable to explain the bizarre and dangerous weather patterns forming out in the toxic soup. It is with a heavy heart that I report the last of the Cairns have been sealed. Of course, all personnel are welcome to a pod downstairs, but there will be no possibility of bringing friends or family into the facility at this time. Conditions outside are too dangerous, and if people had not already been in a secure location, the odds of their continued survival are too low to risk sending anyone out there.*

*We have done all we can. For now, we can only wait and hope the programmers had their game on.*

*Please note that our in-house Cairn will be sealed by 6:00 p.m. today. At that time, the medical staff will enter pods themselves and the vault will lock. Hope to see you all in the future.*

*Col. William D. Mullican, United States Air Force.*

Kiera stared at the status bar, which showed this email hadn't been opened until 7:10 p.m. She backed away from the desk, not wanting to disturb him. "Sorry." She glanced down at the gun, which had a short length of clear tube sticking out the front end. It didn't feel heavy enough to be a real weapon. "Laser pistol? Seriously? Yeah right."

She pointed it at the wall and pulled the trigger.

A brilliant blue line of energy appeared in the dusty air, connecting the tip to the drywall for a split second, starting a small fire and leaving a hole the size of a dime.

"Aah!" she yelled.

The gun hadn't jumped, twitched, or done much but emit a soft hum.

"Holy crap! A real laser gun!" She shook from fear and excitement. "I can trade this for like, *all* the food."

For safety, she didn't put it in the satchel, deciding to carry it to the next desk. A white cube with rounded corners, about the size of a Rubik's puzzle, sat between the keyboard and monitor. Each face had a bowl-shaped pit surrounded by two half-circle ridges.

"Huh... what's that?" She set the laser down and picked up the cube. It weighed more than she thought it would, but appeared to be plastic. The bottom surface differed from the others, having a metal ring with a shimmery purple crystal in it. "Ooh. This is pretty." She turned it over in her hands. One corner had a tiny clear dot, like a power-on light. She picked at with a finger.

The cube beeped and floated up out of her grip. It spun like a top, perched on a fist-sized ball of pale blue light. Energy radiating from it made a few strands of her hair float. After a moment, the cube stopped spinning and hung motionless in midair.

"Wow." She stared at it. "That's cool."

"Hello," said a voice somewhere between little girl and teenager.

Kiera blinked. "Did you just talk?"

The cube glided a few inches to the left and stopped spinning. "Yes. I am talking."

"Hi," said Kiera.

"I am Pet. Or Peta if you prefer, but most people call me Pet. I have a one-petabyte memory core, which is the reason for my name."

Kiera edged after the drifting cube, staring up at it with pure awe. "I guess they didn't want the animal people to get mad."

The feminine voice laughed, the light orb fluttering in time with the sound. "How do you know about that?"

"I'm... uhh, a lot older than I look."

Pet floated up to her face. "Are you afflicted with a disease that prevents aging?"

"No. I'm really eleven. I think I was frozen."

"Cryogenic stasis." Pet orbited her head. "Your identity implant matches. Quinn, Kiera Ann. Birthdate: 9, November, 2022. One moment, accessing network resources. File transfer in progress."

"Identity implant?" She looked at her hand, thinking about waving at the egg every day to pay for her lunch at school. "Oh... now I remember. I've got a chip. Mom made me get one. That's why the door let me in."

The cube's glow flickered rapidly, reminding her of the network activity light on her Supernova 2 console. After a few minutes, it slowed to an intermittent pulse.

"Hey, Kier," said Pet in a slightly different—but still childish—voice as it glided in a lazy circle around her.

She wandered to the next desk, the floating cube following. "What do you do? What did you download?"

"Software update. Mostly I talk. I have wireless, so I can look stuff up for you or send emails or order items. I can navigate, too."

"Umm." She sat on the chair and pulled open the drawer. "None of that is really going to work anymore. The world's broken."

"Broken?"

Kiera told a quick version of her story thus far while collecting a few more bits of electronica from the last of the desks. Pet followed her out into the hallway and across to a conference room, which had nothing of use. An elevator at the end of the hall displayed an error, so she entered a stairwell. Pet's glow created an azure band on the walls that sank in time with their descent. The little cube glided over the railing and sank straight down the middle of the shaft.

"How are you flying?" asked Kiera.

"Micro ion-thruster. I can travel up to ninety miles an hour, which would be dangerous since I'd break myself if I collided with anything."

"Right." She stepped into ankle-deep water at the bottom, cold enough to make her squeal. "Eee!"

"Why did you scream?" asked Pet.

Kiera pointed down. "C-c-cold."

Eerie shadows stretched around the walls as the cube glided to hover by her feet. Small sparks danced across ripples on the water when the ion thruster got close. Kiera sloshed forward a few steps and pushed the door aside, grunting with the effort necessary to shove it. The hallway beyond also had about two inches of water.

She walked from door to door, frustrated at finding yet more places she couldn't open. Windows looked into conference rooms and one that appeared to be a lab or small medical facility. Kiera stopped at a four-way intersection, gazing around while her teeth chattered. It occurred to her that only Pet's light let her see anything.

"Why are the lights off?"

"I don't know," said Pet, "But there is a door straight ahead that is open."

"Okay." Kiera crept forward to avoid splashing the icy water up her legs.

At the end of the corridor, one sliding door on the left had jammed three-quarters of the way closed. She squeezed past it into a huge office with fancy decorations. A glass-top coffee table sat on two silver orbs, fake plants lined the walls, and a desk straight out of a science fiction movie took up most of the distant corner.

She looted a bunch of little puzzles from a bookshelf, as well as a collection of figurines she recognized as comic book characters. They didn't do anything useful, but someone might trade for them to amuse their kids. After, she plopped in the chair, which bounced and rotated. Grinning, she put her feet up on the desk to get them out of the frigid water, and reclined.

*This is nicer than my bed. I shouldn't stay here too long. Dad will be worried. I gotta bring him back here when his leg's better so we can take this chair.*

Still, she couldn't resist kicking off the desk and spinning around in circles a few times. When she stopped herself with a foot on the desk, the screen came to life, a sheet of glowing light that unfurled in midair. This terminal had a holographic display the size of a small TV.

"Wow…" She stuck her hand through it, waved, and pulled back. "That's awesome."

Pet glided around to hover over her left shoulder. "This office was last registered to Quinn, Theresa, R. PhD."

"Mom?" Kiera covered her mouth with both hands. "This was Mom's office? But I don't remember this place at all!"

"That's what the file says." Pet's light fluttered. "Don't cry."

Kiera wiped her eyes. Knowing this chair belonged to her dead mother made sitting in it *much* less fun. "When was the last time she came here?"

"Umm, the file shows she last used this terminal on June 3, 2033. The most recent activity before logout was sending an email message to Michael Quinn that reads: We can't stop it now. The project will never finish in time. If we wait any longer, we're going to die. We have to go in tonight. I'll meet you at home to get Kiera. Don't bother packing anything. We won't need it. Don't be late or we will go without you." Pet paused. "A reply came back, but she never accessed it. The response was: Leaving now. I won't be late."

Kiera pulled her legs up, feet on the chair, and buried her face in dog fur stretched between her knees. Pet muttered comforting things while she cried. After a few minutes, the crippling grief subsided. Still crying, she poked at the computer, searching for 'project.'

The first link she touched brought up a page discussing Citadel Corporation, a manufacturer of technology used to process toxic waste and clean the environment. An embedded video showed a barge sucking trash out of a lake, another had a machine skimming oil off the surface of the ocean. Text explained that while Citadel remained the world leader in environmental purification, even their best technology could not keep up with the damage enough to prevent widespread loss of life. Related articles linked to thousands of lawsuits from private citizens, upset that Citadel hadn't been able to stop the events that would ultimately become Cloudfall.

"That's so stupid. They didn't cause it!" She sighed, shaking her head.

"Some people accused Citadel Corporation of working with the companies responsible for most of the pollution, claiming the cleaning technology was all made up as a scam for money."

"Sorry, Dad, but I don't think anyone needs lawyers now."

Pet laughed. "Oh. I'm sorry. That wasn't funny."

"What's the project Mom was talking about?"

The display shifted on its own, reacting to her voice. A page came up with the title: 'Citadel Rebirth.' Kiera read, dragging the page up a little at a time by swiping a finger into the screen. The file detailed how Citadel Corporation, in cooperation with the remains of multiple national governments, constructed citadels all across the globe. The scientific analysis mostly sailed over her head, but she grasped enough to understand the Earth's biosphere had been dying rapidly. The citadels were enormous machines that could clean the atmosphere... once they were finished. A report put the fastest date to complete them at more than twenty years after estimates predicted every human on the planet would be dead.

"So... people went into freeze tanks waiting for the robots to finish making the citadels?"

She poked a link and a map appeared. Green circles winked in one after the next, each with a flattop pyramid graphic. Lines formed between them, creating a hexagonal grid that wrapped around the planet. The next closest Citadel looked to be north, in Nebraska, with another about fifty miles over the Canadian border. A yellow line circled each one, indicating a radius of a hundred miles. The map areas not inside the circles had dark shading with the word 'toxic' repeating over and over.

"Oh, whoa... no wonder there's villages by the Citadel... it's an air-cleaner. It's making the bubble we're living in." She pictured the tornado perched atop the giant pyramid, and the constant, rotating wind. According to the information on the screen, it took about thirty-six years for the citadels to create these pockets of livable space. A red band at the top marked the Citadel System as offline. "Offline? How can it be offline? It's running...."

"Citadel system awaiting authorization code to initiate primary processing," said an adult woman's voice from the ceiling.

"What does that mean?"

Pet's glow fluttered rapidly for a few seconds. "The citadels are in a standby mode. When they're turned on, they'll clean the air, reseed the biosphere with animal and plant life, and filter toxins from the oceans." The cube glided around and hovered over her feet.

"Why haven't they turned it on yet? That's stupid!" She lowered her feet from the desk, leaned forward, and slapped the glass top on either side of the keyboard. "Turn it on! What are you waiting for?"

The screen flashed black.

"Unauthorized access attempt detected," said a man's voice from the ceiling. "Requested function not permitted from remote. Terminal locked down. Security log recorded."

She sighed. "I guess I need to contact my systems administrator."

"There is no support..." Pet paused. "Oh, duh. You're joking."

Kiera stood, cringing at the cold water. "Yep." She shouldered the fat satchel and picked up the laser. "I need to go home before I get in trouble."

"Can I come with you?" asked Pet.

She grinned, sloshing out the door. "Yeah. And I promise I won't let Dad trade you."

Pet glided after her, a faint hum emanating from its thruster. "That is most reassuring. I do not think I'd like to be traded."

Kiera smirked, thinking of the bandits. "Yeah. I know exactly how you feel."

# LEFT BEHIND

Kiera hurried down the corridor, splashing. "Why wouldn't the system turn itself on when it was finished?"

"I don't know." Pet zipped along behind her and above to the left. "Searching."

She held the laser up to keep it clear of water and ran to the stairway. A few steps up on dry ground, she stopped, shivering. "I can't feel my toes."

Pet glided down, hovering over her feet. The blue glow emanating from its thruster radiated a small amount of warmth, though it tingled.

"Thanks." She giggled.

A few minutes passed before the little floating robot glided up to eye level. "I've found a document. Apparently, once the final citadel had been completed, the system was supposed to thaw out the executives so they could review the situation and make the decision to activate or not."

Kiera patted the overstuffed satchel and headed up the stairs. "Why wouldn't they? Who'd *want* to leave most of the planet deadly? And that machine's going to bring back some animals, right?"

"In theory." Pet glided by her right shoulder. "I've found a few files in the legal drive that refer to a former employee, Jeanne Greer, PhD, who claimed to have found a design flaw. According to her, turning them on would cause all the citadels to detonate in thermonuclear clouds."

"Oh." Kiera nodded on the way up the last set of stairs. "That's a good reason not to turn them on."

"None of the executives appear to believe it. Documents, some of which were written by your father, show that their opinion of Greer's claims amounted to a disgruntled employee attempting to sabotage the project. I've found two other analyses that could not replicate the supposed flaw in computer simulations of the activation process. Also, there are long email chains where both sides accuse each other of lying."

Kiera walked out into the upstairs hallway, smiling at having warm metal beneath her feet instead of icy water. "What happens if they're never turned on?"

"Searching," said Pet.

"So, the company made this giant network of machines that can take all the poison out of the sky, and there's more than one citadel…" Kiera walked around the corner, bursting with eagerness to tell this story to her dad.

"Calculations predict that the current 'passive' mode of operation will result in global restoration in approximately 677.38 years. This estimate would change if new pollution is introduced to the atmosphere, but it is unlikely primitive tribal societies could generate enough contamination to affect the timeline."

"Hmm."

The front door slid open, admitting a human-sized robot of white and silver plastic, with glowing green hexagon eyes. She stopped. The last one of these she'd seen had been friendly, though it had been pinned under tons of concrete. Its eyes had also glowed blue, but maybe this one had turned on night vision.

"Target acquired. Threat detected." The robot drew a laser pistol from a holster on its hip.

"Crap!" She raced around the corner seconds before the walls flickered blue from a laser blast. "Double crap! It's trying to kill me!"

"I believe you are correct." Pet glided ahead of her.

Raising her pistol, she faced the corner and backed up. "Think I'm fast enough to shoot it before it gets me?"

Pet rotated side to side simulating a headshake. "I suggest not allowing them to find you."

"*Them?*" yelled Kiera, glancing sideways at Pet. "What do you mean *them?*"

"There are five androids entering the facility."

She let out an 'eep' and bolted away from the corner. At the end, she slid to a halt and whirled in place, staring at multiple doors. Her voice quaked in fear. "Where should I go?"

Plastic footsteps tromped up the outer corridor.

"Follow." Pet zipped off to the stairs.

*Ugh.* Cold water beat hot laser, so she tore after the little cube. Another barrage of blue light flickered in the corridor a second after she ducked into the stairwell. A spurt of molten metal sprayed from the doorjamb, sizzling when it hit the ground. She raced down the stairs, clinging to the railing, the satchel swinging up with each turn of the switchback.

At the bottom, she jumped into the frozen water and pointed her pistol straight up the channel in the middle, but the stairs blocked the doorway. Pet zipped into the hallway. She hesitated, debating her odds of ambushing, but chickened out and chased the flying cube back to her mother's office.

"This is a dead end. Now what?" She whined, staring at the window to the hall, shaking at the approaching sound of robot footsteps.

"Over here." Pet hovered past a tall plastic plant to a ventilation duct in the wall. A tiny prod snapped out of the cube's side, a motorized screwdriver. It removed eight screws, freeing the vent cover. "Go in here to hide. Pull the cover back in place."

Kiera dove to all fours and shimmied in, dragging the satchel with her. Four-inch-deep icy water continued into the ventilation duct ahead of her. "Yeah… I played this game." She pushed the bag forward, turned around, and pulled the vent cover back up.

Pet replaced one screw and tapped itself into the cover. "Pull the slats apart."

She stuck her hands between and pushed, bending the thin metal enough for the cube to fit. It bobbed over her head and went on down the shaft. Kiera backed away from the vent opening, pushing the satchel along ahead of her.

"Is it stupid for me to try and shoot them?" whispered Kiera.

"It is unlikely you will walk away from five on one. You may disable one or two units before you suffer a fatal injury."

Kiera shivered and stuck the laser pistol into the satchel to free her hands. "You could've just said yes."

She followed Pet past a series of turns. After a mild incline that allowed her to crawl out of the water, she entered a long duct that went so far into the distance she couldn't see a wall at the end. Pausing, she whispered, "Wow… are they still after me?"

"There is too much signal interference with all this metal. I cannot tell. But, I think that means they will not be able to find you either."

Kiera exhaled a sigh of relief. "I hate stealth games."

"I don't understand."

"Shooting stuff in the face is much faster."

Pet tilted at an angle. "But then you will get 'shot in the face,' too."

"Good point." She grumbled. "Does this lead outside?"

"Yes, eventually."

Kiera grinned. "You're awesome."

"Aww, thank you." Pet glided over and rubbed against her cheek while making a kiss noise.

A few minutes of crawling brought her to a vent opening in the floor, from which light shone up into the duct. She slowed and peered down into an enormous chamber full of pods like the one she'd awakened in. All contained human shadows trapped in milky haze. She gawked, unsure if she should scream in horror or gasp in amazement.

"What is this?" Kiera pointed down. "Pet?"

The cube stopped and zipped back over. "This is a Cairn."

"English please?"

"Citadel Corporation, working in partnership with multinational governments, established a series of Cairns across the globe. Each Cairn holds ten thousand people in cryogenic stasis."

She looked around at all the pods, whistling with awe. Soon, her need to get home overpowered her curiosity, and she crawled on. Pet flew for hundred or so yards more before swerving left. A short distance past the turn, the cube hovered over a hatch.

"That goes down," said Kiera.

"Yes. There is another access way which leads to the surface, but to get to it, you must go down."

She shuffled over to the hatch without comment and twisted the handle to open it. The metal flap fell in like a trapdoor, revealing a steel ladder. Kiera again pulled the satchel onto her shoulder and tightened the strap. She sat on the edge, scooting forward until her feet found the first rung. A few steps down, a blast of icy air shot up under her poncho and made her shriek. Shivering, she hurried to climb as fast as her courage allowed. The ladder descended about five stories' distance to metal flooring as cold as the water she'd been walking in. Shin-deep fog stretched across a smaller room containing a few desks, ending at a thick wall with a heavy door. Reinforced windows on either side offered a view into the chamber full of pods.

A terminal winked on when she walked by. She stopped, easing herself to sit on an expensive looking chair with a bunch of leather-covered bar-shaped cushions mounted to a thick steel bar in an ergonomic curve.

The screen displayed an email client.

*I DON'T CARE IF THEY FIND OUT. I'M DOING WHAT'S RIGHT. SO WHAT IF I OVER packed a few chambers? They're kids. Three or four of them have the same biomass as some fat executive. Who's going to be alive long enough to care if I put unregistered kids in with other people? I've already given up my pod, 7044, and I know what that means for me. I'm at peace with it. I'm fifty-two. I've had a good run. Those kids don't deserve to die. I don't know how they chose who got in and who had to stay outside. All these strays... Watching their parents stand there as the kids go in, knowing they'll never see them again. Yeah... I'm totally okay with riding this toxic cloud into whatever's on the other side. For what it's worth, if any of you kids ever find this message, I want you to know I have no regrets. You don't need to feel guilty or even thank me. But if you want to, you can thank me by doing one thing: live. – Dianne Webb, Director of Cryogenics Operations, Citadel Corporation.*

KIERA TOUCHED THE 7044 IN THE MESSAGE, WHICH LOOKED LIKE A LINK. A SUB screen opened with four pictures: a teenaged boy, two tween girls, and a five- or six-year-old boy. The pod's registration still showed it held the Cryogenics Director and not four random children.

She choked up, unable to resist scrolling down.

*I'VE TRIED, ALAN, I'VE TRIED EVERYTHING I CAN. THE VPS ARE ADAMANT. CUTOFF age of forty. No one even an hour into forty-one is allowed into the pods. Those damn robots. I swear, one more like what just happened and I'm going to start shooting robots myself. Those people are forty-one. That's not elderly! Who writes this policy? – Dianne.*

KIERA POKED THE LINK. A VIDEO FROM A CEILING-LEVEL CAMERA PLAYED showing a woman with shoulder-length brown hair in a neat skirt suit dabbing at her nose while two people a little younger looking clung to a boy sitting on the edge of a tank. Two androids stood on either side of the woman in the suit, pointing stubby assault rifles at the parents. The robots looked similar but not identical to the ones upstairs, probably older models. The boy, about twelve, sobbed and begged to go with his parents before shouting at the woman, asking why they couldn't get in the tank with him.

"I'm sorry. It's just the policy… it's for the good of all humanity." The woman in the suit gave the robots a nasty glare. "I can't change it."

"It's all right, Chris. We'll be right here. Go on and get in," said the mother.

"No it's not," yelled the boy. "Those robots are gonna shoot you if you stay. I don't wanna get frozen. I don't care if I die. I wanna be with you guys. Please don't leave me here!" He leapt from his seat on the edge of the tank and grabbed onto his parents before breaking down sobbing, as did the mother.

The father stared at the robots as if weighing his chances of destroying them before getting mowed down.

A man in a medical smock snuck up behind the boy. The father nodded, holding his son as the worker gave him a needle. Soon, the boy went limp in his father's arms. The man held him a moment longer before carrying him back to the tank and easing him in feet first. Another man in a white jacket fitted him with a familiar facemask. Kiera cringed watching them stuff the feeding tube down his throat. His parents let go, and he slipped into the clear slime bath. The crying parents spent a few minutes hovering over the tank before forcing themselves to walk away.

Kiera cried along with them. "That's so cruel…."

The video jumped to the next file. Two androids dragged a shouting man down a hallway. He raged about being fifty and not worthless, shouting, "Two PhDs!" repeatedly as they hauled him out of camera range.

Additional logs detailed about 294 'off the books' children that Director Webb had stuck in other pods, sometimes with random adults, sometimes four kids to a tank.

Kiera wiped her eyes, turned away from the computer, and wandered over to the glass. She leaned against the frigid window, staring at the endless rows of frozen stasis units. *There's ten thousand pods in there… so many people. Did Mom and Dad get in the tanks next to mine, or did they leave me behind, too?*

# 21

# UNDUE ATTENTION

The dark recesses of the pod chamber lit up from an expanding rectangle of light at the far end of the massive room, a door opening. Five robots marched in, their shadows stretching across a glassy black floor. Kiera ducked out of sight under the level of the window. Echoes of rubber and metal feet didn't break into a running pace, so she held on to hope that they hadn't seen her.

"This way," whispered Pet. "It is time to leave."

Watching the video of those people saying goodbye to their son made her want to run home, grab her parents, and never let go. Pet drifted between two other desks and tapped a solid metal panel about three feet square. Kiera rushed over, skidding to a halt on her knees, and pulled it open. She slipped into the wall, turned around, and pulled the cover back in place so the robots wouldn't know anyone had gone there.

The passage had loads of wires and small plastic pipes, and more room than the air vent. A man could crawl around in here in relative comfort. She stooped with a deep bow and followed the glowing cube. It took a right turn where the spur met a crossing passage, continued for a several minutes and veered down a left offshoot. A few yards later, Pet darted into a short right spur that connected to the bottom of a vertical tunnel.

Kiera stood straight inside the shaft, gazing up past wires, pipes, and hoses. Sunlight glimmered in the slats of a vent about four stories above. She sighed. "Oh, this is great."

"It leads out. I do not think the robots know where you have gone. There is a good chance they didn't get a good look at you. If you can avoid being seen, you should be safe."

"Yeah right. How many kids around here have red hair?"

"It would take me some time to examine the personnel roster of the Citadel," said Pet.

She turned in place examining the walls, and found a ladder on the wall above the tunnel she'd crawled out from. "Well, at least I don't have to climb the wires, and I mean kids outside. How many tribal people have red hair?" Kiera shifted the satchel onto her back, grabbed the ladder, and pulled herself up enough to get her feet on the first rung.

Pet bobbed up to her head level. "I am unable to find personnel files for them."

"You're not serious."

A soft laugh emanated from the cube. "I am trying to make you feel better. You are probably quite scared."

"Yeah. Just a bit." She climbed too fast for comfort. "Shot at by robots, worried I might fall off a ladder and break my neck, crying my eyes out at the saddest thing I've ever seen… Yeah. I'm a little messed up right now. Is that boy still alive?"

"I believe he is. Frozen like you were prior to the virtual reality starting. The official Cairns have a much more robust power system than the small substation where you had been placed into stasis."

A vent on the left about halfway up blasted her with freezing air. She cringed as it buffeted her in the face, and squealed a few rungs later when the airburst from below bloomed her poncho up around her. *Oh that's so cold. I think I just peed.* "I… gotta find some real clothes." The icy gust lessened after she dragged herself up a little higher. Teeth chattering, she held still for a moment, waiting for her legs to stop trembling.

"There is a fabricator not too far from here that could generate more preferable attire, but I don't think it is wise."

"Why not?"

"What I understand of the society out there… dressing like you are from a citadel would attract undue attention. Undue attention of the violent type."

"What do you mean?"

Pet orbited her head. "They may think you are valuable, try to kidnap you to get the people inside the Citadel to trade for you. Or they might assume you have technology and attack you to steal it. Most likely however, the high levels of resentment between the tribes and the people within Citadel Zero would lead to simple violence."

"Okay… okay…" She grumbled, climbing on. "It's hot outside anyway. I don't want to get kidnapped again."

"Again?" Pet asked, concern clear in her voice. "I hope you were not traumatized."

"I got away pretty fast. It's… okay. They didn't hurt me, but it scared me to death. I'm more upset they killed that nice old man. Even if he was nuts."

The air got warmer the farther she climbed. At the top, she pushed a button to release the latch holding the cover in place and it flipped up on a hinge. Kiera tossed her satchel out before pulling herself up onto solid ground. She rolled over, sat up, and closed the hatch, which capped a metal platform only a few inches off the ground.

"Made it…" She basked in the warm light of day.

Kiera rested for a few breaths before the urgent need to be with her parents got her to her feet. Forest surrounded her with no sign of a gorge in sight. "Uhh. Where are we? Do you know which way Exxo is?"

"Yes. This way." Pet zipped off into the woods.

She ran after it, clinging to the satchel to keep stuff from bouncing out. The soft whine of Pet's thruster and the rapid *thumps* of her feet felt loud enough that the entire would could hear them. Not once did she look back. Her legs protested after a while, and she stumbled to a halt, leaning against a tree to catch her breath. She bent forward gasping for air and stared at her toes, grass stuck between them. The last she could remember of the real world, she couldn't go outside without covering every inch of her body in protective clothing. Kiera grinned. *Guess the citadels are working, since my skin isn't melting off.*

Pet floated over. "You have stopped."

"Can't… run… more…" She gasped.

"Oh. Sorry." Pet wobbled side to side. "It has been a long time since I had a human companion. I forget sometimes that your energy cells don't last as long."

When her heart stopped slamming in her chest, she pushed off the tree and walked. A couple of minutes later, she reached the footpath and followed it back to Exxo. As soon as the village came into sight, she veered off the road and bee-lined home. Mala paced around the yard in a frantic circle.

"Mom!" yelled Kiera.

The woman turned, stared at her, and sagged with relief.

Kiera ran into a hug.

"Where have you been!?" Mala squeezed her hard for a few seconds before pushing her out to arms' length. "I've been calling you for at least an hour."

"I wanted to help." She patted the satchel. "Dad can't hunt for stuff, so I went to this place Norven told me about. I found something… big."

"Don't do that to us again, okay?" Mala embraced her.

The video of those people putting their son in the tank hit her hard, and Kiera wound up clinging and sniffling. "Mom…."

"Are you hurt? What happened? Why are you crying?"

Kiera held on for a little while more before leaning back and smiling. "It was *so* sad... Dad needs to hear it, too."

"All right."

She pulled Mala along by the hand, heading inside. Teryn sat on the bed, poking at his leg, an annoyed frown on his face.

At their approach, he looked up and smiled. "Where did you go?"

Kiera swung the satchel off her shoulder and set it on the bed before crawling up to sit next to him. While unpacking her loot, she told them everything that happened. Her father looked over the flashlights, clocks, gimmicky paperweights, DVDs, smartphones, and e-readers with wide eyes.

Mala picked up one of the plastic pouches containing pink hand soap. "What is this?"

"Soap." Kiera explained it. "That and the TP are ours. Oh, and these..." The set of little plastic figures of comic book and video game characters she decided to keep since they had belonged to Bio-Mom.

"That's amazing... There's got to be more stuff in that place." He put his arm around her. "But, you're not to go there alone again, do you understand?"

"Yes, Dad." She snuggled against him. "And yeah, there's *so* much stuff."

"That's a lot to think about." Mala sat on the edge. "There's more than one Citadel?"

"Yes. It's not *the* Citadel; it's *a* citadel. There are hundreds of them." She described the map of the globe.

Teryn chuckled. "If we could travel a thousand miles through the Torment without dying, maybe we would find other tribes to trade with."

"I don't like that the metal men tried to shoot her." Mala kneaded her hands. "That's not right."

"I don't understand why the Exalted would be concerned... or even how they could know she went to that place." Teryn pulled her close.

Kiera curled up against him. "It was so sad watching those people walk away from their son, knowing they were going to die."

"They wanted him to live," said Teryn, his voice soft and somber. "Maybe he is still alive, like you were."

Kiera shrugged. "He is. Those people are still frozen solid. The stuff in the tank was white like milk. When I woke up it was clear, but gooey like syrup."

"Syrup?" asked Mala.

"Ugh." She thought for a second. "Have you ever blown your nose and gotten a handful of clear stuff? *That.* That is what I was floating in... only cold."

Both of her parents shuddered.

"What if they come here?" Mala stood and went to the window, peering out. "We cannot fight the metal men."

"We can." Kiera picked up the laser. "I found this."

Teryn started to laugh, but wound up staring. "That's no toy... it looks like the weapons *they* carry. The firelight."

"Uh huh." She handed it to him. "It works, too."

Teryn aimed it at the wall, closing one eye to look over it. "I have found guns before, but none that have worked... and none that made the firelight."

"It's not hard." Kiera shifted to kneel beside him. "There's a little frame on the back and a green dot at the front. Look at the dot through the little frame and that's where the beam will go."

Pet glided in the window. "Don't point that at a person unless you want to kill them."

Mala screamed.

Teryn stared in awe. "What is that?"

"Pet. She's my friend." Kiera grinned.

"Amazing." He reached out to touch it.

"It talks," said Mala. "What is it?"

"A friend. She knows stuff. She helped me get away from the robots by showing me a way out." Kiera held out her hand. Pet landed on her palm, and she hugged the cube. "Is it okay if she stays with us, too?"

"Of course," said Teryn, earning a suspicious look from Mala. "But I think you should keep her hidden for a little while. Not let anyone else see her."

"Why?" asked Kiera.

Teryn brushed her hair off her face, smiling. "Until we're sure the metal men are no longer looking for you. If someone sees Pet, they'll talk about her, and if there's something going on at the Citadel...."

"Undue attention." Kiera patted the cube.

"Indeed." Pet floated back into the air. "I will avoid detection by others until you decide otherwise."

"Come see my room." Kiera climbed off her parents' bed and darted up the ladder with the satchel of comic book figures.

Pet floated up a second later, rotating in midair. The pale blue light from the ion thruster glowed like a bulb in the dim space. "It is... rustic."

Kiera narrowed her eyes. "That's a nice way of saying it's small, dirty, and simple." She laughed, placing the figures on her shelf. "I guess it is, but it's home."

# 22

# NOOB GUN

Two days later, Kiera spent a few hours in the afternoon with Teryn at the worktable behind the house going over her finds. All of the items she'd recovered still functioned without requiring repair, so he sorted them in value piles based on what he thought Norven would want. Much to her surprise, he put the dead smartphones in the topmost spot.

She blinked. "But there's no network left... why would he want those?"

"The Citadel will pay many numbers for things like that, and those folding computers, or bigger ones. They want the information that might be inside, anything that teaches about the world before Cloudfall. Numbers can become food or medicine."

Kiera grinned. "It's weird to hear you calling it numbers. It's like credits or money or something." Oh." She pointed. "That's toilet paper. We are *not* trading it. It's for us."

"Toilet paper?" He blinked.

She explained.

"Huh... they made paper with no other purpose than cleaning your back end?"

"That's what it's for," she sing-songed. "Butt paper. It's soft. A lot nicer than those old books."

"Well that explains why all the trees died." He chuckled. "I can't believe they'd be so wasteful. Using up paper for *that*."

"Maybe. What else would they do? Laser our butts clean?" She giggled.

He chuckled and ruffled her hair.

She picked up the gun, aiming off into the forest. "This thing looks like the noob gun in TCS."

"It fires noobs?" asked Teryn.

Kiera laughed. "No… I mean it's the weakest weapon in the game, the one you start with. But in the game, it fired balls of orange light. This is a real laser. You can only see the beam if it goes through like dust or fog or something. I bet it wouldn't take shooting someone forty times to kill them like the noob gun."

"You don't have to shoot someone forty times to kill them… unless your aim is poor." Teryn rubbed her back.

"In the game. It's stupid. The gun is weak only because it's the one you start with."

Pet glided out the window and floated over. After landing on the table, the glow ceased, so it looked like one more piece of mysterious salvage. "The weapon has a self-regenerating powercell. It can fire about fifty times before it needs to recharge. If all fifty pulses are used rapidly, the capacitor will be ready to fire again in about four minutes. The powercell will last for a total of about 2,500 pulses before it needs to be replaced."

"Umm, how old is it now?" Kiera looked the pistol over. A small screen above the trigger showed 72% above 100%. "Wait, I think I found it. It's got all fifty pulses ready, and the main cell is at 72%?"

"Correct," said Pet. "Kiera, this is not a video game. If you fire that weapon at someone, they will die."

"I know. I'm eleven, not stupid." She patted Pet. "I don't want to shoot anyone… except maybe those buttheads who kidnapped me, but…."

"They're already gone." Teryn squeezed her shoulder. "They can't hurt you anymore."

"Yeah… How's your leg?" She glanced over at a huge dark bruise on his thigh. "That looks bad."

He rubbed the spot. "Ehh. Still hurts a bunch inside, but not so much I can't put weight on it when I need to."

"But it's so… purple."

He jabbed his finger into a spot a few inches from where the arrow got him, and didn't flinch. "It's blood under the skin. The medicine closed the hole, but the inside parts still bled."

"Oh. So it's okay?"

"Yes. No fever, no sick." He took a deep breath and smiled. "I would catch another bolt in the leg if it kept you away from bandits."

She grabbed on and hugged him. Her other dad probably would've been willing to do the same, but she didn't remember him much. *Did I lose my memory being frozen, or was he never home?*

"Hey, no sad." Teryn ruffled her hair. "You're not going to go running across the refuge and find more bandits to chase you, right?"

"Nope."

He chuckled. "Then don't feel sad. Bandits don't come here anymore... and before you say those three did, they came here to trade, not to be bandits. They didn't expect to find you, and when they did, they got stupid."

"Yeah. Hey... Watch this." Kiera pointed the laser at a distant dead tree stump, aimed for a few seconds, and fired. A wisp of smoke rose from both sides of a clean dime-sized tunnel all the way through the wood, as well as a spot of ground a distance behind it.

Teryn reached over and took the pistol out of her grip. "Perhaps you shouldn't be playing with that."

She grinned sheepishly. It felt kinda weird being treated like a child in a broken world, but also normal enough that she didn't mind. Bio-dad would never have let her touch a real firearm. "Yeah, probably not. But it's cool, right?"

"It's not warm or cold." He brushed his hand over the side.

Kiera laughed. "No... 'cool' means good, fun, interesting. You know... cool."

He shrugged. "Cool."

"Food is ready," called Mala from the door.

Kiera spun around on the box she sat on, facing the house. "I would have helped!" She stood.

"It's all right. It was not a lot of work." Mala walked out to assist Teryn, but he wobbled to his feet before she got to him. "Don't. You'll hurt it more and take longer to heal."

He balanced on one leg while she ran up to take his arm. "I'm fine. It's healing."

They shuffled inside. Teryn put the laser pistol up on a high shelf, and let Mala guide him to a chair at the table, which had been set with metal plates holding long slices of grilled potato as well as the all-too-familiar yellow protein bars. The room smelled like potatoes and omelets, due to the bars having been heated over a fire as well.

Kiera ran over and hugged her parents together. "Thank you for taking me in."

"The Sky Spirits brought you to us for a reason. I had been asking them for a child for many years." Mala kissed her on top of the head. "As soon as you walked up and asked me for food... From the moment I saw the look in your eyes, I knew you needed a home."

Wiping away her happy tears, Kiera took her seat and dusted her potatoes with a pinch of pepper from a small bowl in the middle of the table. She hadn't plunged into a nightmare. Kiera Quinn didn't flop on a bed in perfect suburbia, dreaming about a ruined world. No, this place of tribes and dust was as real as the love she'd developed for two strangers she'd stumbled across a few months ago.

She looked at her parents, who watched her eat with broad smiles.

*This is my world.*

# 23

# THE SEEDS OF GENESIS

Like she did whenever Ashleigh slept over, Kiera stayed up too late talking to Pet.

Her new friend even sounded a bit like her, not by voice so much as the way she glided from topic to topic at random. The cube had perched on the top shelf in the little cabinet, among the row of figurines. She'd left the toy rocket ship and ancient teddy bear in the middle. Though she felt too old to play with either one, they belonged to this room. Also, if ever she had a sibling, she'd give them to the baby.

Pet had happily rambled on about the village, her new friends, even video games and some of the comic characters the figurines represented. Evidently, Bio-Mom had been a massive geek. When Kiera realized she'd forgotten herself and thought she chatted with Ashleigh about some of the bands she liked—in the false VR world—a cloud of gloom came on and she decided to go to sleep.

Kiera awoke in near-total darkness, drowning in sweat. Droplets slid down her cheeks, gathering at her neck. Tickles crawled on her legs wherever her poncho hadn't adhered to her skin. No air moved in her room, leaving her in a cinder block oven. She groaned and sat up, flapping the dog-leather garment at her chest. When that didn't help much, she decided to take it off, which made her feel *much* cooler right away. She lay the swath of hide across the mattress, fur side down, and wobbled to her feet. Dripping trails of perspiration ran over her body as she descended the ladder to the main area, noticeably less stifling than her second-floor bedroom. Her parents slept in their bed, looking content.

A table near the front door held the large plastic pitcher they used to bring water from the collector in the middle of the village. She grasped it in both hands and raised it to her mouth, gulping down mouthful after mouthful. Despite being tepid, it felt like drinking pure life. A fair amount dribbled down her cheeks onto her chest, and on down her legs, but she didn't care. If not for being wasteful of drinkable water, she'd have dumped the whole pitcher over her head to cool off. She squinted at the back door, contemplating a midnight swim, but the river would be cold enough to shock her awake.

Once she couldn't swallow any more, she dragged herself back up the ladder and oozed into an ungainly heap on her mattress, fanning herself. When it struck her that it didn't bother her at all to lie there with nothing on, she chuckled.

*I guess I have become a primitive.*

She lacked the energy to laugh at the reaction Bio-Mom or Bio-Dad would have had to catching her sprawled in bed like that, and managed a weak smile. After a while of staring dazedly at the ceiling, exhaustion won over discomfort, and she drifted off.

SHE OPENED HER EYES TO DAYLIGHT, STILL BAKING. STICKY AND MISERABLE, Kiera groaned and pulled herself up to sit on the edge of her thin mattress. She may as well have been on the floor, but at least it offered cushioning. After wiping her eyes, she crawled to the ladder, turned to go feet first, and wobbled down into the house. The room spun in a disorienting blur of half-awake haze. Between not sleeping well and still being overheated, she couldn't tell if she'd actually gotten out of bed or only dreamed she'd woken up. On autopilot, she felt her way to her chair at the table and sat. The old fake leather cushion squished warm against her sweaty skin.

"You're awake," said Mala. "Something wrong with your dress?"

*It's not a dress; it's a poncho. Just a sheet of hide with a hole in it... and a hood.* "It's *so* hot, and that thing is fur. It's so hot today I can't breathe, even without it. I couldn't sleep."

"I thought so." Her mother set a bowl made of scrap metal in front of her. "That's why we let you rest for a while longer. Are you going to leave it off all day?"

Kiera sniffed at the contents. Beans, roasted over a fire, but allowed to cool. She picked up a spoon. Her mother didn't sound ready to scold her for it, more curious. "Thinking about it. It's horrible today. Too hot for clothes."

"Your face isn't red anymore." Mala sat and slid two pieces of bread across the table.

"Yeah." She shrugged, somber as her mind circled around all the things she no longer had to worry about: tests, school in general, bedtime, laws… No one would yell or make fun of her for not getting dressed. On the other hand, having enough food to survive had become a question mark. "The world isn't the one I remember. I'm part of the tribe."

Mala ruffled her hair.

"It's 110 degrees," said Pet, gliding down from her bedroom.

*It's like April now, right?* "Ugh. It's gonna get hotter."

Pet landed on the table by her right elbow. "It has cooled off somewhat compared to the world you remember. This is unusually warm for the spring. Highs around this time of year have been about 110-112, not the 130 degrees you remember from 2033. It might reach 120 in the dead of summer, though. The worst recorded temperatures before the citadels began processing hit the 150s."

"A hundred and twenty? How do people survive that without air conditioning?" asked Kiera.

"In the summer, most of the village spends the daylight hours in the lake. We often sleep outside on the back porch so the wind is on us. You aren't used to it, but we manage." Mala smiled.

The strong black pepper flavor on the beans made Kiera cough on her first mouthful. She eyed the bowl of it on the table. It had been such a normal thing to see, it didn't strike her as unusual until that moment. "Where'd you get pepper? I thought all the plants died."

"Norven spends his numbers for things from the Citadel he then trades to us," said Mala.

"Probably synthetic." Pet glided over and landed next to the bowl. "Or from the hydroponics farms."

Kiera nodded, shoveling beans into her mouth.

Dad limped in, grinning. "Good morning, sweetie."

She looked up. His chest, shiny with sweat, rose and fell with rapid breathing. He braced a hand on the table and eased himself around to stand by her, not putting any weight on his right leg. Mala gave him a disapproving look and shook her head. Kiera stood and managed an awkward sweaty hug before sitting again.

"Don't sit down so fast." Dad winked. "I brought you something."

Kiera got up again.

Dad took his left arm out from behind his back, and let a bundle of pale beige fabric drape into the form of a child-sized dress. The garment had a plain design, but appeared to be the same thin material as Mala's dress. A few microchips as well as tiny, peanut shaped resistors banded with stripes of blue, red, orange, and green decorated the area around the neck and along either side of a short slit down the front.

"This is a lot lighter than the poncho." Dad held it out to her. "Bela makes them, but it takes her quite a while. I'd asked her to make it for you weeks ago. Seeing you overheat this morning reminded me of it."

Kiera wriggled into it and fluffed her hair out from under the fabric. It breathed a *lot* more than the dog hide poncho, and weighed almost nothing. The hem stopped a hand's width above her knees. She admired it for a few seconds before flinging herself into a firmer hug than before, overcome by a sudden upwelling of emotion, more than when Bio-Dad had given her the Supernova 2 for her eleventh birthday. She'd asked for it, and he'd gotten it. Her reaction had been excitement, but nowhere near as emotional as what hit her over a simple dress. *Six hundred dollar console and I'm a wreck over a dress that makes Walmart clothes seem expensive. This is so weird!* She wiped happy tears. "I love it! Thank you so much!"

*Bio-Dad didn't risk the family not eating when he trad—duh, umm, bought the game console.*

"You're welcome." He grinned. "We did quite well with the stuff you found. Traded some of it this morning. Next time he goes to the Citadel, we're going to get some decent food."

Kiera released her embrace and sat, resuming her attack on breakfast.

Her father set a canvas satchel on the table, groaned, and lowered himself into the next chair.

"It's not *the* Citadel. It's *a* citadel." Kiera lifted a spoonful of beans to her mouth, but hesitated. "There's hundreds of them. The other parents worked for the company that made them, but they couldn't finish them before everyone would die... so they put people in those pods and made robots to keep working on the citadels. They're all over the world. Cairns, too."

"You spoke in a strange tongue when you first approached me," said Mala. "Did people talk like that before you went to sleep?"

Kiera blushed. "Umm, no. I'm sorry. You, uhh, kinda looked like you'd speak Spanish. I'm sorry for assuming."

"Spanish?" asked Mala.

She hurried two spoonfuls of beans and a chomp of bread. "There used to be different countries... Umm, think of them like big tribes. Some had different languages. People from those tribes looked different sometimes. You and Dad kinda look like you're from Mexico or Puerto Rico or something. And Mei, and her mom... I thought she looked Japanese, but I don't know that language."

"Oh. I've never heard those words before." Mala smiled. "Maybe you can teach me this Spanish?"

Kiera shrugged while chewing.

"I did not hear this," said Dad. "She spoke it to you before I walked over."

"I don't know a lot. I only started taking it in sixth grade... but I think I had sixth grade a bunch of times."

"Grade?" asked Dad.

Kiera explained school... which led into a longer explanation of virtual reality. That left her parents sufficiently confused to stop asking questions, despite Pet attempting to help clarify.

Dad scratched at his short beard. "It is both strange and frightening to think that there could be that many more Exalted."

"Exalted?" Kiera raised an eyebrow while sopping bean sauce out of the bowl with a half-piece of bread.

"Those who live within the Citadel." Mala gestured at the wall. "The blue ones. They are Exalted. Most do not even speak to us unless their job task requires it."

Kiera blinked. "They're *blue*?"

"Their clothing," said Pet. "The ones they refer to as Exalted are the descendants of those who remained within the citadels' cryonic storage. Once the processing mechanisms created the livable perimeter—the Refuge as the people here call it—their pods opened and they tended to the machinery within, creating a separate society within the arcology."

"Arcology?" asked Dad. "Is that the name of its shape?"

"No." Pet rotated back and forth to approximate a head shake. "An arcology is a self-contained city in a large enclosed structure. Citadels are eighty-one stories tall and the lowest, widest, level is three-point-four miles on each side."

Kiera whistled. "Wow... it didn't look that big from the tower. Guess it's far away."

"If there are more than one, do they all have Exalted?" asked Mala.

Pet spun around in a series of random motions. "I don't know. The communications links between them have either been disabled or have never been activated. Only a system-level connection remains, isolated. I believe that link's only purpose is to transmit the activation command. No human operator can access it."

"I won't pretend I understood a word of that," said Dad.

Kiera leaned back in her chair. "She said that there's a way for the people inside the citadels to talk to each other, but it's turned off, so they can't. But, if someone turns on the big switch, it should work."

"Oh." Dad nodded. "Hmm. Why wouldn't they talk to each other?"

"Someone likely said something to make Administrator Sokolov angry. He has the temper of a small boy." Mala shook her head.

"So there *could* be more Exalted?" asked Dad.

"They're not exalted. They're greedy." Kiera scraped a few bits of sauce off the sides of her bowl. "Why do they hide in the Citadel instead of building out and sharing technology with us?"

Mala sighed. "That, I do not know. What did you mean by big switch?"

"I found stuff in the computer down in the cursed place," said Kiera. "The citadels are part of a giant network of machines that were made to 'reseec the biosphere,' make animals come back, and clean the whole planet. If no one hits the big switch, it will take like 700 years."

"Clean the whole planet?" Dad raised an eyebrow. "You mean it would destroy the Torment?"

She nodded. "Yeah... if it works. Someone thought they might blow up. That's why they didn't turn them on."

"Blow up?" asked Dad. "That sounds bad."

"They won't," said Kiera. "It's just a crazy person."

"The Exalted look down on us. Risuka says the jobs we do, they pay Exalted ten times the numbers for the same work. The Administrator is the ruler of the whole Refuge." Mala waved her arms around in a wide, sweeping gesture. "Everything inside it, safe from the Torment, follows his laws. If the world is healed, he would lose his power. You are right, child. The man is greedy."

"Risuka?" Kiera tilted her head.

Mala smiled. "Your friend Mei's mother."

"How would the administrator lose his power?" asked Kiera. "He'd still have all the tech, and the robots."

Her mother leaned back, a sad sigh leaking out of her. "The Citadel is the only source of good food, vegetables, medicine... we must work there to get numbers. Our gardens alone cannot support us. If the Earth is healed and gives us food again, we would not need the Citadel—or its numbers."

Teryn drummed his fingers on the table. "I do not think this 'magic button' will fix the world overnight. If, truly, this machine can work on the entire planet, it will take years. Do you think this man is so proud of his crown that he would wish ruin on the Earth?"

"I do." Mala smirked. "Look at them. The robots tried to kill our daughter for what? *Finding* a ruin older than Cloudfall? A tribal child cannot be permitted to see such wonders, or we shall surely question."

"You are angry." Teryn put a hand on Mala's. "If they did not wish us to see their machines, why would they let our people learn to work with and repair them? I do not think they attacked her for the simple offense of *seeing* that place." He glanced at Kiera. "Did you do anything while you were there?"

Kiera shrugged. "I tried to hit the big switch, but I got an error. The computer used to belong to my other mom... and she was an executive. VP of R&D."

"Vee pee of arr and dee?" asked Mala. "I do not understand."

"Ugh." Kiera slapped both hands to her face and leaned her elbows on the table. "It's complicated."

KIERA SQUATTED IN THE GARDEN, HER TOES WEDGED IN DIRT. SHE PEERED UP AT the tattered plastic tarp as a sudden surge of wind made it rustle and lifted her hair off her back. The temperature remained over a hundred, but the steady breeze made it tolerable as long as she stayed outside. Despite living here for two months, it felt like only days ago she'd been eager to get home from school so she could get back to playing TCS. She'd gone seven weeks without touching a controller. Kiera dug around the potato plants looking for mature spuds. Pet hovered nearby, making idle conversation and even cracking a few jokes. It evidently had enough of a sensor array to be able to help her locate potatoes worth digging for.

Never in a thousand years had she imagined she might be rooting around dirt with her bare hands, living like some third-world kid she always saw on commercials where some used-to-be-famous old celebrity begged for donations. Upon finding a decent-sized potato, she plucked it and dropped it in the bowl beside her before repacking the dirt.

It surprised her how little she thought about video games. Then again, she hadn't exactly been sent off to summer camp for two weeks, forced to 'be outside.' This house, this village, this farm… real. No going home after vacation. Somehow, the 'adapt or die' part hadn't scared her anywhere near as much as it should have. She smiled over at Mala, crouched two rows over to check carrots.

*No way would Bio-Mom have put her hands in dirt.*

Her new mother looked up and smiled at her.

Kiera grinned back and scooted around to the next plant, dragging the bowl. *I'd kill for an hour of game time, but this isn't so bad. It's so weird thinking of people I met two months ago as Mom and Dad.* She jammed her hands forearm deep in soil and groped around. *They didn't have to take me in… barely had enough food for themselves.*

A few hours of working in the garden while daydreaming about video games later, Kiera had midfood, eating grilled potato and some of the beans left over from the morning. After eating, she ran into the village to refill the water pitcher and lugged it back to the house. Peter, Osc, Mei, and Sparrow came by, asking if she could play.

Mala and Teryn eagerly gave permission, before making odd faces at each other and gliding close to kiss.

She headed off with her friends, Pet in tow, and spent the rest of the daylight hours swimming in the artificial river, since the day's heat made playing any other games unappealing—especially if they involved running. The floating cube held the other kids' total attention for about a half hour before they regarded it/her as another friend. When daylight began to weaken, the beckoning shouts of several parents (and hers) caused her friends to scramble off home. Kiera pulled herself up out of the water, grabbed her dress, and ran home for dinner.

# 24

# THREATENED

The next morning, Kiera helped prepare breakfast by slicing up a pair of cantaloupes her mother had brought back from Norven's, part of the trade arrangement. Since the fruits had the exact same size and shape—as though they'd been copy and pasted in reality—she figured they'd come from the Citadel. No fruits or vegetables she'd seen growing out here in Exxo looked so healthy.

She picked up Mala's knife, a crude blade made from a sharpened metal flange with leather cording wrapped around the end to serve as a handle. It might have once been a piece of a car or other machine, but Teryn had cut it into a knife shape and sharpened it—sorta. She sawed at the melon with it, forcing the not-quite-sharp edge into the fruit.

*This thing is dull as heck. At least it beats melon armor.* She chuckled. *I've become a peasant. I'm 'NPC child_06.' I'll stand here cutting this same melon for hours and hours until the player interrupts me to talk.* "Hello, I'm only a child. I don't have a quest for you. Talk to my Dad."

"Huh?" asked Dad from the table.

Kiera laughed. "I'm being silly."

She carried the tray (plastic and likely scavenged from a cafeteria somewhere) of melon pieces to the table and sat. While they waited for Mala, she explained the concept of fantasy games, NPCs, and quests. Teryn listened with the intensity of a four-year-old boy being educated about cake. Soon, Mala walked in with a plastic bottle of orange liquid. Another trade from the Citadel.

"Wow, is that OJ?" Kiera blinked.

Mala gathered some misshapen pottery cups and joined them at the table. "It is citrus water. Prevents sickness."

"It looks like OJ." Kiera took her cup when offered, sipped, and nodded. "Yeah, that's OJ."

Teryn raised an eyebrow. "Something more from the past?"

"Yeah it's—"

Osc burst in the door and raced around to Kiera, grabbing her arm in both hands and shaking her. Dust covered him from head to toe. He gasped for breath, winded from running. "Kiera! Kiera! You got hide!"

Mala looked up. "What?"

Teryn grunted and forced himself upright. "What's the matter, boy?"

"Metal men!" Osc shook Kiera again, so hard the scrap of cloth wound about his waist threatened to fall off. "They search for girl with long, red hair. Tell reward. Big reward. From Administrator himself."

"Oh, no." Kiera's gut did a backflip. She shivered. "They're gonna find me… No one else here has red hair."

Mala stared worry at the door. "No one else among all the tribes. Maybe among Exalted there are some."

"How many metal men?" Teryn retrieved the laser pistol from the high shelf.

Osc bounced on his toes, still tugging on Kiera's arm. He stared at him for a second, released his grip, and gazed at his hands. A few seconds later, he held up one hand, all five fingers splayed. "Metal men say who shows where she is gets be Exalted."

Mala gasped. "What could possibly make him feel *that* threatened by a little girl?"

Kiera downed her OJ in three gulps, not wanting to waste such a rare treat. "I dunno."

"Maybe that Child of the Earth talk?" asked Teryn.

"That's nonsense." Kiera shrank in on herself, shivering from fear.

Teryn limped back to the table and pointed the laser at the door. Pet zipped down from her bedroom and hovered over her while Mala pushed melon around her plate. Osc looked back and forth among them all. He sniffed, twisted up his face, and jammed his finger in his nose, digging.

"I don't want you to get hurt." Kiera bowed her head, tears of guilt pattering on her thighs. "It's my fault. Something I did with the computer in that place. I'll go away."

Osc gasped.

"Nothin' doin'." Teryn backed up two steps and grasped Kiera's shoulder, almost firm enough to hurt. "You are not going off on your own."

Mala stretched across the table and put a hand on Kiera's. "You are our daughter. We cannot cast you out or let you cast yourself out. Your fate is our fate. This we knew when offering you our home."

"But you're gonna get hurt," wailed Kiera.

"I am sensing automated patrol units moving around the east portion of the village," said Pet. "This dwelling is at the northwest edge. Based on their search pattern, we have about six minutes before they arrive."

Teryn gestured at the plate. "Eat fast. Don't waste it."

"I'm too scared." Kiera grabbed her gut. "I feel sick."

Pet glided closer, nudging at her cheek.

"It's expensive food." Mala smiled. "Good for you."

Kiera, still crying, picked up a melon slice and bit it. "You eat too, then."

"Fair enough." Mala did the same, though she also seemed uninterested in her meal.

"You should return to your parents." Teryn nudged Osc to the door. "Thank you for the warning."

The boy gave Kiera an urgent stare and ran out.

"I know a place where we can hide for a while. I have used it a few times on scavenge trips." Teryn hurried to the shelves on the other side of the room and tossed some items into a satchel.

Mala devoured her food in seconds before darting to her bed and plucking a compound bow off the wall. The peg next to it held a quiver, also made of dog-fur leather, which she attached around her waist on a cord, seating it on her hip. A dozen or so metal arrows rattled around inside.

"I'm sorry," said Kiera, staring into her empty plate. "I'm sorry. I didn't know I'd get in trouble."

"You're not in trouble in the sense of doing something bad," said Pet. "You're in trouble in the sense of being threatened by a bad person."

Mala chuckled. "Your little friend and I agree on something."

The orb of blue light that Pet floated upon intensified as it zipped around in circles. "Look out! A pair have changed pattern and are coming here."

Teryn lifted Kiera out of her chair, carrying her to the rear of the house. He set her down close to the back door and pointed at the floor by an ancient wooden dresser. "Stay down. If it gets bad, run as fast as you can and don't look back."

"You're suggesting we fight the metal men?" asked Mala. "Shouldn't we *all* run out the back?"

Teryn faced her. "No. It's open out there. They'll see us and pick us off."

"You are right." Mala's expression said she expected to die in either case.

Clattering plastic approached outside.

"Dad!" Kiera pointed at the door and flattened herself on the floor.

A silvery-white humanoid figure started to come in, but Teryn rushed the front door, shoulder-ramming it hard enough to knock the android back. Another one battered into it, pushing in. Teryn's feet slipped over the mismatched linoleum tiles, his one-legged stance lacking anywhere near the strength to hold it. The instant a white robot head with glowing hexagon eyes leaned in, Mala shot it with an arrow, nailing it almost at the center of the forehead with a loud *clack*, but the attack bounced away. Teryn grunted, struggling to hold the door.

A second android flung itself into the mix, smashing the door hard enough to knock Teryn into the air. He bounced off the standing shelf and crashed to the floor. The laser tumbled from his grip and slid across the floor, stopping by one of the table legs. Kiera cringed from the *whump* her father made landing on his back a few feet away.

Two robots stood visible in the doorway, each about the height of a man, their bodies mixed of flat white and shiny silver panels. Neither's mouth-screen displayed an emotion line as they panned their heads back and forth.

She hesitated for half a second before scrambling in a crawl for the laser. Mala shot another arrow, trying and missing for the eye. Again, her arrow bounced away without doing much more than making the robot lean a bit to the side. Kiera grabbed the pistol and fumbled it into a firing grip. Both androids reached for weapons.

Mala tossed her bow aside onto the bed and dove at them, landing draped across their arms while screaming, "Get away from my daughter!"

They threw her to the floor with little effort and little care, but before they could recover their aim, Kiera clicked the trigger. The pistol emitted a faint buzz, and fire burst from the left android's chest. She shot the other one in the head, setting off a geyser of sparks. That android staggered away from the house, spinning in circles while a thick stream of smoke sprayed from the front and back of its head.

She shot the other one twice more in the body. Flaming melt holes appeared at both ends of precise tunnels all the way through it. The robot went rigid like a mannequin and fell over backward, muttering, "System fault" repeatedly.

A handful of villagers outside gasped.

"She throws firelight from her hands," said a man.

"The child is magic!" yelled a woman.

Teryn wheezed and rolled on his side, clutching his thigh.

"Dad?" yelled Kiera, still holding the gun in a two-handed firing grip pointed at the door.

"More are coming," shouted a man outside.

The villagers scrambled to hide behind the waist-high wall surrounding the front yard.

"Grr!" Kiera rushed to the door, feeling like the commando from TCS, and aimed around the wall, copying the character's motions.

"Get back!" shouted Mala.

Kiera sighted over the pistol at the path leading up from the village. Three androids came running out of the area by the water collector. She melted one down before any of them could react to being under fire. Her weapon's trigger barely moved; it felt like the button of a mouse. With the three robots close together, she clicked off a dozen or more shots, sweeping her aim to the right and cutting them all down before they managed to shoot back.

*Ambushing is overpowered.*

Neeta, Abel, Juan, and Paoma, four adults from the village, gawked at her from their positions crouched behind the wall. Neeta, Osc's mother, started to bow worshipfully at her.

"It's not magic." Kiera held up the pistol. "It's a gun. Anyone can pick it up and do the same thing." She pointed. "Look. All the robots dropped ones just like it."

Abel leapt to his feet and ran to the house, taking one while Teryn retrieved the other.

"Kiera!" Mala ran up and grabbed her. "That was foolish! They could've shot you!"

She frowned. "They were going to shoot me anyway. And their AI is stupid. They didn't take cover or anything."

"What?" asked Teryn, Mala, and Abel all at once.

Kiera clung to her mother. "Forget it. What do we do now?"

"I will take a firelight machine to protect the village." Juan leapt the wall and ran down the road to the fallen robots.

"Hide them," yelled Teryn. "If the metal men find us with firelight…"

"Yes." Neeta crept up to one of the dead robots, pointing. "What of the broken metal men?"

"Bring them to Norven." Mala cradled Kiera's head to her chest, holding her tight.

Teryn nodded. "Yes. He will know how to get rid of them without trouble. We will hide ourselves for a time, but will return."

Paoma, a fortyish woman with Chinese features, approached. "I shall watch over your home, despite the curse."

"It's not cursed," muttered Kiera. "Dad plays with dangerous things."

Teryn laughed.

Other villagers collected around the three downed robots at the base of the path connecting home to the middle of Exxo. Juan, a pistol in hand, jogged back up, smiling. He trotted over to Kiera and took a knee. Almost twenty, he still had a bit of excited little boy in his eyes.

"How does it work?" asked Juan. "You command it to make the firelight. Please show me."

Kiera explained the sights and the trigger.

"This is the safety." Pet glided over and projected a red laser pointer on a button near the trigger. "If you push that down, the weapon will not fire. It is a precaution to stop accidents."

"Yeah, I know what a safety is." Kiera pushed it. The background of the power screen went from red to green.

"They do not." Pet wobbled, a gesture Kiera had come to interpret as a smile.

Teryn grasped her shoulder and guided her into the house. "We do not have time. We must move before others come close enough to see us."

"Yes, Dad." Kiera hurried inside.

Mala recovered her bow while Teryn threw the rest of their food stores in a satchel and hoisted it up over his shoulder. Kiera filled a bunch of plastic bottles with water from the pitcher, which she packed in another, smaller satchel.

Soon, Teryn headed out the back door, leading them past the scrapyard, heading in a rapid limp toward the woods. Mala gazed at her garden as they passed it, emitting a soft sigh.

Kiera trudged along, gazing at the half-trailer-half-scrap metal pile of junk that felt like home. Watching it grow distant, not knowing if she'd ever come back, punched her in the gut with a giant guilt fist. She hurried a few steps forward and took Mala's hand. "I'm sorry for making you leave."

"You didn't make us leave. The Administrator did." Mala scowled.

Teryn's voice came strained from the effort it took him to walk. "We will return. A few days, perhaps weeks, they will stop looking for you here."

"It will take days for more robots to arrive," said Pet. "Unless they drive. There are few vehicles, and robots do not tire, so they are more often sent on foot."

"There's not too many places to go," said Teryn. "Gral Tribe in the east are well-defended, but their swords and armor won't hold up to the metal men. We cannot go north or northeast for the New Dominion."

"Slavers," muttered Kiera, squeezing her pistol. "What do you say to a slaver? Bam! Laser to the face!"

Teryn gestured to his right. "Norz Tribe lives close to the Citadel. It would be foolish to go there, and the Sand Striders could be anywhere in the refuge except New Dominion territory, though they favor the south."

"Their village moves?" asked Kiera.

"They don't have a village." Mala held her hands apart to indicate something huge. "They live in long tubes that crawl over the desert. Giant rods at the front where twenty people have to pull to make it go."

"Long tubes?" asked Kiera. "Wait... does it look like the Passage?"

Mala shook her head. "No. The Passage has seeing plates on the side. The Sand Striders' homes are all metal. Only holes cut in to see out."

Kiera pictured semi-truck trailers converted into hand-pulled wagons, like the bandit's cart, only with something much bigger than an aluminum pole and set of bike handlebars at the front.

They walked deeper into the woods, as best she could tell, heading to the northwest. Among the trees, the heat grew heavier due to the lack of wind. Shade somewhat made up for it, but the still air made the world into a sauna. Kiera flapped her dress at her chest, adoring how the thinner fabric could 'breathe.' Even though the poncho had open sides, the leather-and-fur mix was much hotter than whatever material the dress had been made from.

She cringed now and then whenever her feet found a rock or burr, and mostly stared at the ground to avoid stepping on ouch for the better part of the next few hours until they reached the end of the forest. Powdery silt-desert spanned as far as she could see in all directions except behind, where the oasis of trees grew more and more distant. The cushiony ground held far more heat than the woodland mulch, but had no surprising stones or uncomfortable bits to step on.

Mala gasped, pointing up. "Teryn... look! We are blessed."

"What? Oh... there..." He stared.

"Hmm?" Kiera looked up and found her mother gazing into the sky. A huge, bell-shaped shadow glided overhead up in the clouds, past the top of the habitable dome of air. It gave off a faint but constant growling whirr. Two bright spots near the front had the appearance of flickering eyes in an otherwise shadowy apparition. "Whoa...."

"A Sky Spirit," said Teryn, his voice low with reverence.

Kiera squinted at it. The shadow banked to the left, reminding her of a slow airplane. A flying-wing type like that stealth bomber they always had on the news. "It's a plane."

"What?" Teryn glanced at her for a second before turning his attention back to the clouds.

"A plane. A machine that flies." Kiera watched it drift the other way. "It's turning back and forth. Those spots aren't eyes, they're lights... or...."

"Sensor arrays," said Pet. "You're right. It is an aircraft, but not a plane. It's a drone."

"Oh." Kiera raised her arms to the side and let them flap against her body. "Right. They have robot cops, so of course they'd have robot planes."

Mala eyed the cube. "They're not spirits?"

"Apparently not," muttered Kiera.

"What you are seeing is not a spirit. Merely a machine," said Pet. "They've been up there for years, never landing. Solar panels and electric fans keep them airborne with no need to come down."

"Mom…" Kiera grinned and hugged her. "Remember your book, with the tech stuff about the machines you wanted to fix?"

"Yes." Mala squinted against a momentary gust. "You are saying it is like that?"

"Same thing." Kiera kicked her big toe into the silt. "I don't know if there are or aren't Sky Spirits, but that thing above us right now isn't one of them."

"Testing the air and measuring toxin levels." Pet orbited Kiera's head. "They work on automatic, linked to the main computer network of the citadels. Think of them as the processor's eyes."

Teryn tensed. "Will it see us?"

"No. Forgive me for not explaining in a way you would understand." Pet wobbled (smiled) again. "It smells and tastes the air to tell the cleaning machine how it's doing. The administrator cannot interfere with them. Some parts of the system are restricted even to him."

"Like the *big* button?" asked Kiera.

"Correct." Pet bobbed in midair, simulating a nod. "But even if he had access, he would not activate it."

"He likes his power too much." Mala shook her head. "Is that what this is about? He thinks our daughter is a threat?"

Kiera glanced at her. *She keeps calling me 'our daughter' instead of Kiera.* Grinning, she squeezed her mother's hand.

"If he did not consider her dangerous, why send robots to Exxo?" Teryn slowed to a stop. "My leg. I must rest."

"That man has often done things that even our elders cannot explain." Mala spun in a slow circle. "I see no threats."

Kiera wandered off a few paces to pee. After, she stared into the distance, careful not to look behind her, until certain that her parents had finished doing the same. She hurried back to where her father sat and flopped on the silt beside him, leaning against his shoulder. They drank, sharing one water bottle among them. Kiera gazed into the direction they'd been traveling, noticing a darkening of the haze not too far ahead.

"Is that where we're going?"

Teryn put an arm around her. "Yes. There is little else of interest in that ruin. The buildings have been peeled to the bones by the wind, but my refuge is under the ground."

"I'm really sorry for getting in trouble. I didn't know it would do that. I'm… I love you guys." She smiled up at them.

Mala beamed. "I have wanted a daughter since I was not much older than you are now. You are precious to me."

"You make your mother happy and you give an old man hope." Teryn winked. "And, once you get a little older, you'll bring in a fat dowry."

Kiera gawked at him. When he snickered, she poked him in the side and yelled, "Butt!"

"Don't tease her like that." Mala threw a handful of silt at him, laughing.

"You're not old... well for a dad. Bio-Dad was forty something. He had some grey hairs." Kiera fidgeted with her dress and dug her toes into the dirt. *I can't remember what he looked like.*

"At your age, I'd call me old." Teryn grinned.

She leaned her head back, squinting at him. "Twenty-seven?"

"Almost." He winked. "Thirty-two."

Kiera poked his bare ribs again. "Must be that clean paleo lifestyle."

Both of her parents stared in confusion.

"I don't think they understood your joke," said Pet.

"Come, we should be moving." Teryn groaned and got to his feet.

They walked toward the ruin for a little less than an hour, all the while Kiera explained about paleo diets, vegans, calories, and how everyone used to be obsessed with staying thin. A mixed sense of longing and disgust swirled around her head. *All that food people wasted...* "We used to look at menus of so much different food and always complain we couldn't decide *what* to eat. Now... having food at all is...."

"Don't worry." Mala hugged her. "We manage."

Teryn guided them down a path between concrete monoliths. Where buildings once stood, only spires remained, some with the telltale cutouts of window shapes, but no one who didn't understand what a skyscraper was would recognize them. He kept gazing around at the structures until spotting something that caught his interest and making an abrupt turn to the left. A short distance later, he came to a stop and crouched, brushing at the ground to expose a manhole cover.

"Here."

*It's a sewer...* She scrunched up her nose. *No one's pooped in it for almost a century. Maybe it won't smell.*

Teryn took a crowbar from his satchel and worked the manhole cover up. Mala descended first. He waved for Kiera to go next. She edged up to the hole and peered down a concrete pipe with a narrow metal ladder.

"Umm...."

"It's safe," said Mala from below.

Kiera took a deep breath, squatted, and stepped down. Teryn held her steady until she got her balance. He attached a rope to the big satchel of provisions, and lowered it in after her.

Mala's hands grasped her sides when she neared the bottom. Pet glided down and around, its ion emitter giving off a lantern's amount of light. A section of old sewer tunnel had been 'furnished' with a number of rugs and pillows, and a few plastic crates serving as shelves. Teryn kept another compound bow stashed here, as well as some arrows, and several gallon-bottles of water. He'd added a fire pit with a flue patched into a pipe coming out of the ceiling. The tunnel kept going in both directions, too dark to see.

Fortunately, it didn't stink.

Kiera reached up to catch the satchel when it came into view and guided it to the ground.

"Your friend is quite the help," said Mala. "We do not need to waste candles."

Grunting, Teryn dragged the manhole cover closed before descending the ladder. Mala rushed to help him. He hopped to the side and fell seated on the bank of pillows and carpet, clutching his thigh. Pet hung in space, acting like a lamp, its engine giving off a wavering, cyan light that made the space ghostly, and Kiera's skin blue.

She wrapped her arms around herself, close to shivering. "Wow... this place... Do you spend a lot of time here?"

"I found it while scavenging. Slept here a night. Forgot my flashlight. Came back in a couple of months, flashlight was still here, so I figured it a safe place. Been building it up little by little in case the bandits ever came back in large numbers and we had to flee Exxo."

Kiera hurried to sit between her parents. Worry raised her voice with a hint of squeak. "Bandits?"

He palmed the back of her head and pulled her into a hug. "They haven't been around in a long time... longer ago than you've been alive."

*I doubt that.* She curled up. *If there are Sky Spirits, please don't let bandits kidnap me again!*

"You're shaking," said Teryn. "Are you cold or frightened?"

Kiera bit her lip, shifting her eyes up to meet his gaze. "Is 'yes' an answer?"

"Do not worry about bandits." Mala rubbed her back. "They fear the Citadel."

"Is the Citadel good or bad? You keep talking about it like they're cruel, but also like they're keeping us all alive."

Teryn chuckled. "It's not good or bad. It is."

"Both good and bad." Mala combed Kiera's hair with her fingers in slow, soothing strokes. "Because we need a thing does not mean that thing cannot harm us."

Kiera nodded. "Like ice cream. Too much will hurt."

"What?" asked Teryn.

"Diabeetus," said Kiera, making her voice low in an attempt to sound like a man.

Mala and Teryn exchanged a glance.

"I believe you've confused them again." Pet wobbled.

"Okay." Kiera forgot about being afraid of bandits, and put on a teacher-lecture voice, pointing one finger skyward. "I shall explain the greatest creation of all humankind: ice cream."

# 25

# TEN THOUSAND SOULS

**K**iera slept with her parents in a pile that night, huddled for warmth under a thick blanket that smelled of wet dog. The 'bathroom' turned out to be about twenty yards deeper in where a drop off separated the upper section from a longer stretch of sewer half-full of water. The surface rippled about four feet down from the top of the ledge. A ladder offered a way down, so as Teryn put it, "you can either perch at the top or go swimming."

Kiera did *not* like his answer to, "Where are the books?"

"Jump in the water and use your left hand," sounded even worse when the inevitable need occurred a few hours later.

The unwanted bath in a damp underground tunnel had frozen her to the core. Even putting her dress back on once she'd dried off didn't warm her up much. Worse, the disgust of using her bare hand to wipe kept her constantly looking for something to scrub it with. No amount of 'looks clean' chased away her nausea.

Teryn stirred first. The rustle of his motion woke Kiera. She rolled to the left, cuddling against Mala as he stepped over them both, Pet following so he could see. A few seconds later, he exploded. Kiera cringed, pulling the neck of her dress up over her nose. The echoes of a long-ago playful argument between her other parents rose up from her memory, a time when Bio-Dad had dropped a nuclear weapon in the bathroom right before Mom needed to shower. That he'd only laughed at her mother's disgust got her calling him a 'stupid little boy.'

Despite cringing at the noises coming from her new dad, she grinned.

By the grace of the Sky Spirits, no smell followed him back to the area of carpets and pillows.

Soon, Mala woke as well, and they ate a breakfast of raw vegetables from the satchel, munching in silence. She made sure not to touch any food with her left hand.

Teryn picked up the laser pistol. "I am going to hunt. Boar dwell in the woods near the edge. It is not far, fifteen minutes."

Mala grasped his shoulder. "I will hunt. You are still hurt."

He looked up at her, frowned at his thigh, and nodded. "I married her for her brain."

She poked him.

"And a few other parts."

She poked him harder, grinning. "I'll return as soon as I can."

He offered her the laser when she reached for the bow. "This will be faster and you will not need more than one arrow."

Mala studied the pistol, turning it over in her hands. "How do I make this machine go?"

Kiera yawned and scooted closer. "I'll show you."

After teaching her mother how gunsights, the safety, and the trigger worked, Kiera headed to the wall to add some more water to the pool while Mala climbed up and out of their sanctuary. Once finished, she hurried back to the warmth of the carpeted area and reclined over the pillows.

*This is boring.* At least at the house, she had things to do. Chores though they may be, they kept her mind occupied. And tending a garden so you didn't die had a whole different feeling than 'go clean your room' or 'go wash Dad's Benz for allowance money.' Here, in this sewer hideout, she *really* missed her Supernova 2. She didn't even have any homework to eat time.

Glumness must have been radiating from her face, as Teryn tweaked her chin with a finger. "Hey… it's not your fault. You're only a child. We're not upset or angry with you."

Kiera looked up at him, eyes brimming with worry. "I miss home."

He sighed. "I'm sure you do… this is not what you—"

"No." She leaned on him. "*Home.* Where we live."

Teryn put his arm around her. "Mala's heart will fill when she hears you feel at home, but you do not have to forget your other life for our sake."

"I don't." Kiera smiled. "I mean, I forgot a lot of it. I remember more of that fake world than what really happened. But I know it's all made up. I'm sad about missing my best friend, but she's only a sim."

"A what?" asked Teryn.

"A simulation. Computer program. Umm. Kinda like a puppet?"

"Ahh. I'm sorry. I cannot imagine how something like that could be so real to you that you'd feel loss."

She sighed into his chest. "What did I do in there that got me in trouble? I think it was trying to turn the citadels on, but that computer couldn't even do it."

"As a security precaution, the citadels' primary terraforming system can only be activated from a specific physical access point," said Pet. "And that access point is beneath the Citadel."

Kiera squinted up at the glowing cube. "You said *the* Citadel. Not any one?"

"The atmospheric processing facility in this refuge is the primary one designated Citadel Zero. All other citadel nodes are subordinate to it. The initiation command can only originate from the master."

Teryn chuckled. "Well that explains the Administrator. Maybe he knows he's got the king citadel, so he acts like it."

"Heh." Kiera grinned. "Is he really that big a douchebag?"

"What is a douchebag?" asked Teryn.

She rolled her eyes. "Oh, come on...."

He pretended to cower away from her wrath.

"It's like a term for someone who's really annoying. They do stuff because it annoys people and like to see bad things happen to other people and think they're all self-important."

"Oh." Teryn scratched the side of his head. "Doooosh bag?"

She giggled. "It's not really a nice thing to call someone. There's worse, but I'm not allowed to say those."

Pet coughed.

Dad tilted his head.

"Bad words." She laughed. "They're probably not even bad words anymore since no one knows them."

"Maybe."

She stretched and sighed at the dingy ceiling. "Ugh. I am bored."

Pet swooped in, hovering between their faces. "I have a large library of fiction novels. If you like, I can narrate one?"

Kiera shrugged. "Sure."

The floating cube projected a holographic screen, showing book titles. Most appeared familiar, as in coming from the 2030s or earlier. *Guess no one had time to write books when the world was dying.* She flicked her finger at the ghostly screen, spending a few minutes paging down the list until she settled on something fantasy looking.

Pet's somewhere-between-child-and-teenage-girl voice echoed in the sewer. It had to pause often so Kiera could explain concepts and words to Teryn. He had no idea what wizards, magic, or dragons were, and initially thought the 'chronicle' the cube spoke of was historical rather than fictional.

Eventually, Mala returned with a watermelon-sized boar she'd shot in the head. The laser had left a tiny tunnel clear through its skull, the singed pork giving off a smell like bacon. Teryn took a pot from the plastic crate shelves and collected some water from below the wall.

"Eww! We're peeing in there! And... and... doing other things." Kiera shivered.

"It's not for cooking." He set it on the small grill by the flue. "It is for washing our hands."

"Oh." She still eyed it with disgust.

He lit a fire and brought the water to a boil before taking it off the flame and letting it cool. Once it had gone from boiling to merely 'oh crap that's hot,' he washed his hands in it and bid Kiera to do the same. She hissed at the heat, but hoped it killed germs.

"There's so many germs in this... ugh."

"The world's bacterial life perished," said Pet. "Any organisms in that water prior to being boiled are most likely from the three of you."

She cringed. "Are you trying to make me feel better or hurl?"

Pet drooped. "He did boil it. It should be safe. Also, that pool is not stagnant. There is a flow."

Once they'd washed, Teryn rummaged a knife from the bag and dragged the boar closer to the 'bathroom.' He gutted it, tossing the inedible parts into the water, all the while showing Kiera how to clean a kill. She watched with a modicum of controlled horror, her 'aww, but it's an animal' side in a fistfight with 'I don't want to starve.'

Preparing and cooking the boar made time go by quick. When it had cooked through, Kiera sat cross-legged in a circle with her parents, all gnawing on fresh-grilled pork. A scratch of memory told her Bio-Mom would've refused to touch it, due to it being fatty, but she didn't bother talking about it. For one thing, she barely remembered them. For another, she didn't want to make her parents feel bad. Besides, she didn't have the luxury of the modern world to be picky about food. Even Bio-Mom would eat pork if it came down to that or starvation. If she kept reminiscing about the probably-dead-and-barely-remembered other parents, her present ones might think her unhappy. She *was* happy with them.

Well, as happy as one can be going from a comfy room with a brand new Supernova 2 to a destroyed planet overnight.

"What circles your head?" asked Mala.

"Pet," said Kiera.

Mala furrowed her brows. "You are making that face because of your little flying box?"

Kiera chuckled. "No, I was being literal and cracking a joke. Circles my head?"

"Oh." Mala laughed. "I mean what is... Umm."

"What's on my mind?"

"Her hair," said Teryn.

Kiera gasped, feigning surprise, then grinned while leaning in to put a hand on his forehead. "I think a sense of humor is developing. Might be a fever though."

He set his food on his plate before attacking her with tickling fingers. Kiera squealed into a giggling fit and held her dinner in her teeth while flailing and trying to defend her sides.

"Stmmm! Stmmm!" She squirmed.

He relented after a moment, leaving her trying to catch her breath despite laugh-choking.

Mala grinned, as did Teryn.

Kiera smiled back at them, still not fully sure how to process having parents spend actual time with her. At thinking she liked these parents more than her biological ones, a bit of guilt stole some of her happiness. Of course, everything she had seen pointed to them being dead.

They ate the last of their dinner without conversation.

"Is something wrong?" asked Mala, noting Kiera's downcast gaze.

She sighed. "I was wondering about the Cairns. There could be hundreds of thousands of people on ice, stuck in vaults."

"Hundreds of thousands?" Mala thought for a moment. "That is... more people than even the Exalted. Far more than the tribes. There is no room. We would be unable to find a place of ground to stand on that did not have four others in it."

"They're not all *here*." Kiera held her arms out to the sides. "The world is a ball." She made a fist and tapped her finger around it. "There's other citadels all around the planet. The Cairns are spread out, too."

Mala leaned close to her, speaking in a comforting tone. "Are you sure what you saw in that place is true? Because it is on a machine does not make it true."

"I dunno." Kiera shrugged. "But it's true enough to make that douche want to kill me."

"What?" asked Mala.

Kiera and Teryn laughed. She explained the word again.

"It is true," said Pet. "There are multiple citadels across the globe. Most are concentrated on land masses, but some were also constructed in the major oceans."

A daydream of a waterbound citadel filled Kiera's head. She wondered if the people living inside it ever left to go fishing or swimming in the sea? Or if they hid inside from violent storms and listened to the endless crash of waves on the walls, like being in a huge submarine.

"The Citadel radiates a field that keeps the poison away. I learn how to fix the machines that do this." Mala smiled. "Even if there is more than one citadel, the Torment would kill anyone trying to go between them. It does not matter if they exist or do not exist."

Kiera snagged another small piece of boar meat, scarfing it down in three bites. With a groan, she reclined on the pillows and patted her belly, too full to move.

Teryn brushed his fingers at her hair, smiling. "We should come up with a plan. We cannot remain down here forever." He leaned toward Mala. "Or the two of us shall turn as pale as this one."

Kiera gave him a raspberry.

"We could go to the Great Ruin," said Mala. "In the southwest."

"Hmm." Teryn shook his head. "So close to the Torment. If the wind shifted, we could be caught in it."

Mala cleaned off her boar bone and hurled it into the darkness. A watery *ploink* came from the distance. "The wind does not shift that much or that fast. His robots would not like to venture that far."

"Pet said there's a fabricator somewhere. A machine that makes stuff. Maybe it's in a place we could live for a while?"

Pet glided in a lazy figure eight. "I don't have information about what is inside, other than there is a facility on my map and it is marked as having a fabricator. It could be as large as where you found me, or as small as a one-room emergency bunker."

Teryn settled into the pillows. "It is worth more discussion. I think for now, since we are safe and hidden, I would like to know how the boy deals with the witch's bottle trick."

"What?" Mala glanced at him. "There's a witch?"

Kiera laughed herself to tears. "No, Mom. It's a story. Made up."

"Oh." She relaxed.

Pet glided over to hover between them, and resumed narrating the story of a fourteen-year-old wizard's apprentice.

# WHERE THEY CANNOT FOLLOW

A sharp bonk on the head woke Kiera.

She sat up. "What was that for?"

"Shh!" said Pet, her volume down at the level of a whisper, but her voice sounded normal. "Robots are coming."

Kiera leapt onto her father, shaking him until he awoke. As soon as he moaned and raised an arm in protest, she flung herself at Mala and shook her.

"What's wrong?" muttered Teryn.

"Robots," whispered Kiera. "Pet can feel them coming."

Mala grabbed the laser Kiera had been carrying. Teryn raised the one he'd taken from the robot that tried to invade their home. Both aimed at the hole in the ceiling leading to the manhole cover. In the darkness opposite the drop-off to the water-filled tunnel, a swarm of glowing green hexagons appeared.

"Where are they?" whispered Teryn.

Kiera pointed. "There."

"Get down," whisper-shouted Teryn. He shifted aim. A spot of flames burst in the distance, the flare revealing wall-to-wall androids. "Damn."

Mala opened fire as well.

Kiera yelped and backed up, head swiveling about as she searched for a place to hide. Other than plastic crates holding crude plates and bowls, a stack of pillows offered the only other concealment.

Flame sputters appeared and vanished as fast as her parents fired blind in the dark. A scintillating white energy ball streaked out of the tunnel and struck Teryn in the stomach. He convulsed on his feet before flopping to the ground and twitching uncontrollably. White foam leaked out of his mouth.

Pet flew into Kiera's chest. "Go. Follow me."

She backed up two steps. Mala kept firing while weaving side to side. Another flickering white light missed her by inches and hit the wall, where burst into tiny lightning sparks skittering across the concrete. An android advanced close enough to enter Pet's light, raising its arm at Kiera.

"No!" shouted Mala, throwing herself in front of Kiera an instant before another sparking ball came flying from the robot's gun and hit her in the middle of the back. She fell flat on the ground, flopping and twitching like a fish out of water. She tried to shout something, but her jaw refused to unclench.

"Kiera! Run. This way," said Pet. "They will not be able to follow you."

Kiera pounced on the laser pistol lying in front of her feet and backpedaled. *They're using stunners...* She aimed for a second before losing count of the number of arms poised to fire stun balls at her.

With a high-pitched yelp of fear, she whirled on her heel and sprinted, not even realizing where the floating cube led her until she tripped over the short concrete wall at the drop-off and fell headfirst into the water on the other side.

*Eww!* She sank a decent distance under before righting herself and peering up at the distorted blue glow of Pet hanging over the surface. She started to swim up, but a handful of stunners hit the water. Painful shocks raked down her body like an army of extremely irate housecats. She screamed out a bubble, her muscles spasming and jerking from the electricity, but the paralysis didn't last more than a second. Icy water made the pain worse. She swam away from the wall, keeping her head down, until another barrage of stunners pelted the water.

That time, she twitched and twisted from the collective shock. Ten thousand sewing needles stabbed into her everything. She screamed, blowing the last of her air off in a streamer of bubbles. Her head pounded as she tried to command her body to move, to swim for air before she drowned. Limbs on fire, she pulled herself up until her face broke the surface. After taking a quick gulp of air, she dove again before a stunner could strike the back of her head.

Long strokes and kicks pushed her along underwater. Above her, silvery puddles shrank toward the middle, gathering like globs of mercury, suggesting the water touched the top of the sewer passage here. Another group of stunner balls created a dazzling display of white light and sparks some twenty feet behind her, but at that distance, she didn't feel anything.

Kiera swam up, sticking her head into mere inches of air between the surface and the ceiling. Pet scraped forward, dragging a clean spot in the muck on the concrete overhead. *There's gotta be air the whole way... it's not closed off.* She shivered with fear. Being stuck in a pipe full of water made the idea of the robot swarm seem not quite so bad.

Keeping her head above the surface, she swam into the dark, following the pale blue light from Pet up ahead. The sound of her breathing echoed in the tiny air-filled channel. Dark green slime, some kind of moss, grew from every crack. Initial shock had worn off to fear and sadness. Her heartbeat thundered in her ears, her lungs burned, and she couldn't feel her hands or feet after a while. Numb, she let herself drift in the feeble current, lacking the energy to swim any more. She didn't even cry—too exhausted.

Pet glided up to her face. "Put your hand on top of me."

Kiera reached up and grasped the little cube.

It angled forward, the light sphere emanating from its thruster swelled as it pulled her like a tiny tugboat. Thin sparks appeared in the water that steamed away from beneath it, her mouth filling with the taste of ozone. She tightened her grip, content to be dragged along for some time. Eventually, the water level dropped enough to reveal a narrow sidewalk on the side. Pet guided her over to it and hovered.

Kiera grabbed the edge and hauled herself up onto dry concrete. She curled up against the dingy wall, dripping and shivering. The thin fabric of her saturated dress clung like a second skin. "You made me jump in the toilet."

"Nothing you or your family added to that water was still there when you jumped in."

She gulped. "W-what was that stuff they shot at me? Felt like I hugged a cactus naked."

"Electrical-based pacification weapon. You would probably call it a taser, only instead of barbed projectiles connected by wires, they fire micronized darts with embedded single-use power cells."

"Okay, whatever." She shivered. "Are... my parents okay?"

Pet swiveled back and forth. "If the androids wished to kill them, they would not have been using stunners. I believe they were after you, and have no reason to harm your parents."

Kiera hugged her knees tight to her chest, nurturing a tiny glow of warm hope. "Now what?"

"Rest. You are exhausted."

After wringing her dress out, Kiera put it back on, sat, and hid her face against her knees. Droplets trickled down her legs. Every breath brought the taste of damp moss to her tongue.

"You should try to sleep. It is still the middle of the night," said Pet.

Kiera shivered, teeth clicking. "Even if I wasn't scared to death and worried about my parents, I would still have trouble falling asleep on concrete." She closed her eyes, picturing the amazing bed she used to have in... virtual reality. A hazy world where she'd been eleven years old for more than one year. Could that fake life have been overwriting her real memories? *No... virtual reality doesn't work like that. It was real time... compressed, but real time. Not like a memory implant.*

"Pet?"

"Yes?"

She lifted her head to look at it. "That tank was a virtual reality machine, right? They didn't just implant memories or make me forget stuff, did they? Why can't I remember the real world?"

Pet swiveled side to side. "No, Kiera. The VR is not a memory implant. I believe your forgetting what happened before is a side effect of cryogenic preservation coupled with spending too much time in a semi-preserved state."

She gulped. "How long was I half-frozen?"

"You were much more than *half* frozen. The system placed you in a state where your brain could process virtual reality, but your life functions were slowed almost to a standstill. You did not effectively age, though you did expel waste about once every five weeks."

She gazed down. "You didn't answer me. How long was I in sixth grade?"

"You experienced the school year ten times over the course of about two real years."

"*Ten* times?" She stared. "No wonder it felt so messed up. But I'm still eleven?"

"Yes, your body was preserved. Two years is the limit of the technology. After that long in semi-awareness, it would have needed to fully thaw you or risk serious damage to your body. It is not safe to return to full preservation from that state. Since you were kept like that until the very limit, I am not surprised you have memory loss. Also, many repetitions of the same events have created stronger memories which drown out the past like holding a candle against the sun."

She shivered, rubbing her hands up and down her arms for warmth. "Is that what the game meant when it said I didn't have enough time left?"

"Probably."

"But..." She scrunched up her nose at the cube. "Why did it matter if I beat General Xax? That last day at school, everyone—even the lunch lady—kept asking about the game."

"I don't know." Pet bobbed up a bit, an attempt at a shrug. "Maybe they just wanted you to finish it before you had to be unplugged. You know, so you didn't go around moping about being cheated out of victory."

She let her face down against her knees again, closing her eyes. *I can't win. Either too hot to sleep or too cold.* "Why did the tank flush me like a turd?"

"That is the typical procedure for when the occupant becomes deceased."

"I'm not dead." Kiera tried to squeeze herself into a tighter ball from the cold. "Am I? Is this some kind of messed-up purgatory thing?"

Pet hovered near her shoulder. "While my sensors lack any way to perceive things of a supernatural nature, I am quite sure you are alive and not in any manner of alternate dimension."

"Great. So… why did it flush me like a *dead* turd instead of opening?"

"I don't know. But I agree that it is strange."

She sighed.

"Kiera?" asked Pet.

"Hmm?"

The cube nudged the side of her head like an affectionate cat. "I don't think you're a turd."

She smiled into her legs. "Thanks."

# 27

# BROKEN HOME

**K**iera startled awake with a gasp, jerking upright. Her cheeks peeled away from her knees with a sting somewhere past uncomfortable but not quite painful. Heart racing, she looked around, trying to remember how she wound up sitting in cold, total darkness. Her dress had almost dried, except for where still-damp hair pressed it against her back. She slid a hand down her leg to her feet and tried to rub warmth into her numb toes.

Robots. Swimming away from stunners.

Parents.

"Pet?" asked Kiera, her voice shivering along with her.

Her small, cube-shaped friend floated into the air at her left. The sudden appearance of blue light from its thruster made her flinch. "Yes. I am here. I landed so you could sleep."

Kiera grasped the four-inch cube and pulled it into a hug, sniffling. "Thanks for staying with me."

"You're welcome." Pet brushed itself at her chin. "There is a way to the surface further ahead, and you won't have to swim."

She relaxed the embrace a moment later, letting Pet float back up. "Please go check on my parents. Tell them I'm okay?"

"Be right back." Pet zipped off to the left.

A halo of light slid away down a dingy, concrete shaft with square walls and a rounded ceiling. Dark water rippled and glittered below. Soon, the tiny robot glided far enough away that the passage became dark again. Kiera stood, keeping one hand on the wall, and stretched. She tried to rub the cold out of her rear end where the concrete had drained all the warmth.

*How long was I asleep?*

Her breaths echoed in the underground passage, joining a song of dripping and burbling water. Worry for her parents built, making her sick to her stomach. She paced in tiny steps back and forth, fearful of tripping into an icy bath. The minuscule glow of the laser pistol's energy display on the ground nearby tinted her feet green.

"Guess it's waterproof."

She faced the direction she believed to be deeper into the tunnel. *Why didn't the robots come after me from the other side?*

Blue light appeared in the distance after a few minutes. Pet bobbed into view, skimming along the ceiling over the water. She stared at it, kneading her hands in anxiety. When the little robot glided over to her and pressed itself to her chest, she burst into sobs. It trying to hug her couldn't be good news.

Kiera grasped it, sank to her knees, and bawled.

"I'm sorry… they're not there."

"W-what?" She coughed away tears. "Not dead?"

Pet struggled to twist side to side, a headshake. "No. At least I don't believe so. I did not detect any blood. Your parents are missing."

Shaking, she forced herself to stand, picked up the laser, and started to walk back, but turned and went three steps the other way before stopping. Pet kept close to her head, following her pacing. Her hands trembled; her chest tightened. "No… I don't want to be alone."

Pet nudged her shoulder. "You aren't alone."

Two grateful tears slipped out. "I'm scared."

"I would be as well if I were capable of being frightened." The cube nuzzled against her cheek.

Kiera thought… and thought. "Maybe… maybe they think the robots got me and went home all sad?" The idea of her parents believing her dead or abducted weighed like a stone where her heart should be. "I should go home."

"Is that wise?" asked Pet. "The robots can find you there."

She brushed grit off her sole, one hand on the wall for balance. "I don't think they'd expect me to go back there so soon. And if Mom and Dad think the robots got me, they wouldn't stay here in hiding. Besides, you can detect the robots from far away, right? You can warn me."

"All right." Pet hovered up to her shoulder.

Kiera crept along the narrow sidewalk running parallel to the water. "How far is it? It felt like it took us all day to get here."

"Your father's injury slowed you down. You were all walking at the speed of his limp. I think you can make it home in about two hours. Less if you run, but there is no need to make yourself tired. Also, if there is danger at the house, you would need to be able to run. If you are already tired...."

"Yeah, I get it." She grasped a tuft of her hair and showed it to pet. "I'm not blonde."

"What does that have to do with running now or later?" asked Pet.

Kiera laughed nervously. "I'm making a stupid joke to try and not think about how scared and worried I am right now. This girl Brittany in school? She's a blonde, and she's every stereotype you can think of. Such an airhead."

"You realize those children were only computer programs."

"Yeah." Kiera grinned, eyes locked on the ground so she didn't step on anything foul. She placed her feet one in front of the next, following a wavering path of dry concrete between piles of gunk. "I guess they were stereotypes on purpose. Sometimes I felt like I was stuck in a crappy sitcom. Some of the stuff that happened... It makes sense now. I *was* stuck in a TV show. Ashleigh seemed different, but maybe only 'cause she was my best friend. But I guess Ash had been a stereotype too. Fashion-obsessed tween."

Pet giggled. "That dress *was* on sale for $180."

Kiera stared at Pet. "What?"

"I have access to the logs." The floating cube bobbed up and spun rapidly for a second before stabilizing.

"Did that needle in my brain hurt me?"

"Unlikely. The cortical interface lance is extremely thin. Once it is inserted to the proper depth, wires thinner than human hairs emerge from the tip and make connections enabling it to feed you sensory information to create a virtual world. Have you ever heard of the 'brain-in-a-jar' theory?"

Kiera glanced at Pet. "I'm eleven. Sixth grade. I may have repeated it ten times, but I'm still a sixth-grader. So, no... And that sounds disgusting."

"It's not a literal brain in a jar." Pet wobbled side to side, a smile. "It's a philosophical scenario. A brain, removed from a body and placed in a jar while connected to a computer or other machine that simulates reality, would not know that it is a brain in a jar and believe the simulation to be reality."

"Oh." Kiera shrugged while walking. "I dunno about brain in a jar, but what about 'kid in a tank of goop?' I've seen that one."

Pet giggled.

"Are you a kid too, or do you just sound like it?"

The cube glided side to side, playing in the air. "I was designed with this voice to be pleasant to a wider selection of people. It is considered 'cute and appealing.' Each pet cube has a distinct personality that evolves based on our interactions with people. If you do not like my voice, you can change it. I can sound like an adult—man or woman—or an old person if you like. Or even a tiny child."

Kiera stopped, staring at a long stretch of nasty on the ground. "Eww. What is that? And no, your voice is cool. I like it."

"It appears to be a mixture of dirt, moss, mold, and... well, the decades-old decomposing remains of rats and other small animals. I take that back. Decomposed. They are not capable of rotting to any greater degree."

"Ugh."

Even a running jump would land her in the middle of it, so she gritted her teeth and advanced, shoulders scrunched up. Wet, slimy brown funk oozed between her toes with each step. Disturbing it lofted a smell like a dead bird found in the attic. She held her breath, all the muscles in her back tensed, arms raised in disgust. Once she cleared the swath of ick, about ten paces later, she spent a moment swishing one foot then the other back and forth in the water to wash them.

Pet zipped ahead a little ways, and hung in space by a pipe opening high on the wall to the right. "In here."

"Really?" Kiera padded over and stood on tiptoe to stare into an opening about two feet wide. "It's dark and small."

"The passage ahead caves in. You could climb this pipe or swim back up and go out the way you came in. This way does not involve soaking yourself again."

"Again? I'm *still* damp." She sighed. "Fine."

Kiera set the laser pistol in first before grabbing the edge of the pipe and pulling herself up, toes seeking purchase in gaps between bricks. Grunting, she wriggled in, pushing the laser forward as she flattened herself out atop a thin layer of dried mud. The narrow passage didn't give her enough room to get up on her hands and knees. Pet drifted over her and led the way as she elbow crawled forward.

"What time is it?" asked Kiera. "How long did I sleep?"

Pet stopped and spun to face her. "It's 9:07 a.m. You slept from 2:18 a.m. until 8:44 a.m."

"Wow... So long." She pulled herself onward, walking on her forearms down the narrow pipe. "Are you sure I'm not still in some simulation? How did I go from boring suburbs to stuck in a sewer?"

"The VR simulation ended," said Pet. "Your pod was nearly out of power."

Kiera sighed. "Thanks. Umm... this pipe isn't going to like fill up with water when I'm in it, right? That's like major nightmare stuff."

"If it begins to rain hard, there might be water, but I do not think the pipe would fill all the way."

She shuddered and crawled faster, determined gasps echoing for what seemed like miles.

At 9:28 a.m. according to Pet, a patch of sunlight came into view up ahead where the pipe curved around a ninety-degree right and canted upward.

Kiera squirmed past the curve, adoring the warmth of the concrete around her body. It took less than a minute to crawl up the ascending part to an opening full of daylight. Grinning, she shimmied out into a tall, rectangular chamber full of silt, plastic bottles, a few Starbucks cups, and fast food burger cartons. She stood, gazing up at a storm drain opening.

"Oh wow. Thanks for the climbing classes, Dad." She sighed. Confused, she twisted to stare at Pet. "How am I... I mean... I floated in a tank for a long time." She lifted her dress to expose well-defined muscles on her stomach. "How am I like this? I wasn't even this über in real life." She let the dress fall back in place.

Pet tapped itself into her arm. "Before the tank released you, it gave you injections that conditioned your muscles and helped you recover from remaining still so long. During the time you were in VR, the system provided you the bare minimum of nutrients, so you lost some weight."

"*Some* weight? I'm a stick figure." She grumbled, but froze as a memory of Bio-Mom needling her over calories came back. *I don't think I was heavy, but I definitely wasn't ripped like this.* She glanced at her noodle arms. *Okay, maybe I'm not ripped, but....*

"You are healthy." Pet floated straight up to the opening and went out. A moment later, it reappeared. "I don't see any threats."

"Right. Uhh... how am I gonna do this without losing the gun?"

A tiny gripper clamp sprang out of Pet's side. "I will hold it for you. It's not too heavy for me."

The base of the pistol's handle had a small ring intended for a lanyard or something, which Pet closed its tiny pincer on. Swaying from the weight, the cube flew up and out.

Kiera wiped her hands on her arms to get rid of gooey moss, eyed the underside of the storm drain, and jumped. Her first attempt slapped concrete. She squatted deeper on the second try, leaping up as hard as she could shove with her legs. Her fingertips caught the ridge of the metal opening, and held. Feet skidding over the wall, she roared with determination and pulled herself up. Hot, humid air blasted her in the face when she stuck her head out, pushing the chill of the sewer back down into the darkness below.

She slithered onto the soft silt and rolled over onto her back, basking in the heat of day.

Pet dropped the laser on her belly.

"Oof." She grabbed it with both hands. "Thanks."

Within minutes, the ice thawed from her bones. She stood, shaking her head back and forth so the wind caught and dried her hair.

Desolation surrounded her, but the patch of forest at the end of the artificial river remained visible as a dark stretch in the distance to her right. A few piles of rubble dotted the area, but nothing had even enough structure to count as 'used to be a building.'

"Guess it's that way?" She pointed at the trees.

Pet wobbled. "Yes."

She smacked her lips, thirsty. "Okay."

Walking at a brisk stride, Kiera followed Pet across the desert, reaching the edge of the trees in about twenty minutes. Random thuds and snaps kept her spinning, frightened that a pack of wild dogs might find her tasty. Over dozens of scares, only once did she spot anything alive: another boar, this one big enough to ride. It faced her and made a threatening noise, but didn't chase her when she ran. She slowed to a jog, then a walk as soon as she felt confident it wouldn't come after her.

"I'm so thirsty…."

Pet drifted to the right. "We are close to the water."

The cube led her through the woods to the edge of a giant lake surrounded on all sides by trees. She crouched, ankle deep at the bank, and drank handfuls. A heavy snorting grunt startled her paralyzed, water dribbling out of her palms. When it happened again a moment later, she raised her head.

Four of the giant bison-like creatures congregated on the opposite shore a good distance away. One slipped into the water with all the grace of a brand new cruise ship sliding out of dry dock, becoming a shaggy island with eyes and horns. None of the creatures appeared to have noticed her, or if they had, showed no reaction. She drank a few more handfuls before retreating into the woods.

"How did those animals survive?" asked Kiera.

"They didn't." Pet floated closer to her head. "The machines in the citadel made them, like they made this whole forest. I don't think any animals like that existed before Cloudfall. These appear to be the result of a genetic experiment trying to make something resilient enough to survive. Every now and then, they produce animals of different types to test survivability. Few manage to last more than a couple weeks. Those creatures your parents call mammoths are the most hardy, but they also aren't natural."

"Oh." Kiera put her hand on a tree, examining the coarse bark. "There's seeds and stuff floating down the river."

"Yep," chirped Pet.

She started to feel hungry, but thought about drinking water with hands that had been all over a sewer less than an hour earlier—and lost her appetite. *Ugh. I am going to get so sick… Wait… Pet said all the germs died, too.* Kiera stared in horror at the green-tinged clouds overhead, far above the pines. "What kind of awful crap is in the air?"

"Heavy metals, industrial chemicals, burned remnants of petroleum products, various gases. Some of the warfare that occurred in the end of the

2030s involved chemical weapons. There is a large amount of dust from concrete, insulation, other building materials and such. During the toxic period before the citadels were complete, the contaminants in the atmosphere became so concentrated that they dissolved almost all evidence of human construction as well as plant life. Most of the chemical weapons have denatured by now, but there are traces."

"Ugh. Sorry for asking." She marched on, her need to be with her parents growing near to painful. "How much farther?"

"At your current rate of speed, you will arrive home in one hour, twenty two minutes."

Kiera nodded. *Don't run. Need to save up so I can run from robots later.*

Trees dappled with lichen passed all around her for most of the walk. Not hearing birds at all unnerved her and made the woods feel like a video game made by lazy developers. She daydreamed about the citadels and what the world might be like if what she'd read about them had been true. In her mind, she pushed a button and the Earth bloomed to life. Alien clouds shrank back to puffy cotton balls in a blue sky while animals erupted from the pyramid-shaped citadel like a volcano blast of fur, happily chittering off to their homes in a forest that spread over the land like magic.

"It's good to see you smiling," said Pet.

"Somehow I don't think it's going to work like that..." She chuckled.

"Hmm?"

Kiera shrugged. "Just daydreaming about fixing the planet. It's not going to be like a cartoon, right? Boom, life everywhere?"

"Doubtful. The process will take many years. It is more than probable you will not live to see the planet fully restored, but it will improve noticeably within your lifetime."

"Hey, I'm technically an old lady." She puffed up her chest.

Pet laughed.

An hour and change later, Kiera emerged from the forest within sight of home. The ramshackle building grabbed her by the heartstrings and yanked. Pathetic as it was, it had become more a home than anywhere she could ever remember being. Her little bedroom and its sad excuse for a mattress felt like a suit of armor she *needed* to put on.

Abandoning care, she raced across the field behind the house, weaving among Dad's scrap piles to the back door, calling out for her parents. She burst inside, gazing around at an empty building.

"No..." She slouched. Panic gnawed on the back of her mind, bringing trembles. She darted to the front door and stuck her head out to survey the empty front yard. "Where are they?"

Pet, hanging in midair behind her, bounced a few inches with a rapid spin.

"Perhaps they are searching for you? I can travel much faster. Would you like me to go look for them?"

Kiera put a hand on her chest, trying to stop breathing so fast. "Uhh... maybe. Do you think it will be better if I stay here?"

"I am not sure."

She paced around for a little while before sudden need sent her running to the outhouse, overjoyed to have access to her purloined toilet paper instead of the awfulness of what had occurred in the sewer. Once she finished, she walked around the house outside a few times, lonely and heartsick before collecting a few carrots and a potato from the garden. Kiera trudged inside, rinsed them off, and flopped to sit at the table, head down.

Raw vegetables tasted surprisingly good. *Anything's yummy when you're starving.* She sighed past a mouthful of potato. How different a word could be... 'Starving' once meant something far different from the now she found herself in. Her old whine demanding food had become a literal possibility.

Forcing herself to eat, she finished off her meager lunch and leaned back in her chair, heels up on the cushion. She stared between her knees across the house, gazing into nowhere, lost to fear. Her parents might wander for days not realizing she'd come home. Something might happen to them before they got back. What if bandits found them? *Dad's hurt... but he's got a laser.* She clutched her pistol tight.

A small, silver plastic object caught her eye, sitting on the table beside the bowl of pepper. It resembled a USB memory fob, only it had no connector.

She picked it up, turning it over in her fingers. "This is new... Pet?"

The cube drifted over. "It is a wireless memory module."

Kiera set it back on the table in front of her. "It wasn't here before... what's on it?"

"Accessing." Pet landed beside it. Cyan light leaking between the seams of its outer shell dimmed and surged in a continuous cycle. A moment later, the glow became steady. "There is a holo-recording. It appears to be a message for you."

"Can you play it?"

"Yes."

A tiny spot on the cube's front face lit up, projecting a holographic man on the table, about the size of a Ken doll, transparent like a ghost. He appeared to be in his middle forties, black hair with touches of grey above his ears, and didn't look like he got much sunlight. His blue long-sleeved shirt had funny gold marks at the ends of the sleeves and a golden flat-topped pyramid pin on his breast. Loose pants, the same shade of blue as his shirt, bloomed where they met military-style boots. The eight-inch tall man stared down at something in front of him, half a victorious grin on his face.

Merely looking at him filled Kiera with the urge to hit him square in the nose. "I don't know who that is, but he looks like a douche."

"I trust you will have found your way back to this little hovel eventually," said the man.

His voice grated on her nerves, dripping with so much superiority she wanted to choke him. Like those commercials for expensive cars where the announcer guy radiated smugness.

"I am Anton Sokolov, administrator of the Citadel. Despite your primitive inclinations, you should realize that I am in charge of everything that goes on, inside *and* outside of the Citadel. The tribals"—he muted a chuckle—"sorry, your *parents* are they? Have been detained. They are guests of mine in secure custody. I will release them upon your surrender. Robots are terribly resource expensive you know. Await—oh what is it you primitives call the bus... the 'passage' or some such nonsense. It will bring you to the gates. The sentries have been alerted to allow you inside. I trust you do not want your"—he chuckled again—"*parents* to spend the rest of their life in prison, do you? See you soon." He waved. "Ta."

He wagged one eyebrow at her before the image blinked out.

Kiera slammed her fists on the table, making the pepper bowl jump. "I hate him!" She flew from the chair and stormed in circles around the house. Several times, she drew her foot back to kick something in a rage, but thought better of driving bare toes into metal table legs or wooden boxes. Anger fizzled out in moments, and she flopped seated on the edge of her parents' bed. "I'll go. I can't let them sit in jail."

"I believe he is lying," said Pet.

She perked up. "You don't think he's got them?"

"Not lying on that point. I believe he does have them... but I think he is trying to deceive you about his promise to release them. They are only safe as long as he does not have you."

Kiera jumped up, arms out to the sides as she shouted, "Why does he want me?! I'm just a kid!"

"I do not know." Pet drooped in the air.

Again, she paced. "What's wrong with him? What did I do that's so bad? I... can't stay here. I have to do *something*."

Pet followed her around. "I'm not sure what—"

"Kiera!" shouted Osc. He burst in the front door and ran over to hug her.

Peter, Mei, and Sparrow hurried in after. Mei also flung herself into an embrace. Peter smiled, while Sparrow gave her a silly grin.

"They took my parents," said Kiera.

"Sky Spirits..." Peter folded his arms. "That's not good."

Mei clasped her hands in front of herself, her poncho draped over a body that made Kiera feel thick. "My parents will hide you. You can stay with us."

"Whole everyone hide you." Sparrow bounced on his toes. "No one tells metal men. You in 'a Exxo tribe."

"We got firelight now." Osc tugged his tiny cloth-wrap shorts up. "We stop metal men if they try to take you 'gain."

Kiera looked down, her hair gathering around her hips. "They won't. He's not going to send more robots. They cost too much. I've got to go to the Citadel to help my parents."

"They'll never let you in." Peter walked up and put a hand on her shoulder. "We need work permits to get inside the gates, and they don't let tribal children in, ever."

Mei frowned. "I guess they think we're too wild and we'll break stuff."

"More like they think we're dirty." Osc grinned.

Sparrow looked down at his mud-caked self. "We *is* dirty."

"Come on." Mei grabbed her hand and pulled. "You can share my room."

Kiera stared at her dress, missing her parents more for the sight of it. The Citadel wouldn't let a primitive girl in, but they'd be expecting her to show up. What would they do? Shoot her on sight? Stun her? *If I'm going to get caught anyway, I should at least try to be sneaky first.* She blinked. *The fabricator! It can make modern clothes. They won't be looking for that.* "Thank you, Mei... if the worst happens, I'd be happy to stay with you, but I have to try something."

"What?" asked Peter.

"I have an idea." She closed her eyes and made a wish. "I gotta go. Maybe I'll be back."

# 28

# THE FABRICATOR

Kiera climbed to her little bedroom, Mei creeping up behind. Peter, Osc, and Sparrow gathered at the bottom of the ladder. She pulled her beloved dress off, folded it, and set it on the shelf before grabbing the dog-hide poncho from the mattress and putting it on. The heavier material would be better for a long walk, especially if she wound up in a chilly sewer again. It also offered her legs more freedom of movement. Plus, the dress had become a physical symbol of her new family's love. She adored it more than her old Supernova 2 and couldn't risk damaging it or having it taken from her if bandits grabbed her. Surely, they'd steal her clothes and sell them separately for even more trade value.

She fumed quietly to herself at how those men had treated her. For once in her life, she didn't feel at all bad that people died. Those three, the world could do without. And she had no idea what would happen if the Citadel forces caught her. They might take the dress too, and give her 'better' clothes. Kiera picked at one of the resistors lining the neck, thinking of her parents.

*I'm gonna get you guys out.*

"You're leaving?" asked Mei, standing by the ladder.

Kiera turned to face her friend. "I have to. If I stay here and do nothing, Mom and Dad sit in jail forever. He might even hurt them if I take too long."

Her friend shivered. "Such scary."

"Yes." Kiera squeezed her hands into fists. "But I don't have a choice."

Mei backed down the ladder, allowing Kiera to descend into the house.

Peter walked up to her. "I'll go with you."

"No way." Kiera shook her head. "Your father would kill me, even if the robots don't. I can't let any of you get hurt for this. Please stay safe."

The four exchanged uneasy looks.

"How far is it to the fabricator?" asked Kiera.

Pet glided closer. "It will take you two days to walk there from here."

"Okay."

Kiera pulled a small canvas satchel from a shelf. She filled plastic water bottles and packed them along with eight protein bars and some potatoes for variety. Her friends stood in a group watching her prepare. She shouldered the satchel, stuffed the laser pistol in it, and faced the other kids. They stared in awkward silence. She hugged them one after the next, begging them not to follow her and stay safe in Exxo. She also asked them to make sure no one messed with her home until she returned.

Peter grasped her by both shoulders and stared into her eyes. "Promise me you will come back."

"Me too." said Mei. "I hated being the only girl here."

"There's other girls." Osc poked her.

Mei whirled on him. "Yeah but they're all babies or two-year-olds."

"I promise." Kiera gripped the satchel strap. "I've got Pet, too. So I'm not scared." She fidgeted. "Much."

Kiera headed out the back door, the others following. She nabbed a roll of TP from the outhouse and added it to the satchel. *Almost as important as water.* After a final series of farewell hugs, she set off following Pet. Her friends gathered at the edge of the scrapyard, waving.

Hours passed in silence, a trail of footprints stretching off behind her in the powdery silt. A fragment of a vehicle stuck up out of the ground on the left, the long barrel of a tank's cannon bent like a chewed up drinking straw. The stiff breeze blowing across her path kept her cool, aided by sometimes lifting her arms so the air could get under her poncho. She took a water bottle out and sipped it on the move, drinking about a third before capping it and putting it back.

*Gotta make it last.*

"The administrator has to be after me because of my bio parents. They worked for Citadel Corporation."

Pet rotated around to face her, though it kept gliding at the same speed. "Corporations have not existed for a long time."

"I know. Maybe I can find something inside that will explain why he's got a bug up his butt over me."

"I don't understand."

Kiera explained the meaning of having a bug up one's butt while climbing across a field of concrete rubble and downed utility poles at the edge of another ruin. A few still-standing skeletons of buildings remained in the distance. By late afternoon, thunder rolled overhead, booming out over the desert. She plodded onward, leaving the small ruin behind. The sky darkened, and a short while later, opened up with a downpour.

She pulled the hood up, the first time she could remember ever doing so, and gathered her hair around to hang in front of her before double-checking the strap holding the satchel closed. She did *not* want her TP getting ruined. Rain pelted her, turning the ground to a gooey mess in minutes. Her feet occasionally slipped out from under her as she trudged amid the deluge, but she picked herself up each time and kept going.

"Kiera. There is shelter ahead," said Pet after a long while.

"'Kay."

The glowing cube led her through the darkness of a heavy storm. She started to sink to her shins with each step in some places, and had wiped out often enough throughout the day to be covered head to toe in pale grey mud, as if she'd gone swimming in it on purpose. Pet zipped off toward where a giant shadow loomed out of the driving rain. She waved her arms for balance, struggling to walk over ground that kept trying to grab her feet and not let go.

Eventually, she reached a scrap of parking lot that offered solid footing for a short distance in front of an old store. So much of the wall had crumbled that doors and windows lost meaning. She ducked in out of the rain and stood in place dripping for a little while. Eventually, she set the satchel down, pulled the poncho off, and took a rain shower to clean herself of mud.

Once clean, she padded back under the shelter of the roof and used the poncho as a pad to avoid sitting on hard concrete when she flopped on the ground. She ate a meal of a protein bar and the rest of the water in the first bottle. Pet hovered close while reciting the book they'd started. Kiera choked up, thinking of her father being so enthralled with the story.

"Please wait for Dad. You can read a different one if you want." Kiera leaned forward, gazing out at the rain with a sigh. "Ugh. I guess I'm sleeping here tonight. What time is it?"

"It will be dark in about an hour and forty minutes. It does not seem like the rain will stop by then, so it would be a good idea to shelter here."

The wet heat in the air made the choice between using the poncho as a blanket or a mattress simple. She stretched out on top of it, fingers laced together behind her head, and listened to Pet narrate a science fiction type story about a sixteen-year-old girl named Jen stuck alone on a space station after some mysterious event killed everyone.

"Pet?"

It paused the story. "Yes?"

She rolled her head to the side to look up at the flying cube. "I don't want to sound ungrateful, but maybe a story about some girl who lost her parents and everyone she knows and is alone in the middle of nowhere might not be the best thing right now, 'kay?" Her lip quivered.

"Kiera…" Pet sank low, nuzzling her cheek. "I'm sorry. I didn't even think of that."

"I know." She smiled. "That's why I'm not mad. Just… frightened and sad."

"You're not in the same situation as Jen."

Kiera laughed. "Of course not. This isn't a space station. I don't have to worry about running out of air." She rolled on her side, head propped up on her hand, and frowned at the distant clouds. "Well, maybe I do."

"Unlike Jen, *you* are not alone." Pet nudged her arm. "I will never let you be alone again. No matter what happens, I will stay with you."

She curled up, holding Pet close to her heart. "Thank you. You're an awesome friend."

The cube wobbled with happiness.

"Umm. Are your batteries gonna die?"

"Eventually, but you can replace my power cell at the nearest citadel when it runs out in sixty years."

Kiera laughed herself to tears. *I'm so messed up. My best friends are a computer program and a flying cube.* She stroked her fingers over the plastic box. *How lonely am I that they both feel like real people?* "Do you know anything about my life before… the tank?"

"The files I found showed you received decent but not exceptional grades. You got in trouble a little in fifth-grade. A counselor thought you were angry with your parents for leaving you alone so much."

"Yeah." Kiera sighed. Hearing it brought memories of Mr. Bryant rising out of the murky depths. She couldn't quite put a face on the blurry person-shape in her head. "I kinda remember that."

"They loved you, but they were trying to save the whole planet. I'm sure they did not enjoy being away from you."

She choked up, thinking back to her mother's office, the last message she'd ever send. "I know. I saw the email."

Pet made a soothing sort of trill noise and rubbed against her cheek. "You still have parents, and they need you to be strong."

Kiera curled tighter around Pet and caught herself *loving* it like one might a cat or dog—no *more* than that: like a friend. She debated the idea of an artificial intelligence counting as a real person until the exhaustion of walking for most of a day dragged her into sleep.

HER EYES OPENED TO A RAINLESS MORNING, UP EARLY SINCE SHE'D SETTLED down much sooner than usual. After wandering outside to find a spot to relieve herself, she returned, shook dried mud off her poncho, and put it on. One protein bar and half a bottle of water later, she resumed walking.

The desert had become a vast field of muck. At least without the driving downpour, mud only covered her up to the shins, nothing splashed. As the day wore on, fields of syrupy goop sunbaked to a spongy texture like walking over a huge pan of brownies that had been out of the oven for only minutes. Pet drifted by her side, matching her pace. She turned her head about, staring at the vast nothingness in all directions. The clear day let the Citadel appear as a distant shiny darkness off to the right, but except for the occasional glint of metal in that direction, the horizon all around remained featureless.

She looked down at her feet, daydreaming about her closet back in the suburban lie, and all the shoes she had. Flip-flops, jelly shoes, dress shoes, at least four pairs of sneakers, an entire cardboard box stuffed full of floppy ballet flats, and a few pairs of boots. Of course, none of it had been real. Her attempt to grab at reality conjured the image of canvas sneakers, heavy rubberized boots, or sitting around the house barefoot.

*Oh. I guess we didn't go out much. Too dangerous back then. Breathing masks and raincoats and stuff.*

Pet read a different, happier story. Something light about a bunch of teenage vampires getting in love triangles. More like quadrangles... or other bigger shapes that didn't have names. She fantasized about being the Warrior Princess of the Wasteland, which got her wanting a spear. The laser was a far more effective weapon, but it didn't match her outfit. Dog leather flapped at her knees, lofted on the occasional gust of wind.

She snarled at the stupidity of society poisoning itself. It seemed ridiculous that anyone had ever *wanted* to kick the Earth in the balls and knock humanity back to primitive society. More likely, they didn't care how much damage happened as long as they got rich. Bio-Mom had spent hours ranting at the walls about 'stupid politicians.'

*Yeah, all that complaining sure helped.* She sighed.

Kiera stopped and squatted, poncho draping on the ground over her feet. A sudden, crippling sadness came on. She couldn't believe she'd been stranded in the desert with a scrap of dead dog for clothing and no one she'd ever known alive. She must have had real friends at school at some point, but couldn't remember any of them. Whenever she tried to think of school friends, she only saw false children from the VR world. Where once had been cities, roads, trees, animals... everything had become dust. How horrible had the air been to dissolve skyscrapers?

"I'm sorry for your loss," said Pet, nudging her shoulder. "I would cry with you if I could."

"I..." She wiped her cheeks. "I'm scared."

"It's all right to be frightened. You're trying to do something way too big for an eleven-year-old. But… you don't have a better choice. If you get caught, you're no worse off than if you give yourself up. You're a brave girl, Kiera. A lot tougher than you give yourself credit for. You got this."

Kiera grinned. "I'm going to take on the whole Citadel and all those robots with one laser pistol and this?" She indicated the poncho. "I don't have armor."

"Not every map is designed for a head-on charge. You're too fond of the direct approach."

She blinked. "How do you know that?"

Pet wobbled with glee. "Network access."

"Out here?" She held her arm out to the side, gesturing at the nothing. Wind took the opportunity to slip under the poncho and steal some of her sweat away. "Oh, that's nice." She stood and held her arms up to cool off in the breeze. "It's *sooooo* hot."

"No. Not here. Where you found me. C'mon. Cheer up. We are almost there."

"Okay." She let her arms flop back at her sides.

Pet glided off again. She followed at a hopeful pace, spitting out hair every so often when the wind threw it in her face. Hours later, she entered another small bit of ruined city. Three-ish blocks of paved street sparkled and gleamed, coated by a dusting of ice crystals.

"Don't go that way," said Pet. "That's all glass."

Kiera curled her toes and cringed. "Eep."

"Follow." Pet circled to the left, leading her around the outside of the ruin. A cluster of steel barrels protruded a few inches out of the ground, hinting that a good bit of city might be buried. "Almost there."

She stepped past scraps of chain link fence into the back yard of a mostly-solid building with few windows. Some of the steel poles resembled half-molten candles. Tall, narrow strips on the sides of the building where glass had once been gave the structure a sinister look. None of the openings were wide enough for a person to squeeze through, making her wonder what sort of place this had been.

Pet stopped by a set of steel double doors. "Can you open these?"

"No idea." She grabbed the handle and pulled it an inch or so open before it stuck. Grunting, she braced one foot on the other door and hauled with both hands until she dragged the door far enough to create a gap she could squeeze through. "Guess I can."

"Be careful," said Pet, within seconds of entering.

Kiera wriggled past the doors and stopped short at the sight of a large room with most of the floor collapsed into the basement. A few heavy beams formed a grid where the softer parts had given out during years of exposure to the elements. "What was this place?"

"A Citadel office. It used to be a government building, but during the final phase, they let the company use it in hopes more resources might prevent… well, Cloudfall." Pet floated out over the room. "You need to go across this if the beams are safe. Otherwise, find a spot to climb down here and back up on the other side."

Kiera crept closer to the edge, making the floor creak. "Can you tell if it's safe?"

"I do not weigh enough."

She eased her right foot forward onto a six-inch-wide beam. It didn't move or make noise, so she leaned all her weight on that leg. For a few seconds, she balanced on one foot before trusting the beam enough to step forward with her right. Below, the basement promised a painful landing on sharp chunks of former floor, furniture, and unrecognizable machinery. The fall itself wouldn't hurt as much as what pointy object she might land on.

Advancing with short in-line steps, Kiera wobbled across the room, following her narrow path. *The fall won't kill me. It's only one story. I'm not going to fall. Please don't let me get a splinter in my foot.* At the far end, she resisted the temptation to jump back to solid floor. Instead, she got down on all fours and crawled over a fringe of steel mesh between her and cracked tiles where a hallway remained solid.

She rolled around to sit and checked her feet for splinters. Finding none, she slumped with relief, elbows on her knees, head in her hands. "This is stupid. I should go let the robots catch me. How am I going to sneak into the Citadel and bust them out? It's so stupid."

"Even if you are caught, the end result would be no different from you surrendering. At least try."

She stretched her legs out and rubbed her thighs, sore from all the walking. "Yeah… I guess."

"It's right in here." Pet floated past the doorway behind her.

Kiera rolled over and stood, dusting off her knees before stumbling forward. "What am I looking for?"

"This." Pet floated up to a metal door that resembled an elevator.

"Ooo-kay…" She crept over. "It's got no handles."

Pet projected a laser pointer dot on a black square on the wall beside the door. "Try putting your hand there."

*Duh.* "That worked at the place that got me in deep trouble." She reached forward and waved her hand by the dark panel.

The steel doors hissed and snapped open, revealing the elevator she expected it to be.

She leapt back with a yelp.

"What is wrong?" asked Pet, concern in its voice.

"N-nothing. Loud. Didn't expect to like fly open like that." *Guess I go in.*

She crept forward and turned back to face the doors. Pet hovered over her left shoulder. The control panel had two buttons, so she hit the one that didn't glow.

The elevator doors closed as snappishly as they'd opened, and the cab went down.

"Whoa. This place has power! How's that possible?"

"The facility has a small solar array, and superconducting batteries that feed the elevator and the space below. Citadel Corporation used a separate self-contained system from the rest of the building."

"Oh." She lifted and dropped her toes, fidgeting while waiting and amusing herself by leaving silt footprints on the clean steel floor. "Guess it doesn't make sense to build a secret base if it dies when street power goes out."

With a *ping*, the elevator doors parted to reveal a dim hallway with blue-cast steel floors and walls. Though not cold, the corridor made her glad she'd brought the fur poncho. A door went to the left not far from the elevator, opposite another to the right. The hallway continued past that to a third door at the end by a set of metal locker cabinets. A hint of dust lingered in the air, but other than smelling stale, the place appeared clean.

"Wow..." She walked forward, looking around. When she reached the facing doors, she glanced left and right.

The room on the left contained four bunk beds with solid white frames and dark navy sheets, as well as small desks and more lockers. On the right, the doorway led into an area that resembled a cross between a living room and a tiny cafeteria. An enormous eighty-inch flat panel screen took up the far right corner in front of a black leather sectional. Another door led to a room of cubicle workstations.

She leaned in enough to put her foot down on carpet—so she could remember what it felt like.

"The fabricator is down here." Pet drifted to the far door, its glow reflecting in a beautiful blue shimmer off the metal walls and floor.

"Right." Kiera trotted after.

Two shower stalls stood on the left side of a steel bench that divided the innermost room in half. Large storage cabinets covered the wall straight ahead opposite the door. A refrigerator-sized steel box on the right sat beside a chamber with a rounded plastic wall and a metal disc. It made her think teleportation chamber or medical scanner. The machine's left side had two shelves on articulated swing arms like something out of a dentist's office.

"Wow." She set the satchel down on the bench and took the poncho off. "Shower time. Do they work?"

"I am uncertain, but I predict you will find out soon."

Kiera, grinning, stepped into the closer of the two stalls and pulled the sliding glass door shut. Tiny bottles of shampoo and a miniature soap like from a hotel sat in a recessed cubby. Both looked quite old, but not beyond usefulness. She gripped the faucets and turned, squealing with delight when water sprayed all over her. Though it didn't approach hot, it had enough warmth not to make her scream. Unsure how much remained in whatever tanks fed it, she rushed cleaning herself.

Watching dirty water swirl around her feet and into the drain made the past months feel like a dream. The normality of showering in a real stall with actual soap and shampoo hit her hard, and she pined again for friends who had never existed and parents she barely remembered.

*It wasn't real. It stinks, but this is the world.* Kiera took a deep breath and let it out slow before shutting off the water. She stepped out into the much colder-seeming room, dripping.

"Crap. Towels?"

Pet bumped into one of the lockers. "Probably in here."

She wandered over and searched the lockers, finding dry-rotted blue jumpsuits that collapsed at her touch, a few sets of men's underwear that also fell apart, and a plastic pack of white socks that had almost as much dead bug larva in it as it did cloth. "Eww."

"Oh well." She waved her hands over herself. Air-drying on the edge of the artificial river after baths had become the norm and no longer felt weird. Between walking in circles around the bench, and weak air-conditioning, she dried in a few minutes and pulled her poncho back on. "Okay, so… fabricator time."

"You should take that off again and stand in the booth," said Pet.

"Why? It's kinda cold down here." She hugged the poncho.

Pet wobbled, chuckling. "It needs to measure you. Unless you would like some odd-shaped pants, I suggest you allow it to scan an accurate idea of your dimensions."

"Fine." She sighed and disrobed again.

After twisting her long, thick hair up into a fat bun, she stepped into the 'teleportation chamber' and turned to face out. "So… how do I make it work from here?"

"I'll do it," chirped Pet, floating out of view to the right. "Stand still with your arms relaxed at your sides."

The large machine beeped a few times, and a grid of blue laser-lines appeared all over Kiera's body. Glowing boxes shrank and expanded back and forth for a few seconds before disappearing.

"Outfit, juvenile-four, standard," said a robotic voice from the giant cabinet.

Her platform vibrated as the entire device whirred.

"Do I have to stay here?" asked Kiera.

"No, it's done."

She stepped down off the pedestal. One of the shelves swung around front, positioning itself under a slot a second before the machine spat out a pair of high-top black sneakers. A pair of thin white socks followed, then a clingy pair of spandex-y shorts that looked so skimpy they had to be intended as underwear. A tank top came next before two larger bundles of blue fabric burped out onto the plate: a short-sleeved, stretchy shirt and a pair of baggy pants.

"Ooh! Real clothes!"

She pulled on the shorts, which felt incredibly weird and clingy in all the wrong places after going for so long without any undergarments. She fidgeted, unsure if she liked the sensation, but left them on. After putting on the tank top, she stuffed her feet in the socks, which stopped right below her ankles. The shirt fit perfectly, though snug and clingy like the shorts. An elastic waist held the loose pants up without a belt. Last, she stepped into the Velcro-secured sneakers, stood, and stared down at herself.

"This is so weird. I feel like I'm in some kinda space movie." She twisted side-to-side, waving her arms and testing how it felt to wear real clothing again. "Going to the bathroom is going to be a pain... at least, without actual toilets." Still though: *real clothes*. She *squeed* and hugged herself. "Do I look like an Exalted?"

"You do," said Pet.

"It feels like forever since I've had legit clothes on." She fidgeted. "Does it mean I've gone total primitive if it's kinda uncomfortable?"

Pet giggled. "Not to make light of a bad situation, but you have been without clothes from 2033 until 2094. In VR, you had the appearance of clothing, but sensory input from your body would have conflicted. I bet there had been times where you felt strange."

Kiera bit her lip. More than once, she'd gotten odd sensations, like cold gooey slime that didn't match her perceived reality or a sense that she hadn't been wearing anything. "Yeah. Ugh. I'm going to melt if I go outside in this." She stared at the pitiful poncho. "How sad is that? I finally get real clothes and I kinda prefer the rag."

"Well... It would not be wise for you to wear those outside. You would attract unwanted notice. If you encounter other tribes, they would believe you are Exalted and probably be hostile or attempt to abduct you for trade back to the Citadel."

She shivered with a brief flashback of being tied up on a pull cart. "Uhh... Really?"

"If they did not attempt to harm you out of anger at how Exalted treat them, they would take you to the Citadel hoping for a reward, which would defeat the purpose of your attempting to sneak in. If you tried to run away, they would assume you suffered mental issues and forcibly bring you back."

"I have a laser pistol now. No one is kidnapping me again." She folded her arms.

Pet floated up to her nose. "But it is not smart to invite problems when you can sneak past them, O princess of guns blazing."

Kiera smirked, but wound up giggling. "Okay... okay. What else can this thing make?"

"A fabricator can produce a wide variety of items, except for complex machines. Unfortunately, this unit is almost empty of base matter. Whoever was in this facility prior to our finding it used up most of it... likely on food."

"Crap."

She removed her new outfit, packing each item carefully in the satchel, and put on the poncho again. The soft hide against her skin felt like a hug from Dad. Wearing it felt *normal*, more comfortable than the 'real' clothes. Kiera plopped on the bench, sulking with her chin in both hands.

"Ugh. I *have* gone primitive."

# 29

# NORZ

Kiera took advantage of a real, working toilet before crashing in one of the bunk beds for the night. Pet perched on the mattress beside her head, reading her to sleep after agreeing to wake her at 8:00 a.m. The soft murmur of the adventures of a pack of three teenage witches faded to silence. She stared up at the ceiling, unable to tell how long she'd been there. The windowless room would've looked the same at noon as it did at midnight. Only the primitive black fur poncho broke the illusion that she'd somehow found a spaceship. Closing her eyes again didn't help, and after a few minutes, she rolled her head to the left, staring at her companion.

"It is 7:42 a.m.," said Pet.

She pushed the blankets off and sat up. "Mom and Dad aren't getting out of jail any sooner if I stay here."

"I can't sleep either."

Kiera rubbed her eyes and raked her fingers through her hair. "You can't sleep at all." She stuck her tongue out, making Pet giggle. "So... how can I get into the Citadel without being caught?"

Pet bobbed into the air, hovering near her face at eye level. "You could walk another few days. If you keep the wind at your left, you will be heading toward the Citadel. Or, you could enter one of the villages and stow away on the Passage. There are cargo pods along the outside, but I do not know if they are searched upon arrival, or even used. You could sneak into one of those, change on the ride, and sneak out once the Passage arrives in the Citadel. In the clothing you have made, you would not stand out."

She let her legs dangle over the side of the bed. "Both choices kinda stink."

The idea of bandits made walking alone for days scary, but sneaking on the bus that would go right to the gate might get her caught as easily as if she'd walked up to turn herself in. Anton told her to take the bus, so they'd be looking for her on one. "If I walk there, how do I get in?"

"There are numerous vents, drains, pipes... many openings on the outside."

Kiera tilted her head. "Why don't people sneak in all the time?"

The cube giggled. "Because they don't have a Pet to open the hatches." Its light flickered. "I have located a likely entry. Waypoint set."

"You're awesome." Kiera hugged it before jumping down. "Waypoint?"

"I thought you'd recognize the term from your games." Pet wobbled side to side, 'smiling.'

"I do. It's funny to hear it though."

She headed to the bathroom before using the fabricator to print out more ration bars. It produced ten before displaying a 'matter store empty' error. Grumbling, she ate one and packed away the rest. This trip, she'd been smarter, keeping her empty bottles, which she refilled at a sink. A locker offered up two more water bottles, fancier ones like what people often clipped to bicycles—with Citadel Corporation logos on them. Those too, she filled and packed before shouldering her satchel.

One elevator ride later, she approached the crappy floor and sighed. Leaving this little island of modern life sucked in general, but having to cross this ruin sucked even more. Kiera sat and fished the sneakers out of the satchel.

"Careful not to get them too dirty. A kid with muddy shoes will attract notice inside the Citadel," said Pet.

"Right... I don't want splinters. Just gonna wear them to go over this crap. I got lucky last time."

"That is wise." Pet bobbed.

Kiera balance-beam walked across the collapsed floor, leapt to the solid area at the other side, and scurried out. The blast of furnace air made her glad she'd kept the poncho on instead of the full outfit—she'd have saturated it with sweat in seconds. "Holy cow. It's hot."

"It's 107 degrees. You have seen warmer days, but you have recently been in a climate-controlled space. That makes it feel warmer."

"Yeah." She repacked the sneakers in the satchel after swatting dust off them. "I think I'm going crazy."

Pet glided along beside her. "What makes you say that?"

"Being primitive doesn't bother me anymore. It's the world for real, right?" She glared at the dirt. "I don't care about anything but wanting my parents back. I don't even really miss video games."

"Would you play them if you had them?" asked Pet.

Kiera smiled. "Yeah, but I'm not like gonna get all messed up over not having them. Do they still exist inside the Citadel?"

"Yes. Life inside there is not so different from before Cloudfall, only with cooler gadgets."

"You said cooler!" Kiera gasped.

Pet hummed to itself, gliding on ahead. "I did."

*She said pets adapt to different personalities.* Kiera grinned. *She likes me!*

Punishing heat battled the constant wind on and off. Every so often, a gust made her stumble to the right or whipped her poncho up over her head, but for the most part, the heat became tolerable again after a few hours. She nursed her water supply sip by sip while walking, listening to Pet narrate the book for an entire day.

About a half hour before sundown, she took shelter in a deep gulley between dunes that kept her out of sight, and ate the second ration bar of the day. Using the soft silt for a bed, her poncho for a blanket, and the satchel for a pillow, she slept under the open sky. Pet sat on her chest under the poncho, staying close to comfort her.

She awoke with the first signs of daylight, ate, drank, and found a spot to go to the bathroom. Within ten minutes of opening her eyes, she resumed walking. Pet continued reading to her along the way, reassuring her now and then that no robots had come close enough to detect.

Late that afternoon, a village came into view off to the left. Shiny silver trailers, old semi-trucks, huge tents, and numerous more modern-looking boxy dwellings made out of plastic formed a ring around a familiar device. Their water collector looked bigger than the one from Exxo, but also more rickety. It fed a steel trough rather than a round fountain basin. The rotating parts inside the vanes squeaked like an orchestra of tone-deaf mice trying to sing.

Kiera crouched low behind a dune, peering over it at the villagers. As far as the people themselves went, they looked similar to the residents of her village. Most appeared Hispanic, but a handful of other ethnicities were present, exactly like Exxo. However, their clothing had a noticeable difference in style despite the materials being similar. Anyone looking at her would know her as an outsider right away. No one here had anything made of dog leather, and this place had a bizarre fascination with long strands of beads or baubles.

*Great. As if red hair wouldn't stand out enough.*

"You shouldn't go in. I doubt they would hesitate to hold you prisoner so they could give you to the robots," said Pet.

Kiera ducked down, kneeling, and glanced at her friend. "Do you think they know? Did the robots go to every settlement or just mine?"

"This is Norz, the closest village to the Citadel. The prefabricated huts come from there, purchased with credits. Most of the people here have work permits. It is certain that they are aware the administrator is looking for a girl with red hair."

She grumbled. "I could really use water."

"We could wait for dark and sneak in?"

Kiera shook her head. "That'll waste too much time. I'll try sneaking now. I have firelight." She winked. Of course, she hoped she didn't have to shoot anyone. Hopefully, threatening people with it would work.

One advantage of a poncho: no sleeves. She took the laser pistol out of the satchel and held it between her knees long enough to pack her hair into the hood and down her back to keep it hidden. If the wind blew the garment up, her cover would be ruined, but she didn't plan on being in town too long. She stood, grasped the pistol, and held it tight to her chest under the poncho while fast-walking over the silt to the edge of the village. Pet ducked into the satchel to hide.

With any luck, the Norz would disregard her like the people of Exxo had. It soon became apparent a small figure in a black fur poncho shocked these villagers more than walking naked into Exxo had affected the people there. Everyone stared, though no one approached or called out. *Maybe they're curious why a kid's traveling alone?*

She hurried over to the water collector, feeling conspicuous. When she reached the trough, she tucked the pistol between her legs again to hold it, keeping it concealed under the poncho. She struggled to take the cap off a plastic bottle with shaking hands, and fumbled it into the water. Fortunately, the trough only went as deep as her elbow, so she reached down to grab the cap while filling her bottle. The weight of people staring at her continued. She glanced out of the corner of her eye at perhaps twenty adults watching her. Some had stopped walking in the middle of the paths between buildings, others peered from the windows of huts. Few of the local children paid her any mind, and kept darting about and playing as though she didn't exist.

The bizarre notion that she'd have attracted *less* attention with nothing on than wearing a dog-fur poncho with the hood up on a blazing hot day, got her giggling from nerves. Of course, without the poncho, her hair would give her away. Even with it, her pale skin might be too conspicuous.

*I feel like some kind of fugitive.*

She hurried to fill three bottles and took out a fourth. Before she could stick it in the water, a shadow fell on her from behind. Kiera whirled, grabbing the laser pistol. She started to pull it out from under her poncho, but froze in shock when she realized who smiled down at her.

Legacy reached out and patted her shoulder. A roundish scar marked his arm where he'd been shot, but other than the addition of his carrying a metal staff, he looked the same.

"Y-you're alive…" She tucked the gun out of sight again and hugged him.

The old man patted her on the back. "Indeed."

"Uhh. Sorry for leaving you there. I would've helped, but I was kinda tied up." She stared down and twisted her toes into the dirt. "Literally."

"It is I who should be sorry for not suggesting we hurry away from those fools." He rubbed his jaw. "They will regret their choices if I find them again."

"You won't." Kiera spun back to the collector and refilled her last bottle. "Find them again, I mean. I think I need to get out of here fast."

"Indeed. Your cloak is wild dog hide. Such garments are not of the Norz. Seeing a child alone from another tribe has them on edge."

"I'm in trouble," she muttered, packing the last bottle.

He put a hand on her shoulder. "I know this. It is why I have come here. Allow me to assist you."

Kiera held the pistol against her chest, following Legacy out of the village into the dust. Once they'd gone far enough that she could no longer see the trailers and huts, she pulled the laser out from under the poncho and stashed it in the satchel. Pet took the opportunity of an open flap to bob into the air.

"Oh, my… what is that?" Legacy stared in awe.

"Her name is Pet." Kiera pulled down her hood and fluffed her hair out from under the poncho.

"Hello," said Pet. "I am a one-petabyte personal companion unit. Kiera is my friend."

Legacy transferred his staff to his left hand and reached out to cup the floating cube, but hesitated before touching it. "A true marvel. Perhaps *his* avatar. Where did you find this?"

While they walked, Kiera told the story of her journey to the supposedly cursed ruin, the robots, and everything that had happened. She explained how the three bandits kept her tied up for an entire day, and of her escape in the middle of the night.

"Waste of air." Legacy grumbled. "Men like that steal life from others by simply breathing."

Kiera closed her eyes to weather a sudden spike of pain at missing her family. "You don't have to worry about them… they're all dead."

"Oh?" He blinked. "You didn't.…"

She shook her head. "No… my dad."

"But your father—"

"New parents."

The story of what happened at Norven's filled the next twenty minutes. Legacy listened with eager intent, a scary glint of glee in his eyes when she described her father stabbing King to death, and again at her description of Norven returning with blood spatter on his face.

Quiet hung over them for a while after. Kiera stared down at the silt, watching her feet sink over and over into the soft ground.

"I am sorry you had to witness that," said Legacy. "But perhaps because you have seen it, you can be free of your fear that they will find you again."

She shrugged. "I guess. I haven't had nightmares about it, so maybe I'm okay. I'm still scared of bandits grabbing me."

Legacy patted her back. "As long as you stay away from the northeast, where the New Dominion rule, it is unlikely that will happen again. Most bandits would steal your possessions, but not steal *you*." He chuckled. "I doubt they would even bind you, as the rope would be too valuable to leave behind."

Kiera frowned. "The idiots said that too, that the rope was worth a lot. I ripped it up."

"Heh. Good for you." He winked. "If I were you, I would've told them how close they came while you were hiding in that cabinet."

She laughed. "What happened to you? I thought you'd died? I'm really glad you're okay."

He gestured at a huge slab of concrete sticking up out of the ground up ahead, most likely part of a collapsed parking garage buried with only the top floor visible. Tilted at an angle, it formed a roof over a small area of ground. "We can shelter in there for the night. It will be dark soon."

"Okay."

They diverted course toward the ruin. Once inside, he set up a small camp with a tiny e-stove and took plastic-wrapped hamburgers out of his backpack. Kiera stared in awe, even though they looked withered and tiny. Legacy tore open the corner of each packet and poured in a little water. Soon, the burgers took on a more normal appearance and he threw one into a tiny frying pan. He added water to other packets, resurrecting freeze-dried buns from the dead. She scurried outside to relieve herself, grateful to Pet for hovering close to keep an electronic eye out for threats.

By the time she returned to the shelter, Legacy had the second burger in the pot, and offered her the first. She sat next to him and accepted it.

"Thanks."

"You're welcome." He smiled. "Sorry if I don't have any red flavor gel."

"Do you mean ketchup?" She chuckled. "Where did you even find burgers? Is this thing as old as I am?" She sniffed it. *Smells like beef.*

Legacy chuckled. "I have my secrets. My cave is quite well stocked."

"You have a fabricator?" She chomped a big bite off the burger.

"Hah. You are full of surprises, little one. Yes... you are correct. I came a little better prepared this time."

She mumbled with a full mouth.

"To answer your earlier question, I regained awareness some time after you had been carted off. The ground told me that you had tried to flee, but been captured. I followed the cart tracks to a large circular mound of rubble, but no one remained there. Alas, I was too injured to keep searching, so I stumbled back to my cave for medicine and rest. It seemed best to hope *he* guided you, so I remained there to await another message... which I received days ago. For months, *he* said nothing."

"Message?" She forced herself to take smaller bites so the burger lasted longer.

"*He* told me to make haste to the village of Exxo... but when I arrived, you were nowhere to be seen. The locals spoke of the metal men seeking you."

Kiera nodded.

"I tracked you into the woods, but lost your direction. Again, I returned home. Within minutes of me reaching my cave, *he* told me to travel to the Norz village, certain you would be there."

"Wow." Kiera looked up at the sky. "That's kinda eerie. Wait... how does *he* talk to you?"

"In my cave... on the enchanted tablet. His words become light."

*A computer.* "You talk back to him by pushing letters, right?"

"Indeed. You are wise beyond your years, little one." Smiling, Legacy shut off the e-stove and flipped his burger onto its bun. "*He* told me that you had accessed the ancient systems. When you touched the old knowing, the false king became aware of you, and of your threat." He raised his hands skyward, one clutching the burger. "You who are the Child of Earth shall redeem it"

*He's still nuts, but he's nice.* She leaned against him, grateful for the sense of protection he offered. *His 'cave' has to be another Citadel Company hideout. Probably has a computer in it.* "I need to get my parents back, but I have no idea how to 'redeem the Earth.' I don't have magic powers."

The old man chuckled while chewing. "*He* is sure you are the one."

"How?" Kiera yawned and stretched her legs out. *Ugh. I've walked more in a week than eleven years.* "Who is this 'he' you keep talking about?"

Legacy bowed his head. "Thread Alpha. Did I not already tell you this? His name is not to be spoken to others. His very existence is a necessary secret. He has told me that you may encounter some, other than I, who will assist you on your path. Even though they are friends, do not speak of him to them."

*Sure. No problem. I don't need anyone thinking I'm crazy.* She put on an innocent smile. "Right. Understood. No talkie about sky voice."

"It was Thread Alpha who told me where you would be born."

"I wasn't *born*. The tank flushed me down the drain and I crawled from a vent."

Legacy showed no reaction to her comment, eyes still half closed with the distant-seeing gaze of a shaman surrounded by spirit smoke. "I am to guide you to the Citadel. I have been shown the way."

"Okay. Hope there's no more bandits...."

"Ahh." Legacy smiled. He pulled open his backpack and held up a handgun. Shiny, metal, and factory-new. "I will not make the same mistake as last time."

Kiera glanced at it. "That's a gun."

"Yes."

"Not a laser...."

"Those fabricators cannot produce complex machines. A simple mechanical firearm, on the other hand, is possible," said Pet.

"Oh." She settled back, trying to get comfortable enough to sleep.

Legacy put an arm around her. "Rest child. I shall keep you safe."

# 30

# THE EARTH CHILD

The next morning, they left behind the parking garage shelter, eating ration bars while traveling. Kiera worried that the chicken-soup-egg flavor mixture, initially so overpowering, had become bland. Her stomach growled for beans or fresh vegetables... or maybe the plea had come from her heart instead, missing her parents more than the actual food. Glum, she trudged along beside Legacy, with Pet leading the way.

Close to noon, they reached a long, downhill slope covered in shifting whorls. Despite her best effort to be careful, she fell into a tumbling logroll about a third the way down when the dune shifted under her foot. Her scream cut off when her face plowed into the powdery ground, filling her mouth. The dense silt absorbed her impact, and slowed her slide to a stop before too long. Legacy skidded down after her and helped her up.

Kiera spat out a mouthful of blech: part sand, part concrete dust, part ashed-over remains of plants, animals, people, and other things. She came close to throwing up, but held back long enough to rinse her mouth and spit a few times. "Note to self. Don't scream when falling." Another swig. She gagged and coughed it up.

"Hills like this can collapse in places without warning."

She squinted at him, lifting her poncho away enough to dust sand from her body. After, she flapped the fur to knock silt off it. "I noticed. At least there's like no sand fleas or stuff."

He shook his head. "No, but the bore worms are worse. They're too small to see, and they dig into your skin to lay eggs. Itches like hell for days and then you break out in little pimples full of baby worms."

Kiera screamed, shivering in disgust. She swatted at herself, phantom tickles everywhere suggesting millions of tiny worms chewed on her already.

"Hah. Got you." Legacy chuckled. "I am teasing. There are no such thing."

Tears of anger gathered in the corners of her eyes as she blushed. "That wasn't funny. You scared me!"

Pet giggled.

Kiera balled her hands into fists and fumed. "Argh! Why do old people always have to tease kids like that?"

"It's what we do." Legacy winked, still chuckling. "Imparting wisdom. When I was a bit younger than you are, I became upset after swallowing a fruit seed. My mother had told us not to eat them. Well, grandpa had me convinced I'd have a tree growing out my back end in a few days. I cried, and cried...."

Her laugh trailed off to an amused grin that lingered for a while after they reached the bottom of the hill and kept going across more wide-open nothingness. The dark form of the Citadel blocked off a scary amount of sky up ahead, but still seemed quite far away. She stared at it while walking, still unable to make any sense of what had happened.

"Do you have any idea why the administrator would want to hurt me?"

Legacy raised both eyebrows. "Of course. You are the Child of Earth. He is clearly afraid of the threat you pose."

If she hadn't been sick with worry over her parents, the idea of her being a threat would've made her laugh. "Me? A threat? What possible threat could I be to someone like him?"

Legacy planted his staff in the ground with each step, a constant *skiff-skiff-skiff* noise at the regularity of a clock. "He is a priest of Torment. He calls down the poison to burden the Earth and bend it to his will. You will cleanse it and destroy him."

"Uhh." She spared a glance up at him. *Ooo-kay. More than a little bit nuts.* "I don't want to destroy anyone." A few steps later, she shrugged. "I wouldn't mind cleaning up the poison, but I don't know how. I've only taken basic chemistry so far. I have no idea how to fix this."

"Oh, child. It is not a problem of science. You are the Child of Earth. You will redeem the world."

*Right.* She suppressed the urge to roll her eyes. *Just wiggle my fingers and blammo. Magic girl powers activate!*

"You do not believe me." Legacy winked.

"Damn. Saw right through me." She gave him a genuine smile.

Legacy patted her on the head. "If there is nothing to my prophecy, why then does the King of Torment seek you?"

Her brain jammed to a halt. "Uhh...."

He grinned.

They walked on for a while more. Upon cresting a large dune, she squinted at the distant massiveness of the Citadel. Strips of blinding sun glare shimmered on a surface of dark metal. Angled walls that dwarfed the pyramids of Egypt stretched skyward to a flat point upon which sat a permanent tornado, threaded up into the cloud dome. The wind had lost some strength this close, enough to make the heat noticeably worse.

"How are we going to get in?"

Legacy paused to take out a water bottle. "*We* are not going in. I cannot. They will not allow me. *He* has told me of a passage, but you will need to stay out of sight. Tribals are not permitted in without a work permit, and they do not issue permits to children. You would be detained as fast as looked at."

"That's stupid." She followed his lead and drank. Warm, plastic-tasting water had never been so wonderful. "If they want to kick tribals out, why would they detain me?"

"Oh, I mean that they would drag you to the gate and throw you out. Probably after they made you tell them how you got inside."

Kiera grinned and patted her satchel. "No problem. I won't look like a tribal."

"Come. There is a place where we can shelter and wait for dark. It would be foolish to approach too close with the sun in the sky." Legacy stashed his water bottle and kept going.

She hurried a few quick gulps, put the bottle back in the satchel, and ran off. Pet hovered at her side, staying low. Inside of an hour later, they crested the top of a dune and faced another steep downhill. A ruined building stood at the bottom, the top two stories of a larger buried office tower. Skinny metal struts, bent and twisted, along the outside suggested it had been one of those all-glass ones, probably silver or black.

Kiera managed to avoid falling on the way down the hill, though she did slide a few times. They crawled in the open side of the rotting building, taking refuge among mold-covered cubicle walls. Frequent rain had washed out most of the furniture and left a jungle of wires and cables hanging from the gaping ceiling. She crept straight ahead to opposite side, where she crouched to hide behind the decaying remains of a long radiator cabinet beneath the windows and stared up at the giant Citadel.

"We are behind it," said Legacy. "The gate is on the other side, so their sentries will not see us."

The ground between her and the eighty-story pyramid sloped downward in a bowl-shaped depression, the terraforming arcology at the center. Winds roared in the air high above, the sound of the storm's fury didn't match the gentle breeze at ground level. Jagged arcs of green lightning flickered across the top of the cloud dome and sometimes shot down the center of the twister to strike the metal pyramid.

Kiera shivered, feeling tiny. She'd never been a fan of thunderstorms, but she had stopped hiding under her bed by around six years old. She lifted her hands from the top of the radiator, finding them coated in silvery glitter. The same metallic powder covered everything inside the dead building. "Pet? What is this?"

The cube glided up to her hands. "Kiera, dust yourself off, please."

"Okay." She brushed her hands clear and backed up. "Is it bad?"

"Traces of lead, manganese, cadmium, and chromium(VI). I'm also detecting measurable levels of tetraethyl lead, and some radium. Likely, this is contamination stripped from the cloud dome, which rained down over the area outside the Citadel. I think these substances are being processed now, but when the machinery first went into passive mode, it only operated at a fraction of efficiency and ejected incompletely processed materials into the air."

Kiera scooted away from the edge of the building and checked her feet. "Okay, so don't touch it."

"Your friend is quite helpful." Legacy sat on the floor, in a space that looked clear of glittery dust.

She fidgeted, staring worriedly at the ground. "Yeah, she is."

He beckoned her over, patting his leg.

Kiera tiptoed to him and curled up in his lap, leaning against his chest, grateful to be away from the poisonous dust. "Thanks."

"I am not worried. I am old. A few more toxins won't matter to me." He took and held her hand, staring into her eyes. "I know you are the future of our kind. You *will* make a difference."

His hopeful gaze made her feel tiny. How wrong it seemed for an old man to be asking a girl her age to go off and save the world. But... he believed she could do it.

"So, what do I do?"

A broad smile bared Legacy's teeth. "Now? We wait for dark."

# SHADOW OF THE CITADEL

Perched on what could've been her grandfather's lap, the absence of her parents grew more painful. In two months, Kiera had come to regard total strangers more dearly than she did her birth parents. By that logic, why not call the first living person she'd met after waking up in this nightmare grandpa?

It didn't matter that he was black and a person couldn't get much whiter than her. It didn't matter that had she not been frozen (and somehow lived) she should be older than him. She figured him for around sixty, which made him twelve years younger than her by birthdate. Numbers meant nothing. She may as well have stepped through a time machine. His hand, braced against her stomach to keep her from sliding off his lap, conveyed more protection than any words could.

Her lip quivered at the sad realization she couldn't remember her real grandparents at all, not even enough to know why she couldn't. Had they died before she met them? Did her bio parents not get along with them, or did two real years spent in virtual reality overwrite those memories, deleting them out of her brain like unneeded files. Kiera lay back against Legacy's chest, comforted by his presence. Eventually, her sorrow at the past gave way to worry for the future.

"I hope I can do this Earth Child thing. I'm not sure if I can, but I'll try." She rested her hand on his, where he cradled her stomach.

"I'm a tiny cube, and I believe in you," said Pet. "O Child of Earth."

Kiera raspberried it.

Pet giggled.

An hour before sundown, they had a quick meal of protein bars. Once daylight weakened, Kiera got the shivers. Legacy rocked her in an effort to be consoling. Minute by minute, the sky grew darker. Soon, the Citadel changed from a looming shadow to a pyramid-shaped tower of color. Blue, red, and green blinking spots covered it as well as long amber lines where glow leaked out from between panels. The shimmering green radiance from the tornado perched upon the flattened top gave off enough light to illuminate the area like the moon she remembered, almost daylight compared to the natural moon struggling to pierce the clouds.

"*So* nervous. Feels like I'm about to do something stupid and reckless. Like shoplift."

"I do not understand," said Legacy.

Kiera wrapped her arms around herself. "I mean, I'm not a shoplifter... but this is as scary as planning to steal."

"I'm not sure what you are trying to say, child. *He* knows you will succeed. Have faith."

*Easy for you to say... you're not the kid trying to sneak into* that *thing.*

Once it got dark, Legacy picked her up and carried her out of the tainted building, setting her on her feet in the silt a few steps away. "From here on, we should not speak lest we be discovered."

"Zero-eight-four?" asked Pet.

"Yes." Legacy nodded.

Kiera glanced back and forth between them.

"I should hide so I am not seen." Pet glided up to Kiera.

She held out her hands and the small cube set down, its glow fading out.

"I would much rather fly by your side, but I do not wish to cause your discovery," said Pet.

"Yeah." Kiera hugged her digital friend before putting it in the satchel. "I can't stop shaking."

Legacy took her hand. "You have the advantage of surprise. The Priest of Torment will not expect you to come to his door."

"Actually, he is..." She fidgeted, explaining the message she'd received on the little memory fob.

"Hmm. Well, he will not expect you to *sneak* in." Legacy winked. "He is hoping you are frightened and emotional, and choose to trust he will not simply kill your parents once he no longer needs them to control you."

Tears slipped down her cheeks. Somehow, she kept her voice from shaking. "That's what Pet said."

"I hear things, child." Legacy walked on toward the giant pyramid of flickering light. "Not all within the Citadel adore their master. You may find friends within. This battle is not one you are required to face alone."

"You're not alone," said Pet from inside the satchel.

Kiera hugged her bag. "Okay."

The ground leading to the Citadel consisted of hard-packed dirt rather than soft silt. The oddity of walking on a surface she didn't sink into barely registered past her fear. She kept her gaze on the distant thrumming Citadel, attention darting from one flickering light to the next. Pet said the ground floor covered about three and a half square miles, a whole city enclosed in a building. Her jaw hung open at the unabashed massiveness of it.

Constant mechanical droning plus the growl of the tornado funnel above made being quiet a futile point. If she spoke at normal volume, Legacy wouldn't have heard her at all, even right next to her. They scurried at a light jog across a field awash in an unnatural emerald glow that flickered brighter every so often when lightning shot down the tornado with ear-piercing cracks. The distant structure grew and grew, until it became more of an endless wall than a standing building.

Kiera gazed up, noting the utter lack of moving air for the first time since finding herself in a tank of clear ooze. "There's no wind."

Legacy kept going, not reacting.

She tugged on his arm and waved at the air. "No wind."

He bowed close, putting his ear to her face.

"There's no wind here. It's strange."

"Ahh." He leaned his mouth to her ear. "The wind comes from this place. We are in the eye of the storm."

She yawned, ready for sleep, but too nervous to consider it. Eventually, the ground leveled off at the bottom of the bowl-shaped depression. Legacy picked up to a light run. With a grunt of protest, she hurried after him. The one-mile run she'd had to do in phys-ed, or at least the virtual reality version of phys-ed, felt like a short trip compared to the dash across the last section of open ground.

Legacy finally came to a stop at the edge of a metal trench running along the base of the Citadel. The enormous structure's walls went from pyramid angle to vertical like a normal building at ground level, forming the inside of a trench perhaps twenty yards across and the same depth. She leaned forward, peering down. A tangled maze of large pipes ran along the bottom, navigating around enormous openings that led down to turbine chambers with huge blades. Despite none of it operating at the moment, gazing at wide-open drains big enough to swallow a grown man scared her to death.

She clamped onto Legacy, shivering.

He held her close and spoke into her ear. "When you call the Great Cleansing, this will become a raging river, spreading life to the world."

Kiera nodded and gave him a 'what now?' stare.

He pointed to the left and pulled her along at a quick walk for a few minutes, stopping again by a ladder on the side of the trench that led straight to the bottom along a recess in the wall. Without a word, he threw his leg around and climbed down. Kiera stared up the side of the Citadel, feeling like a flea expected to kill an elephant. Worst thing that could happen would be getting caught. *No different from being a chicken and surrendering.* At least she had to try. *Okay, check that. The worst thing would be falling into a pump shaft.*

She turned her back to the Citadel and lowered herself onto the ladder. Warm steel rungs at her feet felt slippery enough to make her grab on tight and take the climb slow. Pipes of various sizes passed behind her, some tiny like her arms, others big enough she could've stood up inside them. Everything thrummed and vibrated with machine activity. She tried not to think of falling into one of the turbine pits, which looked like it would chew her up like a frog in a blender. Of course, none of the turbines operated yet, but that didn't mean crashing down on giant, sharp blades would be pleasant.

Her satchel bounced against her rear end as she made her way down, keeping her gaze focused on the metal wall a few inches away from her face. Looking anywhere else would remind her of the dangerous fall below. Minutes later, Legacy put a hand on her side. She gasped, surprised at being so close to the bottom. She twisted around to look at him. He smiled, plucked her off the ladder, and set her on her feet.

Smooth metal plates beneath her radiated warmth. She'd expected cold, and relaxed a touch at the pleasant sensation. Legacy took her hand and walked along the trench, ducking higher pipes and stepping over others closer to the ground. She crawled under a few he had to climb over, but stopped short at a pipe taller than her. Kiera jumped up and grabbed at it, but couldn't get a grip and slid down the featureless metal. Legacy took hold of a catwalk along the top and pulled himself up before reaching down to lift her as well.

She got her feet under her, clutched a thin railing at the side of the walkway, and gazed around, squinting at the mess of tubes. "What are all these pipes for?"

"For when this becomes a river."

Kiera looked up past the crisscross of thinner pipes overhead at the sky. How much of the cloud dome would the machine reclaim for water? She turned to gaze forward when he dropped to the ground on the far side of the mammoth pipe. He reached up for her, so she sat on the edge, extended her legs, and slid into his arms. After setting her standing beside him, he rushed onward. Trying not to think about her lack of plan for once she got inside, she hurried to keep up.

Pet burst out of the satchel and zipped up to Kiera's ear. "Run! There are robots approaching!"

She tugged on Legacy's arm. When he looked at her, she pointed back and yelled, "Robots!"

A legion of green hexagon eyes appeared behind them amid the darkened maze of pipes, far enough back not to cause instant terror, but her knees still lost strength for a second. Legacy, no trace of surprise on his face, calmly grasped her by the shoulders and pulled her behind him.

"Go. Run. You must find the hatch marked zero-eight-four. The word A04DBBF2 will open it." Legacy placed his hand against her cheek, his smile sad. "I have fulfilled my purpose in life, but only if you succeed. Be quick."

"What? No!" She pulled on his arm, feet sliding on the metal. "You run too!"

"I cannot go inside with you. I suspected where this road would take me." He pulled out his gun and a handful of extra magazines. "I will stop the robots from finding you. Do not waste the time I give you now."

Kiera backed up a step, shaking her head while grabbing the laser pistol from the satchel. "We can take them."

"I'm reading forty-three units approaching," said Pet. "Please, Kiera... do what he's asking."

She aimed the laser with both hands at the androids marching closer and closer, unable to find a clear shot past all the pipes. This man asked her to let him die. "I can't... You're like my grandpa. Please don't do this."

Legacy took cover on one knee behind a fat vertical pipe that bent at an elbow six feet off the ground and went left into the wall. "Child of Earth, you cannot allow yourself to be taken. The entire world depends on you. Do not waste this time I give you." He leaned out and fired.

A flash of orange and a loud rapport made her jump. Kiera kept backing up. He fired twice more, one shot triggering a burst of sparks and a loud, buzzing artificial scream. A flaming hole appeared on Legacy's back. Blood oozed down his skin. He gurgled, but kept firing.

"Go!" roared Legacy. "I am already dead."

Kiera, eyes blurred with tears, shot the one she thought wounded him, sending it to the ground in a shower of electrical arcs.

"They don't know who you are," said Pet. "They are reacting to people in this restricted area. You must flee before they recognize you, or your parents are in big trouble!"

"Go!" Legacy swooned to his knees, firing off the remainder of his magazine in a rapid barrage. Each shot slammed painfully into her ears in the metal canyon. He reloaded, suffering another laser hole to the left shoulder that made him roar in pain. "Please, child, run!"

Kiera stared at the army of androids, hating every single one of them for this... as well as taking her parents. She clicked the laser's trigger a few more times before a pipe near her head hissed and glowed orange. With a sharp scream, she ducked and sprinted away, the flash and thunder of Legacy's gunfire continuing behind her.

"Follow!" shouted Pet, rocketing off among the pipes, diving and dipping, slaloming left and right.

Barely able to see past tears, Kiera scrambled to chase the glowing blue light ball. She glanced back for a second. Legacy hadn't gone down yet. His desperate attack stalled the androids within a few yards from where he'd camped.

"Kiera!" Pet zigzagged in midair while shouting.

Sobbing, she ran on, leaping a series of low-lying pipes one after the next where they crossed her path like giant guitar strings. After ducking under another big tube, she spotted Pet hovering by the inner wall, and another ladder.

She leapt onto it, climbing as fast as her weary limbs would move. Gunfire in the distance slowed, but continued. *He's running out of bullets, aiming carefully. Please run away.* The ladder led up to a narrow catwalk a few feet past where the wall angled away to form the side of the pyramid. Smooth silicon-grey metal plates went as far as she could see to both sides, bathed in the electric green light from above. The upper third of the structure shimmered like a great emerald, reflecting the cataclysm swirling in the air.

Pet darted to the left, jamming to an abrupt midair halt a short distance later. She ran to the spot, peering at the floating cube. It hovered near a square outline on the wall bearing the number 084. Kiera examined what she assumed to be a hatch, and reached with shaking hands for a small protective cover nearby. Tugging it open revealed a laptop-sized keyboard.

"Crap... what's the...."

"A04DBBF2," said Pet.

"Again, slower."

She typed each digit as Pet read it off.

The square plate hissed, extended out a few inches, and slid upward, flush against the side of the Citadel. A dark shaft awaited, tall enough for her to crawl on her hands and knees. She crouched by the opening, glancing toward Legacy.

*Pop... Pop, pop.* Orange flashes accompanied each shot.

"Go tell him to run," yelled Kiera.

Pet nuzzled against her cheek. "He won't."

She bowed her head in grief.

*Pop.*

She waited. Silence. No more shots.

Pet made a sad warble. "They're com—"

"I know!" she cry-shouted. After biting back a sob, she scurried in, Pet zooming over her shoulder.

The hatch motored down, closed with a *clank*, and slid inward to seal again. She clutched her arms around her legs, too terrified to breathe lest the robots hear it. Seconds of quiet passed before the clatter of plastic and metal feet tromped by outside. Once they marched too far away to hear anymore, she squeezed herself into a ball and wept in silence.

# NOBODY HOME

Crippled with grief, Kiera cried, face against her knees, hair draped down her legs covering her feet. Her body shook with sorrowful sobs she failed to hold back, though managed to keep quiet. Moments later, sadness shifted to being angry with herself for running and not fighting beside Legacy. *I've got a laser, dammit! We could have won.* Once the storm of emotion lessened, she sniffled, astounded at how faint the Citadel's machine rumble was inside the passage. Even the roar of the storm had become an almost undetectable background presence. Pet pressed itself against her shoulder, nudging like a cat that wanted attention.

She straightened, letting Pet fly into her hands. "Why did he do that? We should have run."

"He knew going into the trench would likely set off an alarm."

Kiera sniffled. "He knew he'd die?"

"He did not desire to die, but he did know it would be likely."

"I hate those robots." She thought about the damaged one she'd found, how friendly it had been, but now, she wanted to smash them all. "This is *so* stupid!"

"I'm sorry. You cared for him. He would not want you to give up and waste what he did for you, for the whole world."

Kiera squirmed out of the poncho and rolled it up into a log. "He was crazy. There's no magic voice talking to him. I'm not a Child of Earth or whatever he thinks… I'm just a kid."

"You need to believe in yourself, Kiera. Great explosions are set off by tiny sparks."

She sighed, staring at the roll of black furry leather in her lap. "I guess… I'm already in here, but I don't want to set off any explosions."

Kiera pulled the clothing she'd made at the fabricator out of her satchel, then stuffed the poncho in the bag. She squirmed around, getting dressed in cramped passage with only Pet's thruster light to see by. Once she'd finished putting the modern outfit on, she pulled the satchel onto her back and crawled along the shaft. Pet glided past her, blue glow illuminating walls of black metal. A little ways in, the plain walls had dozens of small hatches. She opened one, peeking at racks of circuit boards and wire bundles. Curiosity satisfied, she closed it and moved on.

"Where does this go?"

"Into the Citadel," said Pet.

"I know that. I mean what am I looking for?" She stopped to wipe tears, still blaming herself for Legacy's death.

"I am not sure. The most likely scenario is that you make contact with someone who does not like the administrator, and they will be able to help."

"Great," she mumbled.

Minutes later, she reached a chamber at the end of the tunnel that contained a short ladder, also black, but with rubber coating. Six rungs up, she stepped into a small room with two lockers and a featureless metal door without window or knob. More so than the fabricator bunker, this place made her feel like she'd stowed away on a space ship. *Wow… this is more like I'm in 2090-whatever.* She crept up to the door and stared at a dark panel to the right.

"Well, it's worked every other time." She waved her hand at it.

The door slid open.

Kiera crept out from the little locker room into an office full of glowing holographic screens. Two men and a woman in larger versions of her outfit sat in plain blue chairs, their backs turned, absorbed in the contents of their workstations. Pie charts, bar graphs, and status monitors filled every display. Everyone wore garments the same shade of blue, the shirts clingy, the pants baggy.

*Back through the time machine I guess, only I've gone into the future now. Probably shouldn't be seen in here.* Kiera stashed the laser pistol in the satchel and crept to the right toward the room's only door. She hid behind a desk, peeked to make sure the people hadn't looked back, crawled to another desk, and waited. Seconds later, she got the courage up to peer over the top again. None of the workers seemed aware of her presence. She exhaled with relief and tiptoed over to the door. This one had a mechanical handle, which she opened. *I am silent as a ninja.* Kiera slipped into a corridor and eased the door shut behind her. Both directions had multiple doors and neither one gave off any clear sense of which way led 'out.'

At random, she went left, walking quick and quiet, gazing sideways here and there at windows into offices, conference rooms, and another large room with similar workstations as the first one she emerged in. A constant electronic hum filled the air, like hundreds of computers working hard.

Ahead, the corridor cornered to the right. She stopped by the wall and peeked around. A few fake plants and some black chairs broke the emptiness of the otherwise plain metal décor. In front of her lay more offices, an elevator, and a left turn far off, maybe a hundred yards. Kiera gulped. *I'd give anything to be hiding behind a dune again, trying to be brave enough to streak Exxo. I want my parents! Please let me go back. I swear I won't touch the cursed ruin.*

One minute and no miracles later, she sighed in frustration and slipped around the corner. Clinging to the satchel strap, she walked at as normal a pace as she could make her body go. Running would attract attention and creeping, well, creeping would take too long to get out of here. Maybe if she behaved as though she belonged here, she could get wherever she needed to be without being captured.

"Who are you?" asked a man behind her.

Kiera clenched her jaw not to scream. She played it casual, continuing to walk while glancing back over her shoulder.

"Hey kid…."

*Crap. Well it didn't take me long to get busted.* She stopped and turned around. "Hi."

The man, middle twenties with short, brown hair, folded his arms and stared down at her. "Who are you and what are you doing in here? Did someone bring their kid to the office? It's against regulations. This is a restricted area."

"No. I'm sorry. I'm not from this floor. I went down the wrong hallway and I got lost. I'm Ashleigh Martin."

"Hmm. I can't think of any 'Martin' working here." He grabbed her left wrist. "I can't let you walk around in here unescorted."

She shivered. "Please don't tell my parents. I'll get in *so* much trouble. I *just* got off being grounded. *Please!*"

He sighed. "Maybe I can cut you a break and not report this, but only because I don't want to deal with the mountain of paperwork it would cause to report. Did you touch anything in here?"

"Only doorknobs. I've been trying to find the way out. I haven't gone into any rooms at all, just peeked looking for the way out."

The man grumbled, shook his head, and dragged her off down the hall. He didn't squeeze her wrist or yank her arm too hard, so she tolerated it as he followed the corridor to the end, rounded the leftward corner, and took a right turn a short distance later at a T. They passed a set of sliding, glass double doors and hurried down a white corridor into a room with rows of shelves and plain beige storage crates. The far end had a rolling garage door big enough to accept the rear end of a truck. Her escort approached a smaller door beside it and swiped his hand at its panel, opening it.

She peered out at a glimmering street full of blue-clad people, electric cars, storefronts, and a metal ceiling instead of sky. The vastness and oddity of it caused a momentary hesitation in her step. Other than the steel overhead, it looked like a street in the downtown of a city. The man let go of her arm and prodded her in the back.

"Sorry kid. I'd leave you at the front desk, but the lobby people would get security involved because some kid randomly walked into a place kids aren't supposed to be able to randomly walk into. Again, I don't want to deal with the paperwork." He tugged her around to face him and put a finger under her chin, lifting it.

*Crap. He knows who I am. I'm dead.*

He chuckled, lowering his hand. "You look about ready to wet yourself. Calm down, kid. I don't think you were up to anything in there. No one can fake that kinda face. You in trouble or anything, want me to call the police?"

"No thanks. I'm okay. Just lost and terrified of getting grounded." *Tribals wouldn't say 'grounded.' Please don't be suspicious.*

The man nudged her out the door and closed it.

Kiera stood staring at it for over a minute, too stunned to move.

"The Sky Spirits favor you," said Pet from inside the satchel.

"If I get Mom and Dad out of here, I'll start believing in them." She backed away from the door and faced the street.

The road sat a few inches lower than the sidewalk, also metal but covered in a spray-on coating of rubber flecks that turned it black. Most everything else including the walls, ceiling, and fronts of buildings were the same shade of unpainted steel. Holographic signs advertised coffee, clothing shops, restaurants, and some electronics stores. Her hopes leapt for an instant before she remembered she had no 'numbers,' as her adopted village called them.

At once, this place felt both like the world she'd left behind as well as a distant future she shouldn't have lived long enough to see, comforting and alien all at once. A few people zipped by on Segway-like devices, their faces deep in small holographic screens projected from wristbands. Since they didn't look at all where they were going, she assumed their wheeled platforms either had autopilot, or they drove using an app, which of course, would be completely stupid. Why stare at a little screen showing you where you went when they could simply look up.

She jumped back with a yelp when a scooter rider whooshed by, but the woman swerved around the spot where Kiera had been. Pressed against the building, she glared at the careless rider, who continued zipping among pedestrians, none of whom reacted.

*Crap. If I keep jumping like that, someone will know I don't belong here.*

Kiera looked left and right a few times before heading to the right at a jog. She wanted to get off the street, find somewhere less obvious she could spend a few minutes thinking about where to go. A crowd gathered at the corner, waiting for the traffic signal to change. Not wanting to draw attention to herself, she bit back her impatience and remained among the people, hoping no one questioned her battered canvas satchel. She scrunched her eyebrows in disbelief at how everyone wore the same clothing. Clingy blue shirts, loose blue pants, and black sneakers.

Glowing balls of light hovering over the road changed to green, and the crowd crossed as one. She shuffled along, eyeing buildings and side streets, stores, more offices, and two medical places: one dentist and a 'cosmetic consultant.'

Five blocks from the door she'd been unceremoniously kicked out of, she skidded to a halt when a pair of security robots midway down the next section of city made eye-to-hexagon contact. She pulled an abrupt right turn and walked fast.

*Crap. Crap. Crap.*

As soon as the corner building across the street broke line of sight with the robots, she ran. The passage she'd ducked into appeared to be an alley lined with a handful of unlabeled plain doors. She hurried to the end where the narrow passage bent to the right, and slipped around, back against the wall. Kiera peeked past the corner, emitting a squeak of alarm when the pair of robots entered the other end.

*They're following me. Oh crap!* Shaking, she started to sprint to the right, but stumbled to a halt after a few steps, staring at a pair of trashcans by another plain door in the middle of a dead end wall.

With no other option at ready grasp of her brain, she ran to the door, hissing past her teeth in frustration, and pounded both fists on it.

*Please, someone let me hide.*

A panel beside the door emitted a pleasant chirp.

"Scan authorized," said an electronic female voice as the door opened.

Kiera darted in and whirled around to stare at the alley, dreading the sight of robots. They hadn't reached the corner yet. With a *hiss* that made her jump, the door closed before they appeared. She slouched with relief and finally allowed herself to look at where she'd gone: someone's living room. A reddish sofa faced a small table with a metal bar on it about the size of a submarine sandwich. One small corridor went off to the right, likely to bedrooms/bathrooms, and an archway beside the bizarre television opened to a tiny kitchen.

Since no one came running to see who'd barged into their home, she assumed the owner had gone out.

"Whoa… Crap. This is bad. I just broke into someone's house."

Pet floated up out of the satchel. "Technically, you had the key, so I'm not sure it counts as breaking in."

"What?" Kiera stared at Pet.

"You've got an identity chip, right?"

She clasped her right hand with her left, squeezing her palm between her thumb and fingers. "Yeah. Mom made me get it when I was little I think. Everyone had them."

"Well there you go." Pet drifted in a big circle around the room. "You have permission to be here if it worked on the door."

Kiera slouched with a sigh. "I can't steal someone's apartment or raid their fridge."

Her stomach growled.

She scratched at it, wandering into the kitchen. "Okay, maybe I can raid their fridge… Do you think they'd mind?"

"I am a bad influence on you, Kiera… but they can't mind if they don't know."

Kiera laughed.

# 33

# NEGOTIATIONS

K iera found the contents of the fridge both confusing and familiar. The packaging and labels looked like she'd been sucked into a futuristic movie, but the contents all consisted of recognizable food, not strange 'nutrient goop.' It took her only a few minutes to figure out how to work the holographic controls of the microwave and heat a self-contained entrée of salmon with a side of roast vegetables.

She perched on one of three black, padded stools by the kitchen counter and ate, rehearsing in her head what she might say to whoever lived here if they caught her. Fortunately, at eleven, she hoped she had enough little girl left in her to appeal to the occupant's sense of charity and wouldn't be thought of as a thief or a threat. Worse come to worst, she still had a laser pistol, but felt sick at the idea of having to point it at an innocent person.

"Well, I see you decided to listen," said a man behind her.

Kiera screamed and nearly fell off the stool. She spun around, heart racing.

The shimmery ghost of Anton Sokolov stood in the archway between kitchen and living room, smiling.

*How did he find me?* She shivered, staring like a deer about to be hit by a truck. *What is this... future-world phone calls?*

"I must say your resourcefulness impresses me. You are clearly not the tribal ragamuffin I initially took you for. In fact, with real clothing, you could pass for one of us."

"Please let my parents go."

"But you are still out on your own and at risk." He flashed a saccharin smile. The holographic projector made the white spots in his hair above each ear glow blue. "You will be much safer and happier here in the Citadel. I'm not sure what you expect to accomplish, but again, I commend your ingenuity at somehow getting inside past the security team." He pursed his lips. "I promise you will not be hurt. Good care will be taken of you."

Kiera swung her feet side to side, staring at him. "I don't believe you. You kidnapped my parents. You killed my friend." She swallowed the oncoming need to cry at Legacy's death, keeping a hard, stoic face.

"I implore you to see reason in the situation, child. I do not intend to harm you, but I must prevent you from hurting me... hurting everyone."

Kiera leaned forward, glaring, almost shouting, "What are you afraid of? I'm eleven years old! Besides"—she thrust both arms at him, fingers splayed—"if you didn't send your stupid robots after me in Exxo, I'd still be there, and I wouldn't care about you. The only reason I'm a threat to you at all is because you attacked us! I don't know why I'm so important. All I want is to go home with my parents. Please let them go and I swear I'll go away."

He opened his mouth, but the hologram disappeared in a flash of static and buzz.

Kiera blinked. "He hung up on me? Really?"

Pet floated up beside her. "I did that."

"What? Why?" She pivoted to stare at the cube.

"He was about to threaten to kill them if you didn't surrender. I cut him off so he could not."

She made fists, shaking them at her sides. "He's gonna kill them...."

"No. He did not get the chance to threaten you with it, so they are still safe. You need to hurry up and do whatever it is he is afraid you're going to do."

"I don't know what it is!" she screamed.

Pet drooped, emitting a sorrowful electronic trill.

Kiera bowed her head, sighing. "I'm sorry for yelling at you. It's not your fault."

The cube made another sad chirping noise.

"I'm not angry with you. I'm scared out of my mind and I have no idea what to do. Won't he kill them anyway even if I do whatever this great big thing is?"

Pet tilted back up. "Well, it is a possibility, but I can help there."

"How?"

"Your parents are being held in a detention facility. I can override the system and keep the cell locked so they cannot get to them."

Kiera paced in a circle, shaking her head. "That's not an answer. We can't leave them locked up forever."

"I agree, but you should flee this apartment right away. I've sent those robots out front a false order that you went somewhere else. That should give you some time, but I don't think they will fall for it again."

"Crap."

Kiera wolfed down the rest of the salmon and vegetables on the way to the door. She left the tray on a small table by the sofa and ran outside. Pet trailed after her as she hurried out of the alley and crossed the street. She twitched every time someone on a wheeled thing shot past her, but managed not to act like a doofus and jump into the wall. Once she'd gotten far enough away from that apartment to let her guard down a touch, she stopped at the mouth of another narrow alley between two office buildings.

"What floor is the jail on?"

Pet's light flickered for a few seconds. "There is a primary police facility on this level, the ground floor. It is in the northwest quadrant, close to the center." The cube projected a hologram map, a perfect square depicting the entire first level of the Citadel. A round hollow in the middle appeared to contain nothing but a solid dot with a lot of empty space around it. Major streets split the level into four sections around the core, with smaller streets dividing each area into grids, and so on. A yellow dot flashed on the map up and left of the central hollow.

"What's in the middle?"

"All citadel facilities are terraforming machines."

Kiera nodded. "Yeah, I got that part."

"It's the primary atmosphere processing system core. A great shaft runs all the way up through the facility to the equipment below the ground. Most of the machinery that handles the environmental scrubbing is beneath the surface. The eighty-one floors above are arcology. Residences, stores, hydroponics facilities, leisure centers, medical facilities, manufacturing facilities, and so on. Every citadel is a self-contained city."

"Right, so where are my parents?"

"They are on the seventy-eighth floor. The Citadel's security team has numerous operating bases throughout the arcology. The one they are in is the most secure, and smallest."

Kiera grumbled as Pet shifted to display the map of the upper level, easily a third the size of the ground floor. The yellow dot flashed at a point near the northeastern corner. "Do you think my skeleton hand will let me into the prison?"

"Your hand is not skeletal." Pet's voice oozed confusion.

"I mean like a skeleton key." She winked. "If I can open some random person's apartment, maybe I can wave and let them out?"

Pet remained silent for a few seconds. "It may work. However, your skeleton hand won't deactivate robots or live police personnel."

"Crap." She folded her arms. "What are the odds my powers of cuteness will work on the cops?"

"Marginal at best, and not at all on the robots."

"Double crap." Kiera scowled.

Pet flew into her back. "Move. I detect robots coming. Find a stairwell and go up."

"Not an elevator?"

"No. They will know you're using one."

Kiera ran off in a random direction. "You know I am completely lost, right?"

"Follow." Pet accelerated out in front of her, weaving among pedestrians.

Whenever the cube made an unexpected turn, she followed, trusting that her friend could sense approaching security robots before they got close enough to see her, and wanted to avoid them. She ran down streets, across courtyards, and past food courts. Few people paid her any attention, and the handful who did offered smiles.

A thick-chested man pivoted as she ran by. "Shouldn't you be in school at this hour?"

"Field trip," she yelled. "Trying to catch up."

He seemed to buy it and walked off without a word.

Pet zipped into a narrow alley. A heavy, wet breeze that smelled like a dumpster full of boiling diapers assaulted her nose. She gagged, but staggered after her floating friend. Near to vomiting by the time the alley ended, she swooned against the wall to catch her breath and try not to waste her meal by splattering it all over the floor.

"Are you all right?" Pet drifted back when it realized she'd stopped.

"What was that stink?" She gagged, coughed, and wiped her mouth.

"Off-venting from one of the hydroponics farms."

She shuddered.

"The stairs are close. Few people use them."

Kiera adjusted the satchel on her shoulder and loped onward. "Why? Are they like dangerous or something?"

"Nope," chirped Pet. "They don't use them because elevators."

"Oh, yeah. So I'll use the stairs for reasons." She giggled along with Pet, amused that the AI spoke kid slang.

Mirth didn't last long when she got a look at the stairs. Kiera grumbled and started the long, crappy climb.

# 34

# CRIMINALS

On the eighteenth floor, Kiera's legs refused to go onward—rather, upward. She rested for a little while, sitting on the landing while gazing out an open archway at an empty street. A fair ways down the corridor, the multicolored holographic glow of an active thoroughfare shimmered. Unfamiliar techno music thumped and thudded from the distance.

"Do these stairs go up to the seventy-whateverth floor where my parents are?"

"No, these stop at the twentieth. If they kept going, they'd need to cut a hole in the roof. We're inside a huge pyramid, remember? The walls are angled."

Kiera swallowed and stood. "Good, because I can't walk up seventy flights of stairs."

"I think you could if you had to. You are in better physical condition than almost everyone inside this place. They are spoiled by technology. You've been living a pure, natural life."

"Yeah, but people who lived like that died at forty."

"Medieval villagers could not buy Citadel medicine." Pet blinked on and off, perhaps a wink?

She gazed up. "Two more stories...."

After rounding four more sets of switchback stairs, she trudged out an archway onto the twentieth floor. A long alley stretched outward from the top, nowhere else to go but forward for longer than a city block before the passage connected to a large street. Both walls had numerous ventilation ports, but no doors. She jogged to the end and looked left at the face of a huge hospital. On her right stood an unmarked building, but the front room with tiny mailbox-like cubbies suggested an apartment complex.

Having no specific destination—and a mind whirling with worry and fear—she walked past the hospital and kept going. Stores, restaurants, and happy citizens surrounded her. Some had variations on the 'standard citizen uniform.' A few women wore skirts instead of pants, the same shade of blue as everything else. Aside from that, the only real difference in attire consisted of marks at either the shoulder or the ends of long sleeves. One, two, or three white bars, sometimes diagonal lines, and one man had two dots.

*It's like Army ranks or something.* The shirt the fabricator gave her had no markings at all, which probably made sense for a child. "This is so messed up."

"What is?" asked Pet.

"It's so wrong of these people to let everyone outside live tribal while it's like straight out of a video game in here. I keep waiting to see aliens beam in."

Pet chuckled. "There are no aliens. At least, none that have made contact. If they'd been watching this planet, they probably did a mega facepalm and went home."

"Heh. Where did you hear that?" She giggled.

"I have mysterious sources," said Pet with a foreign accent.

Flashing orange and red caught her eye on the wall up ahead. A large, holographic poster depicted a monochromatic black human figure in a sinister facemask. Bloody red lettering under the figure spelled 'Second Dawn.' A calm, male voice emanated from the area around the poster.

"All citizens, be advised that Administrator Sokolov has authorized rewards of up to fifty thousand credits for anyone who supplies information leading to the discovery and arrest of Second Dawn terrorists. Do not approach these individuals as they are highly dangerous and will kill to protect their secrets."

Three seconds later, the message repeated.

Kiera stared at the poster. The man or woman (an illustration of a facemask didn't give away much clue) radiated malice, seemingly staring into her soul. She flinched and hurried off, skidding to a halt only four steps later when a man on a Segway-like device zoomed by.

"Gah!" she yelled, flailing her arms for balance. She twisted, loaded a "Watch where you're going!" into her lungs, but didn't fire it. Anger leaked out of her nose.

"Quick, go left. Robots," said Pet.

She raced across the street, dodging a passing one-seater electric car with wheels the size of donuts. The pitiful *meeeeep* its horn made wouldn't have frightened a field rabbit—if not for their being extinct. She ignored the car, chasing Pet down a series of streets and alleys. The cube took a few turns, skidded to a stop, and backtracked, going a different way.

Almost out of breath, she rasped, "Are they coming for us?"

"No," said Pet, calm. "We are avoiding patrollers."

"Need... rest."

Pet slowed to a glide once more on a smallish street with a handful of pedestrians. She fell in step beside it, trying not to look winded. At least this place had AC, so the modern clothing hadn't become drenched in sweat. After a few minutes when the ability to breathe returned, she risked a look around. No one appeared close enough to overhear.

"What's the Second Dawn? Are they the friends Legacy was talking about? Or do you think they're as bad as that poster says?"

"They are a small group who are trying to destroy the Citadel, kill Anton, and force everyone to be equal. And I mean equally tribal. They want to shut everything down because they think technology is responsible for the mess the planet's in."

She rolled her eyes. "That's stupid. Wouldn't that let the Torment in? Destroying the citadel would kill everyone living in the Refuge. The clouds would fall again and melt everyone."

"Yes." Pet wobbled in a manner similar to nodding.

"So... either these Second Dawn people are idiots, or that's a lie and it's not what they are trying to do. Where did you find that information on them?"

"Official archives," said Pet.

"That means it's from Anton, or at least the cops." She rolled her eyes. "So it's probably lies."

Pet swerved around a speeding Segway. "Correct."

"Argh. What should I do? This is too much for me. All I want is to find my parents and go home. This place is *so* big. It's really silly, but I miss that filthy little bedroom and the garden, and my friends. And Mom and Dad." Again, the urge to cry knocked on the inside of her eyes. She closed them and held back her emotion. Bursting into tears in the middle of the street would attract attention. Someone merely trying to help a crying child would involve cops and she'd wind up caught.

"Perhaps you should attempt to find people who are used to going places they do not belong."

She smirked. "You mean criminals."

"Who else would know how to break out of jail or hack into a computer network?"

"You can hack." She poked it.

Pet spun side to side, a headshake. "I run programs. While I am sentient, I cannot do anything the programs do not have permission to do. Overriding the prison security system is beyond me. Unless you upload special back door routines I do not currently have or we steal someone's password."

"Fine." Kiera huffed. "So I have to find some criminals. Great. Yeah. Little girl wandering around *looking* for criminals. What could go wrong?"

"Quite a lot," said Pet.

"Grr. You're supposed to be helpful." She walked on. "Why would a criminal even help me?"

"Perhaps you can try invoking your powers of cuteness."

Kiera glanced sideways at Pet, unsure if she should laugh or glare. Pet's innocent whistling got her, and she grinned. "Where would I even find someone like that?"

"There are some areas inside the Citadel where encountering lawbreakers would be more likely."

"Ugh." She patted her satchel, squeezing the laser pistol through the canvas. "This is *so* a bad idea, but I got nothing else."

Pet glided onward. "This way…."

# 35

# MARK OF THE BEAST

Kiera wandered around for a few hours, but no one appeared in the least bit criminal or even seedy looking. She felt like she'd jumped into a reality warp and landed on a starship exploring uncharted civilizations, sent by an advanced society where humans had evolved beyond crime and racism and all the bad stuff. Everyone appeared to be so nice... except for Anton.

"Where's the uhh, 'bad part of town?'"

Pet flickered. "You are going to be upset, but the closest thing I can find to that would be on the second floor at the north end."

The map appeared again, displaying the second story floorplan. Huge streets spread out from the circular core like a giant plus sign cutting the level into four quadrants. Faint lines pointed out the official entrance at the middle of the east side one level down. Maintenance shaft 084 that she'd crawled in from was on the west. Pet added a red blob highlight around the end of the northern street, spreading about a half mile into both sides, close to the outer wall.

"All the way back downstairs." She gazed at the ceiling. "Let me guess, if I use an elevator, they'll know."

"I assume they are running face-matching software on all the security cameras. While it is easy enough to keep out of sight on the street, the elevators are small."

Kiera shook her head hard, covering her face with hair. "How about this? Are there a lot of redheads inside?"

"Perhaps nine percent of the population. If you consider only girls your age with long hair, likely so few that robots will investigate. I am sure they are bothering other children who resemble you as well."

"Fine." She huffed. "Where are the stairs?"

Pet zipped ahead. "We will take a different set, closer to the north."

"Right...."

She followed her flying cube, which stuck to smaller streets and alleys, avoiding crowds. Whenever the cube stopped short, she waited for robots to walk by the intersections up ahead. A touch over a mile later, Pet raced backward without warning. Kiera sprinted, chasing it around a corner, down another alley, and north again. It stopped a few paces short of where the alley met a cross street.

"Robot?"

"Yes. We were not seen, but it walked directly at us."

Kiera nodded, hand on her chest. "I'm okay."

"We are clear." Pet glided onward.

She followed across the street, hooked a right at the next alley, and ducked left around a row of fast food shops. The smell of hamburgers, grilling chicken, and spices got her stomach growling, but Pet didn't slow down. At the end of the food court, it headed left. A familiar archway waited at the end of a short street. Kiera trotted up to it, glancing at a sign indicating the stairwell went up four more levels as well as down to the first floor. She groaned at the idea of more steps, but raced along, whirling around turns at each switchback, hand on the railing. At least down didn't wear her out as much as going up did.

Soon after reaching the second floor, she wandered along a street larger than the ones Pet had been using before. Fearing cameras, she shrouded her face with her hair, but not so much she couldn't see. The farther north she walked, the less pristine the area became. A few tribal people moved among the pedestrians, some with strong tans and bright yellow jumpsuits.

Kiera blinked at them and whispered, "Why are they in yellow? Are they prisoners?"

Pet shook side to side. "No. Tribals. They are not permitted into the Citadel to work without clothing. The yellow garments are issued temporarily. They leave them at the gate when they go back to their villages at night."

"Oh." Kiera shivered. "Who'd *want* to be naked in here anyway? It's too cold."

"I cannot say if they do or do not prefer it. They merely don't have anything, or what they do have is not enough for the law. It is sparse outside."

She sighed. "Yeah. I miss when my biggest problem was trying to find something to wear."

Pet chuckled. "A problem feels like the end of the world right up until you solve it."

Kiera waited with a pack of citizens and tribals at a light, crossing once it changed. "I didn't solve it... Dad gave me the poncho. *He* solved that problem."

"But you approached them and asked for help, did you not? So you took the first step that led to the problem being solved."

"I guess."

A familiar barefoot Japanese woman in a plain beige cloth dress with microchips and resistors decorating her neckline walked by going the other way. She carried a toolkit and appeared to be in a hurry. Kiera spun to watch her pass.

"That's Mei's mom... Risuka." Kiera considered waving, but didn't.

Three cross streets later, only a handful of blue-clothed citizens remained in sight. The surroundings grew dirtier, left untended or avoided by those who lived inside the Citadel. Large men with dog-fur hide skirts and bright yellow 'temporary' shirts gathered by the fronts of bars, standing under the baleful red glow of holographic signs. A few glanced at her, and not in friendly ways. She thought back to Pet's warning not to wear modern clothing out among the villages, and thanked nothing in particular that she'd listened.

Kiera kept her head down and hurried forward. *They don't know I'm one of them... That dude with the shaved head looks like he wants to hit me.* The street opened into a bazaar of sorts, filled with tribals and pushcart merchants trading everything from flashy trinkets to haircuts, tattoos, and other things they'd spent their credits on in hopes of trading to other tribals. "Why would they buy stuff only to sell it?"

Pet halted, hovering over her shoulder. "They buy up rare products like candy or drugs and sell them for a few credits more to others. In the end, they generate money."

Kiera sighed. "This place is giving me the serious creeps. I don't like it here. Did you see the way that one guy stared at me?"

"They believe you are an Exalted. The citizens of the Citadel are not too friendly to the tribes, so there is hostility and bad feelings."

"You don't think they'd hurt me?"

Pet bobbed, a shrug. "Since you are inside, they will most likely not harm you because of the police. Outside, you would not have that protection. I think you should still stay away from them. They'd be mean to you if they had the chance."

Kiera wandered for a little while more before coming to a stop and staring in the open door of another bar that didn't look quite as scary as the first. "Hmm. Bartenders know criminals, right?"

"I don't know," said Pet.

"Oh, why not? It works in movies...."

She crossed the courtyard and wandered into a dim room full of round tables and booth seats as well as an empty stage tucked up against the innermost wall with a small drum-pad kit and microphone stand. The woman behind the bar looked on the older end of teenage, with bright violet hair and a nose ring... but the same plain blue outfit as the rest of everyone who lived in the Citadel wore.

Kiera walked up to the bar. She looked side to side, grasped the edge, and leaned forward, whispering. "Hey. I need to find someone with a... certain skill set. Can you—?"

"Get outta here, kid." The woman pointed at the door. "You're way too little to be in this place."

"But I—"

"Move it, brat. I ain't getting shut down over an underage drinking citation."

"I'm not dri—"

"Another two seconds, and I'm going to physically drag you out the door."

Kiera grumbled.

The woman took a step to the side, her attitude softening. "Look, kid. Get out of here before you wind up stabbed or worse. It ain't safe here for you. Mostly tribals come in here."

"All right..." Kiera raised her hands. "Geez."

She hurried out the door. A few steps into the courtyard, she yawned. "What time is it?"

"It is 10:48 p.m.," said Pet, gliding up to float beside her head.

"Wow. So many outsiders still here... don't they kick them out at night?"

Pet followed as she roamed. "The buses leave at 7:00 p.m., but they do not forcibly remove anyone with a work-permit after dark. We're in an area with hotel space. Some from faraway villages spend the entire week inside, working. Some go back on the weekends, and some live here all the time."

"Oh." Again, she yawned.

Kiera headed into a place that looked like a fast food restaurant. Booth seats lined the walls, bright yellow-cushioned benches facing red tables. The red tile floor triggered a faint memory of a hamburger place she'd been in before being frozen. Nervous, Kiera entered, stomach growling harder at the smell of fried potatoes and possibly chicken in the air. A woman in a dog-fur hide dress behind the counter gave her a surprised stare, but said nothing as Kiera went into the back hallway toward a bathroom. In the Citadel, she'd probably get in trouble for peeing in an alley. That the idea of doing so didn't feel wrong anymore worried her. On the way to the bathroom, she thought about her fake life and being 'civilized,' but it only made her miss her new parents more.

After washing her hands, which also felt bizarre, she trudged back to the seating area and over to an empty booth, where she curled up on the bench, using her arm for a pillow.

Pet landed beside her.

Right as she felt herself slipping off to sleep, a hand on her sneaker jostled her.

Kiera lifted her head, squinting at the woman in the dog-hide dress and sandals made of tire rubber. "What?"

The woman, a year or so past twenty, offered a weak smile, but didn't look her in the eye. "I'm sorry, sweetie. I have to ask you to buy some food or you can't stay inside here. It's policy. I'll lose my job if I don't follow it."

"Ugh." Kiera sat up and wiped her eyes. "Sorry. I'll go. I don't have any numbers."

The woman blinked. "Your parents' account is empty? That can't be possible. I've never seen an Exalted who didn't have numbers. Or an Exalted who called it 'numbers.'"

"Uhh...."

"You're hungry, aren't you? Is something wrong at home?" The woman edged closer, still looking down.

"Why are you afraid of me?"

The tribal woman clasped her hands in front of herself. "You're so nice for an Exalted. If you get angry with me, I could be in trouble."

"Yes, something is wrong at home. My parents have been kidnapped." She slid to her feet. "I need to find a hacker or something."

"What?" The woman gawked. "You're far too small for violence. No... you shouldn't!"

Kiera looked up at her with half-closed eyes. "You don't know what a hacker is, do you? It's not an axe. Forget it... I'll go."

The woman gestured at the counter. "You're hungry. Please try to pick something. I'm sure you have numbers. All Exalted do."

*Whatever. She won't believe me until the computer tells her I'm broke.* She stumbled over to the counter. When the woman took her position behind it, Kiera pointed at a fried chicken sandwich combo. The terminal beeped a few times, and a holographic arrow appeared bouncing above a black square on the counter.

"Surprised this isn't all robotic." Kiera held her hand out, expecting a buzz, but got a happy chirp.

"We don't usually have Exalted in here." The woman grabbed something out of a steel cabinet and dropped it in a fryer. "It's really to be nice to us tribals, ya know? They let someone have a job a machine can do."

"That's cool." Kiera smiled, rubbing her hand. *Huh... Maybe Bio-Mom had a café account with her work that's still in the system.*

A few minutes later, the woman set a tray on the counter in front of her. "It's hot. You should let it sit before you bite it."

"Okay." *Too tired to argue.* Kiera picked up the tray and returned to her booth to feast on her grilled chicken and fries.

Pet landed nearby on the table. "You should leave soon."

"But I wanna sleep here," she muttered.

"You scanned your chip. They know where you are."

She scowled. "Crap. I'm so tired I wasn't thinking."

"It's all right."

Kiera stared at her hand, trying to picture the chip inside. A flicker of memory where Bio-Dad called them the 'Mark of the Beast' surfaced. She didn't remember what he meant by that, other than thinking the chips were somehow evil. Having killer robots start hunting her every time she used it *did* seem evil. The brief peek into what had been her life only made her maudlin, wondering how much else—happy moments—she'd lost. *It doesn't matter. That world's gone.* She stuffed fries into her mouth, chewing them into a mush while a black cloud gathered over her head. Pet twirled around on the table, chirping and twittering.

The little robot's antics let a tiny smile creep out from under the gloom. She hurried the rest of her dinner, earned an astonished look from the girl behind the counter when she carried her tray back, and darted out the door.

Pet took off, so Kiera jogged up to a light run to keep pace down an alley leading away from the courtyard. After passing two crossing streets, Pet slowed to walking speed. Kiera held her gut and burped, groaning at having to run so soon after eating fast. They entered a small atrium with ivy-covered walls arranged beneath artificial sun lamps, currently off. On the right, large elevated panels contained swaths of grass, some with benches. Plants covered almost every inch of the space that attempted to be a 'park.' Despite the relative grunge, the air smelled clean. Pet drifted over to a capsule-shaped fountain that resembled an aboveground swimming pool, but it only came up to her thighs. The cube hovered by an access hatch between two benches.

Kiera crawled up to it, close to collapsing in the street, but stayed awake long enough to open the panel and tuck inside. Safe from hexagonal eyes among a nest of piping and small pumps, she surrendered to sleep.

# ROCK, PAPER, SCISSORS

Kiera startled awake. A tangle of PVC pipes hovered over her head, the black curve of the fountain basin above them. She grumbled and tried to stretch, but the small chamber didn't have enough room for her to straighten her legs. A yawn paralyzed her for a few seconds, and she set her foggy head back down on her arm and closed her eyes.

A *slam* outside accompanied a few whispered naughty words.

She leaned up to the slatted hatch and peered out. The ceiling lights had dimmed, making the area appear like the middle of the night. Motion and continued grumbling drew her attention to a narrow alley off the 'park' where a man slapped and kicked at a small metal box mounted on the wall. He paused, staring out at the open area full of plants, looking worried. After a few minutes of silence, he seemed relieved and resumed tinkering.

*That guy's trying to break in to some place.* Kiera wiped her eyes and yawned before pushing the hatch open and crawling out. She tugged her satchel up onto her shoulder and walked, yawning every two steps, into the alley.

The man had the most disheveled blue shirt and pants she'd yet seen on any permanent resident of the Citadel as well as shaggy hair, an unshaven face, and a stink like beer. He looked younger than her Dad, and had a wiry, thin frame that—despite his probable status as a lawbreaker—made him far from scary. A metal lunchbox-sized device hung from the man's black nylon belt, one side open to expose electronics and a nest of wires. He kept attaching them to the component on the wall with tiny clamps, occasionally triggering zaps and burned fingers.

Kiera stopped a few paces away, her left arm rested on the satchel, gripping the strap, right arm lax at her side.

He kept working, oblivious to her.

"Excuse me," said Kiera in a small voice. "Can I ask you something?"

The man practically jumped straight out of his clothes. He whirled to face her, yanking a handful of wires off the device on the wall in a flurry of sparks. After a momentary staredown, he drew a knife and pointed it at her.

Kiera stuffed her hand in the satchel and pulled the laser pistol, pointing it at him. "I think I'm gonna win this rock, paper, scissors, don't you?"

The man twitched, shaking, staring at the weapon. "Damn, kid... what the hell?"

"Don't be stupid. Calm down. I only wanna talk. I don't care what you're doing. I'm not gonna get the cops."

"Cops? What?" He fidgeted, squeezing and relaxing his grip on the knife.

Kiera gave him a flat look. "Police?"

He shuddered, shaking his head. "How you get cops outta police?"

"Forget it. I'm not going to get you in trouble. Can we talk? Maybe put weapons away?"

A nervous laugh forced its way past the man's clenched teeth. His random shakes became more of a nod, and he slid the knife back into its sheath on his belt. "Okay... strange kid. What do you want?"

Kiera tucked the laser in the satchel, but not too deep so she could grab it easily if need be. "Do you know any hackers? I need to break some people out of jail."

"Heh." The man covered his mouth and looked around, lost to a fit of giggles. "Where's the camera? This is some kinda prank right? That's not even a real stinger."

"Stinger? Oh, the laser? It's real... I don't want to prove it, please." She stifled a yawn. "I'm serious. The administrator kidnapped my parents and I'm trying to get them back. I need help."

He stared at her for a minute or two, his shaking slowed, finally stopping. "Umm. Not really. Hackers? No. That's kinda high-end. Me? I'm low-end."

Kiera frowned at the box hanging off his belt. "Right... Do you know anything about those Second Dawn people? Is it a lie what they say about them, or are they really dangerous?"

The man blinked, shook his head, and edged back over to the open panel on the wall. "Wow, kid. What kinda mess are you into?"

"Hopefully, I'm in the middle of the worst dream I've ever had... but something tells me I went to sleep in one world and woke up in another world—a broken one." She looked down, heart heavy. "If this was a nightmare, getting chased up a telephone pole by a pack of wild dogs would've woke me up."

"You're one odd kid." The man hooked up two more wires and convulsed at a small shock. "Gah!"

Kiera sighed and looked up at him. "Please... can you help me at all?"

He glanced sideways at her, shook his head, and hooked up another wire without zapping himself.

"You're getting better at that. No smoke that time."

The man bowed his head against the wall, whisper-laughing. "Okay, kid... You should go for ramen in 42-188. Look for a little old Chinese woman. Tessa."

"Okay... thanks." She backed up a few steps.

"You're really not going to call the police?" He twitched.

Kiera tilted her head. "Are you going to kill or hurt anyone?"

"Naw, kid. No one's in there. Just tryin' ta get some stuff ta sell."

"Then, no. I'm not going to call the police."

She trudged out into the sad little park and crawled into the fountain again. After pulling the hatch closed, she tried to get as comfortable as possible on a hard metal floor, closed her eyes, and waited for the continuous whirr from the pumps to lull her to sleep.

# 37

# TESSA

Kiera walked among a crowd of pedestrians, trying to act as normal as possible for being the only child in the area. Pet floated along by her right shoulder, and neither of them attracted much notice. She ducked into a small deli-style restaurant, made use of the bathroom, and ordered a turkey sandwich to go plus a bottle of 'vitamin-infused lemonade.' Again, the chip reader worked to pay for her meal, but she didn't stick around to eat there.

Three stories up, and a few blocks away from the stairwell, she headed into a narrow passageway between two stores, one full of electronic gadgets, the other selling clothing. Of course, its selection consisted of blue shirts, blue pants, and black sneakers in varying sizes.

*Geez, these people are boring.*

A small dumpster box stood against the clothing store wall, which offered a place to hide from the street. She sat on the ground, opened her food, and ate. Pet hovered above her head, watching out for threats.

"What's 42-188?"

Pet dipped down to eye level. "It's a coordinate. Level 42, sector 188." The cube displayed a map of the floor, with a yellow dot indicating a location near the west end. Open space surrounded by many small squares made her think food court or something similar.

"Okay. I need to go there." She swigged lemonade, cringing at the overwhelming sweetness. Months of having only water made the soft drink feel like syrup. "Eww. This is kinda nasty. I used to like soda."

"That is a 'healthy' beverage. Soda has more than twice that much sugar."

She stuck out her tongue. After finishing off her meal, she tossed the empty bottle and plastic sandwich clamshell case into the dumpster and headed off toward the stairs. Pet helped her avoid robot sentries along the way. Several times, she had to crawl under large machine boxes on the walls or duck into maintenance hatches and hide while robots walked by or lingered. The few living people who took note of her fell for her acting casual and calm. While young enough to still attract concern for being alone, eleven seemed to let her pass for having been given errands to run or 'got lost but I'm okay now.'

The eighth time she ducked into a hole in the wall to hide from robots, she scowled at the floor between her sneakers. "This is getting annoying."

Pet wobbled to nod. "I apologize, but you cannot let them see you."

"Yeah," she whispered. "I can't believe no one's grabbed me and dragged me to the cops for being alone. Guess this place is pretty safe if no one is worried."

Pet waited for a pair of security robots to walk by outside. A flash of silver plastic glimmered in the vent slats inches from Kiera's knees. "There is some crime, but violent offenses are rarer than the world you were born in. Few are willing to flee into the outside world to escape the law, and it is difficult to remain hidden inside."

"Yeah." She stared at her hand, rubbing the spot where she assumed the chip sat beneath her skin. "Tell me about it."

"I just did," said Pet.

She stifled a giggle.

"It's clear. Also, you are hiding in places a man would not fit."

Kiera crawled out onto the street and kicked the hatch closed. "Yay for small me."

A nerve-wracking hour of cat and mouse later, Kiera entered a food court on the west side of the forty-second level. Work-permit people shared the space with over a hundred citizens. The tribals cleaned tables, swept the floor, collected empty trays, and so on. She caught more than a few contemptuous glares exchanged between citizens and outsiders. Though she never considered herself much of an outdoors-type person before, Kiera missed having sky over her head.

She heaved a sad sigh and wandered in. A man in a skirt made of the same thin cloth as her precious dress walked by, bumping her so hard she almost fell flat on her face.

"Sorry, I did not see," said the man, sounding fake.

Kiera glared up at him.

He scoffed and walked away. Glaring had likely been the exact reaction he'd expected.

"Butt," she muttered.

Wandering the edges of the food court, she examined the various tiny shops and restaurants. Three noodle counters served ramen, but only one had an old Chinese woman behind it. Kiera glanced up at a hologram sign, 'Zhou Ramen,' and down at the white-haired elder behind the counter. The woman, in the typical blue shirt/pants of the Exalted, smiled at her in a grandmotherly way.

Kiera approached and leaned on the counter. "Hi. Can I talk to you?"

"Hello, child. What can I get for you?"

*Might as well put it out there.* "I am hungry, but if I buy anything, they will find me here. I need help, and someone told me to look for you. Are you Tessa?"

The woman glanced around, narrowing her eyes. "Where did you hear that name from?"

"Some guy in an alley. I asked him if those Second Dawn people are really as bad as everyone says, or if it's a lie."

"You're running away, aren't you?" Tessa chuckled. "I get two or three a week, you know. It's not at all romantic out there. Most never make it outside, but the handful who do come crawling back to their parents in a day or two."

Kiera lowered her voice to a whisper. "I'm from Exxo. I lived outside for months. It's hard, but it's also kinda nice in a way. I miss video games though." She grumbled. "The administrator is trying to kill me, and he's kidnapped my parents. I'm not running away from home. I'm trying to go back."

"Hmm." Tessa stared at her for an uncomfortably long time. "Why are you asking about the Dawn?"

"Saw a poster. What the police say the Second Dawn are trying to do sounds so stupid I can't believe anyone would be that dumb. It's gotta be a lie. Legacy told me there are people inside the Citadel who will help me." She bowed her head. "He died trying to me get inside."

Tessa took the top bowl off a stack of upside-down bowls. She grabbed a pinch of scallions, chopped seaweed, bean sprouts, and some powdered ingredients from bins, dropping each in the bowl before adding a large wad of noodles. After tossing the tongs aside, she ladled some thick brown broth over it all. "Come around, child."

"Thank you." Kiera followed the old one in behind the counter to a back room.

Steel shelves held various cans and jars of food products. A long metal table on the right had a machine generating more noodles next to three huge pots of cooking broth. The fragrance of pork saturated the entire place. Kiera took a seat at a little folding table against the back wall, next to a cramped corridor leading to a bathroom and a closet with a sink and mops.

Tessa set the bowl in front of her and sat catty-corner. "So, what is your story, child?"

"I had a really weird day at school..." Kiera ate while explaining how she'd gone from suburban San Antonio to wandering a desert after the apocalypse, to sneaking into the Citadel to rescue her parents. Or at least attempt to rescue her parents and get caught rather than simply turning herself in. The parts involving Legacy seemed to interest Tessa most.

"Yes... there are some people inside who are aware of the mechanism. Sokolov has tried to make people believe there is no greater capacity for the citadels to function. He will never activate it, but he uses it as a threat. Administrators of other citadels live like kings and queens since they control their habitable zones. People are forced to depend on the citadels for decent food and in some places, even water."

Kiera stabbed chopsticks into her almost-gone soup. "Mom thinks he likes being king too much."

"That is no doubt a large part of it, but there are also rumors that the robots that were left behind to finish constructing the citadels made errors, and attempting to turn it on will go boom."

Kiera nodded. "I saw that too, but it sounded nuts."

"It's something to keep in the back of the mind."

"Is that why no one's ever turned it on before?" asked Kiera. "It's going to take hundreds of years to clean the planet in standby mode."

Tessa leaned back, hand at her chin. "No one has turned it on yet because no one can. Not that I think Sokolov has any intention to. For whatever reason, the system was designed to only accept the activation command from a senior executive. This all used to be a corporation before the world fell apart, you know."

"Yeah, I know. My parents worked for them." She slurped up the last of the broth. "Thanks for the soup. I've never had it before... it's really good."

Tessa stared at her. "Your parents are work-permit people?"

"I don't mean to be rude, but you didn't listen to me, did you? I was frozen. My parents worked for Citadel Corporation back in the 2030s. Mom was a VP of R&D and my dad was the VP in charge of their legal department."

"Child..." Tessa grabbed her hand. "Your parents were executives...."

"Yeah." She fought the urge to roll her eyes.

"So there is—" Tessa glanced off into space for a second. "Quick, child. With me."

She grabbed Kiera by the wrist and dragged her to the back corner of the room. The old one pressed her hand against what appeared to be plain steel wall, and a panel opened. Without a word, Tessa shoved her into a small cubby. Kiera stumbled in to sit, knees crammed against her chest, feet forced to twist inward. Pet zipped in before the old woman could close the panel, compressing her against the inside wall.

"Stay quiet," said Tessa.

Kiera looked around in the flickering blue glow of Pet's thruster. The hidden closet had smooth walls without any handles, buttons, or hatches to let her out, and not enough room for her to stand up in, or much move at all. Fear made her shove at the panel, but it didn't even rattle. Dread that she'd picked the wrong old lady to confide in got her shaking. She hated the feeling of being basically locked in a cage, but screaming for help would only attract attention and police. If Tessa intended to betray her to the administrator, sitting still and keeping quiet as ordered would have the same result as shouting.

She grunted and elbowed the panel. It took only a few seconds of struggling to convince herself that she'd been hopelessly trapped. Kiera rested her head against her knees and sighed, unable to stop shaking. At a light nudge from Pet, she reached up and cradled the small cube, clinging to it like a child hoping her teddy bear would keep away the closet monster.

# 38

# SECOND DAWN

**K**iera sat in silent darkness for almost forever before whispering, "What time is it?"

A small hologram appeared with clock numbers: 3:17 p.m.

She pushed at the cabinet door, still unable to move it. Grabbing her shins in both hands, she grunted and wriggled, shifting position so the cramped space didn't force her feet to twist so much. "Ow. Ugh. Why did she lock me in here?"

"I do not know," said Pet, at low volume.

At 3:41, Kiera's feet ached, her butt had gone numb, and she couldn't stop fidgeting. The inability to unfold herself made the confinement maddening. Worse, she really had to go. She wasted a few more minutes shoving at the door, despite already being convinced she could not possibly get out of the chamber on her own.

"I'm gonna pee my pants," she grumbled. "I can't hold it anymore."

Pet's inner glow came on, flickering. "I'm not detecting any security robots, but this metal enclosure may be blocking my signal."

"Ngh…" She grabbed herself, whining from how bad she had to go. "Please let me out."

When Pet's hologram clock read 3:54, footsteps approached outside. Kiera shivered with the effort it took not to soil herself. A metallic *click* came from somewhere above her head and the panel swung open to reveal Tessa.

Kiera glared at her.

"Forgive me, child. The police were searching the area."

"'Kay." Kiera fell out onto her hands, dragged herself forward, and scrambled into a limping run to the bathroom. She shoved her pants down and jumped with a spin onto the bowl, then pulled the door closed.

Tessa approached outside, standing close. "Robots and police officers went store to store around the food court here. Your bag is in another hidden compartment. They did not find it."

"Thanks," rasped Kiera, too lost in the wonderfulness of relief to think about much else.

"There are cameras everywhere, and you must have been spotted walking in the concourse."

Kiera gazed at the ceiling. *Umm, could you maybe wait until I'm done to talk to me?* "Probably."

"I have made contact with some people who can help. We will talk more once you are finished in there."

"'Kay."

Tessa walked off.

For a while after she finished, Kiera slouched on the bowl, trying to recover the desire to move. Eventually, she forced herself to stop being lazy and wobbled back to the table where she'd eaten before. One at a time, she pulled her legs up and stretched them, trying to get rid of the soreness from being crammed in such a small cabinet for almost three hours.

"I'm sorry, child," said Tessa, carrying over cups of hot green tea.

Kiera shrugged one shoulder. "You scared me to death, but it's better than getting caught."

"Indeed." Tessa looked at Pet. "You have a reference map of Citadel Zero?"

"Yes," said Pet.

Tessa shifted her gaze to the cube. "You will need to lead her to 12-90. 244.18 by 70. It would be best to keep her in conduits and out of sight."

"Route calculation complete," said Pet.

"Waypoint?" asked Kiera.

Tessa smiled, sipping tea. "Yes. Your little friend will bring you to my associates. They will help you as your goals are the same as theirs."

"Great." Kiera sipped her tea.

Following an awkward twenty minutes of tea drinking, Kiera thanked Tessa again for the food and help. She followed Pet away from the restaurant into another cramped alley. At the back end, she pulled herself into a vent shaft and closed the square hatch behind her.

"Being fully enclosed, citadels have a vast network of ducts that allow air to reach every inch of livable space. While there are some passages too small even for you, between the airways and maintenance passages, we will be able to get there far away from where cameras are watching."

"All right." Kiera tugged her satchel snug, and crawled on.

Pet led her to the left, following a frigid section of ductwork. A few turns later, it stopped at a vent hatch. Beyond, a room with black walls brimmed with technology. One woman sat at a desk nearby, facing to the right, but she had a clear view of the vent. The rest of the small chamber held racks of electronics, computer components most likely.

The word 'wait' appeared in a tiny hologram behind Pet before shifting to 'quiet.'

Kiera put on a 'duh' face. She crouched behind the slats, watching the woman work at a hologram-screen terminal. After a while, the woman got up and walked off to the right. A door squeaked open.

"Be right back. Gotta hit the bathroom," said a female voice.

"Don't hit it too hard," replied a man.

"That wasn't funny the first twenty times you used it."

The door closed with a faint *pssh* noise.

Pet tapped itself into the vent cover.

"Right." Kiera crawled into the room and closed the hatch behind her. "Now what?"

"Here." Pet floated across the room, past the desk where the woman had been, and down a short section of refrigerator-sized computer cabinets to a larger, square opening in the wall below a sign announcing 'hardhat required.' Black metal walls laced with seams and raised rectangular sections went in about ten feet before cornering left.

Kiera stooped and walked in, following Pet. She passed more racks of computer equipment, cable bundles, and winking lights. The passage cornered to the right again and continued for a while before opening out to a catwalk hanging on the side of a terrifying open shaft that spanned multiple floors. Left and right, the walls held more component cabinets and network cable bundles. She peered down through the metal grating at a long stretch of wall glimmering with thin traces of blue light and blinking spots.

"This goes all the way to the bottom, doesn't it?"

"Not all the way. It stops at the ground floor."

Kiera stared at Pet. "If you tell me that I have to climb forty-two stories of spaceship hull by sticking my fingers and toes in these tiny gaps, I'm going to laugh at you."

"No." Pet rubbed against her cheek. "I would not have agreed to that either. Too dangerous. This way."

The cube floated off to the right, following the catwalk.

Kiera tiptoed forward, clinging to the railing with both hands as her hair tossed about in random blasts of wind. She kept her stare on the cube ahead of her, not thinking that only a bouncing metal catwalk separated her from a forty-two story fall. A few frightening minutes later, Pet froze inches shy of going around where the catwalk turned a rightward corner. A hologram screen appeared with, 'Robot! Crap.' The screen blanked and displayed, 'Double crap.'

Kiera grinned despite being terrified. *One robot I can deal with... no one can see us here.*

She pulled the laser pistol out of the satchel.

'No! No! No!' appeared on the screen while Pet twisted back and forth.

She pointed at her eyes and tilted her head questioningly.

Pet projected a holographic drawing that showed a security robot standing by the railing sixteen feet away from the corner. Kiera crept up, flattening herself against the wall an inch from the end. She decided to go low and dropped to her knees. Pet trembled.

Kiera leaned one eye past the corner. The robot stood at the end of the catwalk, faced out over the shaft with its left side to her. Not trusting a real world robot to obey computer game 'vision cones,' she eased herself back out of sight. Minutes later, the clank of it shuffling around rose up and faded.

Again, she peeked. The security android had turned to the right, putting its back to her.

She flowed out from behind the corner on her knees, raised the laser pistol to sight on the back of its head, and held her breath. At the *click* of the trigger button, the android's head burst into flames. She lowered her aim point to the upper chest and clicked the button three more times. A burning plastic-and-metal body tumbled over the railing and plummeted into the darkness, bumping the wall or other catwalks as it fell with a series of echoing *bangs*.

"Backstab rules," whispered Kiera.

Pet zipped into her face. "You are so reckless! Please don't scare me like that again."

"Sorry, but what else should I have done? I don't think it would've moved. It doesn't work shifts or ever need to go to the bathroom. It stands there forever."

The crashing from below ended with a louder *whap* that announced the android's meeting with the ground.

"Come on." Pet glided ahead and ducked into another conduit behind where the robot had been standing. "Someone will be here soon to investigate why that unit went offline."

She ran on the bouncing grating to the opening and crawled in. The next maintenance passage led to a vertical shaft with a black-and-yellow striped ladder. Kiera jumped on and climbed down to the twelfth floor, where she collapsed on a small platform in front of another crawlspace entrance.

"Need... minute... Thirty stories of ladder... jelly legs." She helped herself to one of her water bottles.

Pet hovered patiently beside her until she regained the ability/desire to move.

Kiera pushed herself up to all fours. "Why does this feel like a video game?"

"Maybe because robots built it?" asked Pet. "Their design called for installing components and providing a way for human workers and robots to access them. No live people made this place. They were all dead or frozen before the citadels were larger than bunkers. The design is based on computer efficiency, not being tolerant of human limitations."

"So where did the Exalted idiots come from?" asked Kiera, crawling on.

"Each citadel had a large Cairn. Those Cairns opened once the citadel structure had been completed, years before the air bubble pushed away the clouds."

"Okay, so how did the tribes happen? More Cairns?" She took a right turn.

Pet bobbed left and right while gliding along. "No one seems to really know. Some think there are people who found ways to survive Cloudfall in caves or old subways. Others believe the tribes to be the descendants of dissidents who fled the Citadels as soon as breathable air existed again."

"That's dumb. Why would they go out there when it's nice in here?"

"You miss the sky, don't you? You miss your friends, the way the villagers all protect and know each other?"

Kiera slowed as Pet ducked down a left turn. As silly as it felt, she *did* miss her crappy little bedroom and ramshackle house. Despite its technology, being here made her feel like hamster in a cage. "I guess. But... they have medicine here. Maybe it's a nice place to visit, but humans weren't made to live in boxes. You're right though. I still even miss Ashleigh, even though she wasn't real."

Pet cuddled against her cheek for a moment. "Maybe, but I think you just like not having to go to school."

Kiera laughed. "Yeah. But I did sixth-grade like ten times so I deserve a break."

"Good excuse." Pet giggled.

She came to a stop at an opening into another component room with no hatch to hide behind. A red-haired man slumped over a desk, snoring. The vent cover she felt certain Pet wanted her to enter sat fifteen feet away in a straight line across the room. If she kept quiet, she could crawl right past the front of his desk and disappear into the other duct. She bit her lip and eased the vent cover open, hoping the man stayed asleep.

A buzz came from above when she'd gotten about halfway. Kiera bit back a shriek of fright and pressed herself against the front of the desk, staring across dingy grey carpet at the room's only door. Two bookshelves stocked with three-ring binders and DVD cases stood on either side of the exit. Voices murmured in the distant hallway.

"Huh? What?" asked the man. "Oh, right. Yeah. System was chuggin' on the data for those reports. Packet traffic analysis for the entire northeast, all eighty-one floors over six months. It's gonna take a while."

Kiera put both hands over her chest, trying to keep her heart from bursting out. The man made a series of "mm-hmms" and "yeahs," likely into a phone.

She almost threw up when a shadow fell over the door in front of her. Kiera glanced at the crawlspace, debating going for it, but the door opened before she had the chance. A twenty-something woman with black hair stuck her head in, mouth open to speak, but froze at the sight of her lying on the floor in front of the desk.

Paralyzed with dread, Kiera stared up at her.

"I didn't know you had a daughter, Eric," said the woman.

"One sec, I'm on the phone. Williams is riding me about the quarterly traffic report... yeah yeah, I'm working on it. I can't give it to you any faster than the damn computer will spit out the data. Unless you want me to just make up numbers."

The woman cringed, gave Kiera a little wave, and backed out.

Eric slammed something on the desk and yelled, "Moron."

*Crap. Crap.* She bit her knuckle. *I'm dead.*

Fluttering key taps continued for a few minutes while Kiera squeezed herself against the desk, staring at the door and asking the Sky Spirits to keep people away.

"Coffee time. Hell with this stupid progress bar." The man stood.

Kiera rolled flat on her stomach, shimmying under the desk as he stomped around it and stormed off without looking back. She caught a glimpse of him in the hallway a second before the door closed, and clamped a hand over her mouth to keep from laughing at his red hair and beard.

*She thought I was his kid! Crap, I got lucky.*

Pet zipped over to the vent. Kiera didn't bother standing, crawling across the room into the duct before anyone else showed up. The passage varied in size from sections she could walk while stooped over in to narrows that forced her to crawl, as well as a few shafts so cramped she had to flatten out and pull herself forward one arm's length at a time. Navigating the Citadel by its ventilation system may have been safe from cameras, but it took forever to get anywhere. Almost three hours after leaving Tessa Zhou's restaurant, she slithered out of a duct into a larger chamber where four telephone-booth sized machines spanned from floor to ceiling. All thrummed and vibrated. The air tasted like metal, cold enough to get her shivering in seconds.

"Over here." Pet glided to the middle part of the left side.

A blast of arctic wind streaming out from the center of the four machines almost knocked her over when she walked past the gap.

"Okay… there *is* such a thing as too much air conditioning." She rubbed her hands up and down her arms, studying the wall. "What am I looking for?"

"You know as much as I do, except for not having an integral map function."

She stuck out her tongue. "It's a wall." She felt around seams and poked her finger at recessed screws, hunting for a switch to open a hidden passage. Her chip must've triggered a sensor somewhere, as a faint *beep* sounded after a few seconds. Kiera stepped back as a door-sized panel swung inward. The enormous chamber beyond, at least double the size of her VR classrooms, held numerous vent ducts and two giant air handler machines. A little past the center, a group of men and women in dirty blue clothes congregated, mumbling among themselves.

Kiera stepped in. The door closed itself behind her with a quiet *clank*. Though soft, the noise attracted attention. All six people stared at her in stunned silence. An e-cigarette dangled from the lip of one dark-skinned man. She raised a hand to wave, but they all went for laser pistols.

With a shriek, Kiera dove behind the nearby air handler and yanked her weapon from the satchel, holding it in both hands. Butt on the ground, her back to the metal, she shivered.

The group mumbled quite a few nasty words.

"Hands up. Come out," said a man. "Drop the gun."

"You first," said Kiera.

A moment passed in silence.

"Kill 'em and let's get out of here," said a man.

Kiera squeezed the rubberized pistol grip. "I don't wanna shoot anyone."

Another man laughed. "Good. I don't want to be shot."

"How did you find us?" yelled a woman.

"Shh. Keep it down," whisper-shouted someone.

"Tessa sent me. She said you could help me."

A woman cleared her throat. "Wait… everyone calm down. Sounds like a damn kid, too. Put the stingers away."

"Little bugger's armed," said a man.

"So are you." Kiera thought about peeking, but chickened out. "Please don't shoot me."

"Weapons down," said the same woman, louder.

Grumbling and whispering followed.

"Zhou said she was gonna send someone who can help us. What's a little kid doing here?" asked a soft-voiced man.

"Well," said the 'weapons down' woman, "why don't we ask her?"

"We didn't last this long trusting random people who stumble right into our supposedly secure base of operations," said Mr. 'Kill 'em.'

"The administrator is a giant douche," said Kiera. "Someone needs to punch him in his stupid face."

Quiet footsteps got closer. "It's all right, sweetie. If any of these idiots point a gun at you, it's going into a body cavity."

Heart racing, Kiera risked a peek at the approaching person. The woman appeared to be in her later twenties or early thirties with a short—almost nonexistent—afro and large brown eyes. As soon as their stares met, the woman's expression of curiosity became pitying.

"Relax you guys. She's terrified. Come on out, sweetie. And 'put it down' goes for you, too."

Kiera leaned farther to the side, peering past the woman at the others. All had replaced their weapons on their belts, save a man with shaggy, brown hair who still held it, but pointed the barrel at the floor.

"All right." She stuck the laser in the satchel and stood, gripping the strap where it met the canvas bag at her hip in both hands.

"Aww, look at her," said an Asian guy, the owner of the soft voice. "She's so small. The heck is Tessa doing?"

"C'mon." The woman put a hand on Kiera's shoulder and guided her to the back end of the room where long folding tables held a mess of computers and other electronics. "There's gotta be somethin' to this kid for Tess to send her our way."

An Indian woman also in her thirties dragged a metal chair over.

With everyone staring at her, Kiera took the seat, satchel in her lap, and felt like a prisoner about to face a firing squad.

"Is this what we've come down to?" asked the shaggy-haired man. The voice matched Mr. 'just kill her.' "Relying on children?"

"Cool it, Rand." The woman who coaxed her out from her hiding place appeared to be in charge. She nudged a metal box closer and sat, eye-level with her. "Why don't you tell us what made that old bat send you here?"

"Are you Second Dawn?" asked Kiera.

Rand almost pointed his gun at her. "Some kinda questions you shouldn't ask in your position."

"Rand!" The dark-skinned woman glared back at him. "Knock it off."

An older teen girl with long, straight black hair stared at her with sad, blue eyes. "Yeah, Rand. She's just a little girl."

"Exactly why it don't make no sense." Rand turned away, pacing around.

"I'm Nata," said the woman in charge. "Why don't we start with your name?"

"Kiera."

"Hello, Kiera." Nata smiled. "Guys?"

"I'm Pash," said the teen.

The woman who'd brought her the chair nodded in greeting. "Preeti."

"Ford." A blond man with slate-grey eyes folded his arms.

"Min," said the Chinese man.

"Well ain't this a damn reunion," grumbled Rand.

Kiera clutched the satchel to her chest. "You guys *are* Second Dawn... you're not like gonna sacrifice me or anything, are you?"

Nata laughed. "Is that what he's saying about us now? No... Our goal is not one of destruction."

"You want to turn the citadels on." Kiera relaxed a little. "I *knew* they were lying about you."

The others calmed as well, standing less rigid. A few even smiled.

"We have been trying to hack into the system for years so we can start the process." Nata shook her head. "We haven't had much luck."

Kiera shook her head. "You won't. There's no connection. Only one terminal works, but if you're hackers... can you help me? The administrator's taken my parents. I need to get them out."

"Oh, that figures." Rand threw his hands up in frustration. "The old woman's gone soft. Kid's not here to help us, she's here beggin' *for* help. Like we don't have enough to do."

Pet, hovering behind Kiera's ear, spoke low so only she could hear. "Now would be a good time to unleash your powers of cuteness."

"Pleeease..." Kiera perked up, eyes wide. "I don't have anyone else to take care of me, and he's going to kill them."

The Second Dawn people, standing in a horseshoe around her, stared.

Kiera shrank in on herself, and tried again in a tiny voice. "Please?"

# CITADEL CORPORATION

Kiera sat still in the chair while the Second Dawn group clustered over by the table of computers, muttering over what to do about her. Rand didn't want to let her leave, fearing she'd blow their cover and ruin everything they'd worked for over the last twenty years. Fortunately, the rest showed more sympathy. Min rambled on about various automated scripts he'd set loose in the system, as well as the odds of infiltrating a police subnet and taking control of security cameras, pacification modules, and cell doors. Ford and Preeti, while sympathetic, didn't think 'the Dawn' could spare the time or resources.

Pash brought Kiera a bottle of water and sat on the box nearby. "I'm sorry about your parents. You must be frightened."

"Yeah. Thanks." Kiera drank a few mouthfuls. "I promise I won't tell anyone about you guys."

"It's okay. Don't pay any attention to Rand. He's our pet paranoid. He wouldn't trust a baby in a crib."

"I heard that. And those babies are shifty." Rand pointed two fingers at his eyes. "Gotta watch them."

Kiera chuckled.

"You look so sad." Pash brushed Kiera's hair out of her face.

"Yeah, well. I am." She sighed. "Lost one set of parents that I don't even really remember... woke up in a nightmare world. Didn't even have any clothes. Got kidnapped by bandits, escaped, adopted by my new parents... and now they're gone."

Pash hugged her. "Aww. It's awful to have such scary dreams."

*She thinks I'm making it up.*

"...so if the kid's right about one terminal, we have to get to the Concordant Sequence if we're going to do anything." Min scowled.

"What?" Kiera perked up. "Min? Did you say Concordant Sequence?"

Everyone looked at her.

"Uhh, yeah. Why?" He quirked an eyebrow.

"That's so weird. I used to have a video game called that." She frowned. "But I guess it wasn't real. Just virtual reality."

Nata swooped over. "What? Virtual reality? What are you talking about? How do you even know about the Sequence? That's about the toppest top secret thing in the whole Citadel."

"Umm." Kiera fidgeted under six sets of staring eyes. "You're probably not going to believe me."

"Spill it," said Rand. "Or we'll strap you down and tickle until you talk."

She gasped.

The Second Dawn people all snickered.

Hoping he'd only teased about that, she took a few breaths and explained everything that had happened so far. Her audience listened with rapt attention, most of their mouths gaping open when she mentioned the tank and being frozen. Once her story ended with her arrival here, she looked up at them, on the verge of tears over her parents.

Min paced around, wagging his finger. "It's bizarre, but it makes sense in a kind of odd way. Tell me more about this game."

"Well... Aliens took over the earth, and there's tons of open-world content. Going from settlement to settlement where the humans are trying to survive. You get missions to do stuff, and you push the aliens back. The last mission is going after General Xax, a big fat blob in the main alien stronghold. It's four levels deep and full of aliens and turrets and stuff. I think it was harder getting *to* the boss than killing him."

"Hang on." Min ran over to the table, rummaged among some e-tablets, and hurried back with one. He tapped at the screen and held up an image of a hallway, straight out of the game. "Do you recognize this?"

"Yeah." She nodded. "That's an intersection on level one, near the start. It's got two laser turrets in the ceiling and a pressure-sensitive floor. There's an alien on each side. Only way through without blowing everything up is to crawl into a vent duct at the corner"—she leaned forward and pointed—"right there."

He swiped to another image. "What about this?"

"Umm. That room's on level two, bottom right corner. I have no idea what those glowing round towers are, but they hurt if you get too close to them. I used to think it was useless 'cause it's a dead end with no loot, but there's a panel in the floor you can climb down to level three with, and skip like half the second floor. I had to do that 'cause the stairs had too much defense to get by without being seen."

Min flipped to another image. "This?"

"Level four. That's the room right after the stairway."

"You've memorized that game, haven't you?" asked Min.

Nata glanced between them, eyebrow raised. "Where are you going with video games?"

Min bounced with glee. "It's... I don't know why, but this kid has memorized the Concordant Sequence."

"Yeah, so? It took me forever to beat that damn game. I—" She stared. "Uhh. I got stuck in virtual reality for ten years playing it over and over until I finally decided to sneak instead of blow everything up. Right before the world melted, my game console told me it was glad I did it because I had almost run out of time."

Silence hung heavy over the room.

Nata appeared lost in thought. Min and Ford stared at each other with awe in their eyes.

Pash kept petting Kiera's hair like a cat.

"Umm," said Kiera.

"I don't really understand why," said Min, "but you've been trained how to run the Concordant Sequence."

Kiera blinked. "Yeah... it's a game."

"No, child." Nata grasped her cheeks like a doting aunt. "The Concordant Sequence is the name of the four floors below the Citadel that hold all the guts of the terraforming machines. If the only way to turn this thing on is to physically go down there, that's huge. Sokolov has put so much security in the way it would be near suicide to try."

"The AI." Min snapped his fingers. "The AI did that on purpose. Making you play that game over and over until you knew every hallway by heart, every duct, every turret."

Kiera fidgeted at the satchel. "Umm, but why me? I'm only a kid."

"Small for the vents?" asked Preeti.

"They shouldn't be *that* tight. I could fit. So could Ford or Pash." Min drummed his fingers on the tablet.

"Who are your parents?" asked Nata.

"Teryn and Mala. They're from Exxo."

Nata shook her head. "No... who gave birth to you in 2030-whatever."

"I was born in 2022. Theresa is my mom, and my dad's Michael. Umm, Quinn."

"Of course." Min jabbed his finger at the tablet screen, reading. "Right here. There's two people named Quinn on the list. Theresa and Michael. Both executives. They would have authorization to turn it on."

Kiera shrugged. "Yeah. Great for them, but they're dead."

"There could've been an inheritance of permissions," said Rand. "Maybe in case something went wrong, or maybe that computer's got a mind of its own."

*Thread Alpha.* Kiera tasted the word on the tip of her tongue, but at Legacy's warning not to tell anyone, she kept her mouth shut.

"If it's gonna change its own rules, why not let anyone turn it on?" Pash continued playing with Kiera's hair.

"That would depend on the programming. It might have a series of preset conditions for stepping down the access." Min shrugged.

Rand picked up a pistol-sized device from the table and walked over to hold it up to her face. Green laser-flash from a small lens made her squint. A few seconds later, it chirped. "Well, damn. Look at that."

"What?" asked Kiera.

"We've been working on a way to bypass the final authentication for the command. Facial recognition of the executive board, likely backed up with an identity chip implant." Nata glanced sideways at Rand's device. "That little box just told me you are a key."

"Double crap." Kiera shivered. "Actually... *triple* crap."

"That is why Anton wants you," said Pet.

Nata bit her lip, grasping Kiera's shoulders. "You're a genetic key to unlock the vault that holds the survival of this planet. That fool Sokolov thinks it'll set off a rain of nuclear explosions."

"I guess I *am* the Child of the Earth," muttered Kiera.

"You cannot let him capture you," said Pash. "He'd kill you and burn you to ashes so no scrap of your DNA remained."

Kiera trembled.

"Don't scare the poor kid," said Rand.

"Too late." Kiera shivered. After a few seconds, she stilled, glancing up at him, utterly confused. "Didn't you want to shoot me an hour ago?"

"Ehh. I'm paranoid, remember?" He winked.

"I don't think he'd kill her." Min shook his head. "If she died, the system might step down access so anyone could do it. I don't think the programming would allow a situation where it became impossible to activate. He'd want to keep her alive as long as possible—and far away from 'the button.'"

"It wouldn't go wide open." Pash shook her head. "Based on what I've seen in the code, I think permission would go to the administrator of Citadel Zero. If that happened, it might as well become impossible."

"This can't wait." Nata stood. "We can't miss this chance. She can guide us through the Sequence."

Kiera clutched her satchel tight. "But... if I do it, he might kill my parents." She weathered their earnest stares for only seconds before bowing her head. "If I don't, the entire Earth suffers."

Pet rubbed against her cheek, emitting a cooing tone.

"I… I can't do that. You can't ask me to do it. My parents don't deserve to die."

"But the whole planet," said Preeti. "You must."

Kiera looked up at them. "Get my parents out first. I don't care. I'm not going to get them killed. I don't *have* to do anything—other than not die—fast. It's not like the planet's getting worse. It'll take decades even after it's turned on. A couple more days won't matter."

The Second Dawn people sighed in unison. Except for Pash, who kept fawning over her, the others drifted off to have a muttered conference. Kiera stared at her lap. *I'm being selfish.* Putting two people's lives above an entire planet gnawed at her guilt, but she couldn't bring herself to abandon them. Her need to be back in her room, even if she baked in the oven-like heat, became painful, a hot ember in her chest.

"Kiera…" Nata approached and held her chin high, an air of authority surrounding her. "The situation we are in is delicate. Anton is doing everything possible to find and kill us. No matter what happens, neither you nor your parents will be in any way safe until the citadels are activated. It is true he may kill them as revenge, but once he can no longer stop you from initiating the process, he has no real need to threaten them anymore. He may accept defeat and release them."

She smirked. "I doubt it."

"We will help you, child. Pash and Ford will go with you and protect you as though you represent every life on the planet. While you go to the Sequence, the rest of us will simultaneously conduct an electronic attack on the detention area holding your parents. They may be free before you reach the terminal."

"It is foolish to delay," said Min. "That man who died in the water processing conduit gave his life so that you can do this. Much could go wrong with wasted time."

Kiera cried into her hands. Guilt at Legacy's death crashed into guilt that she might cause her parents to die, and crushed her straight face. Pash rubbed her back while Pet trilled at her left ear. The odds of her lasting much longer in here without being captured didn't feel too great. Only slightly worse than the odds that she'd have even made it inside in the first place. As much as she wanted to stamp her feet and demand her parents be freed before she did anything else, she had to agree with Nata on one point: none of them had lots of time. For all she knew, Teryn and Mala might already have been killed. If not for the ridiculous thought that the fate of the Earth relied on her running a video game level over again, she would've wound up sobbing. Instead, she stared off into space for a few seconds.

"All right." She looked Nata in the eye. "I'll go."

# 40

# LOADING SCREEN

K iera crawled through a series of ventilation shafts and maintenance tunnels, following Pash and Ford. Pet glided along behind her, content to let the Second Dawn lead. They avoided any chambers with people, preferring two long detours on their way to a scary climb down a narrow metal ladder from the twelfth story to the third. Ford got stuck in a vent too small for him, causing a backtrack and alternate route that came to an unexpected halt when the passageway expanded to a larger chamber containing a deadly-looking fan with blades as long as Kiera stood tall.

"Sec." Pash took a small, round object from a belt pouch and threw it at the fan motor. It stuck against the housing with a sharp *click* like a magnet. Seconds later, sparks lapped out of it at the metal, and the fan shut down.

As soon as the huge blades glided to a stop, they slipped past. Pash reclaimed her disk, which sparked again when it came free, allowing the fan to resume spinning. The group continued down the main air duct for a while before Ford pried open a hatch into a maintenance crawlspace with enough room for Kiera to walk with a slight stoop. That led to a room packed with computer equipment but no desks. Pash picked a physical lock on a hatch cover, which exposed another black-walled maintenance conduit. Ford headed in first, hurrying over to another ladder chamber that led down to the first floor. The conduit out of that room required all three of them to crawl on their hands and knees.

"Now for the hard part," whispered Ford.

He advanced a short distance to a T-junction, went left, and hustled along for a few minutes before a right turn.

"This part is the worst," whispered Pash. "A little over two miles."

Kiera groaned. "Did they get my parents out yet?"

"I'm sorry, kid. No idea. We don't have radios. Even if we did… too much metal in the way."

Crawling for two-point-two miles in a tunnel ranked up there on the list of 'ugh' with taking a hundred-question robotics quiz thirty times. Eventually, the shaft ended at a cube-shaped chamber. Numerous square boxes jutted out from the walls, everything black, suffused with blue light underneath and glowing from the seams between panels. At the chamber's center, cable bundles as thick as Kiera's waist flowed over an edge, disappearing down a hole into darkness.

"Rest." Ford flopped to sit.

Kiera didn't protest. She took a water bottle from her satchel and drank some.

Pash and Ford stared at her.

She pulled out another bottle and handed it to them. "The water's from a collector machine in my village."

"Don't matter." Ford chugged half of it before sipping.

"That's clean. It's taken from the air and filtered. My brother works making the machines and spare parts, too." Pash drank as well.

Kiera tilted her head. "The water collectors are made here? But they look like scrap heaps."

"What the villagers decorate them with isn't made here… but the guts are." Pash smiled. "Usually takes a whole village worth of work-permits to afford one, but repair parts aren't as expensive."

"So, now what?" asked Kiera.

"The hard part." Ford winked.

She frowned. "I thought that long crawl was the hard part."

"Heh." Pash grinned. "He always says that."

Kiera peered into the hole. The wires continued for about ten feet at a forty-five degree angle before diving down into a tube. "In here, right?"

"Kid's smart." Ford smiled.

After everyone had rested, Ford ducked headfirst into the opening, pulling himself along on top of the cable bundle. Kiera sat on the edge of the hole, frozen with nerves for a little while before dropping down to straddle the giant wire like a horse. She stretched forward, following Ford's lead, and shimmied after him. The rustle of Pash climbing in behind her seemed like the loudest sound in the world.

At the point where the wire plunged downward, Ford controlled his fall by releasing his grip of the cable and clamping on in a series of short slides. The first time Kiera tried to let go, she sailed headfirst into his rear end.

"Oof!" said Ford, groaning. "Why do kids always nail me in the balls?" He wheezed in between complaints about his sister's two sons.

"Ow." Kiera gripped the cable with her legs so she could cradle the top of her head. "Sorry. Accident."

"Need a minute." Ford clung to the cable bundle like a koala, gasping for air.

Pash's snickering made him grumble.

Ford cleared his throat a little while later. "Whoo. Okay. I'm good." He resumed sliding forward.

Careful to avoid crashing into him again, Kiera scooted down the steep passage until the conduit leveled out. She crawled for quite some time, arms and legs on either side of the huge cable bundle. Ford stopped short without warning, but Kiera caught herself before running into him again.

"Here we are," whispered Ford. He sat on the cable and pushed a section of ceiling up.

The panel moved with little resistance, rising on a strut that held it open. He grabbed the edges and pulled himself out of the tunnel. Kiera crawled forward, standing in the opening with the floor of a huge chamber at shoulder level. Ford grabbed her hands and lifted her out of the hole.

Kiera stared in awe at the giant doorway in front of them. Patterns of black and silver on the walls, the angles of the bulkheads, hoses and tubes hanging from the ceiling, even the round part in the middle of the door matched the entrance to the final mission.

"Whoa..." whispered Kiera. "This place is exactly like the start of the last bunker in TCS. That's the same door as the alien general's bunker."

Pash climbed out of the floor and closed the hatch. "This is the entrance to the Concordant Sequence.

Behind her, a normal sized door sat at the center of an otherwise plain wall opposite the massive gate, forty yards away. In her memory, it led to a cave that ascended to the wasteland, the open world portion of the game, but here, it held a metal stairwell.

"All right, kid. This is your show. What do we do now?"

Kiera walked up to the big door. "There's a way to get under the floor in the first hallway. Or we can fight past four aliens and a commander."

"There's no aliens, kid," said Ford.

Pash fidgeted. "Maybe they're stand-ins for security robots? The AI wouldn't have put aliens there for nothing."

"Could be to make it a game?" asked Kiera.

"I do not think so." Pet orbited her head. "The aliens represent security robots, human officers, or other defenses. It needed to show you how to avoid everything and not be detected."

She looked back and forth at the door, as wide as her new house. "So, how do I open this? Wave at it?"

"Run," said Pet.

"Don't think that'll help." Ford set his fists against his hips, gazing up at the wall.

Kiera whirled to face the small entrance, terror in her eyes.

"Nobody move," shouted a live man. He wore the same blue shirt and pants as everyone else in the Citadel, but had a heavy utility belt and white stars on his shoulders.

Two other men and a woman followed the first man out from the stairwell with pistols raised. Kiera let off an "Eep!" and darted to the spot on the floor where they'd come in.

A buzz of lasers went off. Ford howled in pain and fell. He lost his grip on his stinger pistol, which clattered to the floor. Kiera skidded to a halt on her knees, grabbing at the hatch panel.

One officer ran toward her, gun pointed. "On the ground, kid! Do it now!"

A female officer pointed a smaller weapon off to the left. A long, thin lightning bolt snapped, connecting the tiny pistol to Pet for an instant. The cube went dark and fell with a *clank*.

"Pet!" shouted Kiera.

"Get down!" roared the man pointing a gun at her face.

Pash, emotionless, sank to her knees and stretched out flat on her front. A group of security robots tromped in behind the live cops from the stairwell. Kiera trembled as she lowered herself to the floor, staring at Pet.

The man ran up on her, pressing a knee into her back as he tugged the satchel away and tossed it aside. He forced her arms behind her back and locked handcuffs around her wrists. The others cuffed Pash and Ford, dragging them to their feet despite the man howling in pain. Blood covered his chest and right arm.

Kiera bowed her head, sniveling and crying as two plastic hands grasped her, one around each bicep. She struggled to look back at Pet as a pair of robots walked her up the stairs. They climbed several flights before entering a hallway with two rows of silver spheres embedded in the ceiling, likely laser turrets. A heavy door at the other end opened to a room with a security desk and two more people in uniform. The androids forced her onward, past another intersection and down a hallway to a room with three desks and a group of security officers and robots, all of whom stared at her in silence. Her captors dragged her over to a set of large sliding doors that opened to a city street.

Three tiny cars with flashing police lights sat out front. The robots escorted her to one. Overcome with dread, she doubled over and threw up, hanging on their grip. Both robots waited for her to stop puking before packing her into the rear seat. She trembled, watching Pash and Ford each loaded into a different car. One live officer got in to drive, a robot taking the passenger seat.

She shied away from the window during a short ride to an elevator that fit the whole car. Neither the cop nor the robot said a word, the rattling of her handcuffs as she shivered and the soft hum of the car's electronics the only sounds. The image of Pet careening out of the air kept replaying in her head, as painful as witnessing Legacy's last stand. Worry about her parents got her heaving again. She coughed and sputtered, but nothing came out of her mouth.

The elevator opened minutes later, and the cop drove out onto another street. She didn't bother looking up, instead staring at her knees. Eventually, the car stopped. Kiera glanced out the window at the wall of a building bearing giant lettering 'Security Outpost 28.' Both cop and robot got out and walked around to the left rear door. She sat frozen in terror when he opened it, unable to process the sounds coming out of his mouth as words. He grasped her arm and hauled her out of the car, much to her surprise, not viciously.

Again, the robot grabbed her right bicep, and the two walked her in past a door, a desk, another door, and a hallway. They stopped in a small room with a shelf, an overhead light, and some locker cabinets. A woman with brown skin and short, black hair looked up, saw her, and stared for a moment in astounded shock. Her confusion lasted only seconds.

The female cop read something on her desktop screen, and muttered, "Is he kidding?"

She got up, approached, and patted Kiera down, squeezing her legs, waist, and gripping her body up under her armpits. After, she went over to fetch something from one of the lockers and walked up behind her.

The woman took a knee and grabbed her leg, lifting her foot off the ground. When her sneaker came off, Kiera looked down. The female officer removed Kiera's other shoe, then secured a second pair of handcuffs around her ankles, the metal cold against her skin above the low socks.

"W-what's that for?" asked Kiera, still unable to stop shaking.

"To stop you from running off," said the male officer. "You're evidently a maximum flight risk."

She swallowed. "I mean... why are you taking my shoes?"

The woman emitted a sigh. "So you don't try and hurt yourself with them."

Kiera's stare called the woman a monster.

Both live cops took hold of her arms. She could barely take a step with her ankles connected by such a short chain, and shuffled, grimacing as the metal pinched. They tolerated the pace for only a moment before lifting her off the ground and carrying her into a hallway full of small, armored doors.

"Ow," she whined. "It's not my fault I'm slow." She kicked her legs back and forth. "You shouldn't have put these on me if you wanted me to walk."

They set her down by a small, heavy door near the end. Cold floor chilled her socks in seconds, seeping into the sweaty fabric. After the man hit a button to open the door, a hand at her back nudged her forward into a cell. A cot took up the whole left side of the room from wall to wall. A square vent hatch near the floor straight ahead looked like it could survive a direct hit from a rocket launcher. The far right corner had a combination sink/toilet sitting below a small shelf at the level of a man's head.

She whimpered. "Please don't."

The door slid closed behind her with a metal scrape.

Kiera tugged at her hands, still locked behind her. "Hey! What are you doing? You're supposed to take these off once I'm in jail."

One set of footsteps squeaked off down the hall.

"You haven't been arrested," said the woman, sounding almost regretful. "You've been abducted."

"Please help me," wailed Kiera.

The woman sighed and lingered a moment outside the door before walking away.

Kiera stood there, staring at her socks, listening to chain rattle behind her. She grabbed the ring around her left wrist, pulling and twisting at her hand. When that didn't work, she shuffled over to the cot, flopped down, and tried to force her hands around her rear end. Too tight, the steel dug into her skin. She wriggled and struggled for a little while before giving up due to pain.

Anger came out of nowhere.

She kicked her legs to sit up and screamed at the door. "You can't treat me like this! I have right—" Kiera blinked. *No... I don't... America's gone. I... don't have any rights.* She shrank into a ball. "I'm in deep crap."

For a while, she stared at the floor, fidgeting at her restraints. She couldn't reach to wipe the tears from her face or the snot bubble from her nose. When the tickle got to be too much, she wiped her nose off on her knee.

The room had no clock or anything close to a window. Maybe the glaring overhead lights would turn off at night. She scooted back into the corner, sitting on the cot. Despair, anger, and fear traded places, and at one point, she wound up laughing. Sliding out of a vent into the desert with no food or clothes seemed far less scary than her present situation. Out there, she didn't have anyone actively trying to kill her... and burn away all traces she ever existed.

She tucked tighter into the corner, lost to uncontrollable shaking and panic.

"Mommy," shouted Kiera. "Daddy!" She broke down, crying out again and again for her parents until her throat hurt.

But no one answered.

# 41

# LESSER EVILS

**K**iera huddled in a ball, staring down hatefully at the restraints on her ankles after crying herself out to blah silence. Her thoughts drifted from the bloody floor in the tank room to how happy she'd been when Dad gave her the poncho. That had felt like her welcome to the family, the first act of her parents providing for her. Remembering the joy she felt at the dress made her super homesick for her ramshackle little bedroom.

That the security people had taken her poncho away from her felt the same as if they'd magically stolen the happiness that came along with her finding a family. Growling, she tugged at her wrists while shouting at the walls, calling everyone here awful. When her energy ran out, she shivered at the memory of Mala jumping in the path of a stunner heading for her face. A random thought of Legacy got her crying in silence again. The man had walked for days knowing he most likely marched to his death. He died to help her, and she'd messed up, wasted it, gotten caught.

They'd even killed Pet.

Growling, she squirmed around trying to get a hand up to wipe her tears, but couldn't reach. Failing that, she flopped flat on the bed and dragged her face back and forth over the blanket. Wanting to sob over a little electronic box made no sense, but she couldn't help it. Pet had been real to her.

Footsteps approached outside her cell. She flipped over onto her back and scooted against the wall, pushing at the bed with her heels, trying to become part of the wall. The door slid open, revealing the same two cops who'd put her in there.

Wild-eyed, she screamed, "No! Go away! Please don't kill me!"

They both spoke, but her panicking brain rejected their words as meaningless warbles. When they walked into the cell, she thrashed and screamed, expecting to be dragged off to her death. The woman wouldn't look her in the eye. The male officer held her down against the cot, grabbed her cheek and forced her to make eye contact.

"Calm down, kid. You're not going to be hurt. It's an interview."

Panting and covered in sweat, Kiera lay there shaking, gazing up at this 'police officer.' His expression held sympathy and regret, but also resignation. The woman peeked at her but turned away, staring at the floor.

"Really." He let go and pulled her seated. "Just talking. No need to be frightened."

The female officer fidgeted at her belt.

Kiera tried to give her a pleading stare, but the woman kept dodging eye contact.

They took her by the arms again, lifting her into the air so her toes dragged along the floor. The thin socks didn't do much for warmth. She coughed and shivered as they carried her past other cells, around a corner, and down another hall to a room at the end.

The male officer knocked.

"Enter," said Anton.

Kiera gurgled. She convulsed but had nothing in her to throw up.

The officer thumped his fist on a panel and the door slid open. A plain steel bench inside against the left wall had two eyebolts sticking up from it. To the right, Administrator Anton Sokolov stood behind a simple metal desk, upon which sat one terminal screen—and an inactive Pet.

Kiera went wide-eyed, staring at her friend. *She might not be dead!* Whimpering, she struggled. "Pet... Please can I have her back?"

The cops ushered her over to the bench and pushed her to sit, one standing on either side of her.

"Thank you. You may wait outside," said Anton.

"Are you sure, sir?" asked the male officer. "Perhaps we shouldn't leave you alone with such a *dangerous* prisoner? Full shackles may not be enough to keep you safe. We should probably lock her down to the bench for your protection. Maybe put a mask on her so she can't bite you?"

Anton frowned.

"Pet," whispered Kiera, "are you okay?"

Her friend didn't move.

The officers exchanged a glance, seeming reluctant to walk off. When Anton cleared his throat, they shuffled out and closed the door. Their evident concern for her made her feel a little better... for a few seconds.

*Why don't they wanna leave me alone with him?* She gulped.

Anton stood with one arm tucked behind his back, other hand poking the keyboard, reading something on the holographic screen. She grabbed the cuff around her right wrist, trying to squeeze her hand past the metal, but it hurt too much.

"Miss Quinn," said Anton over a long sigh. After a melodramatic pause, he looked up with a pleasant smile. "I must say I am not sure how it is you are alive. I admit that when we found your tank and saw the failure status, I felt no small amount of sorrow believing you dead. So young…" He shook his head again. "The files mentioned Theresa had a daughter, but did not reveal your age. I thought it tragic."

Kiera shivered, mostly due to the cold steel floor and bench. Words didn't want to squeeze past the giant lump in her throat.

"I cannot allow you to assist the terrorists in destroying the entire world." He paced back and forth behind the desk. "Though I am relieved to find you are alive."

"I don't want to destroy anything!" shouted Kiera. "I just wanna go home with my parents… even if it's tribal. I don't care!"

Anton's expression hardened. He swiped Pet from the desk and hurled it against the wall, shattering the cube into fragments.

Kiera screamed. When her lungs ran out of air, she lapsed into heavy sobs. The door slid open; the male officer peered in at them, but backed out again. Anton waited, tapping his finger on the desk.

Eventually, she collected herself enough to speak, though her voice warped with sorrow. "Why? Why did you kill her?"

"Now that I have your attention." Anton leaned his weight on his knuckles, making the desk creak. "You are too dangerous to let out of my sight. I do pity you though. How awful it must be to wake one day in a world so much like a nightmare to you."

Kiera stared at the scattered electronic bits on the ground, and wept. Tears she couldn't reach to wipe gathered on her chin, dripping onto her legs. She murmured, "You didn't need to kill her."

"Hmph." He poked the keyboard.

The holographic screen rotated to face her side of the room and expanded to the size of a modest television. Video, likely from a helmet-mounted camera, showed someone walking into a chamber full of cryogenic tanks. Milky white haze surrounded the bodies within, a sign the ooze remained frozen solid. Police robots filed in behind the person wearing the camera. Two other men in blue suits and helmets went from station to station, working at the controls of each tank. The camera panned left and zeroed in on the last tank in the row, the only one showing red lights instead of green. The person wearing the camera walked down the line, knocking over a privacy screen separating the last three tanks from the rest, and approached the red-lit control panel.

*Quinn, Kiera, A.*
*Sex: F DOB: 9 NOV 2022*
*Ingress Age: 11 Chrono Age: 70*
*System malfunction. Cryonic process failure.*
*Subject deceased.*

The view leaned forward. Beyond the white pearlescent haze of frozen gel, Kiera's pallid face stared back at the camera, surrounded by a darkish cloud of billowing red hair. Staring at herself on the screen, eyes closed, mouth and nose covered by black plastic, chilled her worse than the goo had. Obviously, she hadn't *really* been dead, but she certainly looked like it.

A breathy sigh came from the video.

"Now that's a shame," said a static-laced version of Anton's voice. "Poor kid."

"All set, sir." A man walked up to him.

Anton faced the next tank. The gel had gone clear, revealing a woman in her later thirties with short black hair and only a facemask on. When the upper half of the tank rose open, two robots reached in and grasped her by the arms. Buzzing and beeping alarms came from the terminal. Needles tore from the woman's arms and legs, spewing blood. The robots dropped her face down on the floor and shot her over and over again with lasers. Her mother had never even opened her eyes.

Kiera screamed and looked away.

"Pause," said Anton.

She huddled against the wall. Anton walked around the desk and sat beside her on the bench. Two uncomfortably warm hands, soft, smooth, and coated in sweat, gripped her by the jaw and back of the head, forcing her to face the monitor. The man smelled like a leather jacket wrapped around pumpkin spice candles. Kiera tried to curl up so she couldn't see the display, but his grip tightened, holding her head upright.

"Don't close your eyes, dear. I'd much rather not become angry with you."

She struggled, cuffs on her hands and feet clicking.

"Play," said Anton.

From the second tank, the robots extracted her biological father, also limp and wearing only a breathing mask. Kiera sobbed, unable to look away due to Anton's delicate hands keeping her in place. She squirmed and twisted, desperate *not* to watch what she knew was coming. Anton held her tighter, keeping her face pointed at the screen while the robots shot her father full of holes as he lay on the floor. Once the rapid buzzing of lasers ceased, Anton let go.

Kiera recoiled from him and dry heaved until she choked. "You're awful. Why did you make me watch that?"

"Stop playback." Anton stood and walked around behind the desk. Bits of Pet crunched under his shoes.

She flinched with every crack and scrape.

"They were only first for being all the way at the end of the row. Nothing personal. That facility held the entire executive board. Fools. They would've trusted the machines they never bothered to remain awake to oversee. But, I suppose it's their own fault for being elitist. If they hadn't set their system to thaw them out *after* our little bubble formed, I wouldn't have had the chance to delay them." He chuckled. "I bet they never saw that coming."

She scowled at him. "You're lucky I can't move."

"Oh, perhaps I should have the security officers tether you to the bench for my protection." He smirked at her.

Snarling, Kiera leapt to her feet, but lost her balance and fell over sideways, banging her elbow on the floor. "You're lying. The Refuge has existed for a long time."

"Just because I was not the administrator at the time does not mean I lacked forethought. Once I delayed their awakening, I had all the time I needed."

Kiera rolled around to sit up. She grabbed the bench behind her back and hauled herself onto it, still glaring. Never had she hated another human being so much.

"The entire system is flawed. Citadels are not going to heal the planet, Kiera. They're going to incinerate it. Activating the machines will cause a cataclysm. On the off chance they do not trigger thousands of nuclear detonations, they will malfunction. The current processing will shut down, bringing the clouds down on our heads."

"You're lying," mumbled Kiera, no emotion in her voice. She felt like a wrung-out dishtowel. "You like being king and having power."

"I truly hope that you are young enough that you will come to understand in time." Anton sighed. "The idea of harming a child is so distasteful."

Kiera lifted her head, staring at him past a wall of hair. "Would you have killed me if I didn't look dead in the tank?"

"I..." Anton glanced away and down. "Might have brought you here. I doubt you knew of the override before being exposed to those terrorists. You could have enjoyed a pleasant life had you been ignorant of the danger you presented."

She lifted her legs to wipe tears and snot off her face with her knees. "You would've had your robots kill me when you didn't watch."

Anton drew a breath past his teeth. "I am a businessman at heart, so I will offer you one of two choices. Since you are a child and may yet see reason, the first option is that you will live in a secure suite instead of a prison cell.

Your"—he chuckled—"*parents* and those Second Dawn fools will remain in detention, unharmed. Attempt to run away or disobey, they will die."

Kiera glared at him.

"Option two. Despite the threat you pose to the entire planet, I am loathe to consider killing a little girl. You will find a pill waiting for you in your holding cell upon your return. If you swallow it, you will fall asleep and die peacefully. After, I will release those tribals."

Another wave of nausea twisted her gut into knots.

"I will give you forty-eight hours to think. If you refuse the pill, you will be moved to nicer accommodations and treated well. The others will remain in secure custody as a guarantee of your compliance."

She bit her lip, scrunching her feet together. "For how long?"

He smiled a broad smile, free of regret or guilt. "Until one of us dies. I don't care if you want to destroy the world after I'm gone."

Kiera glared, snarling.

"Oh, no." Anton's eyebrows rose together. "The prisoner has become agitated. Whatever shall I do?"

She kept staring at him.

"Anyway. You do not need to make a decision right away." He poked the keyboard and leaned down, raising his voice at the terminal. "We are done here."

The door opened and the two cops walked in.

"Can I have—" Her lip quivered, but she refused to cry more. "P-Pet's remains?"

Anton blinked. "It's a simple companion bot. They're a dime a dozen. If you're still with us in forty-eight hours, I'll make sure you are brought a new one."

"But it's not Pet! You killed Pet!"

Anton rolled his eyes as the cops took hold of her arms.

"Come on, kid," muttered the man.

"No! Please let me keep her. She's my friend!" She tried to kick and squirm, but they dragged her backward out of the room despite her protests, heels dragging. "Pet! No! Please let me have her back!"

A few steps down the hall, when she could no longer see any of the shattered pieces on the floor, she sagged limp and let them carry her away.

# 42

# OPTION THREE

The officers set her on her feet inside her cell. Above the toilet/sink combo, the shelf held a small plastic cup with a green pill in it next to a glass of water. She held her hands up behind her, hopeful. The female cop grabbed the chain between her wrists as if to unlock them, but hesitated, sighed, and let go. Kiera's hands fell against her butt as the door snapped closed.

Kiera bowed her head. Stumbling, she turned to face the door, red-faced, and screamed, "How am I supposed to eat like this?! Or use the toilet?"

Silence.

"Please," she said in a small voice. "It's really cruel to leave me in handcuffs."

She bounced on her toes, fighting and kicking at the chains until she tripped herself and fell sitting. "You're so mean! Take them off!"

A shadow by the door hinted that someone hovered outside.

Kiera growled and struggled for a few seconds before gazing at the 'kill pill' way up on a shelf. She yelled, "How am I supposed to even take that stupid pill with my hands stuck behind my back?"

The shadow at the door glided off.

"Crap." She bowed her head.

For a while, she slouched on the floor, stunned into an emotional wasteland at Pet's death and that horrible video coming within minutes of each other. She'd expected her bio parents to be dead, but *seeing* them killed triggered a cascade of brief camera-flash memories. Smiling Mom. Smiling

Dad. Birthday party here, mall trip there, laughter muted by breathing masks… and long hours home alone.

She stepped on the cuff around her left ankle, pushing and squirming at it, but her efforts only made a red mark. With a grumbling sigh, she scooted over to the cot and pushed herself up onto it. Flat on her back with her feet still on the floor, she glared at the plain metal ceiling. After a while, she wriggled into a sitting position, leaning against the wall. She spent some time throwing hateful glares up at the suicide pill before another wave of sadness came on, and her gaze fell to her sock-covered feet.

Kiera flexed her toes. "Good thing they took my shoes. I might have hurt myself."

In the stillness of an isolation cell, the video of her parents' death played on repeat in her head. Every so often, the *crack* of Pet exploding on impact with the wall interrupted the thrum of laser pistols.

*He's going to keep Mom and Dad locked up forever in rooms like this.* She glanced again at the pill. Could she accept being responsible for that? *He showed me that video to make me sad. He wants me to take that pill.*

Kiera fidgeted at the metal pinning her wrists behind her. "Not like I could get to it if I wanted to." She swished her feet back and forth, tapping her big toes together. "I don't want to take it."

Barely being able to move made her want to run in circles. She absentmindedly chafed at the cuffs for a while, more out of irritation than any sincere effort to get loose.

"Legacy died for this. I'm not going to give up." Sorrow morphed to anger. Every time she pictured Anton's smug smile, she wanted to kick him straight in the teeth.

She rolled onto her stomach, folded her legs up behind her back, and grabbed the metal around her right ankle. Twisting and pulling failed to break it off. She squirmed and screamed in rage, spending another few minutes working up a sweat in a futile battle to force her arms around her rear end.

Out of breath, she collapsed on the cot, panting. Her wrists ached, as did her shoulders.

"Hey!" she yelled. "Please take these off me. It hurts."

*That woman sounded sad when she said I was abducted, not arrested. Maybe she'll feel sorry for me.* She sat up, faced the door, and shouted, "Help me! Please! Don't let him do this!"

Silence hung heavy for a while before she lost hope and curled up on her side. The pill haunted the edge of her vision. The more she tried *not* to look at it, the more she found herself staring at it. Could she live with knowing her mom and dad would be locked up for years? They wanted more kids, but they couldn't have that in jail. If she swallowed that pill, they could be happy again. In only two months, she'd come to love them as much or even more than she had loved her bio parents, and they in turn had become loving and protective. If she took that pill, they'd be devastated. Kiera sniffled and cried at the idea her parents might never be happy again.

She closed her eyes, thinking of Pet scattered across the floor. Her friend had promised she'd never be alone again.

Stuck in a tiny cell, Kiera had never felt so alone.

# 43

# MOUSE IN THE WALL

Sadness and apathy waltzed together in Kiera's mind. She lacked the will to move. In her current mood, if she had to pee, she'd have let go without even getting up. Not like she could use the toilet the way the cops had left her shackled. If she hadn't been the one locked up, the idea of a grown man being so frightened of an eleven-year-old girl that he'd ordered her not only jailed, but kept in chains would have been hilarious.

What did anything matter anymore? Every option stank. She couldn't even trust that he'd actually let her parents go free if she died. A butthead who would smash Pet just because she screamed at him would probably kill them anyway. Face mushed against the cot, she stared at the door, wondering if they would force her to eat like a dog from a bowl, or at least free her hands long enough to have a meal.

*Grr. What's wrong with these people! I'm a kid. Why are they so mean!*

Anger got her sitting upright, fuming. She hopped to her feet and shuffled over to the back corner, glaring up at the pill in its little plastic cup. The shelf at the height of a grown man's head would've been difficult to reach even with her hands free. What would Legacy say if he hadn't died to help her? She huffed, slouching.

"He'd say something like *he* is going to help and *he* is looking out for me. I shouldn't lose hope and stuff."

Grumbling, she paced around her cell in three-inch steps, looking for anything she might use to fiddle with the locks on the cuffs. The cleanliness of the place astounded and saddened her. What had happened that clean and modern surroundings made her long for her pathetic little overheating bedroom that perpetually smelled of wet wood? Again, she sat on the side of the cot and fidgeted at the chains.

"Why did they lock me up so tight? What are they afraid of? I'm just a kid." She sighed. "Not like I can kill anyone with my bare hands and stuff. I'm not gonna grab a knife and go crazy." Her head sagged. "They're seriously being buttheads."

The complete silence, the lack of the familiar faint whirring noise circling around her, made her sad all over again for Pet. Trying not to think about the video of her parents' murder proved impossible. On the screen, her tank still appeared frozen, but that had been over two years ago. *I hadn't been thawed yet.* Of course, it made sense... her parents had brought her to the Citadel Corporation's main headquarters. Thread Alpha would have had access to everything—the pods, as well as the virtual reality suburban paradise in which she'd repeated the same year ten times. *It probably thawed me out and started training me as soon as Anton left... after he killed Mom and Dad.* Reading Mom's last email proved that her parents *had* loved her. They'd only worked so much because they had to save the whole planet.

"I hate him." She bounced in time with repeating, "I hate him," over and over.

As much as she wanted to wipe the tears off her face, the steel around her wrists refused to let her.

"Argh!" she screamed. "Please let me out of these cuffs!"

Her voice echoed around the cell, but no one answered. She struggled trying to squeeze her right hand out of the metal ring for a little while more before sagging, out of breath and defeated. She daydreamed of Teryn or Mala kicking in the door and rescuing her, but they also sat in a similar cell somewhere with no chance to escape. Well... they had *one* chance to escape. If she killed herself, they'd go free.

"No," she muttered. "I'm not gonna let him win. I don't care how long it takes me. I'll never stop trying to escape. And then I'm gonna kick him right in his stupid, perfect teeth."

*Click.*

Kiera wiped her tears on her knee and looked up toward the door. Nothing appeared different. She shifted her gaze left. The reinforced vent grille along the cell's narrow inner wall had drifted open half an inch, enough to cast a shadow on the floor.

"What the heck?"

She got to her feet and hopped over to it. "Who puts a vent like that in a jail cell? This is a bad video game."

*Robots did build this place....*

She wobbled down to her knees and examined the opening. A small, square shaft went a little ways in before bending to the right. It looked like a tight squeeze, but she might be able to make it.

"Okay. Maybe it's not *that* stupid." She glanced over her shoulder at the door. "They didn't plan on putting kids in jail."

Kiera rolled back to sit and hooked her toes over the armored vent cover. A little tugging pulled it aside on hinged metal struts. She nodded hard to the side to fling her hair behind her, then flopped on her chest. Like an inchworm, she squirmed into the tunnel and wriggled around the turn. The hatch closed behind her on its own with a soft squeak.

*Eep.*

The shaft didn't have enough room for her to turn around. The walls touched her shoulders and hips on both sides. She lifted her butt to scoot her knees up, then pushed with her knees to thrust her chest forward. Over and over, she repeated the motion, slithering the length of a sixty-foot shaft. Every ten feet on the right, an offshoot led to other empty cells. When she reached a right corner at the end of the long strut, she rolled onto her side and got past it with a series of short jerky hops.

Another long passage stretched into the distance with squares of light along the left at regular intervals, lined up with more cells. She puffed to get hair out of her eyes and resumed her caterpillar creep.

Voices muttered from the third passage leading right. Familiar voices.

"...so worried about her. They won't tell us anything," said Mala.

"Mom!" yelled Kiera.

The conversation stopped. Grunting and gasping, Kiera wriggled into the offshoot the voices came from and scooted up to the vent plate.

Her parents, still in their tribal clothes, crouched inside a cell no larger than the one she'd been in. Kiera felt a little better that they'd been allowed to remain together, if a tiny bit jealous that neither of them were handcuffed. Mala burst into tears.

Teryn stuck his fingers between the slats. "Take my hand."

"I can't." Kiera sniveled, rattling the chain behind her back. "I'm still cuffed."

"What?" Mala growled. "How dare they! She's a child!"

Teryn looked furious, but contained it. "Forgive me, Kiera. I wasn't able to protect you."

"It's not your fault. *So* many robots. I'm sorry for running."

"You had to." Mala stuck her fingers in the vent at well. "I do not like this place."

Kiera scooted closer until her parents could touch her cheek. Inch-thick square bars kept her from being with them, but as soon as fingertips met her skin, she cried. "I love you guys so much."

"I love you too, child." Mala tried to rub her cheek.

"They will not hold us here. I will die before I let them harm you." Teryn's calloused fingertip brushed her chin.

All three of them wept, Mala sniffling, Teryn shedding tears in stone-faced silence, and Kiera emitting a weak nasal whine.

"This is not even human how they are treating her," said Teryn.

"They gave us medical care." Mala wiped her eyes with her other hand, refusing to pull back from the grille. "Your father's leg is mended... and..." She looked down. "You're going to have a sibling."

Teryn's expression mixed rage with elation.

"You're having a baby?" Kiera growled, trying again to snap the handcuffs. "Ow."

"Yes." Teryn nodded. "What happened to you after we were taken?"

Kiera rushed an explanation, shocking her parents that she'd dared to attempt to sneak into the Citadel... much less done it. She slowed down when she told them what Anton wanted, and about the pill.

"No," said Teryn. "You are not to harm yourself no matter what happens."

"Yes." Mala pressed her fingers tight to her cheek. "I forbid it. It does not matter. This place is small and cold, but clean, and they are giving us real food. We would rather be here and know you are safe than lose you."

Kiera cried from guilt. "I'm sorry. I promise I won't take the pill."

"That's my girl." Her father smiled. "What are you doing in there?"

"The vent opened on its own." She blinked. "Second Dawn... maybe they're helping me?"

Mala looked back and forth between her and Teryn. "What? No... do as the Administrator asks. Perhaps he can be persuaded to put us together."

"I doubt this man is reasonable." Teryn stroked her chin again. "A reasonable man would not give a child two poor choices."

Kiera narrowed her eyes, letting her anger build. "I'm picking option three."

"What's that?" asked both parents at the same time.

"Me stuck in a vent shaft." She huffed, trying to blow hair off her face. "I don't really know where this is going, but it's not option one or two. Someone let me out of the cell and... I gotta try. I can't just sit there."

Mala stared at her.

"There is courage in you. I see it in your eyes and in your heart." Teryn nodded once. "May the Sky Spirits guide you. Do not let them use us to hurt you."

Kiera spent a few seconds adoring the caress of their fingers upon her cheeks. She steeled herself and squirmed backward. Mala struggled to keep touching her face, turning away to weep onto Teryn's shoulder as soon as she could no longer reach. Her father held eye contact, proud and confident.

*As soon as I can't see him anymore, he's going to cry.*

Tears made it hard to see—a significant problem, as she had no way to reach her face to wipe them clear. She thought about how much she hated Anton, holding that anger up as a shield. Rapid blinking got rid of the blurriness in her vision. She wriggled into the longer duct, straightened out, and resumed her inchworm routine.

After long minutes of fighting to crawl, Kiera rasped for breath, sweating despite the cool air in the vent. A little bit at a time, she advanced, pulling her knees up, slipping forward, and so on. Doubt as to who had opened the vent for her circled her head like a buzzard.

*How far do they think I'm going to get in cuffs?*

Kiera grunted and wriggled to the end of the duct. After passing under a vertical shaft that blew cool air straight down on her back, she rounded short right bend that ended at a vent grille, but rather than a prison cell, it looked out into a room with two rows of lockers against the walls and a steel bench in the middle. The far side of the storage area had an open archway with a view across a corridor into another room with cabinets and a table—holding her satchel and sneakers.

*My stuff!* A brief daydream of using her laser pistol to melt the chain between her ankles gave her hope. At least if she could run, she might have a chance to get back to Tessa.

She inched up and examined the grille, a square of inch-thick steel with slots cut in it to form bars, like all the others. A plate that might laugh off a missile.

"Okay… is this where I'm supposed to go?"

She tapped her foot on air, clicking chain.

Someone walked by in the hall, but didn't go into the locker room or the other one. Seconds later, the vent plate in front of her face squeaked and popped open a little on its own. Kiera squirmed forward, pushing the grille aside with her head as she crawled out into the room.

*I gotta move fast.*

She rolled around to a sitting position, pulled her heels back against her legs, and threw her weight forward, bouncing up to stand. Rapid tiny steps brought her across the room to the archway. Leaning against the wall to hide, she peered out. On the left stood a closed door with a window too high up for her to see through. More hallway ran off to the right, with moving patches of blue reflected on the steel floor and distant murmuring voices.

*Go! The vent waited on purpose.*

Kiera started shuffling, but decided to bunny hop, terrified someone would catch her before she could get out of sight. She bounced across the corridor into the room with the table, cabinets, and her stuff. Once out of the hallway, she shuffled around to the back of the table. A somewhat larger vent grille blew cold air into the room from above a counter. *No way I'm getting up there like this.* She scooted up to her bag, which someone left open. The laser pistol remained inside, as did everything else she'd had.

*They didn't take it? I... guess they thought it's fake.*

She glared down at her raw ankles, burning from the handcuffs. *I said I don't want to kill anyone but... I think I'm going to shoot Anton.* Seconds ticked by. She fidgeted at the restraints. *Someone let me get here... what am I supposed to do now?*

At the approaching squeak of rubber-soled shoes on steel floor, she jumped and stared at the doorway.

*Craaaaaap!*

Kiera squatted to grab the knob of a cabinet behind her back. After pulling the door open, she bumped it away with her hip and fell backward, sitting inside. She scooted deeper and gave the door a strong push with her toes, shoving it hard enough that it swung wide open and bounced back closed.

Mere seconds after it shut, someone walked into the room outside.

She froze, not even breathing, and tensed her arms so the chain didn't rattle. A shadow fell over the light leaking in the gap between the doors. The person had walked right up to where she hid.

*Please don't look in here.*

# 44

# HARDWARE UPGRADE

Shivering in fear, Kiera kept herself as silent as she could be and twisted her hand around, desperate to pull it out of the steel ring, but couldn't. *What am I supposed to do? Hop to freedom?* She scowled at the metal locked around her ankles. *Whoever is helping me needs to help more!* The vent path led her right to this room, and another vent she had no way to get to waited on the wall above this cabinet… *I'd fall and break my neck trying to climb up there like this.*

"I was just thinking," said the male cop who'd been escorting her around. "How much of a shame it would be if that kid got away."

Kiera stifled a gasp, gazing at the cabinet door.

"Yeah. Such a tragedy," said the woman. "I really ought to stop keeping my handcuff key in the same pocket as my noseblow rag. It's careless. I might drop it and not realize."

A tiny metal clatter followed.

Someone blew their nose.

"Yeah, that is kind of dumb," said the man.

Kiera's eyes widened. *She dropped it on purpose!*

"I keep losing the damn thing whenever I sneeze."

The man sighed. "I was getting worried there for a bit."

"Yeah." The woman grumbled. "It's hard to take a pill in cuffs."

Kiera stopped trembling. The metal locking her hands together went from an intolerable sense of captivity to something like a mother holding their kid back from running into traffic. She glanced at the second pair on her ankles, wondering if these two would help her if she showed herself. She started to nudge the door open.

The cabinet creaked from someone leaning on it—right by her, pushing the door shut again.

"I wish we could do more," said the man. "But… those damn robots."

"Yeah." The whole cabinet creaked as more weight pressed into it. "I hate those things, too. They killed Rick when he refused to grab her a day ago. I can't believe Sokolov would turn those things on us." A sneaker tapped the ground nearby.

"Insane. You know, I think I'm going to catch up on *Planet Raider*. That kid's kinda small, in full restraints, and locked in a cell. No sense inspecting it every hour. I doubt she'd escape."

"Yeah, seriously. Those cells could contain a security 'bot. No way a little girl's getting out." The female officer tapped her foot a few times more before muttering, "Sorry…."

Kiera kept quiet, holding on to a moment of silent gratitude. Those two never seemed happy about having to keep her prisoner. Hope bloomed in her heart. She had a way out: a key, her stuff right there, a vent passage. After that, who knows? Maybe something would turn up, and crawling in a vent definitely beat her current situation. Another door might open on its own, or lights, or some kind of message… The two cops walked out, discussing *Planet Raider*, a video game from the sound of it.

She waited four breaths before nudging the cabinet door open with her knee and scanning the room. A glint a few feet away almost made her yelp with glee. Kiera scooted across the floor and stretched to pick up a small key before fumbling with it behind her back. Metal scratched on metal, searching for the keyhole.

*Come on… Come on…* She stared at the door, shaking from anxiety. *Why didn't they just let me out? Do they have cameras on them or something? Dammit!* Having the key in hand and still being trapped frustrated her near to screaming.

The vent above the cabinet rattled.

"I know, I know," she whispered. "Little stuck here."

She stretched her legs out straight, examining the cuffs on her ankles to locate the keyhole. A little finger probing at the one around her left wrist found it, and she managed to slot the key. One twist popped it open and she whipped her hands around in front before unlocking her other arm. After freeing her legs, she jumped up and grabbed her sneakers.

The vent rattled again.

"Working on it," muttered Kiera as she stepped into her shoes and pulled the Velcro tight.

She checked the laser, which appeared functional, and blinked. *They knew. They let me keep it.* Kiera grinned. *They're real cops. They hate Anton, too.* For good measure, she hid the cuffs and key in the cabinet. Another rattle came from the vent. Grumbling at being rushed, no matter how necessary, she climbed up onto the counter and grabbed an ordinary, flimsy aluminum vent cover.

Two feet in, a white and silver cube, about the size of a Rubik puzzle, hovered on a bloom of cyan light.

"Hurry," said Pet.

Speechless, Kiera flung the vent hatch up and scrambled in. She speed-crawled over to the cube, pounced on it, and hugged it to her chest, weeping with joy.

"I promised you'd never be alone," said Pet.

Kiera cried harder, muffling herself by hiding her mouth in her elbow.

"I am happy to be with you again, but you do not have time to cry right now."

She gasped, sucked in a breath, and nodded. "Okay." Again, she squeezed the little robot tight. "How did you come back? I saw you break into little pieces."

"Close the hatch."

Kiera leaned back and pulled the vent closed.

"This is a different unit, but Thread Alpha restored my particular sentience and memory. Basically, same brain, new body. It's even a little bit of an upgrade." Pet zipped into the vent.

"Is he opening these vents for me?"

Pet slowed so she could catch up. "I'm not sure. It could be... or the Second Dawn, or maybe those two officers."

She grumbled, rubbing the sore red marks around her wrists. "They could've unlocked me instead of dropping the key. What if I got caught?"

"If they are seen helping you...."

"Yeah. Robots shoot them." She scurried onward. "I'm going to kill him. Where is he?"

Pet swiveled back and forth. "No. Too much security. As much as the police officers may agree with your decision, if you kill him, they will be forced to arrest you for it. Follow me."

Seething, but deciding to accept that murder wouldn't work for the best, Kiera crawled after her friend, shedding the occasional tear of joy along the way. Pet drifted past turn after turn, but at least she radiated enough light to see. After what felt like a mile of duct, the little cube floated out into the middle of a large vertical shaft. The opposite wall had two tracks with large teeth to engage gears.

Kiera halted, fingers clutching the edge, and stared down a channel so deep her stomach did a backflip. Two more gear tracks ran down the wall she leaned out from. "Ugh... how high up are we?"

"Seventy-eighth floor."

She leaned back. "Am I supposed to climb those tracks?"

"No. Please do not try that. They are lubricated and you will fall. Wait for now."

"Cool." She shifted around to sit and rubbed her sore ankles. "I have the worst luck in the world. I wake up on a dead planet, and in like three months, I get kidnapped *twice*."

Pet nuzzled her cheek. "You are important."

"I'm so glad you're okay." She hugged the cube.

A sad trill came from the little cube. "I am sorry about your parents."

Kiera gasped. "No...."

"Oh." Pet bobbed up. "Not them. I meant your... old parents. I know he showed you that video."

"Yeah." She stared down. "I always kinda knew they were gone. But seeing it...."

"They would have wanted you to finish what they tried to do for the Earth."

Kiera shot a sideways glance at Pet. "You don't need to talk me into anything. I'm going to mash that button like it's Anton's fat face."

"He's not fat."

She started to glare at Pet, but wound up giggling.

"Get ready," said Pet.

Kiera shifted to her hands and knees. "What am I ready for?"

Loud whirring came from the shaft, along with a strong wind that pushed her a few inches back. She fought her way forward to peer out, but Pet whacked into her forehead before she could.

"Stay back!" yelled Pet.

Kiera fell on her seat, holding the spot. "Ow. That hurt!"

An elevator cab shot past, going up. It stopped soon after, leaving the shaft silent.

She squeaked. "That would've hurt."

"You would not have felt much."

"That doesn't make me feel better." Kiera sighed out her nose.

"Be ready."

When the elevator noise resumed, Pet's light flickered. The cab drifted downward, far slower than its ascent, and came to a stop two feet below the vent. Kiera took the hint and jumped out on top of it. Four metal housings, two per side, held gears as big as car tires, locked in the tracks.

Pet floated over to her. Her gaze darted around components before she spotted a set of reinforcing spars bracing a big box in the middle. She wedged herself into them, wrapping one arm under and holding on. *If this thing goes down as fast as it went up, I'm going to go flying.*

It did drop fast, but not enough to make her float. Her hair bloomed straight up in the breeze wrapping around the capsule. Pet chased the elevator down, its light flickering. After a moment or two, the elevator slowed to a graceful stop.

"What is wrong with this stupid thing?" yelled a man inside it. "This isn't the damn floor I hit." Loud plastic button mashing followed. "Hello… stupid thing. Level twenty-two!"

Pet drifted to the side by another duct opening. "Hurry."

She disentangled herself from the spar while the man kept punching the button, and managed two wobbly steps before a bad feeling made her leap at the duct a split second before the elevator dropped out from under her. She seemed to hang in midair for a moment, the whole world frozen in time. Her fingers caught the edge of the air duct as her body slammed against the wall beneath it.

"Oof," she barked.

Pet zipped down, trying to get under her backside to push her up.

Kiera stared up at her hands, breathing hard. *If that elevator comes back up, I'm spaghetti sauce.* She hunted for a foothold, but her sneakers squeaked on the smooth metal wall, offering only a little support. She let out a muted growl and pulled. Pet kept ramming into her from below, trying to shove.

"You're… not… helping," gasped Kiera. She hoisted herself up until she got one leg into the tunnel. A shove with her knee launched her forward, flat on her chest, and she scurried deeper into the passage away from the hole, worried the elevator would run her over. "Ouch."

Pet appeared by her face, brushing against her cheek. "You should have stayed on the elevator. I could have made it come back. Jumping was risky!"

"Bit late." She curled up and cradled her fingers to her chest. "Can I lay here for a while?"

"A few minutes to recover is okay, but you must finish before Anton is aware you are not in that cell anymore."

"Yeah." She closed her eyes, picturing her parents sitting in jail because of her, Mom with a baby coming. "I'm good. Where to?"

The elevator shot by the opening a few feet away, blasting her with a powerful rush of air. She curled up and shuddered, not wanting to know what it would've felt like to be hit by something that big moving *that* fast.

Pet floated into the dark. Kiera's sore fingers protested being used so soon, but she weathered the pain and forced herself to keep moving. A left turn less than a minute away from the elevator shaft led to a fan chamber. Powered off, the massive air mover drifted like a one-ton pinwheel in a faint breeze. Pet didn't slow down, zipping between two blades. Kiera skidded to a stop and tried catching the drifting fan to stop it, but it threw her on her butt. She scrambled upright again and whined at the dangerous obstacle. It kinda felt like one of those swinging axe traps in *Shadow Kingdoms*, so she took a step back and observed the timing of the blades, each one the size of a car hood. Begging the Sky Spirits that it wouldn't turn on, she held her breath and leapt forward when the moment felt right. With a squeal, she jumped through a gap, suffering only a light bump to the shoulder. Pet waited by an opening behind the fan. As soon as she approached, it darted in. Kiera followed into another duct tall enough to let her run upright. Three turns later, she wound up again in a small shaft, crawling on her hands and knees. Midway down a fifty-yard conduit, Pet stopped in front of a metal grille that blocked the way.

"This is not on the map, umm." The cube drifted side to side. "It shouldn't be here."

Kiera prodded the metal grid. "It doesn't look like it can open, it's welded. Hang on. I got this."

She backed up, pulled out the stinger pistol, and aimed between her knees at it. Twelve shots melted the bars where they met the wall, and the barrier fell over with a loud *boom* that echoed back over itself three times.

"Oops."

Pet bobbed up and down. "Maybe they'll think it's a mouse?"

"Big mice." She put the laser away.

"Squeak," said Pet.

Kiera eased herself over the hot grating and followed Pet to a corner and into a section of duct that ended at a brightly lit mesh vent cover. She crawled to the opening, gazing out at a room with a white tile floor and a ton of huge computer cabinets. Men and women too far to the side for her to see chatted about someone's new baby.

"Stay calm," said Pet at low volume. "The floor ahead is raised. When I say 'now,' crawl out, lift the first tile up, and go under the floor."

She nodded.

Pet hovered against the mesh. Kiera tensed, twitching. *One mess up and he kills them... me too probably. He wouldn't have to kill them, but he would just to make me cry.*

"Now," said Pet.

Kiera pushed the vent open and scampered out into a freezing room with a floor of large white tiles. She dug her fingers in the closest seam and lifted, exposing a two-foot tall crawlspace full of blue network wires. She slid in feet first and lowered the tile back in place over her head. Cables ran everywhere, crisscrossing the room around pylons supporting the raised floor. Constant hissing came from thick white plastic tubes.

Pet floated off.

Someone walked overhead, making the tiles shift one after the next. She turned, following the sound of motion with her eyes as they passed. The baby conversation changed to boring stuff about processor monitoring and bandwidth optimization. Kiera crawled forward, freezing still wherever someone walked close.

Pet bobbed up and down near the corner on the right.

She navigated the forest of pylons and cable snakes, pleasant compared to her inches-at-a-time escape from her cell. A puff of dust hit her in the face when a foot came down heavy on a tile in front of her. Kiera clamped her eyes shut.

*Do not sneeze. Do not sneeze.*

Fast losing that battle, she curled up on her side, both hands clamped over her mouth and nose. The technician above her shifted their weight back and forth, making the tile slide and click. They lingered, probably working on something and not likely to move any time soon. She grumbled in her head, but decided to hope he or she wouldn't notice her. One hand pinching her nose, she hurried to where Pet floated over a metal trapdoor with a code panel lock.

She glared at it before giving her friend an urgent glower.

The cube bounced and spun, acting happy.

Still squeezing her nose, she tilted her head.

*Beep.* The panel lit up green.

"Ooh," she whispered.

An unborn sneeze scrunched her face and made her eyes burn when she let go of her nose to grab the hatch with both hands. She couldn't open it all the way without pushing a floor tile up, but managed to shimmy underneath it onto a ladder. Barely able to see, she eased herself down, lowering the trapdoor over her head without a sound. As soon as it closed, she buried her face in the crook of her elbow and sneezed six times.

Once her head stopped spinning, she snot rocketed to the side, then climbed down about ten feet to a chamber at the bottom with black vented cabinets. Everything around her hummed with electrical power infusing the air with the flavor of tingly metal.

"I shouldn't touch anything in here, right?"

"That's a good idea." Pet crossed the room to a door. "We are close now. Here. By the floor."

She walked over.

Pet indicated a tiny shaft that carried cables into the next room through the wall. She sat and tied the satchel strap around her left ankle before pulling herself in, tugging the bag along behind her.

"Only a kid could fit in here and it's even tight for me."

Pet, inches in front of her face, emitted a happy beep. "They did not expect someone your size to do this. Go straight here."

She dragged herself past a four-way intersection. Cables branched off in each direction.

"Next one, go left."

Fifty feet later, she squirmed around the corner and continued a short ways into a small chamber where wires connected to cabinets covered in blinking lights of red, green, and orange, saturating the room with color. She took the satchel off her leg, stood, and put it on her shoulder again. The top of her head came within an inch of the ceiling, but the room appeared to be a dead end.

"Now what?" she whispered.

Pet perched at her shoulder. "Up. There, at the corner."

She walked over, grateful for the short moment of not crawling or slithering, and pushed at the ceiling. Another hatch flipped open. Kiera grabbed the edge and pulled herself up into a huge open chamber, standing at the left side in the shadow of a bulkhead. The great door where the cops ambushed them earlier stood a little ways behind her, still closed, but she'd already gotten past it.

A gasp of awe leaked out of her when she faced forward and stared at the spitting image of the loading screen for *The Concordant Sequence*. No matter how many times she'd seen it on her giant screen, a video game couldn't convey the massiveness of physically being there. An overwhelming presence of technology pressed in on her from all sides, the air emitting a constant thrum of colossal machines. Static crackled on her tongue, filling her mouth with a coppery twang.

She took a hesitant step forward, gazing around at everything. "Whoa. This is it... This is exactly it."

Pet hovered beside her head. "Are you ready?"

Kiera thought back to her hours and hours of time spent bashing her head into a wall trying to beat the final level. She knew every room by heart. "Yeah. I've been practicing this for years."

# 45

# SAVE GAMES

**K**iera gazed down the first corridor of General Xax's base, a T-junction. Two laser turrets in the ceiling waited for her around each corner, plus whatever reality would substitute for video game aliens. The turrets on level one had a short detection radius, enabling her to take them out with rifles before they even opened. She crept a few paces forward, stopping before the turrets came into view past the walls on either side.

"My equipment was better last time... but I know the layout." She hesitated. "And... I'm a kid, not a GSF soldier."

"GSF?" asked Pet.

"Galactic Special Forces. For the game." She shrugged. "It's a shooter. They don't put a lot of effort into the backstory."

"Why do you look angry?"

Kiera held up the laser. "Because I want to blow something up to let off stress. I'm really mad about being locked up for... however long I was in that cell."

"Two hours eighteen minutes," said Pet.

"That's it?" She blinked. "It felt like all day."

Pet rubbed against her shoulder. "Given the circumstances, that is understandable."

"I can't blow the crap out of everything. The game made me keep doing it over and over until I managed to get the stealth run perfect. Blasting stuff is more fun, but real life doesn't have save games. There's auto-turrets, alien—I mean robots, laser grids, pressure plates. If this place really is like TCS, I'm going to die."

"You're not alone." Pet pressed against her arm. "Be smart. Be invisible. If you get spotted, Anton will know you're loose."

"Yes, and then he'll hurt my parents."

Kiera backed up a few steps and went into a vent duct on the wall to the left. She bypassed the first intersection and edged up the grating on the other end where it met an L in the corridor. From her stealth run, she remembered an alien patroller walking back and forth in the section of hallway she observed. Pressure sensors in the floor lined up with the light fixture pairs on the wall. They looked identical to the game, so she assumed the floor would work the same way.

In the game, one alarm equaled failure of the 'perfect dark' achievement. Here, one alarm equaled dead parents.

Instead of an alien, a security robot walked into view, following the same path the video game trooper did. *I hope these things are as stupid as the blobbies.* The robot advanced toward her hiding place at the corner of the hallway. She tensed, holding her breath as it got closer. It kept going to her right without hesitating.

Kiera counted five footsteps after it passed, knowing that would be the earliest point the alien wouldn't see her. She darted out of the vent and leapt over the floor tiles between the light pairs. After two pressure-sensitive areas, she barged through a door on the right, entering an office with desks in it. She climbed up to stand on one, pushed a panel in the ceiling open, and hauled herself up into a crawlspace above the room.

After reseating the panel, she rested a moment, dusting her hands off. "Crap, this is tiring for real."

Pet floated nearby. "What were you expecting?"

"Video game characters do all this crazy stuff and never slow down. Like run six miles and climb everything and they never get tired or worn out. This is really hard." She froze. "Oh crap. The pipe is going to *suck!*"

"The pipe?"

"I gotta walk across this ginormous room on top of a big pipe. There's like a billion aliens on the floor. Trying to clear it Kiera-style used up all eight rockets, two demo charges and sixteen grenades, and I still barely made it out the other side with thirty hit points."

"Kiera?" asked Pet.

"What?"

"How could you possibly have carried all that?"

She rolled her eyes. "It's a game."

Pet flickered.

"Don't say it." She patted the cube. "I know this isn't. And I don't have any missiles, grenades, or health packs. I'm gonna stealth it."

Pet chirped.

Kiera crawled across the ceiling space, bypassing several rooms before lowering herself down a hole in a dead-end corridor. She dangled from her fingertips until she stopped swinging back and forth. The drop left her no way back up into the ceiling without a ladder, but didn't hurt much. A quick dash forward and a right turn entered the start of a U-shaped hallway with the stairs down to level two at the middle of the curve. If she went there, two turrets on either side plus a pair of huge defense robots would force a mini-boss fight before she could get to the door. However... perfect dark stealth run. She crept forward five steps and felt around the wall until she found the seam right where it ought to be.

One push caused a concealed hatch to pop open. She shimmied into a maintenance conduit the instant approaching robot footsteps started in the hall. The hatch closed automatically a breath and a half before the robot walked by outside. Pet pressed against her back and buzzed like a smartphone on mute. Trembling?

The duct ran parallel to the corridor, filled with exposed circuit boards and flat cables. She hurried to a left bend that connected to the stairway behind the door, skipping the combat. Kiera scrambled down the stairs, rounded the corner at the bottom, and went down the second half.

"Stick close," whispered Kiera. "There's a turret in the hall that I have to sneak past. It spins back and forth. Gotta wait 'til it points to the right, then run to a doorway on the left."

Pet approximated a nod.

Kiera peeked past a narrow strip of window on the side of the door. Sure enough, the turret, a ball in the ceiling with a laser-pistol-sized mechanism sticking out of it, panned side to side. For the few seconds the sensor on the front faced away, she'd have a chance to run to the lab. Or at least, it had been a lab in the game. She didn't care about clicking on computers for tidbits of backstory or picking up every scrap of ammunition or health packs—not that anything of the sort existed in reality.

She watched the turret sweep three times before feeling confident the pattern matched the game. As soon as it rotated past its visibility limit a fourth time, she hit the button for the door and sprinted, sliding into the next room with two seconds to spare before the turret caught her.

"Whoa." She tried to catch her breath. Fear wore her out more than the actual running.

Kiera counted seconds, timing a two-robot patrol while imagining the comic banter the alien soldiers would often share before she shot them in the head. The instant they reached the point that would give her the most time, she dashed out the door and huddled against the wall of the corridor where black metal grating ran along the floor at the edge. She stuck her fingers into the grid and lifted a section out of her way so she could slip under it into a trench full of wires and cables. Pet glided in after her, and she lowered the metal plate back in place. Safe from the view of patrolling robots, she crawled along the gutter down the corridor. In the game, this hallway had huge windows on both sides looking in on huge labs where dozens of aliens worked. Despite being weak in comparison to the soldiers, they would still ruin the Perfect Dark achievement if they spotted her, and set off an alarm.

She didn't bother looking to see if the lab 'aliens' existed, as it felt kinda pointless to have so many robots standing around for real, but the shuffle down the conduit kept her out of sight of patrollers and six turrets. Kiera crouched at the end of the trench, peering up through the grating at the next patrolling sentry. She counted it taking seven steps past her position before emerging and darting into a huge, dark room.

Three rows of giant columns, glowing neon green—the universal video game symbol for radioactive badness—stretched to the far wall. She'd thought the game developers considered themselves slick for making a dangerous room that appeared to have no reason to go in, and using it to hide the passageway that bypassed most of the second floor. Most players who commented on the forums didn't even bother with this room due to the radiation damage and lack of anything worth picking up, but she'd pathed the room so much she knew how to navigate the maze using wider gaps where the spacing between the towers varied ever so much. For an instant, she felt selfish for not posting her secret, but then sighed.

*None of them were real. I'm the only person who ever played TCS.*

"This better not be actual radiation or being a few inches closer won't matter."

"I don't sense any radiation, but those pillars are carrying a lot of voltage," said Pet. "If you get too close, you may experience a dangerous shock."

"Bag." She lifted the flap. "You're not getting zapped out of the air again."

Pet landed in the satchel.

She walked back and forth outside the front row of columns, trying to convince herself it matched the game. The more she looked at it, the less sure she felt. *I'm overthinking. Everything has been exact. TCS didn't exist. Thread Alpha was teaching me how to find it for years.*

Between the third and fourth columns, she crept forward, keeping her arms tight at her sides. After passing five rows, she went left one column and forward three more. Since nothing bad happened to her, confidence grew. After going left all the way to the wall, she flattened against it and advanced three rows. Back into the grid she went, past nine pillars before advancing six. Left two, and forward the last three to open space.

"Okay. I can breathe again."

Pet poked out from under the flap. "Nice."

"What the heck are those things?" She put a hand to her chest, trying to calm down.

"Power capacitors, I think. Huge batteries."

"Oh." Kiera squatted by the hidden trapdoor. Hitting an 'interact with environment' button on a game controller didn't translate well to having to find the switch in real life, but a few minutes of poking around worked She stuck her finger in a slot between two floor tiles and pushed a rubber button.

A hatch opened on a motorized strut. She dropped onto a ladder, climbed to the bottom, and dusted her hands off on her shirt in the middle of an empty security office. Beyond a single desk full of monitors, a large window looked out over an enormous chamber. Instead of aliens, hundreds of robots swarmed around. They appeared much different from the security units, all shiny metal with no plastic, and only vaguely human in shape. Some even had four arms.

"Level three." She grinned. "Now I only have to get past nine hallways and a huge pipe."

"You're not alone."

Kiera hugged Pet. "You're awesome. I know you're only a little cube but… you're my friend."

"I'm glad. You're my friend, too."

She skipped searching the desk to see if the giant medpack would be there. The doorway opened to a metal hall that looked in no way designed for humans. No effort had been wasted on appearance, and the sight of it for real caused a shiver of dread. She may as well have been the last human left alive on a derelict spacecraft floating into a black hole.

Pet provided the only light.

"Wow," she whispered. "It wasn't this dark in the game, but the walls look just like it."

The first stretch of corridor had no threats, the same as in TCS. She crawled into a round wire conduit at the corner, concealed behind a removable panel in the wall. Something she'd ran past countless times in 'blow stuff up' mode without ever realizing it had been there. Of course, the massive stash of ammunition and health packs hidden inside didn't exist in reality. *This looks like the game, but it's so cramped. A soldier wouldn't fit in here…* She blinked. *Thread Alpha made the game for* me. *It showed me a path only a kid could take!* She crawled to the end, unsure if she felt special or used. *If I was older, would I be shooting my way in?*

Two ducts later, she climbed into the ceiling and balance-beam walked across a metal spar between foam drop-ceiling tiles. An army of robot footsteps clicked and clattered below her. *Oh, that sounds like a buttload.* She glanced down at her feet. Of all the times she'd played TCS, she'd never messed up this part and fallen in. She had no idea what the room underneath her looked like, and from the sound of it, did not want to learn.

She crept forward extra slow, holding on to bracing struts as much as possible, heading for a wide, rectangular vent in a separating wall to the next chamber. Her legs cramped up from the hunched over, careful walk, and after crawling past the hole in the wall onto the roof of a raised observation deck, she sprawled flat to rest.

In the game, the giant room below her had two sniper aliens. She *hated* those since their rifles outranged hers. The pipe walk ticked her off because on a Perfect Dark run, she didn't get to kill those annoying snipers. From her perch, she stared out at the fat purple tube wide enough for an adult to walk inside with plenty of headroom. It crossed the main chamber at the center of the third floor. The area below teemed with worker robots tending to giant machines of mysterious function. *Terraforming stuff.* Some appeared to be tanks of fluid, perhaps where all the animal embryos and stuff waited. Where the snipers had been in the game, reality offered a pair of large security cameras.

Kiera sat up. "Well, at least those won't shoot me. Okay. I'm wasting time."

She got to her feet and crept to the edge of the angled roof. From there, she jumped up to hang from a metal spar and climbed to a grating. It didn't look intended as a walkway, more of a support, but it served the purpose and brought her to the start of the giant pipe.

"Oh, crap. I guess it's a good thing I'm not terrified of heights."

"That is good," said Pet.

Kiera smiled weakly. "I'm terrified of falling."

She stepped onto the purple metal. The huge tube emerged from the wall below her and went about sixty feet into the room where it curved to the right in a short S bend before turning back to the left, connecting to the far wall. A minor detail for a video game character, but the absolute worst part of this stealth run for a real person waited at the opposite end. She'd have to jump from the pipe to the top of a wall, and climb down a shield plate surrounding some giant alien machine—which her current viewpoint suggested would likely be the terraformer core.

"That's gonna hurt."

"What?" asked Pet.

"The jump at the end of this pipe."

"It will hurt if you miss?"

Kiera chuckled. "No. If I miss, I won't feel a thing."

"That's not funny, Kier." Pet wobbled.

"I'm kidding. It's only twenty or thirty feet. I'll probably break both legs and my back and scream so hard I faint."

Pet pushed into her chest. "Stop then. It's too dangerous. Thread Alpha must have made a mistake."

"Maybe it's a representation. I'll be careful. I'm too far in now. Those robots will kill me."

Pet trilled, sprouting its grippy claw to tug at her sleeve, trying to keep her from continuing. "Maybe you shouldn't."

She walked out onto the pipe, holding her arms out for balance. Warm air swirled around the machines below, occasionally blowing upward, blasting her with an overpowering chemical smell that watered her eyes. Pet stopped pulling on her shirt, retracted the grabber, and hovered close to her shoulder. Every twenty feet, a collar wrapped around the pipe connected to a telephone-pole-sized strut bracing it to the ceiling. She allowed thirty seconds of rest each time she hugged a support post. Segment by segment, she advanced, refusing to look down.

"Round purple road. Nothing but flowers and unicorns under me. One foot in front of the next."

Kiera negotiated the first bend of the S and advanced to the closest post after it. She shimmied around it while clinging, faced forward, and advanced. Six steps later, her right sneaker shot out from under her on a wet spot. Arms flailing, she fought for balance and fell on her chest, sliding to the left. She scrambled, hands squeaking on the pipe, and managed to stop herself from falling off. Two seconds later, a sharp *splat* echoed up from below.

Her heart slammed in her chest. Barely able to think or breathe, she pulled herself back to the top of the pipe and held on, flat on her belly.

"You're safe," whispered Pet.

She closed her eyes, shaking. "What was that noise?"

"A water bottle fell out of the satchel and burst on the floor."

"Crap."

"The robots are gathering around it. I don't think they know what it is." Pet drifted to the side. "One has picked it up and is studying it."

"Get back!" whisper-shouted Kiera. "Before they see you glowing."

Pet zipped over and landed in front of her face. She lay motionless on top of the pipe, clinging while listening to the shuffle and clatter of robots milling around below. Something as simple as a bottle falling out of her bag could kill her. Worse, that minor error stabbed a knife into her confidence.

Ever since she'd slithered out of a vent into the desert, she'd clung to a tiny scrap of hope that everything had been some bizarre dream or perhaps she remained in virtual reality. No video game character ever dropped a random inventory item at an inconvenient moment. No matter what kind of crazy leaps, rolls, or acrobatics they performed, video game characters never had stuff fall out of their bags. One random event cemented reality around her—the reality of being twenty feet in the air over a hard, metal floor and an army of killer robots. She twitched whenever it felt like she started sliding off the pipe again.

Pet nudged her cheek, speaking in such a low volume its voice barely made it past the machinery roar from below. "The robots are back to routine. I think you can continue. None saw you, but they were looking up for a while."

She kept her eyes closed, cheek to the pipe, too frightened to move.

"Kiera?" asked Pet. "Are you hurt?"

"No. Scared."

Pet nudged her cheek again. "I'm here. Don't be frightened."

"It's real," muttered Kiera. "Water bottles don't fall in VR. No one programs that."

"And brave girls don't fall in real life."

Kiera whimpered into a chuckle. "Yeah, we do. A lot. Thanks for trying to make me feel better. I'm not that brave. I'm scared so bad right now."

"Brave girls get up when they fall. Weak ones stay down."

She shivered, still unable to bring herself to move.

"The cave led into the mountain to a stairwell carved by the ancients. It descended far into the depths of the world, deeper than anyone had gone in a thousand years. Alonna knew the shadow walkers had followed them up the trail, and would discover the door soon. The Kingdom of Thalinor's only hope rested in her hands..." Pet continued narrating the story of a sixteen-year-old with a wizard mother and pirate father.

Kiera smiled a little, thinking the girl too perfect. Great with swords, great with magic, and brave. As silly as it sounded for a teenager to take on groups of twenty or more darklings at a time—and win—the story *was* fun... and it took her mind off her situation. She lifted her face off the pipe and opened her eyes a few minutes later when Alonna reached the bottom of the two-mile stairway. "I should probably get going."

Pet stopped 'reading' to her. "Be careful. You're doing great. I haven't seen anything bad yet on the network. We still have time."

"Yeah. I was more thinking I don't wanna be stuck up here when I gotta pee again."

Pet tilted a bit to the right.

"Joke." Kiera dragged herself forward like a snake the last few feet to a support pylon, and braced herself on it to stand. While clinging to the strut, she peered over the side at the legion of shiny metal robots going about their tasks on the machines, tanks, pipes, and tall cylinders below. Fear at being so high off the ground collided with her relief at escaping notice, leaving her neither happy nor trembling.

She shimmied around the pylon and walked on, arms raised to the sides for balance. Heel to toe, she focused only on reaching the next brace, then the next. Before she realized it, dark metal greeted her where she expected a post.

The subway-train-sized pipe met the wall near a semicircular barrier that blocked the room off from a shaft that plunged two stories down. The opening between the core and the curved wall would let her reach the fourth floor below ground level, and bring her that much closer to General Xax's room.

"You made it," said Pet.

"Yeah, but..." She cringed. "In the game, I jumped from here to the top of that round wall. There's like yellow handholds on the inside and the character just automatically leaps and holds on." Kiera shook her head. "I don't wanna jump that. I'm scared of falling. I'm not a video game character."

Pet drifted over the opening. "We should trust that Thread Alpha is aware you're a child, not a video game. There must be something else here."

"Hmm." She wobbled, waving her arms to keep from slipping, and looked around. The wall in front of her had thick plates separated by inch-wide seams filled with bluish-purple light. Each square panel was about as tall as from her feet to her stomach. "I think I see something."

"Be careful. Are you sure?"

"No, but... I don't see any ladders and I'm *not* jumping."

Kiera crept to the end of the pipe. She grabbed a seam above her head and wedged the tips of her sneakers into the opening below it, testing support. *I'd get more of a foothold if I took my shoes off, but the edges look sharp.* She bounced up and down, feeling secure.

"Like the rock climbing place..." She grumbled. "Dad didn't bring me there. Thread Alpha did."

"Oh, Kier, please be careful."

"If I was careful, I'd be sitting in my jail cell behaving myself."

Pet giggled.

Kiera shimmied to the left away from the pipe and made the mistake of looking down the shaft. *Crap.* Fear-paralysis kept her stuck to the wall like a bug smashed into a windshield for a few minutes. *Deep breaths. I can't hang here too long. My arms will stop working.* She scooted left another plate and stretched down to wedge her foot into the next seam. Strong wind blew up from the depths, heavy with a pleasant scent like forest after rain. She gave up trying to see anything with her hair constantly in her face, and worked by feel on the metal.

Panel by panel, she climbed down the wall, sticking her feet and hands in the seams between square panels like rungs of a ladder. Once she descended past the top of the curved barrier, hidden from the robots in the massive room, she breathed easier. Pet bobbed and weaved, trying to hover beside her, but had to fight the wind. Something told her the stiff breeze went all the way up and out the top of the Citadel, becoming that tornado. She felt grateful at wearing the fabricated clothes; the powerful upward wind would've ripped her poncho clear off and shot it out into the sky.

A long, uncomfortable climb later, her sneaker found floor instead of a seam. She let go of the wall and held her hands out, stretching her fingers and cringing. So much static electricity hung in the air here, her hair floofed up. Again, Pet giggled.

"Ow. I can't feel my hands anymore."

"You forgot to use powder."

Kiera stuck her tongue out. She turned away from the wall, examining a D-shaped chamber filled with a sideways breeze. While the curved part lacked the convenient handholds her video game alter ego had bounced down so easily, the hatch in the middle near the floor was right where it should be. She hurried over to it, skidding into a baseball slide against the wall. Remembering what the fictional commando had done, she grabbed a bar inside the circle part and tried to twist it counterclockwise—but it didn't move.

"Ugh. Think it's stuck, or is it my noodle arms?"

Pet hovered up to her cheek. "You are not weak for your age and size."

"No, but I'm also a kid, not a Galactic Special Forces commando with cyber-muscles. I'm weak compared to a grown-up soldier." She grasped the handle again, grunting and straining to turn it.

"Are you sure it rotates that way?" asked Pet.

She rested a few breaths. "Game went that way... but." She tried clockwise, but it didn't move either. Annoyed, she stood, half turned away, and stomped her heel down on the left half. The third time her sneaker made contact, the bar moved an inch. "Yes!"

Kiera knelt and grabbed the right side of the bar in both hands, pushing against the wall with her legs for extra power. She grunted, yanking it an inch at a time with a series of tugs before the mechanism popped free and tossed her over on her back.

Flat on her back, she took a few breaths before thrusting her arm up in victory. "Got it!"

Once she caught her second wind, she crawled back to the opening. The wheel spun with little resistance, opening the hatch that led to a smaller pipe. While an adult commando would've struggled to fit, she had enough room to crawl on her hands and knees. After a long rightward curve, the pipe straightened out and brought her to a hollow in the floor beneath another room.

A grid of light shining down from a grating overhead painted the walls of the square chamber blue. Four giant electronic boxes, each big enough for her to stand inside of, hung on the walls, flickering with green lights. Black flexible hoses as big around as her arms crisscrossed the floor of a space half the size of her former prison cell, and only three feet tall. Kiera duck-walked to the opposite corner, expecting the grating overhead would offer passage to a safe hiding place.

Sure enough, she peered up at the underside of a giant tank of dark metal, banded with blue light. What lurked inside, she had no idea, but by size, it could hold an entire swimming pool's worth of water. Kiera lifted the grating and pushed it aside before pulling herself out of the recessed chamber onto the floor. Compared to the room around it, the tank seemed tiny. Four rows of identical storage vessels occupied a chamber that had to be over a mile long.

"I gotta sneak across to the end. Need to wait and watch for alien—uhh, robot—patrols, and run across walkways between tanks." If reality worked like the game, she'd be safe under the tanks and at risk only when crossing between them.

Pet made a chirp of acknowledgement.

"Wish I had a minimap. This was so much easier when I could see dots."

"I could project one," said Pet. "I can estimate their position based on wireless network signal. But the light... They might see it."

Kiera shifted her jaw side to side, thinking. "Can you tell me when to go?"

"Yes."

She clutched Pet so it didn't have to fly and make light, and scooted to the end of the first tank. Metal feet clanked and scraped in an endless symphony of badness. After looking around at tons of distant spindly legs, she figured there had to be over a hundred androids.

"Go," said Pet.

Kiera darted across a walkway between tanks and slid under the next one. Five seconds later, a robot walked past behind her. She closed her eyes and tried not to breathe loud enough to be heard. The cube in her hand vibrated like a cell phone on mute again, a nudge to keep going. She crept to the far end of the second tank. Hoses along the bottom as wide as her thigh twitched and hissed, fluid of some unknown type coursing through them. As chilly as the Citadel had been everywhere else, the space under the tanks rivaled the outside for warmth, perhaps even hotter. While waiting at the end, she peeled the neck of her shirt away to fan herself, missing the airiness of her poncho.

"Now," said Pet.

One after the next, she rushed across walkways and slid under tanks. Sometimes she had to wait for several minutes at the end; sometimes she didn't get a rest at all. Whenever Pet prodded her to go, she went. In her friend's electronic brain, an overhead map with dots and vision cones said when she could move without being caught. Tank by tank, she crossed the gargantuan chamber.

When she reached the second to last row, she held Pet up to her mouth and whispered, "I need to go left two tanks, under the row by the wall."

"Okay. Get ready."

At Pet's prompting, she ran, slid, waited, ran, and slid again.

After crawling under the second to last tank on the far left side, she pulled up another grating panel and dropped into a chamber beneath the floor similar to the first one. From there, a maintenance duct took her beyond the wall at the end of the room. A short way past that, she stood inside a vertical shaft and gazed into another duct at face level. Being close to the end got her hands shaking like they did every time she played the game. Inches from obtaining the perfect achievement for sneaking, she feared a screw-up at the last minute. Only, a screw-up now would have far worse consequences than being forced to replay a video game map from the start.

"Is something wrong?" asked Pet. "Why are you standing still?"

She brushed her hand over the cube, petting Pet. "We're almost there. I don't want to choke."

"I am not reading any smoke or fumes in the air."

Kiera bit her arm to muffle a laugh.

Pet emitted a faint giggle. "You got this, Kier."

She grabbed the duct and pulled one leg up, but froze as a realization smashed into her brain. "Pet?"

"Yes?"

"Are you Ashleigh?"

The cube remained quiet for a moment. "When you first activated this pet cube, I downloaded myself into it so I could still be your friend. The other children at school were programs, but Thread Alpha created me as a fully sentient AI so you wouldn't be completely alone. It would be more accurate to say Ashleigh was me, but I am not exactly Ashleigh either. In that world, I had certain rules I couldn't break."

Kiera laughed and wiped happy tears before hugging Pet again. "Yeah... You're not obsessed with clothes."

"I don't need them here."

"Yeah." Kiera climbed into the duct, giggling. "I kinda don't either... outside. It's so messed up how they don't care."

"Remember Powers' class? The people in the rainforest? Different societies have different rules."

"Okay. So does that mean it's okay if I go tribal?"

Pet glided along by her head. "Are you happy?"

Kiera pictured herself sitting at her new home in a loincloth like the one Sparrow wore, plus the rainforest tribe's war paint on her face, while playing a video game. The absurd mental image made her laugh. "Maybe."

Pet emitted Ashleigh's giggle.

"Wait." Kiera grabbed the cube. "You knew the whole time that we were in VR? Why didn't you ever say anything? If it was so important... why act like some fashion-obsessed kid?"

"I'm sorry, Kier." Pet trilled. "I wanted to, but I couldn't. Thread Alpha, or maybe my programming, didn't let me break the illusion. You needed to stay comfortable so you didn't freak out. It was too important that you get the perfect dark, you couldn't be distracted by worrying the whole planet was going to die."

Kiera rolled her eyes. "The whole planet *was* going to die... but only in the game. Alien bombardment."

Pet giggled again.

"Still sucks." She frowned, but patted the flying cube. "But I guess it makes sense."

The duct in front of her led to an absolute maze of passageways, but after doing it over and over so many times, she hurried along without a shred of hesitation. Seventeen turns later, she entered the final stretch of conduit and scurried up to another heavy vent cover, the same reinforced metal square like in the prison. Touching it brought back the sense of her parents' fingers at her cheeks.

"How am I going to—?"

With a faint *pssh* sound, the vent lock released and popped open a half-inch.

*Thanks whoever is watching.* She pushed it outward on its struts and slipped into a D-shaped chamber from an opening at the middle of the curve. One corridor went left, another hallway continued off to the right. Dark blue metal glimmered in the light of pulsating strips set in the ceiling. The flat wall in front of her stalled the breath in her throat—a huge trapezoid-shaped door. She'd skipped the two nasty fights in either side corridor. Those passages going to the sides didn't lead toward her objective; they went back *out*, straight into robots and turrets she'd bypassed.

"General Xax's room. This is it." She swallowed and pulled out her laser pistol. "No save games. Run inside, jump in a hole. Go back and forth and shoot it in the back of the head after it stops searching. Wow. I guess I got the *Perfect Dark* achievement for real."

She hummed the little musical score the game played for obtaining the achievement.

"Kier?"

"What?" she whispered.

"One, there's two robots approaching from both hallways. You have twenty-eight seconds before all four of them see you. Two, Thread Alpha didn't plan on you finding—or using—a weapon. I don't think there's a boss in there at all. Don't be scared. Hurry."

"Right." She ran up to the giant circle in the middle of the door and pressed her right hand flat against it.

The three-foot-wide disc rotated half a turn to the left and stopped with a heavy *thud* that shook the floor. A seam at the height of her chin expanded as the two halves of door separated, the larger part sinking while the upper part retracted into the ceiling. Eager to escape the approaching robots, Kiera jumped over it before the lower section finished going down.

General Xax's chamber looked exactly like the video game down to the open vent covers scattered all over. She eyed the one nearby on the left, the fastest way into the network of tunnels under the floor. The room was, however, missing one small detail: no giant blob-shaped alien overlord on a flying disk bristling with missile launchers and cannons. The constant whirring thrum of machinery made the ceiling rumble, and the air had an electric charge that tingled her cheeks.

Massive tubes ran across the ceiling, all converging on a round, raised column at the far wall, some forty yards away. Near the base, a holographic monitor screen displayed the Citadel Corporation logo, which she recognized as the arcology-building-slash-terraformer. Taken by sudden fear something would go wrong, she sprinted across the room, sneakers chirping on the polished metal.

Kiera waved her arms for balance as she stopped short by the column. The terminal screen had no visible keyboard or any other controls. Sticking her finger into the intangible graphic did nothing. "No... this is stupid. What am I supposed to do now?" She looked around, heart racing, breathing too fast. Below the screen, an angled shelf had a darker metal square in the middle. "Hmm."

*The chip!* On a lark, she placed her right hand on it.

A second later, a small panel to the right of the monitor popped open, flickering blue laser light glimmering within. She remembered Min saying something about facial scanning. Squinting, she leaned closer. Bright gridlines appeared over her blurry reflection on the shiny steel around the screen. Soon, the terminal beeped.

"Access granted," said a pleasant voice, mostly robotic, but enough like a mature woman to feel calming. "Emergency authorization provision enabled. Welcome, Quinn, Kiera A."

A bright orange holographic man shimmered into existence beside her. Bald, indeterminate age neither too young nor too old, and wearing a Chinese jacket and pants, he smiled with the meditative calm of the Shaolin monk he appeared to be. "Welcome, child."

"Who..." She blinked, afraid to pick her hand up from the panel.

"I am Thread Alpha, and I am grateful to you for having undertaken this task."

She managed a feeble smile. "Is it done? How do I turn on the citadels?"

Thread Alpha bowed. "As an authorized user from the senior leadership team, you have only to issue the directive."

"So, tell you to do it, and you do it?"

"That is correct," said the hologram.

She narrowed her eyes at the console. *I win.* She opened her mouth to issue the command, but hesitated. *Is Anton right? Am I going to blow up the planet?*

# THE CONCORDANT SEQUENCE

isions of nuclear mushrooms filled her mind, helped along by the bright orange apparition standing beside her. Kiera opened and closed her mouth a few times. She glanced at Pet for support, but her friend said nothing, hovering quiet nearby.

"Stop!" roared Anton.

She screamed and whirled toward the voice, but only a hologram version of the Administrator loomed over her. Still, she pointed her gun at him.

The red in Anton's face showed clear despite the blue, ghostly holographic projection. "Stupid child! What are you doing! How on Earth did you get in there!" he shrieked. "You're going to destroy us all! What little we've managed to get back will be wasted." He cleared his throat and tried to put on an authoritative voice. "You will do nothing and wait for security units to bring you safely back out of there."

"I don't believe you." Kiera looked at Thread Alpha's ghost. "Will it explode?"

"The report claiming the citadels will malfunction or experience a reactor core breach, and concerns of subsequent thermonuclear detonation were derived from a mathematical error in a simulation. I am certain there is no risk. The report is false."

"Of course it lies," yelled Anton. "You're a little girl. Easy to fool with stories of flowers and happy little animals prancing around again in the woods. Do you really believe you'll hit that button and the world will be fixed? It's a computer. The AIs changed while we were all asleep. They don't want humans back! They were made to kill us all. It's trying to trick you!"

Kiera looked down at her shoes. "You gave me two choices. I could kill myself or let you keep me and my parents locked up. Both your choices were evil. I choose option three."

"Wait!" roared Anton. "Run that sequence and we're all dead! Those... those dirt-rakers you call parents will die first—and not quickly. It'll take a few minutes for everything to explode and I promise you, they will suffer. The insurgents as well. I'll raze your whole village before the clouds take us."

Kiera shot a laser through Anton's face, but the hologram didn't care. "Don't you dare hurt them!"

"Projections indicate the citadels will achieve restoration of the Earth sufficient to permit reseeding the biosphere in 677.37 years without activating the primary sequence. However, the machinery will not last that long, Kiera. By my calculations, the terraforming cores will last 140 years at most before the installations in the harshest conditions break down."

"It lies!" shouted Anton. "Even if it's true, that's almost two more centuries to figure something out. You're going to nuke us!"

Tromping echoed on the other side of the giant door, an army of security androids approaching.

Kiera stared at the console screen, full of text that appeared to be a checklist for 'The Concordant Sequence Initiation Protocol.' If she did it, she'd kill her parents by making Anton furious. If she didn't, she'd doom the whole planet. The citadels would fall apart before completing their work. She didn't believe the citadels would go nuclear, but considering her parents would die either way, couldn't find the ability to care if the machines exploded or not. She looked from the console to Anton's glaring phantom.

"You killed my mom and dad before they even woke up. You killed Pet. You killed all the executives in that place, and even that cop who refused to arrest me. You want me to die too, and I'm only a kid. I don't know how many people you'll kill in the future. No, I think no matter what I do, you will kill everyone I love anyway. I can't let everyone in the world die."

"Wait," said Anton in a twitchy voice. "I-I'll let all of you go back to your hovels if you stay out of the Citadel forever."

*I don't trust you.* Hot tears ran down her cheeks as she closed her eyes, grief for the parents she prepared to sentence to death. "Initiate the Concordant Sequence. Run it. Go. Do it. I grant permission."

"No!" roared Anton. He made a funny gurgling noise and grabbed his chest.

His scream cut off when the entire chamber fell dark. Only the glow of Pet's thruster remained, its soft whirr filling her ears. Kiera looked around at the chamber. Except for distant reflections of Pet's light gleaming from metal high over her head, she couldn't see anything. The absence of the heavy mechanical noises, so constant that she had tuned them out, became a suffocating silence. Each breath in and out of her throat carried over the chamber like a shout.

"Was that supposed to happen?" asked Kiera.

Pet drifted close. "I'm not sure. The network went down. I have no connection to anything."

"Crap."

A deep *thud* shook the floor. The chamber shuddered. Kiera screamed, falling to the ground amid the earthquake and curling up in a ball. Violent shaking stopped a few seconds later. The lights flickered on again. Distant mechanical whirring wound up, like an entire fleet of jets starting their engines at the same time. Heavier rumbles followed soon after. Panels lit up along the walls, racing along the paths of pipes.

"Did I break it?" asked Kiera.

"I don't know." Pet flew into her arms.

The orange apparition of Thread Alpha reappeared, surrounded in a halo of blue static. "Sequence Initiated. Commencement signal successfully transmitted to all other citadels. Primary atmospheric filtering and terraforming systems are coming online throughout the globe. Estimated time until restoration of atmosphere: 387 days. Once complete, biomass regeneration will begin via bacterial organism distribution, seed release, wildlife cloning, and water processing. In approximately 962 days from initiation, conditions will meet baseline for Cairn Activation Protocol. Preliminary CAP initiation has been scheduled."

Kiera didn't bother standing, instead staring glumly at the floor. Somewhere, Anton would be doing horrible things to Mom and Dad. "Uhh, yeah, that's great."

"I am detecting an unexpected emotional response to such good news," said Thread Alpha.

"How many kids lose *two* sets of parents?" She clutched Pet/Ashleigh tight, all she had left in the world.

Thread Alpha stared quizzically at her.

A group of ten silver and white security androids walked in. She made no move to run, raise her hands, or shoot at them, remaining slumped in place as they approached and formed a half-circle around her.

"You guys are too late," said Kiera at the floor. "You can't stop it. It doesn't matter what you do to me now."

# DANGEROUS POWERS

K iera stared at the blurry mixture of color on the steel surface in front of her knees. After a moment of no lasers piercing her body or plastic hands grabbing her, she looked up in confusion. The androids all faced her, heads tilted down to stare with their unblinking blue hexagon eyes. None of them pointed a weapon at her.

She hung her head, hoping her parents had gone peacefully, like the ones who never even woke up. "I'm not gonna roll over and put my hands behind my back. If you're gonna arrest me, you'll have to carry me."

They continued standing there, silent and motionless.

"What?" She looked up at them.

"Kiera," said Thread Alpha. "The security units are here to protect you, not harm you."

She whipped her head around to gawk at the hologram. "Huh?"

"When you gave the command, you unlocked the system to me. I obtained root level access to the entire citadel network. I am the primary process that controls the restoration. My functions were shadowed to prevent tampering by unauthorized users. You rebooted Citadel Zero, and I have moved to a foreground process. Anton Sokolov no longer has any clearance in the system. I revoked it. The robots listen to you now, as you have been granted equivalent access to a senior executive. Also, Assistant Administrator Alan Chan has been promoted to administrator. The director of law enforcement, Melanie Stanton, also has the authority to issue commands to the robots."

She trembled from a collision of worry and hope. It occurred to her at that instant that the robots' eyes glowed blue, like the one she found trapped—not green like they had been when they killed Legacy or chased her before. "Are... are my parents...?"

"Anton can order them to kill as much as he likes, but they will not obey. You have the same authorization as Theresa Quinn, SVP of Research and Development."

Kiera tilted her head. "Alpha? He said when he went there to kill them, my bio parents, that I was dead. Is this a dream? Am I a robot or something?"

"No, child." Thread Alpha's smile radiated the placidity of a monk. "Prior to you initiating the restart, my ability to affect systems was limited. I became aware of his plan to murder the executives so the authorization to initiate the Sequence defaulted to him. Before he arrived at the facility, I altered your stasis pod to falsely show your vital signs as dead, hoping he would leave you alone."

"It worked." She shivered. "Thanks for flushing me, by the way."

"An unavoidable side effect. The false status triggered a flag in ROM software that resulted in postmortem processing of the tank's occupant. That portion of code resided in hardware and could not be changed."

"So, my parents were dead for two years before I woke up? Why didn't you make them look dead, too?"

Thread Alpha nodded. "Yes. A few months plus two years. I initiated the virtual world to prepare you for this. Their pods had executive access restrictions. I could not. You were inserted with dependent child permission. Additionally, multiple 'dead' occupants would have increased the risk of detection to an unacceptable level. As you are a child, I predicted Anton would not expect you to even be aware of the Sequence and thus, not a threat."

Pet nuzzled her cheek. "I'm sorry you lost your parents, Kiera. The whole world owes you thanks."

"It's okay." She stood, hoping the AI's words meant Teryn and Mala were alive. If the robots wouldn't listen to Anton anymore, maybe they survived. *He wouldn't do it himself, and even if he tried, Dad would kick his butt.* Hope tingled inside her chest and made her hands shake. "I... I've still got parents." She looked at the line of androids. "Take me to the seventy-eighth floor."

---

KIERA HURRIED OFF THE ELEVATOR, SURROUNDED BY TEN LAW ENFORCEMENT robots. Ever since the lights came back on, the Citadel building rumbled more noticeably than before, a constant vibration in the ground. Outside, *cracks* and *booms* from a great thunderstorm lashed the walls. Every so often, the lights faltered. She made her way down the street behind the two androids leading their group. A few minutes later, she spotted Mala and Teryn walking out from a doorway beside a group of small electric police cars. Behind them, Pash and Ford staggered, both looking like they'd lost fistfights. Two androids and about a dozen live police officers escorted them, including the two who had tried to help her.

"Dad! Mom!" shouted Kiera.

Pash and Ford looked up with hope.

She broke away from the group of androids and ran into her parents' arms.

Mala burst into tears, squeezing all the air out of her. Teryn wrapped his arms around them both. Having her mother cry set Kiera off with sobs of joy. She clung to them as if letting go would cause their death. Her emotion sapped the strength from her legs, but Teryn picked her up, rocking her while Mala held on. Pet orbited the three of them, chirping and beeping merrily.

It took quite some time before she could manage words. "I'm so sorry. I thought I killed you."

At their astonished expressions, she explained 'hitting the button' despite Anton's threat to kill them. "I knew he'd do it anyway."

"I'm proud of you." Teryn squeezed her. "A father could not ask for a braver daughter."

"The choice was not easy, but you made the right one." Mala kissed her atop the head.

Kiera sniveled. "But you've got a baby."

"Who would have been lost when that"—Mala's face gave away a word she chose not to speak out loud—"man... killed us anyway."

"He showed you what he did to your parents once before," said Pet. "The man does not possess mercy."

Kiera wiped her cheeks dry, almost smiling. "Yeah. Well... we didn't blow up."

The two cops who assisted her escape walked over, looking much less somber.

"Nice job, kid," said the woman. "I'm really sorry for how we treated you. We couldn't help you, or your parents, if Anton turned his robots on us."

"I know." Kiera hugged her. "Thanks for helping me get out... and I guess for leaving the cuffs on. I don't think I would've taken that pill, but not having a choice helped."

The woman cringed, shaking her head. "That place is nowhere for a child to be. I'm sorry we had to do any of it."

"Yeah. Anton didn't have a high opinion of us... lower than his robots even." The male cop patted her shoulder. "By the way, I also swapped the pill. That was a vitamin."

His partner gasped. "You should've told me. I wouldn't have left her in restraints."

Kiera stared at him, on the verge of laughing.

"Didn't want to risk getting overheard. Anton's got a vicious streak," said the male cop. "It's almost hard to believe he didn't... uhh, hurt her."

"I don't think he was lying when he said he didn't like hurting kids." Kiera frowned. "But if he thought I was going to blow up the whole planet...."

"Most likely, he never believed you had any chance of getting past all the security to reach the terminal four levels down." The female cop scratched above her ear. "I'm still not sure how you managed it."

"I had a lot of practice." Kiera clung to her father. "Is Anton gonna try to hurt me?"

The woman gave her parents an apologetic look before shaking her head at Kiera. "When you issued the command to the system, he had a heart attack."

"He really believed you were about to blow us up." The male cop chuckled. "He's in the hospital now, probably going to survive. Although, he will face trial once he recovers. Administrator Chan has ordered him arrested."

"Trial?" Kiera narrowed her eyes. "For kidnapping my parents... and me? And killing everyone in those tanks?"

Both cops nodded.

"And there have been a few officials and police officers who have gone missing or been killed at the hands of his robots for disagreeing with him." The woman's expression mixed angry with pleased. "He will answer for everything."

Ford and Pash got into a car, headed to a hospital as well from what Kiera overheard. When the cop preparing to drive them passed along that the Citadel had been activated, they both cheered at her.

She grinned at them, waving as the car pulled off.

"We have a lot of work ahead of us with the new administrator. I think we're in for quite a few changes here." The female cop smiled. "Please don't be afraid of us anymore."

Kiera smiled. "Thanks for helping me get out and for being nice to my parents."

The cops spent a moment apologizing and shaking hands with her mother and father before going back inside the police building.

"The world is shuddering." Teryn looked at the ceiling. "I cannot get used to seeing metal sky. Come, child. Let us return home."

"Umm." Kiera glanced at the robots. "I think I kinda control this place now. We could stay here if you want."

Mala fidgeted. "What of your friends? Won't you miss them? I thought you liked our garden."

"I do! I really miss my room." She looked up. "And being inside all the time *is* kinda weird. I have a *lot* of numbers... from my old parents. We don't have to worry about food, and we can get stuff to make the garden healthy. Maybe we can build up Exxo? When the Cairns open, we'll need to build a lot more houses. And work permits are going away. The gates will open. I'm going to tell the new administrator to treat everyone fair."

"Kiera," said Thread Alpha's voice out of a nearby android. "While you have network access like an executive, you are still eleven. I am sorry, but you cannot tell the administration what to do."

"Then I'll *ask*." She held her chin up. "I have dangerous powers of cuteness."

# EPILOGUE

## The Blue Ring

**K**iera wandered the garden beside her home, adoring the feel of damp soil between her toes. Her thin cloth dress breathed in the wind, comfortable despite the temperature being past a hundred. She didn't sweat quite as much as right after she'd awakened from VR. A clean breeze laced with the scent of the nearby forest kept the air from being stagnant. Her 'citadel clothes' sat folded on the shelf in her room, waiting for the next journey with her parents to get supplies.

She sprayed nutrient liquid from a plastic bottle over healthy tomato plants and carrots, cringing from the 'somewhere-between-poop-and-dirt' smell of it. Pet floated along at knee-level, scanning each plant and commenting on which ones needed more water, less water, or another few squirts from her bottle.

Her mother, too round with baby to work in the garden, rested on a padded bench by the back door, watching her with a smile. Dad went into town to work with the other villagers and a group of androids, setting up solar panels and batteries that would, within a couple weeks, provide electrical power to the entire town instead of a few individual homes. Thread Alpha had told her she had a balance of 847,300 credits, the remainder of her bio parents' accounts that she'd inherited.

Once the town could support it, she'd buy herself a holographic TV and video game system. Living in a world where going outside wouldn't cause death in ten minutes from heatstroke or inhaling toxins as well as having four real live friends—not to mention chores—would cut into her game time... but, she'd deal.

*Permanent summer! I don't have to wear pants ever again, there's no school, and no more tests!* Kiera frowned playfully. *I wouldn't mind a nice set of PJs though. Those I miss. But gah. Too hot. Maybe when I'm like fifteen, it might get cool enough for PJs in the winter sometimes.*

Plant by plant, Kiera made her way down the row, spritzing at the leaves, until she reached the end of the fluttering plastic canopy. She stepped out into the sun, grinning at the sky. Already, a donut of clear blue circled the top of the tornado sprouting from the Citadel. Similar rings probably existed above all the citadels, expanding over the coming weeks and months until the sky once more looked like it did before Cloudfall.

An hour or so later, she finished her work in the garden and set the bottle of plant food on a shelf by the house.

"Kiera? Would you fetch me water, please?" asked Mala.

"Okay, Mom."

She darted inside, filled a plastic cup from the pitcher, and carried it outside to her mother. While Mala drank, Kiera rested her hand on her mother's swollen belly, hoping to feel the baby inside move.

Peter, Mei, Osc, and Sparrow ran around the corner of the house and gathered beside her.

"We're going to the river to swim," said Mei. "Wanna come?"

"Can I?" Kiera looked to her mother.

"Who's watching you all?" asked Mala.

"I am," said Peter. "I'm thirteen."

Mala made a hesitant face, but relented. "All right. Please be careful. I'm in no shape to run if you get in trouble."

Kiera stooped and hugged her. "I'll be careful."

"I know you will." Mala winked. "It's the little one I'm worried about."

Sparrow put on an innocent face.

After the group of kids crossed the scrapyard behind the house, Kiera diverted to the left. "Hang on. I'll be right there."

Her friends waited in a group while she hurried over to a mound about a hundred yards behind the house with an irregular chunk of concrete protruding from the ground at one end. She'd laser-burned 'Legacy' into the slab. The Citadel's administration had released his body to her father, and they buried him here out of thanks.

Kiera knelt by the grave, head bowed, Pet hovering at her left shoulder. "Thanks doesn't seem like enough. I wish you told me you knew you'd die... I would've insisted we do something else." She let out a sad chuckle. "Guess that's why you didn't say anything. There's a ring of blue in the sky now. The machine's working. If Mom has a boy, I'm going to ask her to name him

Legacy, but I don't know if she will. If I have a kid when I grow up, I'm going to name him after you... even if it's a girl. Unless my brother gets named that, then it'd be kinda weird." She smiled. "I'll never forget what you did for me. Guess you were right. I am the Child of Earth."

"I liked him, too," said Pet.

She stood, pausing for a moment of silence before running to rejoin her friends.

"What are you talking about?" asked Peter.

Mei pointed toward the Citadel, a dark haze in the distant sky. "We're gonna have to go to school soon."

"What's that?" Sparrow scrunched up his face.

Kiera froze in horror. "What?!"

Mei looked at her. "Inna couple months. Mom said. There's gonna be another Passage for all the kids in all the villages, takin' us to the Citadel 'couple hours a day for school. 'Ministrator changed his mind. We're not dumb as dogs, so we gotta do school now."

"No!" Kiera leaned back with a desperate, overacted wail.

Peter raised an eyebrow. "Is it that bad?"

Kiera laughed. "No, I'm being a drama queen. I thought I was free. Just my luck. Two things survive the end of the world: cockroaches *and* school."

"What's a cockroach?" asked Osc.

"Forget it." Kiera stuck out her tongue and grimaced. "It's a bug. People always said they would survive the end of the world."

"Come on!" Sparrow shouted and ran off toward the river.

The others followed.

Sparrow shed his loincloth and hurried to the edge, standing on the concrete rim for a few seconds before holding his nose and falling forward like a plank.

Mei flung her poncho off and dove into the water. Osc jumped in after her, not bothering to unwind the cloth around his middle. Peter left his skirt on and hurled himself in.

Kiera approached the edge, grinning at the sky. She dropped her precious dress beside Mei's and dove headfirst into the river. The shock of going from such heat to freezing paralyzed her for a few seconds, but wound up feeling awesome. Swimming deeper, she glided out of a cloud of dirt as the water washed garden soil from her arms and legs. After touching her hands to the bottom, she spun around, kicked off, and broke the surface, finally able to release a squeal at the cold. Basking in the relief from the heat, she floated on her back, gazing up at the clouds. Lightning flickered far overhead in the haze, but didn't look as green anymore. Kiera took a deep breath in her nose, grinning at the giggling coming from the other three splashing each other.

A high-pitched shriek of glee preceded Sparrow's scrawny body flying over her. He hit the water nearby, splashing her with a rain of droplets.

"My turn!" yelled Mei. "Peter! Throw me next!"

Kiera started to laugh, but stared straight up in awe at a little moving dark spot.

An actual sparrow sailed overhead, gliding into the forest.

She pointed and opened her mouth to shout, 'Look!' but Sparrow (the boy) pounced on her and dragged her under. Laughs bubbled out of her as she wriggled away from the over-energetic seven-year-old and swam back up. She splashed him in the face, which made him laugh and fling water back at her.

Kiera looked around in a hurry, but the bird had disappeared into the trees. Still, seeing one filled her with hope.

*There'll be more.*

*fin*

# ACKNOWLEDGMENTS

Thank you for reading Citadel: The Concordant Sequence!

My sincerest appreciation to **Merethe Najjar** for her help editing this novel.

Additional thanks to **Alexandria Thompson** for the cover art!

# ABOUT THE AUTHOR

Originally from South Amboy NJ, Matthew has been creating science fiction and fantasy worlds for most of his reasoning life. Since 1996, he has developed the "Divergent Fates" world, in which *Division Zero, Virtual Immortality, The Awakened Series, The Harmony Paradox, and the Daughter of Mars series* take place. Along with being an editor at Curiosity Quills press, he has worked in IT and technical support.

Matthew is an avid gamer, a recovered WoW addict, Gamemaster for two custom RPG systems, and a fan of anime, British humour, and intellectual science fiction that questions the nature of reality, life, and what happens after it.

He is also fond of cats.

Visit me online at:
Facebook: https://www.facebook.com/MatthewSCoxAuthor
Amazon: https://www.amazon.com/author/mscox
Pinterest: https://www.pinterest.com/matthewcox10420/
Goodreads: https://www.goodreads.com/author/show/7712730.Matthew_S_Cox
Email: mcox2112@gmail.com

# OTHER BOOKS BY MATTHEW S. COX

- Dead Man's Number

- New Moon Rising
- Moon Mourning

Maddy Wimsey series (with J.R. Rain)

- The Devil's Eye
- The Drifting Gloom

Samantha Moon Case Files series (with J.R. Rain)

- Blood Moon
- Dead Moon

Young Adult Novels

- Caller 107
- The Summer the World Ended
- Nine Candles of Deepest Black
- The Eldritch Heart
- The Forest Beyond the Earth
- Out of Sight
- Evergreen

Middle Grade Novels

Tales of Widowswood series

- Emma and the Banderwigh
- Emma and the Silk Thieves
- Emma and the Silverbell Faeries
- Emma and the Elixir of Madness
- Emma and the Weeping Spirit

Standalones

- Citadel: The Concordant Sequence
- The Cursed Codex
- The Menagerie of Jenkins Bailey
- Sophie's Light

www.ingramcontent.com/pod-product-compliance
Lightning Source LLC
Chambersburg PA
CBHW031649210626
46816CB00023B/1572